THE WOU

Maggie Makepeace was born in Buckinghamshire and went to school in Devon. She has a BSc in Zoology from Newcastle University and an MSc in Ecology from Aberdeen. She has worked as a TV presenter, for the Scottish Wildlife Trust and in the Wales office of the RSPB. She is married and lives in Somerset. Maggie Makepeace's two previous novels, *Breaking the Chain* and *Travelling Hopefully,* are available in Arrow.

ALSO BY MAGGIE MAKEPEACE:

Breaking the Chain
Travelling Hopefully

THE
WOULD-BEGETTER

Maggie Makepeace

ARROW

Published by Arrow Books in 1998

1 3 5 7 9 10 8 6 4 2

Copyright © Maggie Makepeace 1997

Maggie Makepeace has asserted her right under the Copyright,
Designs and Patents Act, 1988 to be identified as the author of this work

First published in the United Kingdom in 1997 by Century

Arrow Books Limited
20 Vauxhall Bridge Road, London SW1V 2SA

Random House Australia (Pty) Limited
20 Alfred Street, Milsons Point, Sydney
New South Wales 2061, Australia

Random House New Zealand Limited
18 Poland Road, Glenfield, Auckland 10, New Zealand

Random House South Africa (Pty) Limited
Endulini, 5a Jubilee Road, Parktown 2193, South Africa

Random House UK Limited Reg. No. 954009

A CIP catalogue record for this book
is available from the British Library

Papers used by Random House UK Limited
are natural, recyclable products made from wood grown in
sustainable forests. The manufacturing processes conform to
the environmental regulations of the country of origin

ISBN 0 09 922462 3

Printed and bound in the Great Britain by
Mackays of Chatham PLC, Chatham, Kent

ACKNOWLEDGEMENTS

My thanks to Tessa Lorant Warburg, Janet Laurence and Shelley Bovey, for excellent soup, invaluable criticism and unfailing support.
To Laurian Bowring for friendship and proof-reading.
To Sarah and John Ford of the *Weston Mercury* for advice and help.
To my husband Tim, for solidarity.

M.M. Somerset, spring 1997.

BOOK ONE

1983

I

'BUT what if your wife's here?' Jess asked anxiously as she and her colleague turned in at the gate and drove up towards the house. It was an imposing drive which led to a preposterous mansion with turrets.

'My soon to be ex-wife,' Hector corrected, 'and she won't be. She's a workaholic, always has been. I always assumed it was a form of displacement activity. You know what I mean? I thought she was unable to do what she really wanted, i.e. have babies, so she was busying herself with her job with a kind of manic energy as a distraction from her inner conflict. I saw a nice example of that kind of thing last night, as a matter of fact, on one of those *Survival* programmes. These two big fat herring-gulls were facing each other and yanking up great beakfuls of grass, when what they were bursting to do (but daren't) was peck each other senseless.'

'I've never found Megan particularly aggressive?'

'You should try living with her!' Hector raised both eyebrows expressively. 'No, what I'm trying to say is that it just never occurred to me that she might not have normal maternal instincts.'

'But you both married quite late on?'

'Well she was thirty, but that's common enough these days.'

'So you thought she was just waiting for the right moment to marry and start a family?'

'The right moment and the right man.' Hector frowned. 'I suppose I just took it for granted that we'd have kids. Doesn't everyone?'

'Not really,' Jess said, letting out a small sigh.

Hector didn't appear to notice it. 'I mean, I thought we'd been trying for a baby and Megan was just failing to conceive. I was really supportive to the bloody female. I even went to

3

the length of getting myself *tested* for God's sake! And all the time . . . I'll never understand the woman. How could she do it to me? She was taking the pill all along, you know, *secretly.* She never even discussed it with me; a major issue like that! Then on my birthday, my fortieth birthday no less, when a chap needs something *positive* to counteract the horrors of middle-age-made-manifest, what does she do, but calmly tell me that not only has she never wanted children, but now she's worried about the long-term effects of the pill, so she's decided to go the whole hog and get herself *sterilized!*'

'It must have been awful for you,' Jess said. She glanced at him as he drove and was surprised to see the tension in him. His handsome face was flushed and he was gripping the steering wheel with two clenched fists.

It had been a standing joke for some time amongst the other employees of the *Westcountry Chronicle,* that Hector Mudgeley, after seven unproductive years of marriage, must surely be several sperm short of a dynasty. It was no secret that he wanted an heir to keep the Mudgeley name alive, so they had been keeping a book, and the odds got longer as each year passed.

Jess had often wondered why someone like Hector would want to stay in an undistinguished small town like Woodspring-on-Sea, but concluded that he must enjoy being a big noise in a confined space. He seemed to be involved in every important decision that was ever taken locally. He was a Councillor, a School Governor, and a member of several committees concerned with planning and the conservation of wildlife and landscape, yet he still found time to work on the *Chronicle.* Jess was unfailingly impressed by his vigour and enthusiasm. She wondered if he had ambitions to be Editor. There was no obvious line of succession, the present one being about his age, and Hector's immediate boss, the News Editor, several years younger than him. Perhaps he would be content to go on being Senior Reporter until he retired? Jess hoped that she too would continue in her post as Photographer for many more years. She got on well with most of her fellows, and she had no hankerings for the uncertainty of the freelance life.

Poor Hector, she thought, glancing round and seeing his

expression, I shouldn't have encouraged him to talk about children. I must try to take his mind off the subject.

'Well then of course I had no option,' Hector continued, braking hard and stalling the car outside the front door, 'I just had to start divorce proceedings.'

'Better than chopping her head off,' Jess said, thinking of Henry VIII.

Hector got out of the car and, bending his long back, looked at her through the open door. 'Sometimes, Jess Hazelrigg, I really worry about you.'

Why do men always say things like that to me? Jess thought crossly. I don't want to be worried about. I want *passion*. Inside the porch she looked about her with some trepidation. What if Megan were to be lurking somewhere? She felt uncomfortable but vaguely excited at the thought.

'What are we doing here?' she asked. 'I thought we were going straight to do the interview with Caroline Moffat. I've got to be at the garage to collect the Jeep by lunchtime (if they've managed to fix it) and then I'm supposed to be up on the Mendips at one thirty, with a chap who says he's seen a puma.'

'I want you to take some pics of the house,' Hector said. 'Relax. It won't take a moment. I've brought a colour film with me. Here . . .'

'For the paper?' Jess asked, taking it.

'No, strictly unofficial. I just want some photos, especially of the interiors. It's morally just as much mine as Megan's, you know. I put a lot of time and money into this house.'

'So why is she living here now, and not you?'

Hector sighed. 'It's been in her family for a long time,' he said. 'It's her home. Then seven years ago her parents gave it to us as a wedding present and moved to Wales. So I can hardly throw her out now, can I?'

Lost ancestral homes were another touchy subject for Hector, Jess remembered just in time, so she said the first thing that came into her head. 'Why do you need the photos then?'

'Inquisitive little madam, aren't you? Simply because if I'm never to be allowed to live here again, I want a record of what a lovely house I once had.' He stood aside politely to let her go through the door first, and then added, 'But also, if I'm honest, because I like to make hay whilst the cat's away!'

Jess snorted at this. 'But you can see the house any time, presumably, since you've got a key?'

'Not a lot escapes those fine brown eyes, does it?' Hector said. 'Those specs of yours must be bionic.' He patted her arm. 'Just call it forethought,' he said. 'Sooner or later the stupid woman is bound to wake up to reality and get the locks changed. But when that happens, I'll still have my pics. Why don't you come up here? It's a great vantage point.' He led her upstairs into one of the round turret rooms, which was papered with blue elephants and an alphabet frieze.

They stood side by side at the arc of windows and looked down the long view to a distant river. 'This was to have been Morgan's room,' Hector said. 'Megan let me go ahead and get it decorated specially; never said a word!'

'Morgan who?'

'My future son. Morgan Caradoc, named after my grand-father. Goes well doesn't it, Morgan Caradoc Mudgeley?'

'But you can't name someone before they're even born, can you?' Jess asked. 'I mean, what if you called a daughter Melanie and her hair turned out to be blonde, instead of black? Don't you have to wait and see? A baby might not look like a Morgan, after all.'

'Mine will,' Hector said, staring at the horizon.

'But . . .?'

'Oh this won't be his room now,' Hector said, turning to face her. 'I'm quite aware of that, but there'll be other rooms.' He nodded as if to convince himself further. 'I've no choice, you see. Ifor, my elder brother, has a gaggle of sweet girls, but he and his wife have just announced that they reckon they've bred enough, and to hell with posterity. So if he's not going to beget a son to carry on the name, it falls to me. I'm duty bound to produce the heir myself.'

'With a little help from a friend?'

'That's the only inconvenient bit,' Hector said, breaking into an unexpectedly warm grin. 'But there's still time. I'm sure it can be arranged.'

Jess thought, he's so good-looking, and his face really softens when he smiles.

'I don't know how it is that you've managed to snare me into this full and frank discussion,' Hector said, now looking rather embarrassed, 'but you will keep it to yourself, won't you?'

'Don't worry,' Jess said happily. 'I'm the very soul of discretion.'

Hector hadn't meant to discuss his personal problems with Jess. He had temporarily overlooked the fact that she was a woman, and therefore predisposed to gossip. He had got so used to working with her that to him she had become virtually sexless; just a good mate. In any event, he consoled himself, he hadn't confided in her too recklessly. He hadn't told her his latest plan of campaign. It would probably be politic not to divulge that to anyone, yet. He regarded her with an avuncular smile. How old was she, mid-twenties? She was far too young and much too feminist; she wouldn't understand.

He wondered how many people would. It wasn't fashionable, in these days of equal opportunity, to be so determined to produce a son to keep the bloodline going, but then most people were carelessly unaware of their own distant ancestry. Hector could trace his family back seven generations to Sir John Mudgeley, the third Baronet, who had built himself an elegant country house in 1765 and named it Zoyland Park . . . Hector sighed, and stared out of the window trying to think of something else.

He supposed it must be a recent piece he'd done for the paper that had been responsible for getting him into this imperative frame of mind . . . It had been about a man of his own age, about to marry, but dying from a sudden heart attack on his stag night . . . The story had affected Hector more than usual; given him intimations of mortality? Yes, he thought, that must be it. After all, my father and his father and *his* father all died in their sixties. It could happen to me. Maybe I've got less than twenty years left? If only bloody Megan hadn't put me on hold for seven years, I might have had three or four sons by now. And then of course I could be killed in a road accident tomorrow. Who knows? There's no time to waste. But I might only get one shot at it, so it's got to be right *first time*. I can't afford another empty marriage . . .

He had decided upon a plan, and he had structured it in such a way that he would feel bound to stick to it and not be distracted, as he had been so often in the past, by mere dalliance and sexual adventure. This idea of his was designed to concentrate his mind on the job in hand (even if it might appear a trifle artificial and cold-blooded); the serious business of getting an heir.

'Right,' Jess said, aiming her loaded camera, and making him jump. 'Do you want to be in these ones, or are you too busy day-dreaming?'

'Oh . . . why not?' Hector moved round the room as she popped off several shots, putting himself in the foreground of each one so as to direct her towards what he considered to be the best composition. 'Wide-angled lens?'

'Of course,' Jess said. 'Teach your grandmother!'

'Sorry.' He went on smiling at her until she dropped her eyes from his. She was a sweetie. He was sure she wouldn't rat on him at the office. The last thing he wanted was to be an object of pity, or worse still a laughing stock. He thought he might have mentioned wanting a son to the odd person here and there, in passing, but he doubted whether they'd really registered it.

'One more?' Jess asked.

'If you like.' At least, Hector thought, at least I'll have something to show the boy – something along the lines of *Pictures of your father in the elegant house in which you were conceived*.

When they got outside again it was raining, but Hector wanted a few exterior shots. Jess watched him with a half-smile as he posed beside the high lion knocker on the heavy oak front door.

These are going to come out just like my Uncle Fred's holiday snaps, Jess thought – Aunty Kath in Egypt, with the pyramids somewhere under her left elbow; Aunty Kath in Sicily, with Mount Etna smoking from the back of her neck; Aunty Kath headless in Gaza, and so on. I wonder why Hector wants to be in all of them? I always run a mile if anyone points a camera at me. I suppose if you look as good as he does, it's easy.

'Excellent,' Hector said. 'That should do it. Thanks Jess. Now we'd better get going prestissimo.'

Jess got back into the passenger seat of the car. It was a novel experience to be driven by Hector, and one she was not in a hurry to repeat. She hoped her official Photographer's Jeep would indeed be repaired by lunchtime. This unfortunate vehicle was the smallest of the half-dozen company cars available, and the one which Hector most despised. He had already bumped it into several hard objects in the hope of ending its natural life, so far to no avail. Jess looked back at the house as they drove rather jerkily away.

'It's very large,' she said, 'especially for one person.'

'Yes,' Hector agreed bitterly. 'It's crying out to be a family home, isn't it? What makes it even worse is that Megan is hardly ever in it. Most weekends she buggers off to Wales to see to her geriatric father, so the place stands empty. It's a wicked waste and, what's more, an open invitation to any passing yob who fancies helping himself to the television and the video and God knows what else.' He sighed. 'I've tried to make her see sense, but it just makes her more bloody-minded. Women!'

'Some of us are quite pleasant,' Jess suggested.

'Some of you are little gems,' Hector agreed, taking his eyes off the road for rather too long. 'It'll be a lucky young bloke who turns your head.'

'It's odd, but I've always been attracted to the older man,' Jess ventured.

'Is that a fact?' Hector said, taking a bend too fast, but recovering with panache. 'Oh God, what am I going to say to this Moffat woman? As far as I can see she's some pushy superwoman who's been brought in as new MD to our biggest local employers hereabouts, at the unripe old age of thirty, no doubt over the backs of legions of hard-pressed married men with babies to support. Not the ideal person with whom to spend half an hour, but I suppose it's better than being in the Newsroom glued to the bloody phone, which seems to be mostly where I find myself these days. You photographer bods don't know you're born, you know, gadding about all day, special transport, mobile phone . . .'

'Long hours' Jess put in.

'I used to work long hours too, but I didn't mind that. I was out and about all the time in the old days, with my ear to the ground, getting contacts, being given tip-offs. I was a proper reporter then, but nowadays it's all cuts; less money, fewer staff . . . boring, boring, boring.'

'Cheer up,' Jess said. 'You don't know it but you've got a treat in store. I actually know your so-called superwoman and she's not pushy at all. In fact I'm really looking forward to seeing her again. She was my role model years ago, when we were at school together. In fact I had quite a crush on her, would you believe, when I was in the third form. Haven't seen her since.'

'All-girls' school, eh?' Hector smiled knowingly. 'Ah . . . That explains a lot. Hothouses of repression and misandry. No wonder she's a bra-burner.'

'I suppose you do realise that you're an appalling chauvinist?'

'Nonsense,' Hector said cheerfully. 'You wouldn't have me any different.' Jess raised two sceptical eyebrows. 'I do it on purpose,' Hector assured her. 'Works a charm every time. You rise to the bait just like a sheep.'

'Right,' the surprisingly suave reporter said to Caroline, with biro poised above his notepad. 'Shall we get started then? I'm Hector Mudgeley, and I believe you already know Jessamy Hazelrigg our photographer.'

'Hello. Jess! How lovely to see you again. It's years since we last met! I didn't realise you worked for the *Chronicle*.'

'Yes. It's twelve years actually and you look just the same.'

'You don't! We must talk later.'

'Yes!'

Hector waited with studied patience for a moment or two, until Caroline had rewarded him with her full attention. Then he continued, 'And you are Caroline Moffat; two *f*'s, one *t*? Now, may I reveal your age?'

'Why not?' Caroline said, 'Since it's pertinent to the whole thrust of the article.'

'Quite. And are you . . . ah . . . married at all?'

'Not even slightly.'

'Oh.' He looked up and caught her eye with a humorous

glance. 'Right, and how long were you with your previous company?'

As the interview progressed, Caroline thought, why is it that I always have to play games; see if I can disconcert them? This one is different though; a cut above your average Press reptile. Could it be because he's from a wholesome and straightforward provincial weekly? No, I think there's more to it than that. Mmmm . . . But how odd to see Jess grown up! I remember her so clearly at thirteen, very shy, rather plain, the vulnerable sort.

When the questions were finished, and Hector had shut up his notepad with a satisfied snap, Caroline asked him, 'Are you any relation to Ifor Mudgeley of Mudgeley Goggles Ltd?'

'He's my brother,' Hector said, 'Why?'

'Just wondered,' Caroline said. 'Wasn't Mudgeley a big name around here at one time? Didn't they used to own most of Woodspring?'

'And the *Chronicle* too,' Hector agreed ruefully. 'Not any more.'

'But you never wanted to join the family firm?'

'I never found the manufacture of protective clothing to be particularly stimulating,' Hector said, holding her glance.

Caroline detected a definite gleam in his eye, and debated within herself whether to respond in kind. She estimated that he was about ten years her senior and surprisingly well dressed. He was taller than she was (even in her highest heels) and had pleasant symmetrical features and thick greying hair. The thing however that most attracted her, was his habit of direct eye contact and his air of effortless self-confidence. She wondered whether it was justified, and found herself wanting to find out.

He'd make a pleasant change from Vivian, she thought; less artistic but definitely more sensual . . . Not that I can actually do anything about him at this precise moment, with Jess here . . .

Caroline collected her thoughts. 'Do you work freelance?' she asked her.

'Nope,' Hector answered for her. 'She's a wage slave, aren't you Jess.'

'I sometimes take photos for friends on days off or weekends,' Jess said. 'And I've been known to do the odd wedding.'

'Mmmm,' Caroline said. 'Perhaps we could get together professionally? Not for a wedding (God forbid!) but I'm doing a presentation brochure and I need some mug shots of the Directors. The last ones we had done were quite ghastly; made them all look like delinquents. I'll give you a ring, yes?'

'Yes. I'd love to, but time could be a prob . . .' Jess looked doubtful.

'Excellent idea' Hector enthused. 'Industry and the Press will be all the better for a spot of mutual co-operation. I'll square it with our Editor.'

From the outset, Hector had been impressed by Caroline Moffat and now, with a bit of luck, Jess would be in touch with her further, which might create more opportunities for him to meet her too. He reckoned she was smart in every sense of the word. She was the type he could certainly fancy in a big way but mindful of the task ahead, as he and Jess drove back to the *Chronicle* building, he forced himself dutifully to run through his carefully considered list of 'essential wifely qualities' to assess her marks out of ten:

Beauty – 6ish
Personality – bit sharp, 5?
Sex appeal – 7, maybe 8?
Poise/Elegance – 10 definitely
Intelligence – 9 (maybe a mixed blessing?)
Wealth – 8 or more?
Class/Accent – 10
Suitable age range – 30ish. Perfect – 10
Child-bearing hips – Mmmm, only 3
Maternal potential – Hard to tell, 5+?
Genetic endowment, diseases etc. – Unknown, but promising
Politics – unknown
Status – unmarried, available? 10 or nil.
Useful connections – 9?

Bingo! he thought, screwing up his face with the effort of mental arithmetic. That comes to a minimum of . . . 82, and potentially a great deal more, especially if she can cook. I must do some research. Caroline Moffat could be THE ONE!

'Have you got a pain?' Jess asked.

'What?'

'Well, you're making awful faces.'

'I'm thinking.' Should I put my life-plan suggestion to Caroline, Hector wondered, or should I go ahead with it and not tell her? I know, I'll sound out the female response — maybe not a universal one, but adequate. I'll ask Jess.

'Must be agonising,' Jess said, 'activating all those little synapses in the brain, and simultaneously too.'

'Very funny. Look Jess, supposing someone made you a proposition along the lines of, "Would you be prepared to have my baby first and then get married afterwards," what would you say?'

'You don't mean . . .?' Jess flushed scarlet.

'*No*! Not you, you complete and utter noodle. Good Lord, whatever next! I was speaking purely theoretically; asking your opinion, as a woman.'

There was a pregnant silence. Hector glanced sideways and saw, to his consternation, that Jess looked about to burst into tears.

'Hey!' he said, slowing the car down. 'I haven't upset you, have I? I wouldn't do that for the world, Jessy-boot, you know that. I just wanted an intelligent, unbiased womanly opinion, so who better to ask than you?'

'It's okay,' Jess said, smiling hard. 'It's nothing. I've just got . . . an eyelash . . . in my eye.' She reached into the sleeve of her jersey and then, taking her glasses off, dabbed at her face with a tissue.

'Better now?'

'Fine.'

'So what do you think Miss Average would reply to such a proposition?' Hector stepped on the accelerator again.

'I'm not a great expert in such matters,' Jess said, flung back against her seat by the unexpected thrust, 'but I think she'd probably tell you to get knotted!'

'Putting you through,' Wendy Bing cooed in her carefully modulated telephone voice. She pressed a button and looked up from the switchboard just as Hector and Jess came in through the *Chronicle*'s swing doors. Wendy wondered why Jess didn't make more of herself. With a body as skinny as hers, she could wear anything, so why did she have to choose such coarse mannish fabrics, and such a determinedly unfeminine look? And why, while she was about it, didn't she get herself some contact lenses and make herself less owl-like? Wendy exhaled in disapproval and stroked her own right shoulder reflectively. Beneath her fingers the pink angora sweater felt baby-soft, and she deliberately left her hand where it was whilst Hector approached, so that he would be bound to notice that its fourth finger was now invitingly ring-free.

When she had passed thirty and yet remained puzzlingly single, Wendy had invented a fiancé to keep her end up. But when she had gathered that Hector was getting divorced, she had chucked the fake diamond into the bin and had lived in hope ever since.

'Hi Wend,' Hector said breezily. 'I really must stop saying that, mustn't I? Sounds just like "High wind". Any messages for me?'

Wendy smiled brilliantly at him. 'Just the one, on that poaching story,' she said, handing him a small oblong of yellow paper with a telephone number. 'Can you phone a Mr Milligan?'

'That it?' Hector said, taking it and stuffing it into his pocket.

'That's your lot.'

'Right.'

Wendy watched him as he disappeared up the stairs to the Newsroom. She felt rather let down. Today he hadn't said anything special to her. On good days he'd admire her hair or wink at her as though they had secrets in common. Of course, Wendy mused, they did indeed share secrets, although Hector himself wasn't strictly aware of this fact. As the chief Receptionist of three, Wendy had always considered herself to be the nerve-centre of the *Westcountry Chronicle* and thus felt justified in being in the know about everything that was happening throughout the building. She didn't exactly eavesdrop on conversations; that would be more than her job was worth. She just happened to overhear snippets as she switched calls about and made connections. It was strange but when Megan, Hector's wife, called him at work, Wendy was often the unwilling recipient of a great deal of information, ranging from the mildly interesting to the very personal indeed. She knew for instance that Hector was seven years older than herself, that Hector's marriage was in trouble long before he publicly admitted as much, that his and Megan's arguments were invariably about starting a family, but that Hector's sperm count – whatever wicked things her workmates were saying – was absolutely up to scratch.

Wendy sighed and stopped stroking her shoulder. She had been wracking her brains for some foolproof scheme which would ensure that Hector actually saw her as a *woman*, not just as part of Reception. Next month's office Christmas party seemed to be her best bet, but it was fancy dress this year and she couldn't for the life of her decide what costume to wear. Should she go as somebody famous; Marilyn Monroe? No, she wasn't blonde and she didn't fancy a wig. Maybe something connected with one of Hector's special articles? That way he'd be bound to notice her.

Hector came down the stairs again and said, 'Wendy? Don't suppose you have any ideas on cooking pheasants do you? This poaching story is producing some rather tasty perks!'

'Roast, casseroled or what?'

'You're wonderful,' Hector said. 'In a microwave for preference. I think I could just about manage that. Could you jot it down for me?'

And it was whilst she was writing, from memory, the essentials of the recipe on another little yellow Post-it, that Wendy had her fateful idea.

2

'TIME to go?' Barry Poole said, suddenly arriving in the doorway of Jess's office, puffed, and flourishing a press release.

Jess jumped. 'I didn't know you were coming with me today.' Barry was the *Chronicle*'s most recent graduate trainee, working on the paper whilst he studied for his qualifications in journalism. He seemed to Jess to spend most of his time alternately eating crisps, and in a day-dream about his future prospects. She quite liked him, in spite of the fact that he had been the main instigator of the ribaldry about Hector. Of course, from what she now knew, the taunts were quite unfounded, but she wouldn't be able to tell Barry that. She'd promised.

'Yeah. Nige says he wants a few supplementary questions. D'you know Jess, I really covet that man's job. D'you think I'll have made News Editor by the time I'm his age?'

'Doubt it,' Jess teased. 'Come on then if you're coming.' She led the way out to the car park and climbed into the yellow Jeep which had the *Chronicle*'s logo painted prominently on both doors. Since she was out and about more than most of the staff, and on call at any time of day or night, she was the one who drove it the most often and considered it virtually hers.

Ever since its visit to the garage, it had started perfectly, as it did now. They drove out of the High Street and left along Marine Parade. It had been a mild and unusually wet winter so far. Jess, glancing sideways briefly as she drove, could see another squall approaching across the flat grey sea.

'Looks like we're going to get soaked,' Barry observed.

'Mmmmm.'

'You know Jess, I've been getting really hacked off with

only rewriting press releases and doing wedding reports. I mean, what I'd ideally like is a good juicy human-interest story, but since I'm not offered one, I was thinking of doing an environmental piece on unpredictable rainfall. What d'you think?'

'Hector usually does all the green issues. It's his special interest.'

'But not his only one, so I hear.' Barry cackled. Jess was silent. 'Well go on then. That was your cue to ask me . . .' His plump cheeks quivered in anticipation.

'I've heard all the cracks about him,' Jess said, stopping at a red traffic light and turning to face him, 'and I think they're pathetic.'

'Nah,' Barry brushed them aside. 'Ancient news. This is bang up to the minute. You know that classy female who was on the front page a couple of weeks ago; the top executive?'

'Caroline Moffat?'

'That's the one. Well we all reckon that her and Hector are an item.'

'*You what?*'

'True as I'm sitting here. One of the Subs saw them together at the Purple Matador the other night. He said H.M. was all over her!'

'But she's quite wrong for him,' Jess protested. 'I knew her years ago, and she isn't Hector's type at all.'

'No accounting for taste,' Barry said.

'You're having me on?'

'No, honest, straight up.' A car behind them hooted. 'It's green,' Barry observed, 'and at this point in time, I believe it's normal to be in gear?'

So far, Hector thought complacently, things with Caroline are motoring along nicely. He stretched himself back against the leather upholstery of his old and trusty Jaguar, and drummed his fingers cheerfully on the steering wheel in time to a burst of Wagner from Classic FM. Caroline clearly quite fancied him, and was happy to talk about herself. Up to now it had been light superficial stuff, but Hector had hopes of doing some in-depth research on her antecedents pretty soon. He wasn't quite sure how he would go about the questions he wanted to put to her on the subject of genetics. He could hardly turn to her and ask baldly, 'Any madness in your family?' Yet if he merely said, 'You look as though you come from fine healthy stock?' she might just laugh and he'd be none the wiser. How to elicit vital facts without subjecting the woman to a cross-examination – that was the question.

The more he thought about it logically, the more he was amazed at how casually people got together to procreate, with no thought of the Pandora's box of concealed and potentially, heritable disasters. I mean, he told himself, people don't go into business ventures until they've sussed out all the pros and cons. They don't buy anything large or important until they've priced it in at least two different shops, so why on earth do they let themselves be conned by their hormones into choosing totally unsuitable breeding partners merely on the transient pretext of 'love'? You only have to look about you at modern relationships, to realise that whole idea is doomed.

Looking at things dispassionately, Hector thought, (which is what I must train myself to do, in spite of my normal human instincts) I've clearly got to try to find an ideal set of genes for my son to inherit. It's not at all the same thing as eugenics – that whole concept is clearly abhorrent – it's more like a positive affirmation of the best that humankind can offer . . .

He avoided a wobbly cyclist by inches, but managed to hang on to his train of thought: after all, man had perfected his livestock by generations of selective breeding, so perhaps this wasn't such a huge step . . .? Hector was still partly unconvinced . . . Maybe it was a little extreme? But this sort of thing would come – of that he had no doubt. It was just a pity that designer babies weren't yet on-stream . . . Anyway, whatever happened it was obvious that an arranged marriage would be the best compromise he could realistically achieve – providing of course that he could arrange it in his own way.

Hector drew the car in towards the kerb and stopped outside an ugly 1930's house, the ground floor of which he was renting (very temporarily) as a flat. The sooner my divorce goes through and I can move from this dump, the better, he thought. I'm certainly not going to entertain Caroline here. Thank the Lord I've got an alternative venue. It might be a little tricky, but I'm pretty sure I can pull it off. He let himself in, and went straight to the living room where he poured himself a large whisky and sank reflectively into the depths of his capacious leather chair.

Of course, he thought, body chemistry has to come into the equation. There's no way I could contemplate getting together with a woman I didn't desire, but again, that mustn't be allowed to cloud the issue. It's so easy to get carried away . . . He went over his plan in his head. If Jess's reaction had been anything to go by, and Hector thought it most probably was, then he couldn't afford to be open about his aims. He'd have to employ a bit of subterfuge; maybe tell the successful female candidate that he'd had a vasectomy? There were well-documented cases where the operation hadn't worked, which would let him off the hook if subsequently necessary. Of course he'd have to make sure she hadn't got a coil, or wasn't taking the pill . . . Then, if a baby came along, all well and good, and if one didn't, then back to the drawing-board and the search for another suitable partner. It was all so beautifully simple in theory.

Hector took a long swig of Scotch and let out a sigh of contentment. Then of course he'd have to buy himself a proper house, in keeping with his status in life, but he would have to delay that until after the divorce and the question of the settlement had all been decided. Once it was safely completed, and with Megan out of the picture, he would be free to liberate the funds he'd prudently stashed offshore, and begin again; maybe even recreate the same room for his son? Hector, in his mind's eye, saw the young Morgan gurgling happily in a brand new cot, with the blue elephants and the alphabet frieze on the wall above the child's precious head . . . the pit of his stomach did a little flip, as fanciful paternal pride swelled within him.

After Hector had downed his Scotch and glanced at the early evening news on BBC1, he eased himself out of the chair to go to his bedroom and sort out a change of clothes for the evening ahead with Caroline. That night he had planned a quiet dinner in a discreet restaurant where each table was cosily boxed into its own alcove, the ambience illuminated by candlelight and mellowed by revolving Mozart. He debated out loud on his choice of shirt. The cotton or the silk? He stood in front of his full-length mirror and held each one up to his chest in turn. Then he leant forward rather smugly and inspected his hairline. Maybe the gods haven't always been kind to me, he thought, and maybe I am going a little grey but at least, thank God, I'm not bald!

Caroline dressed with care for her dinner with Hector, putting her hair up in a chignon and applying eye make-up with a steady hand; mouth half open to aid concentration. She regarded the finished product with some satisfaction. Vivian would approve. She hoped Hector would too.

Caroline thought about Vivian as she drove towards her rendezvous with Hector. They had met years before when she had gone into his art gallery in Bath to buy a painting, and they had been friends and occasional lovers ever since. She had wondered initially whether he was gay, but had eventually concluded that he was just not all that fired-up about sex, rather like herself in fact. On the occasions when they did go to bed together, he made a good job of it (being a perfectionist at heart), but for both of them, a little seemed to go a long way. It did have the great advantage that they never got bored, or possessive, or took each other for granted. There were worse arrangements.

So what am I doing with Hector? she asked herself, as she walked into the restaurant. Toying with a minor aristocrat – 'a bit of smooth'? Having a fling? Recharging the old batteries? Whatever. So I fancy him; and why not? There he is, over by the bar. Here goes . . .

'Caroline! Lovely to see you,' Hector said, coming to meet her. 'You look wonderful.'

'Thank you.'

'Now, what will you drink before we're bidden to our table?'

Caroline noticed that Hector drank rather a lot during the course of the evening, but appeared none the worse for it. For her part, she stuck mainly to mineral water, the better to stay in control. Hector seemed fascinated by every aspect of her past life. She felt flattered, but still inclined to tease him. For his part, he was clearly eager to demonstrate his authority, summoning waiters with a flick of the fingers, and sending his fork back to be replaced by a clean one. He also demanded a fresh candle and a different kind of bread roll.

'I've just been reading an article on the Human Genome project' he had said over the starter, tucking in with gusto now that he had everything arranged to his satisfaction. 'You've heard of the thing? They're mapping all the millions of genes on our chromosomes. It's quite fascinating. Just imagine if you had the blueprint for your entire genetic, make-up right there in front of you, on paper! Now wouldn't that be something?'

'I'm not a great believer in genetics, actually,' Caroline said, sipping some of the liquor from her *moules marinières* from half a mussel shell, and then wiping her mouth with a napkin. 'I'm convinced that nurture has far more influence on the developing person than nature. You've only got to look at the way that poor environments produce problem children. And then they all too often develop into adults with psychiatric problems who eventually get "cared for" in the "community" which, as far as I can see, is a fate worse than death. But if they'd been born into good homes and given proper parenting, then who knows?'

'Oh I can't agree with you there,' Hector leant forward earnestly, 'It's well documented that manic depressive illness, for instance, is passed on down through families, regardless of social status. You must have come across examples of that yourself?'

'Not really.'

'You don't have those sorts of problems in your family?'

'Oh I didn't say that. No, what we're talking about here is not the occurrence, but the mechanism, right?'

'Well . . . yes . . . but personal experience is always relevant, isn't it.'

'I always try to keep off the personal when exploring issues,' Caroline said. 'Anecdotal evidence can be very suspect.'

'But still valid, surely?'

Caroline laughed. 'You'd have to defend it. It's your stock-in-trade as a journalist.'

'I'm not being a journalist now,' Hector said, reaching forwards and taking her hand. 'I want to know all about *you*.'

'Why?'

'Because you fascinate me. Tell me for instance about your parents. What sort of people are they?'

'They live in a small castle in Scotland, and have a guard dog called Offenbach. I think that says it all.' Caroline suppressed a giggle.

'Really?' Hector looked impressed.

Caroline relented. 'No,' she said, 'actually they live in a semi in Watford and have a Jack Russell terrier called Fergus. They're very ordinary and elderly and lovely, but I'm afraid of no possible interest to the Press.'

'Please' Hector said, 'I'm being serious you know, and I'm not the Press. I just happen to think you're someone rather special, and I want to fill out this mental picture I have of you; give it depth, foundations . . .'

'You mean you want to find out which pigeon-hole to file me in?'

'Well, yes if you like. I mean, if a person had spent his adolescence in hospital, say, he might turn out rather differently than if he hadn't. History leaves its mark, and I find people's scars interesting.'

'Oh I *see*,' Caroline said, breaking into a wide smile. 'You're after the skeletons in my cupboard: deceived lovers, drug abuse, corruption in high places . . . yes?'

Hector sat back as their main course was served. He was frowning and his face looked flushed. I must be careful, Caroline thought, not to push him too far or he'll go right off me, and this whole evening will be a complete waste of time. As the waiter withdrew, they both started talking at once.

'You've got me all wrong . . .' Hector began.

'Forget it,' Caroline said, 'I'm . . .'

'Sorry?'

'I'm sorry too. I can never resist a tease. Just tell me what it is you want to know and I'll do my best to give you straight answers.'

'How about if I tell you things about me, and then you tell me things about you in return? Then we could really get to know each other.'

'If you like.'

'Right. Shall I start?' Hector drew a deep breath. 'I've had a vasectomy.'

'Did it hurt?'

'NO! You're supposed to say something relevant in reply to that, such as, "I'm on the pill".'

'Does it have to be the truth?' she asked. Hector looked as if he might give up in disgust at any moment. 'Well I could say I was,' Caroline explained hurriedly, 'but I'm not, so it would be a lie. But I'm glad you've been tied off. It's always such a reassuring thought, isn't it?'

'You're not keen on children then?'

'Oh I didn't say that. It's just that at the moment my career is more important to me than babies.'

'Women tend to change their attitude once they've got one, or so I'm led to believe,' Hector said.

'Well this one isn't likely to. When, if, it ever happens, I have absolutely no intention of giving up my job.'

'Oh,' Hector frowned again.

'Well, go on then.'

'I will, when you've said yours,' Hector said. 'Otherwise it's not fair.'

'Oh OK. I give in. I use a cap and spermicide.'

The waiter, who was holding a bottle over Hector's glass at this moment, jumped, and spilt red wine on to the table. Hector, strangely, appeared not to notice. He was smiling broadly. He paused calmly whilst the nervous waiter reappeared with a cloth and mopped up the mess, and then he leaned towards Caroline confidentially and said, 'My sister has diabetes'.

'Oh that's tough . . .' Then she saw the irritated look on Hector's face and said hastily, 'Well I haven't actually got a sister, but . . . um . . . I had measles when I was four. Will that do?'

Hector sighed. 'My IQ is 140,' he said.

'Heavens! Mine's 125 . . . I think. Or is that the beginning of my PIN number? I never can remember.'

'I vote Conservative,' Hector said grimly.

'Yes, you would. I'm a Lib Dem myself.'

'I'm divorced.'

'I guessed as much. I've never made the mistake of getting married.'

'I have a private income on top of my salary.'

'I'm fabulously wealthy too.'

'Now you're just pissing me about.' Hector looked hurt.

'Well, it's just that this strikes me as a most peculiar way to conduct a conversation. Is this how you normally chat someone up?'

'Would you like a sweet?' the waiter enquired.

'Go away!' Hector growled. 'We're not ready.'

'Certainly sir.'

'OK,' Hector said to her. 'One more, and then we'll stop. Right?'

'If you say so.'

'C-haugh!' He cleared his throat. 'Last one. Um . . . several of my wife's family suffer from achondroplasia (that's hereditary dwarfism, you know).'

'Were they much in demand during the pantomime season? Sorry, sorry . . . er . . . right, well my brother is a congenital idiot, or so I'm always telling him. Look, I'm sorry Hector, but this is ridiculous. It isn't getting us anywhere. If we must go on playing silly games, I'd rather do word-association. Better idea – why don't you take your mind off disease and destiny, by having a nice sticky pud from the trolley over there? I'll just have coffee, thanks.'

Jess took off her boots and curled up in one of Caroline's plush sofas.

'Glass of wine, a G & T or what?' Caroline asked her.

'I don't suppose you've got any cider?'

'Sorry.'

'White wine would be lovely then.'

'So,' Caroline said, bringing it over, 'tell me all about what's been happening to you since school. The five years between us seemed a chasm then didn't they? They hardly register at all now.' She sat back opposite Jess, smiling, sipping a gin and tonic.

'You're still streets ahead of me,' Jess said, looking round the room. 'This flat's marvellous, and I love that painting.'

'It's one I bought from Vivian, a friend of mine who runs a gallery. You must meet him one day, you'd like him. You're not married then?'

'No,' Jess blushed.

24

'No children?'

'God, no!'

'Very wise. I have absolutely no intention of breeding just yet either – maybe not ever.'

Jess thought, well, that wasn't exactly what I . . . I mean, chance would be a fine thing . . . 'Oh,' she said.

'It always infuriates me that people with families who are replicating their own narcissistic, imperfect, egocentric genes down the millennia (and vastly overpopulating the world in the process) then have the nerve to complain that the voluntarily childless are *selfish*!' Caroline said.

Jess laughed. I needn't have been concerned about Caroline and Hector, she thought amusedly; they won't last a moment. They're totally incompatible!

'Talking about selfish genes reminds me,' Caroline went on, 'your Hector Mudgeley seems fascinated by heredity?'

'Oh?' Jess was startled by the coincidence of thoughts.

'Yes, we've been out together a bit, as I expect you know. Actually, I'm feeling rather guilty about him. I think I went a little too far last time.'

'In what way?'

'Teasing him.'

'Oh Hector's got a very good sense of humour.'

'Yes, he's an amusing chap,' Caroline agreed.

There was a pause, during which Jess searched for something intelligent to say. 'Tell me about Vivian's gallery,' she said. 'I could do with some education in modern art.'

The rest of the evening went well. Jess was flattered that Caroline would bother with someone like her, who had previously been so insignificant in her life. It's probably because she's newly back in the area, Jess thought, and finds she doesn't know anyone now. Well that's fine by me. They compared notes about the progress of fellow pupils and members of staff, and laughed about trivial things which had once loomed large. At eleven thirty she got reluctantly to her feet and said she really ought to be going. 'I expect you'll be busy tomorrow?'

'As ever,' Caroline agreed, escorting her to the front door, 'but thanks so much for coming. It's been really lovely to see you. We must make a regular thing of it.'

'I'd like that,' Jess said, bending down and thrusting her left foot back into its boot.

'Oh, and Jess?'

'Mmmmm?'

'I have to ask . . . you're not by any chance smitten with Hector yourself?'

'Oh . . .' Jess wobbled and clutched at the hall table to steady herself. She pressed her right foot firmly down into the second boot. Then she stood up straight again, pink in the face and smiled shyly at Caroline. 'Heavens . . . no, of course not. Perish the thought!'

'Oh good,' Caroline said, giving her a quick peck on the cheek. 'That's a great relief to me. You see, I just suddenly thought . . . I mean, I'd hate to step on your toes.'

3

HECTOR felt vaguely uncomfortable about all the lies he had told Caroline in his attempts to draw her out and obtain some hard data. Well, some of it was true, he reminded himself. I *do* vote Conservative, and the private income and the divorce (well, the impending divorce), are real too. It was just the illnesses . . . He wondered if he'd made a complete prat of himself. Perhaps Caroline wouldn't want to see him again? Did he, in fact, want to see her? She was a trifle sharp; a bit too ready to take the piss, but in truth, he had probably asked for it. The only really important question was her apparent dislike of full-time motherhood. Hector wondered how well-thought-out that idea of hers had been, and felt inclined to discount it. He decided that it was a common enough attitude in successful young career women, until time and the advent of the right man combined to transmute it into comfortable domesticity. It was not an insuperable obstacle. Hector poured himself a whisky and sat back, watching the pictures on his silent television. He always zapped the sound off during the advertisements. The telephone rang.

'Hector!' Caroline said. 'I've had a bad conscience about you . . .'

Excellent, Hector thought. That's a good sign. 'Oh?' he said.

'Yes. I hope you didn't think I was laughing at you, last time we met? I'm afraid we tend to be a bit cutting in our family. My brother's just the same . . .'

'Oh, I'm all for sharp wits,' Hector said, 'especially when packaged so beautifully.'

'Ah,' Caroline said, 'under the circumstances I suppose I'd better take that one on the chin, and thank you prettily.'

'Come round to my house this Saturday evening,' Hector said, 'and do it in person. I'll organise some food.'

'Lovely idea. How do I get to you?'

'It's difficult to find,' Hector said carefully. 'Best thing would be for me to meet you in the pub in the village and drive you there, . . . here, myself.'

'Well . . . all right then.'

They arranged to meet at eight thirty. That should give me time, Hector thought, to do the necessary preliminaries, and also to get us a Chinese takeaway for supper. That cool-box thing of Megan's keeps things hot as well, doesn't it? Now, I must organise sheets . . .

'Have you noticed,' Barry asked Jess over a snatched snack lunch in the *Chronicle*'s coffee area, 'Wendy's not wearing her engagement ring any more?'

'Can't say I have.'

'Perhaps it's all off?'

'Mmmm.'

'Jess? You wouldn't find out for me, would you?'

'Why?'

Barry choked on a bit of cheese and onion crisp, and Jess beat him on the back. 'Stop! Enough!'

'Are you keen on her yourself, then? Surely not?' Jess broke into a broad grin. 'She's *years* older than you!'

'Fourteen.'

'But Barry . . .!'

'Aren't we being just a teensy bit ageist here, Jess? And, no, I'm not admitting to anything. I'd just like to know, OK? I wouldn't ask anyone else, but I know you won't tell on me.'

'So how am I supposed to find out?'

Several people came in and stood at the coffee machine, chatting. Barry frowned a warning and started flipping through a pile of photographs on the table in front of Jess. 'Who are all these stuffed shirts?'

'Don't get greasy fingerprints all over them! They're Caroline Moffat's Board of Directors, and they're works of art.'

Barry sniffed. 'I've got a gut feeling about that woman,' he said. 'Bet you ten pounds that H.M. gets into her knickers within the month. It's a doddle; can't fail!'

'Now then,' Hector said on Saturday evening as he ushered Caroline out of the pub and into his Jaguar. 'Your car will be fine here in the car park. We could always go in convoy, of course, but it's much more friendly like this, isn't it?' He seems a bit jumpy, Caroline thought. I wonder if he's planning a big seduction scene. 'Let me know if you happen to see a red Mini, will you?' Hector went on, 'only my cleaning lady drives one and I forgot . . . to pay her.'

'She doesn't work evenings, does she?' Caroline said, surprised.

'Sometimes, yes. She's a little unpredictable.'

In the event, no red Mini was sighted, and they travelled rapidly along country lanes in a confusing moonlit journey, during which Caroline was almost sure she'd seen the same crossroads twice, lit up in the headlights, but approached from different directions.

'What's that picnic bag for?' she asked.

'Supper,' Hector said. 'I'm no great shakes as a cook, I'm afraid. Hope you like Chinese?'

'And if I don't?' Caroline wrinkled her nose. Hector stared at her. 'Look where you're going! I was only joking.'

'Just as well,' Hector said, turning the car into a driveway, 'because we're here.'

'Oh,' Caroline said, getting out and looking up at the moon. 'Turrets, fancy!'

Megan Mudgeley drove angrily eastwards across the Severn bridge in the moonlight. Her Mini seemed to be firing on only three cylinders, and the beams from the headlamps were even more feeble than usual. In Megan's mind the two problems were clearly correlated, and she worried about making it home before the lights and/or the engine failed altogether.

I ought to get myself a decent car, she thought. It's ridiculous, constantly driving between Somerset and Wales in this rustbucket. Can't afford one now though, especially after getting that brand new cooker (which cost me a flaming fortune), but when the divorce is all settled (if it ever is) *then* I'll buy myself a VW Golf. She had said as much to her father that morning. That was what had caused their row. He'd never liked Hector, but he didn't hold with divorce either. Oh dear, Megan thought, I shouldn't have stormed out like that. He's an old man. He can't help being grumpy. I should've stayed on until after chapel tomorrow morning at the very least. It'll be a judgement upon me if the bloody Mini gives out and strands me halfway.

Barry stared out through the window of his mum's house at the full moon and felt wistful. It was a clear frosty night, and there was most probably a great skyful of stars out there, twinkling away, which he'd be able to see if only the moon weren't so bright. An analogy occurred to him. Perhaps Wendy would notice him, now that the fiancé had waned, if he really had. He put a smoky bacon crisp into his mouth and crunched it, debating whether he had enough courage to ring her and find out for himself. He convinced himself it would be OK if he didn't ask her directly. Then he keyed-in her number with a sweaty finger.

'Uh, hello Wendy. It's Barry.'

'Who?'

'Barry Poole, you know . . . from work.'

'Oh, Barry. This is a surprise!'

'How are you?'

'I'm fine. I've just been washing my hair. In fact if you'd rung a second earlier, I wouldn't have heard the phone over the noise of my hairdryer. It's really clapped out. I keep meaning to get a new one, but you know how it is. Was there something you wanted?'

'No, yes, well . . . you see I found this ring and I wondered if you'd lost yours because I noticed you weren't wearing . . .'

'You found a ring? Where?'

'Oh, um, on the pavement outside the office. So I wondered . . .'

'Can't be mine,' Wendy said, 'because I threw . . . gave it back. We had one heck of a row if you must know. I told him where he could stick it.'

'So the engagement's off then?'

'You're telling me! I'm not bothered though. He wasn't worth it. No, I'm seeing ever such a nice new bloke, seven years older than me, a professional man, you know.'

'Do I?'

'Do you what?'

'Know this new bloke?'

'Ah, now that'd be telling, wouldn't it?' Wendy sounded arch.

'It's just that I wondered . . .?'

'Ye . . . es?'

'If you'd like to see a film with me tonight . . . or tomorrow . . . or maybe next week, if you're busy . . .?'

'You're asking me out?'

'Well, yes.'

'You?' She laughed, a merry little giggle which stopped abruptly. He knew she had clapped a hand over her mouth. Then she said, 'Don't get me wrong Barry. I'm ever so flattered of course, but it'd be like cradle-snatching, wouldn't it? It's really sweet of you to ask though. You're a nice boy.'

'Oh. Right. 'Bye.' Barry put the phone down. He could feel his face was scarlet with mortification. He glanced quickly all round to make sure his call hadn't been overheard. No. At least his humiliation hadn't been public. God, he felt such a wally! Jess was right, he thought. I should have listened to her. He debated whether he could phone Jess and ask her out instead, but then he thought she might think he *fancied* her, and he didn't think he could handle any more embarrassment in one day. Then he thought, Hey! If Wendy's really got this wonderful new bloke, then what's she doing at home alone, washing her hair on a Saturday night? And he began to feel marginally better.

Caroline noticed that the sitting room of the house into which Hector ushered her seemed to be only partly furnished. There was a sofa but no chairs, a TV cabinet but no television, and a substantial but mostly empty bookcase. But then, as she looked further, she saw that parts of the room were very thoroughly co-ordinated indeed. The curtains all had immaculate pelmets and swags and tie-back sashes, and matched the sofa *and* the carpet. The paintwork and radiators harmonised. The walls toned in, but there were several dark rectangles where large pictures must once have protected the wallpaper from fading. Over some of these, smaller undistinguished prints now hung. It wasn't at all what she would have expected from someone like Hector. Caroline allowed herself to be shown to the sofa, and looked about her in puzzlement as he went to the sideboard and opened a new bottle of gin. There was a bowl of assorted citrus fruits and some shelves with nasty glass ornaments, but no decent books at all. Bad news, Caroline thought. This is probably a ghastly mistake. Why am I here?

'Gin and tonic,' Hector said, coming over with a full glass and standing beside her. 'Ice?'

'No ice thanks, but a slice of lemon would be good.'

'Ah . . .' Hector said, 'I didn't think of that. Bother.'

'There's a lemon over there, in that bowl.'

'Oh? Oh yes, so there is. Not started though . . . but I suppose . . .'

'Are you worried about it drying up once it's cut? Only I . . .'

'No, no,' Hector said hastily. 'Not a problem.' He took the lemon from the bowl and went into the kitchen with it to find a sharp knife.

I'm here, Caroline reminded herself, because I detect a certain earthy vigour in Hector, which I find definitely attractive (and which is decidedly lacking in Vivian). I hope I'm right. She got to her feet and wandered after him into the kitchen. The lemon had already been cut into five thick slices on a plate. Next to it on the melamine working surface, several metallic take-away cartons stood, unopened, cooling. Hector was down on his knees beside the gas cooker, peering inside the oven, with a dead match in his hand.

'What on earth are you doing?' Caroline asked.

He scrambled to his feet looking flustered. 'I was just going to make sure the food was hot enough,' he said, 'but the damn cooker's playing up.' There was a strong smell of gas.

'For goodness sake!' Caroline exclaimed, rushing forwards to turn it off. 'You'll blow us all up! How about opening a window before we try again, eh?' Hector rather sulkily did as he was bidden, and when the worst of the gas had cleared, Caroline closed the oven door and turned the gas on again. 'You surely don't need matches for a state-of-the-art cooker like this?' she said. 'There must be a pilot light?' There was a popping noise as the gas ignited. 'There you are!'

'Oh good,' Hector looked annoyed. Then he opened the oven door again and began putting their supper inside it.

'Do you cook here often?' Caroline grinned.

'What d'you mean?' Hector's head jerked up.

'Nothing! Nothing. It's just that you don't exactly strike me as a new man. Unreconstructed is a word which springs readily to mind!'

'Lemon's there,' Hector said, pointing. 'Be with you in a moment.'

Caroline speared the thinnest ring with the knife, and slipped it into her glass. Then she went back into the sitting room and admired the shine on the ornaments. Hector's cleaning lady might work odd hours, but she clearly knew her job.

'That's all right then,' he said, coming in smiling. 'I think quarter of an hour should do it. Hope you don't mind eating in the kitchen? It's so much easier. In the meantime, let's have some music in here. Did I mention earlier how lovely you look tonight, *cariad*?'

'*Cariad*?'

'Welsh for love, or darling.'

'But you're not Welsh are you?'

'My great-grandmother Gwladys was, and she had an enormous influence on my family in the 1880s. That's a portrait of her.' Hector, without turning, indicated the wall behind his head. Caroline followed his pointing finger and was confronted by an Easter bonnet full of kittens.

'She was a Welsh tabby then?'

'Eh?' Hector jerked round and then laughed in some embarrassment. 'Oh, how ridiculous of me. For a moment there I'd forgotten I'd sent her off to be . . . restored!'

'Something for all of us to look forward to, maybe?' Caroline murmured.

What followed was entirely predictable, she thought, but none the less acceptable for all that. Whilst she drank two gins, Hector admired her clothes, her hair and her intellect. They ate the Chinese food (which had survived its ordeal triumphantly) and then Hector began to kiss her feverishly and mumble briefly about beauty, fate and desire. Then he led her upstairs.

'Here we . . . no, up here,' Hector said, pulling her urgently after him. 'It's actually the spare room, but the view's better.'

'I shouldn't have thought that matt . . .' but he was kissing her again, and fumbling to disconnect hooks and eyes somewhere at the level of her shoulderblades. 'Lower down,' she instructed him when he removed his mouth from hers to take a breath, and then, 'Don't you have a double bed in your room?'

'Lumpy,' Hector explained, between kisses. 'Belonged to my parents, N.B.G, pre-war . . . God, your skin is so soft and smooth . . . and the curve of your neck is . . . exquisite . . . Mmmmmmmmmm'

Caroline lay on her back and counted the blue elephants on the wall closest to her, that is, until she found herself being drawn into the spirit of the occasion. Then she was obliged to close her eyes and go with the flow. Only later did she have time to think to herself, I was right! Hector *is* one of those unusual men who, despite being rich and handsome, is also remarkably good in bed.

Yes, Hector thought, yes, yes, YES! This is it; I'm home and dry! Home, eh? that's ironic. I'm not exactly dry either. I do love the way sweat sticks naked bodies together, once it begins to evaporate. I could lie like this for ever. Now, the only problem is – I shall have to replace Megan's damn lemon. She'll be bound to notice it's gone. And then there's the sheets. I didn't bring any spare single ones . . . I'll just have to check the bed for hairs later. Thank Christ I remembered just in time about Megan's stupid slimming magazine on her bedside table (but only *after* I'd gone to all the trouble of putting clean sheets on the flaming bed). It wouldn't have taken a moment to hide the wretched thing, if only I'd thought, but sod's law I didn't remember it until I was half-way up the stairs with Caroline . . . Mmmm, what a woman!

But, *revenons à nos moutons* Hector thought, what I'll have to do next, is to take her back to the pub to collect her car. Then I'll come straight back here and cover my tracks – I've no idea when Megan is due home. I must put her sheets back on the double bed, wash up, take the food containers and my own bottles of gin and tonic home and . . . Hell! where in heaven's name am I going to find another sodding lemon in the middle of the night?

'D'you by any chance know of a 24-hour supermarket nearby?' he asked.

'You do say the most romantic things.' Caroline yawned and stretched. 'I was almost asleep. Why the sudden interest in shopping?'

'Oh, I was just thinking ahead.'

'Doesn't take you long to switch from the divine to the mundane, does it?'

'Sorry,' Hector said, kissing her silken shoulder. 'Insensitive of me. You are divine – there's no denying it, but I suppose all good things must come to an end sooner or later. I hate to suggest it, but I suppose it's almost time to drive you back to your car, isn't it?'

'What's the rush? Let's not move just yet. I'm so very comfortable . . .' She closed her eyes, 'and anyway, I don't have to be home until tomorrow. We could spend the whole night together.'

'Oh, but is that wise?' Hector hadn't even considered this possibility.

'Why ever not?'

'Well . . . you wouldn't get a wink of sleep,' Hector said. 'I'm afraid I snore horribly. Much better stick to the original plan.'

Caroline's eyes snapped open. 'OK, I get the message,' she said crisply. 'It's amazing how quickly the thrill of the chase evaporates, once the quarry has been well and truly overmastered, isn't it?' Then she threw back the duvet and, standing between the bed and the window, began putting her bra on.

'Please,' Hector said. 'Don't take it the wrong way. I only meant . . .'

'It's quite obvious what you meant. Oh, are you expecting someone?'

'Why?'

'Because there's a car coming up the drive.' Caroline peered through the gap between the curtains.

'*Hellfire!*' Hector cried, leaping out of bed, and scrabbling about on the floor for his clothes.

'Don't panic, Hector. I don't have a reputation that needs

protecting. Ah, yes, I can identify the make of car now, in the light from the front porch. Good Lord! It must be your cleaning lady. She's parking next to your Jag. What an extraordinary hour to turn up. Does she "do" for you daily, eh? Is that why you were so keen to get rid of me?'

'*Of course not!*' Hector gibbered, 'Don't get the wrong idea – old girlfriend – won't take no for an answer – so embarrassing – mustn't involve you – better get your clothes? Oh God! Why the bloody hell . . .? Where's my sodding . . .?'

'If you're looking for your shirt, it's there under the bed,' Caroline observed coldly. 'And what exactly are you hoping I'll do now; shin nimbly down the drainpipe and leg it?'

Hector was speechless.

The front door banged shut, and a powerful woman's voice bellowed, 'Hector? What the fuck do you think you're doing in *my* house? Come downstairs AT ONCE, d'you hear?'

'If I didn't know any better,' Caroline smiled, tight-lipped, 'I'd say that sounded exactly like a wife.'

4

I FEEL a bit concerned about Hector, Jess thought, as she drove home from work. He's seemed very down recently. I wonder what's wrong? She had hoped all day that he would unburden himself to her, but a public meeting about a proposed new housing development had taken up all his time and attention and besides, Hector didn't seem to be in the mood for confidences. Perhaps he's had a falling-out with Caroline, and perhaps she will enlighten me this evening, Jess wondered.

She had invited Caroline to supper rather tentatively, not really supposing that she would want to come, and was both delighted and alarmed when she had accepted with alacrity. What on earth will we talk about, Jess worried, once we've flogged to death all the old tales from school? I'm not sure we have anything else in common.

In the event, it was not a problem. Caroline arrived and from the outset was entirely at ease. She congratulated Jess on the quality of her photographs of the Directors, and proceeded to walk round her flat admiring more of her work on the walls, even asking to see some of her old stuff. Then she sat on the futon with a glass of wine in her hand and said, 'Isn't this lovely? So civilised! D'you know, all my other women friends have small children, and quite honestly it's a waste of time going to visit them these days. If you speak more than three consecutive words to any of them, at least one of their tiresome offspring feels neglected and has to chip in with its say, and from then on any intelligent conversation is totally out of the question. How people survive that kind of stultifying boredom, beats me!'

Oh I see, Jess thought. So she's bothering to befriend me partly because she's lonely, but mostly because everyone else she knows is 'a mother'. I hope she doesn't want me to join her in an association for the glorification of superior childlessness. I mean, I'm not against having children. Perhaps I should say so? As long as she doesn't expect me to swear an oath of eternal . . .

'You're looking very serious all of a sudden?' Caroline said.

'I'm stuck for a word. I've never realised before that there isn't an English noun for the state of being-happily-without-children. "Childlessness" sounds so involuntary somehow. There ought to be one — non-procreatorship . . . barren-itude . . . no . . . Why isn't there, d'you think?'

'Perhaps because it's unthinkable? Although that's less and less true, if you believe the statistics. Apparently these days as many as one in five women are choosing not to have any. I've got a good term for it, actually. So far at any rate, I'm child-free.'

'So's Hector' Jess said, fishing.

'There's a lot of us about,' Caroline said casually. 'Perhaps we're the beginning of the end of the human race?'

Jess didn't take her up on this. 'Of course, unlike you, Hector isn't happy about it,' she persevered.

'Bit late now; crying over snipped tubes, I mean.' Caroline expelled air down her nose in a brief snort.

'What d'you mean?'

'Oh dear, hasn't he told you about his vasectomy? I rather assumed . . .'

'You are joking?'

'No, seriously. I'm sorry, I shouldn't have mentioned it. It's no business of mine. Anyway, it's academic now. He can tie his neck in a knot as far as I'm concerned.'

Jess struggled to make sense of what she was hearing. 'So . . . it didn't work out then?' she ventured, 'between you and Hector . . .?'

'In a word, no.' Caroline smiled. 'No great tragedy. It just didn't get off the ground. No big deal; not even a single tear shed.'

Jess smiled back. 'I'm so glad,' she said. 'I thought you were totally wrong for each other, but I didn't like to say . . . It's just that Hector is mad keen to have children. I probably shouldn't tell you this, but it seems to have become a sort of obsession with him. I expect he's mentioned it?'

'*No?*' Caroline was clearly taken aback.

Jess frowned, 'Oh yes, it's his major preoccupation these days, so I don't understand why on earth you thought he'd had a vasectomy? He'd rather kill himself than do that!' Then an appalling idea occurred to her, rendering her uncharacteristically blunt.

'Oh my goodness, you didn't go to bed with him . . .?'

'Good God, no,' Caroline said, flushing. 'There are limits!'

'Oh, that's all right then. Heavens, you had me worried there for a moment!'

Then over another glass of wine, Jess told her about Hector's suggested strategy for a baby first, followed by marriage, and after Caroline's first horrified reaction at the callousness of the man, they both laughed rather a lot.

Caroline went home quite early and Jess, as she washed up, had a sudden attack of conscience and wished she hadn't said anything about Hector's private life, especially when she'd promised she wouldn't. Then she thought, I don't suppose it matters. It doesn't look as though Caroline will be seeing him again anyway. Thank goodness for that. It was all wrong. I'm glad that she and I are friends. I only hope she's all right though; I thought she was looking a bit pale when she left.

Hector spent a whole week being browned off with himself, taciturn to everyone at work, and furious with Megan. If there was one thing he couldn't stand, it was being made to look a fool. He realised, bitterly, that he had well and truly blown the Caroline option. That was it; finished! Once your dignity had been demolished, to the extent that his had that evening, then there was no going back. He resented the amount of time and effort he'd put into the woman, not to mention the money he'd spent on her, and now here he was, no nearer parenthood; back to square one. Megan's remembered sarcasm still stung him. He winced at the thought.

To take his mind off her, he glanced at his diary. Hell! He really wasn't in the mood for letting his hair down and having fun, and he most certainly didn't feel like making himself look stupid on purpose by wearing fancy dress for the wretched office party this coming weekend.

Whatever it is I go as, he thought (and I suppose there's no way I can get out of going altogether?), then it'll have to be something warm. It's genuine brass-monkey weather these days. I haven't time to mess about making anything, not that I'd have the first idea anyway, so I'll just have to go to that theatrical costume-hire place. And I'll get something with a mask – a little anonymity at this juncture would be most welcome.

By Saturday, Hector had worked out a plan for arriving incognito. The party was to take place in one of the large public rooms on the sea front, where there was ample parking space and good catering facilities. The proprietors of the paper and a handful of local dignitaries had been invited as usual, but this year there was no one that Hector was currently trying to cultivate. He was grateful for this respite. It meant that he could lurk inside his costume for the minimum time required, and then when duty had been served, and without the necessity for any bootlicking, he could get the hell out good and early and bugger off home.

He pondered on this idea with grim satisfaction as he parked his car in the far corner of the car park. Over on the other side he could see the lights of people arriving and hear the whoops and giggles as they identified each other. No one would see him getting out of his Jag. It was nice and dark so no one would know who he was. I'll get out and walk all round the edge until I'm there, he thought. Good thing it's not a garish costume; couldn't be better actually. Right, here goes.

He got out of the car, reached in for the top of his outfit and put it over his head. Seeing out was a little tricky in the dark, and the cold wind whistled in through the slits and made his eyes water, but he finally managed to locate the door lock and turn the key in it. OK, Hector thought, let's get this over with! As he walked briskly round the perimeter of the car park, he patted his hips, chest and bottom in turn, trying to locate somewhere safe to stow his keys and his wallet. There were no pockets. Stupid bloody get-up; clearly not designed by a man, Hector snorted in disgust. I'll have to find some female with spare handbag capacity, to look after them for me. What a bore.

The room was already crowded and noisy when he approached the door, and he was seized by a moment of panic, during which he seriously considered beating a hasty retreat. But then the frivolous atmosphere engulfed him like a kick in the pants, and Hector found himself seduced into an impromptu performance.

As Barry had predicted, there were several pirates in the room. He was glad that he had rejected that notion out of hand. He had been surprised how hard it had been to think up a witty idea for a costume, and he would not have admitted to anyone that he'd finally got his from an old university rag magazine from the 1960s which he'd found behind that filing cabinet he was helping to move from the Sales room. Now though, Barry was sorry that he hadn't had the courage to approach Jess to collaborate in a double act. He should have dressed himself as a clown; Jess could just have come as herself. Then he would have given her a piggyback, and bingo! – *virgin on the ridiculous*. No, it would have been too unkind to Jess, who was a good sort, but not feminine enough for his taste.

Barry looked round for Wendy. He was determined not to appear sheepish. There she was! She looked so sweet. She was a mass of feathers, all brown and grey, stripy, barred and spotted, even down to the matching shoulder bag. She had a little downy head-dress, obviously home-made, with a beak on it, and a long tail hanging down over her bottom. Her shapely legs were revealed in tight brown leggings, and she even had little yellow claws fastened over the front of her high-heeled shoes.

'You look terrific,' Barry said, going over to her. 'What are you?'

'I'm a game bird,' Wendy giggled.

'Are you indeed? Way-hey!' he smirked.

'Now don't you go getting any saucy ideas, Barry Poole. What are you?'

Barry looked down at himself; at the sandwich-boards of thick white card on which he had printed things very carefully in black ink:

MONSIEUR BARRIE CASANOVA,
RUE DE JOIE,
PARIS, FRANCE . . .

This appeared on the front, with a big, red postage stamp at the top right-hand corner. On the back, he'd written *S.W.A.L.K.* (Sealed With A Loving Kiss) and two lines to mark where the flap went. He hoped everyone would get the joke, but worried that it was too out-of-date a euphemism. Nowadays most people simply called them condoms. So, when Wendy asked him, 'What are you?' he really should have told her. It was a heaven-sent publicity opportunity. Knowing Wendy, he would only have had to say it once, and it would have been all round the room in no time.

'I'm a French . . .' His nerve failed him. 'I'm an envelope,' he said.

'How peculiar,' Wendy giggled again. 'Oh no! Look at that!'

A gorilla had bounded into the room, grunting and swinging the knuckles of its large paws close to the floor, and everyone fell silent and stood back to let it into the centre. Once there, it started to beat its chest, but the heroic effect was slightly marred when it dropped something on the floor and had to pat about between people's feet to find it.

'Whoever is it?' Wendy wondered. 'You just can't tell, can you? It's amazing. Oooh it's coming this way. Perhaps it's a gorilla-gram!'

It's a cheat, Barry thought, *hiring* a costume. Any fool can do that. It isn't the least bit clever. 'So, what are you game for, then?' he asked Wendy, but she wasn't listening. The gorilla was advancing towards her, holding out what looked like a bunch of keys and something else.

'Hi Wend,' it said gruffly in a disguised bass voice. 'You wouldn't be an angel and look after these for me, would you; pop them into your reticule?'

Wendy let out a little shriek of pleasure. 'It's *you*!' she breathed. 'It is, isn't it?'

The gorilla put a fat digit to its lips. 'Sssssh,' it said.

Wendy laughed delightedly. 'I haven't got a retic . . . whatever it was you said,' she apologised, taking the wallet and keys, 'but I'll keep them safe in my handbag if you like.'

'Perfect' the gorilla said, patting her feathery bottom with a hairy paw. 'And what species of sporting birdy are you, then? If I snipe, duck and dive, or even goose you, will you grouse or quail or just be pheasant to me?'

Oh wonderful! Barry thought bitterly, as they moved away together. Thank you God, so much. Would-be Lothario upstaged by Pun-man wrapped in hearthrug; how stunningly incompetent!

Jess knew at once that the gorilla was Hector, and thought, How clever! I wish I'd got myself covered up so that I could pretend I'm not who I am. If only I wasn't me, I could be the life and soul of this party, but reality is so dreadfully inhibiting. She had realised as soon as she had arrived that she should have spent more time trying to think of something clever and topical to wear. Even Wendy seemed to have hit the spot. Jess had simply come as 'Westcountry Year' and had stapled some of her best photos of the previous twelve months on to an old kaftan, including as many amusing ones as she could find. It wasn't daring or original as she now acknowledged to herself, but it was warm and safe, and a surprising number of people came up and peered at her.

'Lift your arm up a bit,' Barry said, beside her. 'I don't remember that one?' He was looking at a moody photograph of a drainage ditch on the Somerset Levels under louring clouds, in which the gleaming silver rhyne sliced through the flat fields into the middle distance in a hard straight line. In the foreground an untidy bay had been cut into its bank and a drunken hand-painted notice beside it read: NO FISHING IN COW DRINK.

'No,' Jess agreed, 'it was just one I liked. I quite often walk down there on the moor for fun, you know. I take binoculars and watch birds.'

'What, in this weather?'

'Well no, it's far too wet at the moment. Most of the droves are under water; have been for weeks.'

'I'd hate to live down there,' Barry said, making a face. 'Horrible foggy, boggy sort of place, full of peat mumps and far too much sky. Looks like it's in the process of getting even wetter too.' He inclined his head towards the large dark windows. Someone had forgotten to draw the curtains, so it was possible to look out over the sea front. Jess did so. In the yellow glare from the street lamps she could see that it was raining hard. The wind had got up too, bowling an empty fish and chip wrapper at speed along the promenade, and sending odd waves high over the sea wall in a flurry of froth and sand. She could imagine the combined noises of wind, waves and rain, but the thick glazing of the windows and the swell of party voices kept it at bay for the moment.

Leaving here is going to be horrible, Jess thought. But I won't think about that now. Maybe the weather will have calmed down by then?

'If it carries on like this, I'll be papier mâché by the time I get home,' Barry said, echoing her thoughts. 'I knew I should have come as a frogman.'

He wandered off to get his glass refilled, and Jess looked round to find someone else to talk to. Hector was not far off, in the centre of a group of people. He had taken his gorilla head off and left it somewhere, and his paws dangled from his wrists on bits of elastic, like a child's gloves. Jess smiled. Then Hector turned in mid-sentence and saw her, beckoning her to join them with a gesture of his head and an answering smile.

'Nice get-up,' Jess said when she arrived beside him. 'Suits you.'

'No pockets,' Hector said. 'Honestly, how do gorillas manage?'

Hector was enjoying himself in spite of overheating in his tight-fitting costume. To cool himself off, he drank a lot of ice-cold lager and wiped his damp forehead from time to time on a hairy arm. As he was exchanging friendly banter with Jess, the food was announced and they went through to the buffet together.

'It's simply pouring down outside,' she said to him. 'There'll be more floods at this rate.'

'I'll be OK,' Hector said. 'I'm on a slight hill. Your flat's high up too, isn't it?'

'Oh yes. I was thinking more of the cottages on the edge of the Levels.' They joined the queue for food.

'Daft place to live if you ask me; just asking for trouble.'

'I've got some lovely photos down there, over the years.'

'You're a good photographer. Ever thought of going free-lance, moving to London even?'

'You trying to get rid of me?'

"Course not. Fancy a vol-au-vent?'

I mustn't talk to Jess too long, Hector thought. I'd be more gainfully employed having a good look round just in case Caroline's successor-in-title happens to be here; unlikely but always a possibility. Mustn't miss a trick. No time to lose! He piled his plate high with goodies from the buffet table and then moved through the crowd, eating as he went, exchanging polite but brief chit-chat with those he bumped into or couldn't avoid. After another hour, when it was obvious that there was not a single woman at the party who was remotely eligible, Hector decided to push off.

It was a bit on the early side, so he slipped out into the storm without making any demonstrations of farewell, and walked briskly across the car park to his car. Even before he got there, he was soaked to the skin. The gorilla suit which had trapped his sweat on the inside all too efficiently, was now leaking like a colander the other way round! He'd put the headpiece on to act as a hat, but the rain was oozing in at the join and dripping down the back of his neck. Then he couldn't see through the eye slits to find his car in the semi-darkness, so he was obliged to take the head off again and carry it under one arm. Not long now, he thought, thank God. Home and a hot bath, whisky and bed. It had never seemed so welcome. He located his car with a sigh of relief and felt for his key . . .

'SHIT!' Hector cursed loudly, dumped the head on the bonnet of the Jaguar and stumped angrily back through the rain in search of Wendy and her handbag.

Wendy had noticed Hector slipping out into the night and had been on the verge of running after him, calling, 'Hey! Don't forget your things!' when a much better idea had occurred to her. It was so fiendishly good that she nearly gasped aloud. Instead she made a dash for the cloakroom, grabbed her mackintosh and umbrella, and then set off to walk home through the wind and rain as fast as her unsuitable shoes would carry her. As she passed a line of stationary taxis at the rank, her umbrella blew inside-out for the third time and Wendy, hanging the expense, took one for the rest of the way home. Then she kicked off her high heels, ran upstairs, tore all her feathers off, put on her best silky robe and a liberal spraying of perfume, repaired her make-up, brushed her hair and sat down to wait.

Hector took an inordinately long time to arrive. Wendy almost gave up on him and went to bed, but kept waiting for five minutes more each time, just in case, yawning all the while and having great difficulty in keeping her eyes open. She rehearsed what she would say when he did eventually show up, and hoped it would sound convincing. In the meantime she cuddled up in her big armchair in front of the gas fire and crossed her fingers.

The chiming of the front-door bell threw her into an instant tizzy. She leapt out of the armchair, discovering as she did so that one leg had gone to sleep and was now all prickly with pins and needles. She clutched the front edges of her robe together with one hand and, rubbing her leg with the other, limped to the door and opened it only as far as the chain would allow.

'Who is it?'

'It's me, Hector,' he sounded cross.

'Oh, Hector! Just a minute, I'll open the door.' She undid the chain and the force of the wind burst the door wide open. Wendy clutched at herself and gabbled, 'Oh! Come in. You look wet through! I'm ever so sorry about your stuff in my bag. I looked everywhere for you to give them back, but I couldn't find you anywhere. I didn't know what to do. I thought maybe someone had given you a lift home, or even a bed for . . .'

'No,' Hector said shortly, stepping over the threshold and leaning his full weight against the door to close it again. 'I've been looking for you too. If only you'd stayed at the party a little longer, then I wouldn't have had all this trouble.' He looked down at his feet. Water was dripping from the black fur and forming dark patches on Wendy's hall carpet. 'Hell! I'm wet to the bloody bone.'

'You'll catch your death like that,' Wendy said. 'I'm really sorry. I just didn't know what to do for the best. Look, you mustn't stay all cold and wet. How about having a hot bath here, now? I could pop the gorilla suit into the tumble dryer – I mean, you really can't go out again like that, can you?'

'Oh I don't know . . .' Hector began, then a shiver went right through him, making his teeth chatter, and he grudgingly agreed. 'Oh, all right then. God, what a farce.'

Hector had found it hard to believe that Wendy had left the party without giving him his things from her bag. Surely no one could be that dim? How the hell did she think he was going to get home without them? He had wasted a lot of time rushing round all the party rooms, the cloakroom, the bogs, the entrance hall, every-bloody-where looking for the stupid woman. Then, when he concluded that she really must have gone home, he couldn't find anyone who knew where she lived! Oh he knew roughly where it was, but roughly wasn't good enough on a night like this and in such a ridiculous get-up. So he went to look for a phone book, but there wasn't one. He tried Directory Enquiries and they gave him her number but refused to divulge her address. Then he saw it was a payphone, but he didn't have any money, and by the time he'd realised this, he'd forgotten the number, because he hadn't anything to write it down on. By this time, he was incandescent with frustration, jumping up and down and beating his head with his fists.

'Something wrong?' Barry enquired, on his way to the cloakroom.

'You don't happen to know Wendy's phone number by any extraordinary chance, do you?' Hector was clutching at straws.

''Course I do. Why?'

'She's only taken my bloody keys . . . You DO know it? Thank Christ for that! I don't suppose you've got change for the phone as well?'

'Sorry. Spent it all on booze. You could always reverse the charge, or, better still, I could pop round there for you, if you like. Have to be on foot though; I left the car at home so's I could drink.'

'You mean you *know her address?*'

'Yeah.'

'Well why the blazes didn't you say so in the first place?'

'Well you never asked m . . .' but Hector interrupted him and made him say it twice, and slowly so that he could get it properly memorised.

'D'you want me to go then?' Barry asked. He seemed eager to do so for some reason.

Hector stared at him. 'What, like that?'

Barry looked down at his sandwich-boards and then out at the gale. 'Well, on second thoughts, perhaps not.'

'No,' Hector said. 'Thanks, but no thanks. This is my disaster. I'll sort it out myself.'

He walked briskly through the wind and rain, and was grateful the weather was so bad that there were few people around to jeer at his costume. A few cars hooted, and one youth wound down a window and wolf-whistled, but he strode on regardless. He felt very irritated with Wendy, but he made himself concentrate on the task in hand. He would get his keys etc. and then leave, walking fast (which would keep him warm – rather like wearing a wet suit actually) back to his car and finally, God willing, get *home*.

When Wendy opened her front door to him, Hector was taken aback. She was clearly ready for bed, and equally obviously wasn't wearing anything at all under that dressing-gown thing! He hadn't realised before what good legs she had. She looked younger too, and even fluffier than usual. He had intended waiting on the doorstep whilst she fetched his things, but with the gale roaring into the house as it was, he really had no option but to go inside and close the door.

Now, as he lay in a bath full of foaming scented oil, warm again, he felt enormously relaxed. There was something about coming to a house run by a woman that was curiously soothing. He supposed it was the feminine touch. He glanced around him at the lacy curtains, at the pink and white towels, at the pink knitted cover on the lavatory seat, and felt comforted and pampered. This is a good idea, he thought. Next, I must persuade Wendy to give me a lift to my Jag in her car, once she's dried the gorilla suit.

There was a knock at the door. 'Er . . . hang on,' Hector called, ' . . . I'm still in the bath.'

'It's OK,' Wendy's voice said, 'I've just brought you a cup of hot milk and honey. Don't want you getting a chill. I'll leave it out here, shall I?'

'Oh . . . well, thanks. Yes.' Whatever next! Hector thought, I suppose I can always throw it down the bog. Hot milk!

However, once he was out, and dried, and had wrapped a bath towel firmly round his waist, he emerged and picked up the mug. He sipped it experimentally. It was delicious! He drank it all down, and wiped his mouth on the back of his hand. Right, he thought, now I feel well and truly restored. Time to go!

'Hector?' Wendy called up the stairs. 'Something awful's happened . . .'

'What?' He went to the top of the stairs and looked down. Wendy was standing at the bottom, holding up something small and black.

'I don't know how to tell you this,' Wendy began. 'I thought it'd be OK, but it seems to have shrunk somehow in the dryer. I'm ever so sorry . . .'

Hector clutched the towel with one hand, and the banisters with the other. Then he went down the stairs. He took the gorilla costume from her and held it up. It was now the size of a child's romper suit; totally shrivelled.

'But I can't wear this!' he exclaimed in horror. 'It's completely f . . . *ruined*! What in hell am I going to do now?'

'I'm afraid I haven't any clothes that would fit you,' Wendy said. 'You'll just have to stay the night . . . Yes, that's the answer. Then tomorrow, I'll drive over to your place and get some of your proper clothes, and come back, and you can put them on and then I'll take you to pick up your car!'

'But I've got a busy day tomorrow,' Hector said, looking agitated. 'Couldn't you go now?'

'Oh I would, Hector. It's just that I'm really exhausted . . . and I've had quite a bit to drink . . . and anyway, it's Sunday tomorrow. You're not working this weekend, are you?'

'Well, no.' Hector conceded reluctantly.

'Don't worry,' Wendy went on eagerly, 'we can get up really early. It'd be no bother.' Hector fancied she was blushing and wondered why. She led him into the lounge and sat herself down on a settee.

'Well . . .'

'It'll be fine, Hector. Don't worry. Come and keep warm by the fire a minute,' and she motioned him to sit down next to her.

'Well, if you're sure?'

'Positive.'

'Well, all right then.' He sat down.

'Actually, I'm rather pleased,' Wendy said, leaning towards him. He became aware that she was wearing a very seductive scent, and that the dressing gown which she had been holding closed at the front had slipped and was now revealing rather a lot of cleavage.

Good grief! Hector suddenly thought. Is this all leading where I think it is? Surely not?

5

THE gale seemed to have worsened as Jess drove home from the fancy dress party. She had taken off the photograph-covered kaftan, and in its place had put on a heavy sweater and a scarf. She was grateful for their warmth. The gusty force of the wind was causing the Jeep to tremble like a jelly and veer unexpectedly. The rain was a horizontal monsoon, hitting the road in front of her like smoke, with volleys of drops as large as five pence coins gleaming in the beams of her head-lights. She was relieved to get safely back to her flat, and closed the door thankfully behind her. As parties go, it hadn't been such a bad one, but it wasn't especially good either. Jess sighed and got ready for bed.

Two hours later the telephone shrilled, waking her from a deep sleep. It was Nigel, her News Editor.

'Sorry Jess,' he said. 'Bad timing I know, but there's some fairly dramatic flooding going on – great stuff!'

'Uhhh . . . where?'

'South of Woodspring. Apart from all the rain, we've apparently got an extra-high spring tide with half a hurricane behind it, and it's smashed through the coastal defences. People are having to be rescued by boats and God knows what else!'

'Right.' Jess struggled upright. 'I'm there.' She reached for her glasses.

'So, d'you have any idea where Hector is? I can't raise him. He's not at home and his car phone isn't answering; not like him at all.'

'I hope he's OK,' Jess said, stretching for her clothes with one hand.

'Oh he'll be fine. You know Hector. It's just that it's a bloody good story and I need you both there.'

'I could go via his flat, just in case?' Jess volunteered.

'Great. Thanks.' He gave her the location details ending with, 'Don't forget your wellies!' and rang off.

Jess yawned widely, took off her glasses in order to rub her eyelids with her knuckles and then put them on again, before starting to dress.

When she arrived at Hector's flat it was in darkness, but she could see by the street lights that none of the curtains were drawn. He can't be there, she thought. Where on earth is he? She tried ringing the bell but to no avail, so, after a few minutes she went without him.

It was impossible to get down to the breached sea wall that night, and anyway there was little point in the dark. Jess went instead to the edge of an inland village which was still accessible by road, and where the largest of the *ad hoc* shelters had been set up. This was in the village hall, on higher ground which had so far escaped the inundation. Half of the rest of the place was under three feet of fast flowing water, and by the time Jess had arrived the evacuation of the inhabitants was almost over. It was pitch black but for the emergency lighting, still teeming with rain and about as unpromising for photography as could be. She got a fireman who was taking a short break to hold a brolly for her so that she could attempt a few flash photos of the arrival on dry land of the last boat. Then she followed the trail of resigned old people, harassed parents and excited children clutching pets, up to their temporary refuge.

Once inside, she dried her specs with a tissue and her camera lens with its special cloth, pushed the wet hair out of her eyes, and then took a few more shots as the refugees began to bed down for the remainder of the night in borrowed blankets in uncomfortable heaps on the floor. The pictures would be graphic enough, Jess thought, but they wouldn't be able to capture the real drama of the event; the noise of the storm and the roaring water, and the vibration of the ground shaking underfoot as the roadway nearby was undermined by the flood and great chunks of tarmac were swept away. But above everything there was the *smell* of it all. Few people in the village hall were entirely dry, and their dampness was caused not simply by rainwater, but by saturated peat and mud and the contents of a large number of backed-up sewers and septic tanks. The authorities had brought in portable gas fires, and people were huddling in front of them with their clothes steaming, rendering the entire atmosphere of the room redolent of old wet dog, and worse.

Hector should be here, Jess thought, screwing up her nose in distaste. He could have written a brilliant piece on all this, and he could have interviewed the more forthcoming victims and really gone to town on it. I'd better get some names and addresses for him, although they won't be back in their own homes for weeks, I don't suppose, so finding them again could be tricky. Thank goodness it's only Saturday (well, actually it's Sunday by now), so there's plenty of time to get it together before the Thursday news deadline, and who knows, there may be some dramatic developments between now and then. Goodness, I almost forgot, it's Christmas next week.

Wendy registered the exact moment when Hector finally got the message, and felt a surge of triumph. All at once, Hector's face had become flushed, his eyes seemed somehow darker and more intense, and the hand which had been holding the towel tightly round his middle relaxed a fraction, allowing it to sag round his hips in a casually suggestive manner. He no longer looked like a fool in a farce, caught with his trousers down. All traces of embarrassment seemed to have vanished. He was still dishy in spite of not being exactly young, Wendy decided. He was forty-two, after all, but was wearing it well. His torso was solid and muscular and only moderately hairy, and his demeanour was eminently reassuring. He looked jaunty, in control, appraising. Please, Wendy thought, *please* God make him fancy me. I'll never get a better chance . . .

Hector leant towards her. 'And what would your fiancé have to say about this then?' he enquired softly.

'Oh, that's all off,' Wendy said at once, displaying ringless fingers with pride. 'I'm free again. I can do what I like.'

'I see.' Hector smiled wolfishly. 'And just what is it that you do like?'

'I like you,' Wendy said. She kept her eyes demurely downcast, but allowed the edges of the robe to part a fraction more.

Hector shuffled himself up so that he was sitting right next to her and then, letting go of his towel, he put his left arm along the back of the sofa and smoothly inserted his right hand under her silky gown, cupping her breast and squeezing it gently. 'Like this?' he asked. Wendy gasped, and abandoned all pretence at holding her robe. 'Or like this?' Hector continued, sliding his hand over her stomach and down between her thighs.

'Ohhh . . .' Wendy sank backwards so that her head was resting on the arm of the sofa. Her naked body felt exposed and disconcertingly vulnerable, so she closed her eyes tightly and hoped against hope that she was doing what Hector wanted, and that he wouldn't be disappointed or find her unattractive or worse still, too easy . . .

Then he must have got to his feet, because he was lifting her legs up on to the seat until she was lying full length, and he was kissing her shins and her knees (*her knees?*) with little warm dry nibbles of his lips. She lay still, trying to relax, mystified, but already won over by the unaccustomed sensations and her unbelievable delight in the knowledge that at long last it really was *Hector* who was making love to her . . . His hands crept up her legs, fondling them, easing them apart. Wendy squirmed and, relinquishing all prudish thoughts, prepared to abandon herself completely to anything and everything that he might expect of her.

But, just as he was about to lower himself on top of her, he appeared to be having second thoughts. He paused. Wendy, roused prematurely from her rapturous trance, opened both eyes and held her breath in suspense.

'You're so beautiful, cariad,' Hector began, 'but I'm sorry, I haven't brought . . . you see, I didn't expect . . . I mean, we mustn't take any chances . . .'

'Oh . . .' Wendy almost laughed with relief. 'Is that all? Don't worry. Everything's fine.' She made her voice sound as casually convincing as she could. 'You see, I'm still on the pill.' She looked up at him with love.

'You are?' Hector smiled broadly. 'You wonderful woman, you! Now are you warm enough, or would this be a good moment for us to move over on to that rug in front of the fire? I don't know about you, but I'm finding it a bit awkward and cramped here. Yes? Good . . . Now then, mmmmmm . . . where were we?'

★

When Hector had realised what was afoot at Wendy's, he had been well and truly taken aback. He had never even contemplated her as a possible conquest. She was – well to put it kindly – not quite up to the mark in the brains department. She would certainly be no good as a prospective mother; her children might be as thick as she was! This had completely debarred her from consideration, since Hector was unwilling (these days) to waste precious time on dalliance. It had to be the real thing. Then he remembered all the time he had expended on that Caroline woman, and it occurred to him that he was owed a bit of fun, especially as it was so obviously on offer. He wondered as he began to touch her, whether Wendy had fancied him for some time? The idea appealed to him. She has a good mouth for a gift-horse, he thought, kissing it; not brood-mare material, but a tasty little filly nevertheless. Then suddenly, shrinkingly, he remembered that he had no means of contraception to hand. He'd almost convinced himself with his own vasectomy story! Now that would be ironic, he thought wryly. So with great reluctance he'd had to make himself stop just as it was getting damply interesting. But then she'd laughed and had reassured him that she was on the pill, and in his relief and enthusiasm (and in spite of knowing he was absolutely knackered) he'd got carried away and had gone right through his entire repertoire, all in the one night. Somehow Hector felt, when one was doing it simply for fun rather than for serious procreative purposes, one could be much more relaxed and inventive . . .

Then, just before he had slumped off her, quite exhausted, he had allowed a preliminary verdict – *Bit passive, but OK as a stop-gap?* – to wander idly through his head, before falling deeply into a sticky, satiated sleep for the remainder of the night.

In the morning he felt different altogether. He woke with a start and wondered where the hell he was. Then Wendy turned over sleepily and woke too, with a little gasp of excitement and pleasure. Oh Christ! Hector thought, wishing immediately that he could deflate her and pack her away out of sight in a convenient box, until the next time his sex drive got the better of his critical faculties. He shuddered. God forbid! Then to avoid having to talk to her, he reached over to her bedside radio and switched on the news. Flooding in Somerset was the top story.

'Jesus!' he cried, and shot out of bed. 'SHIT!'

'Wha?'

'I've only been missing the drama of the decade!'

'But you're not s'posed to be working . . . this weekend?'

Hector had great trouble in convincing Wendy of the urgency of his situation; that at a time like this, no self-respecting journalist could consider himself off duty. And now here he was with no trousers, no notebook, no *car* even, and a great elemental story wasting away out there in his absence. He switched the radio off before the end of the news and said abruptly, 'Look I'm sorry, Wendy, but I've really got to GO. So if you could just slip over to my flat now and get me some clothes; the trousers and shirt and jacket are on the chair, by my bed, shoes of course, and socks in the bottom drawer. Here's the keys. It's the ground floor of the house. OK?'

''Nother cuddle . . .' Wendy said sleepily, reaching for him. 'NO!'

He finally persuaded her to go, and then waited for what seemed an age for her to return with his things. When she did so, he was pleasantly surprised to find that she had got it right, even down to matching socks, a jersey and a tie. He took them from her briskly, and dumped them in a heap on the bedroom carpet while he dressed.

'Yours is quite a small flat, isn't it?' she remarked.

'Yes.' Hector was struggling into his trousers.

'And it's rather dark. I reckon it could do with a bit of painting up.'

'Mmm. ' He picked the jersey up off the floor and pulled it over his head.

'I could go over and do it for you, if you like?'

'What?'

'Decorating. I'm quite good at it. I did this place all by myself; only finished the lounge a month ago, and it looks nice, doesn't it?'

'Can't say I noticed really,' Hector said, putting on his shoes and doing up the laces. 'And anyway, I hope I won't be in that grotty flat for long. I'll be buying myself a proper house soon. Right!' He stood up straight. 'I can't tell you how much better I feel to be properly dressed again. Now, how about running me to my car?'

Later as Hector, alone again, drove the Jaguar away from the deserted car park, he squirted the washers and put the wipers on to clear the smoked-glass effect of the previous night's salt spray, and reached for his car phone to get in touch with his News Editor. I'm going to have a lot of explaining to do, he thought; to Nigel, to the wretched costume hirers, even to Jess, who's probably been out all night getting epic photos. I only hope Wendy has the sense to keep her mouth shut. I really do not want it noised abroad that she and I . . .

A nasty thought struck him. I hope to goodness she isn't expecting a repeat performance? No, she'll understand that it was just a one-off office party thing – surely? Now, I must make up for lost time . . .

Some months later, Hector would look back on the rest of that day and realise that it had been fate all along. He had been meant to go to the village hall the day *after* the flood, when everyone was beginning to get used to what had happened, and were therefore more open to telling the tale. If he had been there the night before, they would understandably have been tired, wet, cross, scared, and probably in no mood to talk to him. As it was, he got some first rate stuff, but better still, he met the ultimate contender for the rank and position of Mrs H. Mudgeley. She might have been born especially! It was love at first sight; there was no denying it. Hector had never felt quite so carried away by a woman. He didn't even bother to go through his mental list of 'essential wifely qualities'. There was no need. She was perfect! I must take care, he admonished himself. I must be . . . cool . . . That was the word her son had used, when he had given him his surprisingly articulate account of the drama. Hector thought, now I mustn't rush things . . .

Nevertheless, he found his writing hand was clumsy, making his shorthand even less decipherable than usual, and the hand holding the notebook trembled as he took down her story. She and the boy had been alone in their cottage beside the Levels when the floods had struck. They had been asleep, and then they'd heard the water pouring in. They had no telephone. They'd had to jump from the back bedroom window on to a shed roof, and from there, climb into the boy's tree house where they'd waited hours to be rescued. They had no relatives in the area; nowhere else to go . . .

'It all sounds quite dreadful,' Hector said to her. 'You must have been so frightened?'

'No,' she said, giving him a Mona Lisa smile. 'I'm never frightened. There's no point.'

Wendy looked up hopefully every time someone came in through the swing doors and passed Reception. Hector was never usually this late on a Monday. He couldn't be ill – he'd been bursting with rude health only the morning before! Wendy smiled to herself, but carefully so that the other girl on the desk with her wouldn't see and get nosy. There would be plenty of time to talk openly about Hector and herself – maybe when she had a ring to show off? – but in the meantime it was a wonderful secret.

Only one small cloud was crossing the clear sky of her contentment and causing her a brief frown. She was worried that Hector would be cross with her about the gorilla suit. It really hadn't been part of her plan to ruin it. She had genuinely wanted to dry it for him, but of course in the end it had turned out to be a real piece of luck; the whole idea had worked like magic! She was however a little concerned about what the theatrical costume-hire place would have to say. Not only had the suit been shrunk to uselessness, but the gorilla head had been missing from the bonnet of Hector's car when she had taken him back to it yesterday morning. Someone had nicked it! Would they make him pay the full replacement price? Should she offer to chip in?

No, she thought, Hector wouldn't allow that. He's a real gentleman – even if he does want to do rather dodgy things in bed . . . I'm not a prude, Wendy thought, justifying herself, and it isn't the first time I've been to bed with a man, but I do think that sort of thing ought to be on the level. I don't really like anything . . . funny . . .

So between looking out for him, and taking classified ads from members of the public, and answering the telephone, Wendy day-dreamed about the future and wondered what Hector would do next. Poor love – he really did need a woman to look after that flat – and him. And what about Christmas? He had seemed a little gruff yesterday when they had woken up together, and he hadn't phoned or been to see her since. Perhaps in spite of being such a man of the world, he was shy? The idea both charmed and amused her.

'Share the joke?' Barry suggested in passing, 'and a crisp?' He proffered a packet of prawn flavour.

'No thanks,' Wendy said. 'I've got to keep my figure for my new man,' and she smiled even more broadly, because this time it was true.

'Please yourself,' Barry said. 'Hector get his keys back OK?'

'Oh yes,' Wendy said. 'No problem.'

Jess came past at that moment and stopped to collect her messages. 'By the way, Barry,' she said. 'You lost your bet over H.M. and Caroline Moffat, so you'd better pay up the ten pounds you owe me!'

'How d'you know?'

'Caroline's a friend of mine. She told me. Apparently the relationship crashed even before take-off. And while we're on the subject of Hector, where the hell is he?' she asked. Barry shrugged.

'What bet?' Wendy enquired. Barry told her. 'Oh,' Wendy said loftily, 'I could have told you nothing would come of that. Hector doesn't go for her type at all.' Then she saw identical frowns on both Jess and Barry's faces, and burst into giggles. She heard Jess say to Barry as they walked away, 'What's up with our Wendy today then?' and heard with satisfaction Barry's reply, 'Dunno. She's totally out of her cage isn't she?'

'So, where've you *been*?' Jess asked Hector as he appeared at her open darkroom door, halfway through Monday morning, 'and have you spoken to Nigel?'

'Yes, I phoned him yesterday afternoon,' Hector said. 'Tasty bit of flooding, eh? I got some brilliant heart-rending stuff down at that village hall of yours, with tea and buns thrown in!'

'You never ate their emergency rations?'

'They wouldn't take no for an answer. But enough idle chatter. Where's your pics? There's one I particularly hope you've got . . .' He leafed quickly through the photographs Jess offered him, ignoring her best daylight shots of the broken coastal defences and the newly formed inland sea, and going instead for the technically less good ones from the village hall. He gave an exclamation of pleasure, 'Ha! Good one, and with the boy too.' He flourished a picture of a young woman with long dark hair and gipsy earrings who was wrapping a lovely child of about nine in blankets, and making a rueful face at the camera as she did so. 'That is one beautiful woman,' Hector said, inspecting it closely, 'and she has a very unusual name too.'

'Something like Shakespeare, as I remember?'

'Brakespear – Zillah Brakespear. You wouldn't believe it, but she's actually an Oxford don's daughter who's down-shifted – a real wild child! D'you know, she even quoted *Socrates* at me? I made a note of it. Here . . .' Hector felt about in his pocket, produced a sheet torn from his notebook and unfolded it. *The desire for things is unlimited, so there are two ways to approach your material life: increase your income, or decrease your wants* he read aloud. 'I think that says it all.'

'Maybe in theory,' Jess said.

Hector clearly wasn't going to brook any criticism. He went on enthusing regardless, ' . . . and the boy's called Christian – pretty bright too, I think. He insisted on giving me an interview first, before his mum, and told me an amazing story about snakes . . .'

'You still haven't told me where you were,' Jess insisted, picking bits off his jersey, out of habit, 'and you've got feathers all over your back.'

'Hangover,' Hector said abruptly. 'No excuses, just a plain boring old hangover. No, this Christian child told me that as the water rose higher and higher in their cottage – they live right out in the wilds you see – half a dozen grass snakes swam in through a broken window and swarmed up the stairs! Can you believe it? So I asked him if his mother had screamed, and he said, no, she was . . .' Hector adopted a falsetto treble, ' . . . totally cool, like it happens every day.'

'Must be a witch,' Jess said.

'Well I'll most likely be finding that out,' Hector said airily, shuffling the photographs into a pack and tapping the bottom edges on the bench. 'I decided that it was time I did a festive Good Deed, so that's where I've been this morning – inviting Zillah and son to come and stay with me for Christmas.'

6

ZILLAH Brakespear wrestled with pride versus ethics, and pride won. I am definitely NOT running home to Daddy at the first sign of real trouble, so that he can say 'I told you so', she thought. He's just waiting for my lifestyle (and my relationship with Clive) to fail, and I'm damned if I'm going to give him that satisfaction, *ever*! After all, there is always Hector Mudgeley.

In normal circumstances she and Clive managed well enough. Zillah sold her pots to passing trade in the summer, and Clive took what cargo he was offered, and was away a lot, driving his lorry across the continent. But it didn't generate enough income to cope with a sudden crisis like this flood. Where would they stay? They wouldn't be able to afford hotel bills, and she hated the thought of B & B in this cold weather. If ever I needed a sugar-daddy, she thought, it's now.

Zillah had seen at once that Hector fancied her, but she was well used to wandering hands, sheep's-eyes and grovellers; men in general trying it on, so she'd very nearly given him her *not-if-you-were-the-last-man-alive* look. She was stopped only by the realisation that she was in no position to dismiss such a good offer out of hand. She was in no doubt that there would be a price to pay; she just hoped it would be worth it. Eyeing Hector dispassionately, she supposed he was much like any other tall, middle-aged, greying man, but he did have a very handsome profile, an appealing smile and a sexy laugh. She could do worse. And it was Christmas . . . and it was a long time since anyone had given her presents . . . and Christian seemed keen to go . . .

The day after the storm, the authorities organised transport for a round trip for people to visit their flooded houses (where the water had receded enough) to collect clothes and anything vital that was needed for the ensuing days before normality might return. Zillah had been horrified at the state of her cottage. The building itself still appeared sound, but the mess of mud and slime in the bottom three feet of the ground floor was daunting, and the smell overpowering. She thought, There's nothing I can do, not with Christmas so imminent. I'll have to wait for my landlord to sort it all out anyway, and it's bound to take ages to dry out. It's obvious we can't live here for some time. No, we've no real alternative, we'd better cross our fingers and go and stay with the Mudgeley man.

Hector had offered to come and collect them, so whilst they waited for him in the village hall, Zillah scribbled Z.B. and his name and address on a note and stuck it on the newly organised communications board. Then she exchanged small talk with some of the other families who were still without somewhere to stay, and were waiting to be interviewed by Social Services and the Housing Department.

'Lucky you,' a menopausal Social Worker observed, on hearing of her plans, 'Christmas in style, eh? What it is to be nubile.'

Huh! Zillah thought, curling her lip, she probably doesn't even know the meaning of the word. Then she thought – marriageable; yes, technically speaking I suppose I am, although Clive certainly wouldn't think so!

'Here's Hector now, Mum,' Christian said, pulling at her arm, 'but he's got a really old car, look!'

Barry had resigned himself to spending Christmas with his mum, as usual. Since his father's decampment they had always done so, and this year he saw no way of absenting himself without causing her pain, but he decided to make up for this dutifulness by going out boozing with his mates both the day before, and on Boxing Day. He wondered what Wendy's plans were. When he had passed Reception and had asked her as casually as he could manage, she had been very bright and positive.

'I'm spending it with my man, of course,' she said. 'He's going to take me all over the place; shows, restaurants, night-clubs, you name it. I've had to buy myself that many new clothes!'

It sounded good, but why was Barry getting the distinct impression that she was being brave? This feeling of slight disbelief niggled him all through the 23rd and finally, on Christmas Eve just before he was due down at the pub, he gave in to it and telephoned her. She answered at once.

'Hello?' So she *was* at home. 'Hello, is that you?' She sounded anxious.

'It's me, Barry.'

'Oh.' Her disappointment was palpable.

Barry clutched the receiver more tightly and thought, the bastard's let her down! I could still be in with a chance. 'You doing anything tonight?'

'Oh Barry. You never give up, do you?'

'Well, are you?'

'Well of course I am. I told you . . .'

'So what time are you leaving?'

'Oh, any time now. I was just waiting for him to ring . . . In fact, I thought you were him . . .'

'Really?'

'What d'you mean, really?'

'I mean, is he really going to phone you?'

There was a small pause before she answered. Then she said, all in a rush, 'There's someone at the door. That'll be him now. Sorry, got to go,' and she put the phone down.

Hmmm, Barry thought sceptically, and went out for his drink with a hopeful heart.

Hector looked round at his flat in despair. He had only unpacked the essentials when he'd moved in, and the front hall was still full of boxes of books and papers. This was not the sort of place in which to entertain anyone, let alone one's lady love. It wasn't nearly good enough. It hadn't really mattered how shabby it looked before, how dingy the wallpaper, how faded the curtains, but now it was crucial. What the hell could he DO about it? He couldn't possibly repeat his ploy with Caroline, and take Zillah to Megan's house. He would just have to sort this place out, explain to her that he didn't own it; that it was just a temporary expedient.

God! Where should he start? He rushed around, hoovering, dusting, shoving clothes into drawers, junk into cupboards. He discovered some Jif and cleaned the basin, the bath and the lavatory. He wiped down the surfaces in the kitchen, sniffed inside the fridge to check that nothing was flagrantly off, but balked at mucking-out the cooker. Then he made up the single bed in the only spare room for Christian, stuffing the duvet into the brand-new cover he had bought especially, and which depicted the latest, most popular Walt Disney character. To Hector it appeared simplistic and crude in the extreme, and it looked even worse on the bed than it had on the packet illustration. It'll have to do, he thought, seizing double bedclothes from the airing cupboard and preparing to fit them lovingly on to the only other bed in the flat – his. If she's reluctant to sleep with me, he thought, plumping up the pillows (and one must expect a certain token resistance in a properly brought-up girl), then I shall offer to sleep on the sofa, but I'll make sure I've only got one thin blanket. She surely won't allow me to freeze to death?

He glanced at the clock; nearly time to go! He had a quick shower, dressed with the maximum amount of care and attention to achieve the greatest casual effect and then, suffering from unaccustomed nerves, got into his Jaguar and set off for the village hall.

The boy, Christian, came running out to meet him.

'My dad's lorry's a lot newer than your car,' he said.

'This,' Hector said, 'is a classic car, I'll have you know. Where is your father these days, then?'

'Europe somewhere. I dunno.'

Good, Hector thought. We can do without him. He and Zillah must surely have split up, or he'd be here helping her now? He was just about to ask the boy a few more pertinent questions, when he saw Zillah approaching. They were clearly not well off but she looked marvellous anyway. She had changed her clothes and was wearing a short orange coat with a button missing, a rather tatty, long, black skirt and little lace-up boots. She had a bright scarf round her neck and a suitcase in either hand. Her facial expression was strictly neutral. Next time, Hector promised himself, next time she'll look positively eager to see me – I'll make sure of that or I'll die in the attempt. He jumped out of the car and went to help her with the cases.

'Hello!' he said. Was he sounding ridiculously hearty? 'Is this it?'

'There wasn't much else left,' Zillah said.

'No, of course not, stupid of me. Right, climb in then and off we go.'

'Have you got a computer?' Christian asked him as they drove away.

'Well, only a fairly basic one at home,' Hector admitted. 'I use it for word-processing; for letters and the odd unofficial article here and there, that sort of thing.'

'So what games have you got?'

'Games? Oh, I see . . . I don't think it does games as such.'

'Oh,' Christian was clearly disappointed.

'I've got lots of books though.' As he said this, Hector nerved himself for the usual scathing response from the younger generation: 'Nah, books are crap'. It didn't come.

'Hey, have you? That's excellent!'

Hector felt a surge of happiness. It was all going to work out wonderfully. Zillah was both beautiful and fertile. She had already proved herself by producing a son with a literary bent. If that didn't bode well for a future Morgan, then what could? He turned and smiled widely at her. In response, she raised a quizzical eyebrow, and twitched her mouth just a little at the corners, but it was definitely upwards.

When they arrived at his flat, Hector watched Zillah's face intently, to see what her reaction to it would be. She didn't register anything.

'I'm just staying here temporarily,' he said hastily. 'It's not my usual sort of place, but I thought I'd get it decorated anyway. I know a woman who's very experienced in interior decor.'

'Why bother?' Zillah asked. 'Looks fine to me.'

How kind of her, Hector thought fondly. She's only saying that to make me feel better. 'Now then, what would you like,' he asked, 'cup of tea, or a drink?'

'Where am I sleeping?' Christian interrupted.

'Oh yes, first things first.' Hector led the way. 'You're in here. All right?'

Christian went inside, made a face at the duvet cover, but

sat and bounced on it anyway. 'Yeah, it's . . . okay.' He went
on bouncing.

'Kitchen in here, living room, bathroom, lavatory,' Hector
demonstrated, opening the doors in turn to show Zillah round.

'And I suppose we're in here then?' she asked quietly,
opening the door of the main bedroom and taking a cursory
glance.

'Oh, well . . . er . . . yes.' Yippee! Hector thought triumphantly, and then wondered why he felt strangely
disappointed.

'Can I have a bath?' Zillah asked.

'Yes, of course. Plenty of hot water.'

'I'll need a towel.'

'I'll get you one.' Hector was cross with himself for forgetting. 'Would you like a G & T to drink in your bath?' he
asked, as he handed her his best bath sheet.

'Sorry?'

'Gin and tonic.'

'Oh no. A glass of white wine would do.'

'Damn! I don't think I've got any white . . .'

'Forget it. I'm fine.'

'You're sure?'

'Quite sure.'

'I thought I'd get us a Chinese take-away for supper?' Hector
suggested.

'Fine.'

'Can we have prawn crackers and spare ribs and sweet and
sour?' Christian asked eagerly, catching up with them.

'Whatever you like.'

'Great!'

Well I'm glad someone's enthusiastic, Hector thought. His
mother is too laid-back to be true. Never mind, I've got a
tried and tested method for drawing out emotional responses
from inhibited women, and maybe when she sees all the
goodies I've bought for her and the boy, she'll realise how
serious I am about her?

Hector waited impatiently for Christian's bedtime, but it
came much later than he expected, or thought good for the
child. He found himself fidgeting with impatience, and unable
to think of anything remotely intelligent to say. Zillah appeared

unsettingly calm and relaxed. Hector drank several glasses of whisky and covertly inspected his watch from time to time.

Even after Christian had been read to, and finally settled, Zillah insisted on waiting for an hour to be sure that he was asleep, before stuffing a large red sock with the few presents she had brought with her plus the extra ones proferred by Hector, and creeping in to hang it from the end of his bed.

'Right,' she said, coming back into the sitting room at last. 'Well that's that. I'm about ready for bed myself. How about you?'

Now that the time had actually arrived for Hector's great performance, he was dismayed to find himself nonplussed. He'd been keenly anticipating a friendly contest. No, more than that, he had looked forward to making a conquest; gaining ascendancy over Zillah through sheer force of character and animal magnetism. He'd planned to overcome her understand-able resistance by his own subtle but powerful techniques, which slowly but inevitably would open the floodgates to all her pent-up passions . . . But when they both got into his bedroom and had safely locked the door, she just stripped off all her clothes and climbed matter-of-factly into his bed (as though she were doing a routine job . . . the notion leapt into Hector's mind with a horrible clarity, and temporarily para-lysed him), and he discovered that he was not only deeply confused, but much worse; not even particularly lustful.

Oh God! he thought. There has to be a first time for everything. What if I can't get it up?

Zillah yawned widely and reached for the bedside light. 'Hurry up,' she said, 'I'm knackered. D'you want to do it with the light on or off?'

Jess's parents were on a cruise this year, so she had arranged to spend most of Christmas day with Caroline. They sipped celebratory glasses of champagne and orange juice for elev-enses, and Jess felt pleasantly tipsy almost at once. Caroline had given her a present for her flat; a large green earthenware bowl, perfect for fruit, wrapped in scarlet tissue paper. In turn, Jess had given her an enlargement of one of her own photographs of the Levels in winter, which Caroline had previously admired. She had had it properly framed and, as she glanced at it now, propped against the sofa, it didn't look bad.

'It's good,' Caroline said. 'How clever you are. Now why don't we drink up and go out for a nice healthy walk by the sea? I thought we'd eat properly this evening. Vivian may turn up then too. Hope that's all right with you?'

'Sounds lovely.'

Most of the rubble and detritus from the recent storms had been cleared away from the sea front, but parts of the wall were missing and there were several areas where the surface tarmac had been stripped off, revealing its underlying hardcore. Jess noticed that a few of the more vulnerable hotels still had sandbags piled across their entrances, just in case. The beach was deserted but for the odd gull, and the sea had withdrawn far out beyond the sand and further still, behind wide expanses of smooth grey mud, so that the breakers were visible only as a thin white line in the distance. All the donkey droppings and the trippers' litter of the summer had long since been scoured out by the winter tides, and the sand was hard and clean as they walked side by side along it. A fresh wind made Jess's eyes water and bleared her vision, so she was obliged to to take off her glasses and hunt for a tissue. She looked about her myopically at this newly Impressionistic seascape, and smiled.

'What?' Caroline asked.

'I was just thinking that this would be a great place for a hero on a white charger — lots of galloping space. And I wouldn't be able to see him properly until the very last minute, without my specs, so it would be just like the man in black on the camel in the heat haze in *Lawrence of Arabia*, only colder.'

'Unlike real life, where you'd see him coming a mile away, and take cover sharpish,' Caroline said.

'Don't be so boringly rational,' Jess admonished her. 'Let yourself go a little.'

'Can't,' Caroline said briskly, 'or I might never get back.'

'Don't you dream about the future at all?'

'Not really. Too busy coping with the present.'

'D'you think you'll ever get married?'

'Shouldn't think so.'

'I hope I will, one day,' Jess said, polishing the lenses of her glasses and holding them up to the light for inspection. 'I used to think I'd like at least four children; two of each, but now I'm not so sure . . .'

Caroline smiled ruefully. 'I feel very ambivalent about children,' she confessed.

'I thought you were dead against the whole idea?'

'Not really. I seem to swing wildly from one extreme to the other. I've been feeling rather broody lately to be honest, but I expect it will pass.'

'Isn't it usually more specific than that?' Jess asked. 'I mean, isn't it usually all bound up with one man who is special to you, so you want *his* children, rather than kids in general?'

'Not in my case,' Caroline said. 'But perhaps I've never met anyone that special.'

'Haven't you?'

'Well, have you?'

Jess reddened. 'Probably not,' she said.

Caroline gave her a long look and then, 'Let's run,' she suggested. 'We need the exercise before we stuff ourselves with calories this evening. Race you to that bit of old driftwood over there!'

'Where?'

But Caroline had already set off, and called over her shoulder in friendly mockery, 'Get your specs back on! You can't miss it.' She pointed. 'See? Just in front of that magic white stallion.'

When they eventually got back to Caroline's flat, puffed and laughing, they took it in turns to use the shower. Then Caroline sat Jess down in front of the fire with a drink, and busied herself in the kitchen.

'What can I do?' Jess called.

'It's all right. Everything's under control.'

'But I ought to help with something.'

'Why? Stay put. I'm not good at being helped.'

Marvellous, Jess thought, relaxing. What luxury!

Vivian, when he arrived, seemed not at all put out on finding her there too. After greeting his hostess, he stooped and picked up Jess's present from its position propped against the sofa. He held it by the frame at arm's length and narrowed his eyes as he examined it.

'This one of yours?' he asked her.

'Yes.'

'It's very good indeed. Ever thought of going freelance?'

On Christmas morning at twelve noon, Wendy discovered that she was unable to park by Hector's as there was a large articulated lorry manoeuvring right outside it. It was about to block his drive, Wendy noticed and thought, Hector won't be pleased about that. Oh dear, I wonder what he'll say when he sees me? She got out of her car and walked towards her destination, worrying all the way.

Perhaps it's the wrong time to come? Perhaps I shouldn't have come at all? Perhaps I should just have phoned? Perhaps he's in the middle of cooking lunch? No, I just had to come; I couldn't stand not knowing . . . But what if he doesn't celebrate Christmas? Or what if he's gone away? Or what if he's regretting the whole thing? Perhaps I was a disappointment to him? Perhaps it was only a one-night stand . . . Oh . . .

As Wendy crossed the road and wavered in painful indecision beside Hector's front gate, a large unshaven young man with red hair jumped casually down from the cab of the lorry and came round it on to the pavement beside her.

'This number 42?' he asked her.

'Yes it is. I was just going in there myself, actually.'

'Oh, right. You must be Mrs Mudgeley then?'

Wendy blushed scarlet with pleasure. 'Oh . . .! Well not yet, no, I'm Wendy . . .'

'Pleased to meet you. Name's Clive. It was right nice of you to take us in, like, specially at Christmas. Really appreciate it. Didn't think I was going to make it back through the tunnel in time; got the last train by a whisker, so here I am.' He rang the front doorbell. 'God, what a state my house is in though; mud every-bloody-where! Good thing I saw Zillah's note up the village hall or I'd never have found . . .'

'*Dad!*'

The door had opened and a young boy had rushed out and flung himself at the man beside Wendy. Totally confused, she looked wildly around, checking she was at the right house. 'But . . . What . . .?' was all she managed to say. Then a young woman with long dark hair came out as well and joined in the welcome, kissing the red-haired man and pretending to complain about his bristly chin.

'What's going on?' It was Hector's voice. Wendy turned in relief and saw him standing in the doorway, awkward in a striped apron and with an oven glove over one hand. He looked harassed, surprised and annoyed all at the same time. 'Zillah – Who's this? And Wendy – what on earth are you doing here? And do you two know each . . .? He gave up.

The young woman with the peculiar name (who looked distinctly hippy) laughed, and taking the lorry driver by the hand, presented him to her host.

'This is Clive, Hector; Christian's dad, you know? Isn't it great he's made it back for Christmas? I never thought he would. Perfect timing, eh?' Wendy saw Hector looking anything but impressed.

'It's a gift.' Clive said modestly.

'And who have we here then?' Zillah asked, turning to Wendy with an incurious smile. 'You're not a friend of Clive's?'

'No!' Wendy said, rather too vehemently. 'I'm Wendy. I'm . . .'

She was about to explain her romantic connection with Hector, when Hector himself hurriedly interjected, 'Oh I've told you all about Wendy, Zillah, don't you remember? She's my home decorating expert.'

7

HECTOR had assumed that when Zillah came to stay, she would automatically take over the cooking for the three of them. But to save her from having to buckle down to it immediately on their first night, he had got a take-away. Then he had sat back, congratulating himself on his consideration and forethought. He had, after all, gone and done a large amount of shopping, buying all sorts of delicacies from Marks & Spencer, and getting a last minute goose at a bargain price. He had definitely made a big effort. He reckoned it would keep them going until the shops opened again, when he would press crisp tenners into Zillah's long, strong fingers, and give her *carte blanche* to select anything she fancied to feed them through the New Year. He wasn't sure how long the two of them might be staying. Zillah had told him that her landlord had promised to get her house cleaned and dried out and some of the furniture and carpets replaced, but that it would take time. As far as Hector was concerned, the longer the better. He would never get tired of looking at her.

On that first night together after an unpromising start, he had lain in bed beside the now sleeping Zillah and assessed the situation so far. Things hadn't gone entirely to plan. He had (thank God!) managed to make love to her; old habits swiftly reasserting themselves at the touch of her hot acquiescent skin. She had even flattered him afterwards by sounding surprised, even if it had been a bit of a backhanded compliment.

'You're not bad in the sack, are you?' she said. 'Good-looking men are usually appallingly selfish in my experience.'

I wonder, Hector thought, eyes wide to the dark of the room, how many men she's actually had? And did she take the initiative with them as well? Maybe I'm too conservative;

out of touch? Perhaps the young feel able to dispense with the conventional hypocrisy of pursuit and conquest, with the man always taking the lead? It's far more honest and straightforward after all, just to see what you want and go for it. I ought to be pleased that she jumped straight into my bed without any pretence at playing hard-to-get. She obviously fancies me, and why not? He turned over on his side, still thinking. He had wanted some sport, but he wasn't so inflexible that he couldn't adapt his aims and pleasures accordingly, was he? After all, he shouldn't have expected her to be predictable; she was far too exciting for that. Comforted, he fell asleep.

In the morning he was woken at some God-forsaken hour by Zillah digging him in the ribs.

'Wha . . .?' he said, coming to with difficulty.

'Hurry up,' Zillah said urgently. 'It's gone five o'clock and Christian always wakes up early on Christmas day.'

'Sorry. What?'

'You'd better go and pretend you've been sleeping on the sofa, under that old blanket. That is what it's for, isn't it?'

'Oh . . . well, yes.'

'Go on then. I don't want Christian to find us together.'

Hector dragged himself sleepily upright and put on his dressing-gown and slippers. Then he gathered his pillow to his chest and tip-toed as quietly as possible to the living room. The sofa was cold. The blanket was thin. It was all a little unconvincing, Hector thought grumpily. He settled himself down as best he could, and tried to get back to sleep again. When it's really morning, he thought hopefully, maybe she'll bring me a cup of tea?

Zillah woke again at six o'clock when Christian came in and slid into bed beside her, putting his two cold feet on to her warm calves.

'Aaaah! You're freezing! Been awake long?'

'Six and a half minutes; just as long as it takes to open a stocking.'

'Was it all right?'

'Great!'

'Happy Christmas then.' She put her arms around him and held him close.

'Happy Christmas Mum.'

'Sleep well?'

'Yeah. How long do we have to stay here?'

'Why? Don't you like it?'

'I thought he'd have a big house and a huge garden and peacocks and stuff. I thought you said he was rich?'

'Mmmm. Well maybe I was wrong. Don't worry darling, we'll be home again as soon as we can be.'

'D'you think he'll lend me some of his books?'

'He might.'

'And will he give us presents?'

'I hope so.'

'Have we got anything for him?'

'Oh I've already given him his.'

'What was it?'

'I think you could call it payment in kind.'

'What's that?'

'Oh, it's much too boring to explain.' Zillah yawned.

'You mean you're not going to tell me?'

'That's about it.' She yawned again.

Christian sighed. 'So, are we going to get up then?'

'Not for a while. He might bring us breakfast in bed, if we're lucky.'

At eight thirty Zillah heard Hector running water in the bathroom, but by nine o'clock, when not even tea had appeared, she got up and went into the kitchen. Hector was sitting at the table in a plaid dressing-gown and carpet slippers, nursing a full mug between his palms. He leapt to his feet, smiling a welcome.

'Good morning, and a happy Christmas to you! I would have brought you tea, but thought you might welcome a bit of a lie-in. Now then, how about a spot of grub? What do you normally cook for breakfast?'

'Me?'

'Well, I'm sure you're far more experienced in these matters than I am.'

'Nice try,' Zillah said firmly, 'but doing the cooking is definitely not part of our deal, you know.'

From then on, it became an unspoken contest as to who could manipulate whom most effectively on the catering front.

Zillah knew she had the advantage; she was not aiming to impress anyone. She and Christian both opted for cereals for breakfast and watched with mild curiosity as Hector cooked himself a hard-boiled egg.

'I like the white hard and the yolk runny,' Christian observed.

'So do I,' Hector agreed mournfully, adding a lump of butter to the pale yellow lump in the egg cup in front of him, in an attempt to soften it.

Afterwards he produced presents, wrapped in fancy paper with stuck-on rosettes of shiny ribbon. Zillah had to admit to herself that the man really was trying. She even felt touched. Christian opened his first and was clearly delighted with them. He set them out on the table in front of him; a jar of sweets, a book token, and a compact camera with two films and a carrying case.

He beamed at Hector. '*Thanks*,' he said. 'They're excellent.' Then he opened the camera and began putting the first film in straight away.

'I wasn't sure what sort of thing you read,' Hector explained. 'So I thought you could choose a book yourself.'

'It's very kind of you, Hector,' Zillah said, pleased.

'It's a pleasure. Go on, open yours.'

Zillah found that he had given her a large bottle of Givenchy perfume, some chocolate truffles and a multi-coloured silk scarf. She leant across the kitchen table and kissed his cheek.

'You're very generous,' she said, 'thank you.'

Hector, flushed with pleasure, got up and went over to a shelf where a few dusty cookery books were stacked. He selected one and brought it back to the table, smiling. 'I seem to remember,' he said, 'that if one wants any sort of a Christmas lunch, then one has to spend the whole morning cooking it. I've got us a goose, you see, and I'm not sure how long they take.'

'No more golden eggs then . . .?' Zillah said, *sotto voce*.

'Eh? . . . So I thought I'd better look up how long to cook it for.'

'Good idea.'

'You haven't ever done one?'

'Never.'

'Pity.'

Zillah knew that if she were patient, Hector would be the first to crack. He was. Over the next few hours he put on a butcher's striped pinny, lit the oven, and muttered a lot to himself. Zillah volunteered to wash and cut up vegetables. Christian took photographs of her doing it, and some of Hector stuffing the goose with sage and onion, oblivious to the large greasy mark on his forehead, where he'd forgotten and wiped it with the back of his hand. Then, whilst transferring the bird on to the roasting rack, Hector stumbled, and dropped it on to the kitchen floor with a dull thud. Christian took another picture. This was Zillah's cue to step forward authoritatively and say, 'Here, let me,' but she was far too clever to be caught like that. She'd seen controlled incompetence before, and she wasn't fooled by it.

'Hell!' Hector exclaimed, picking the goose up and dusting it off with a damp dishcloth. Some of the stuffing had fallen out on to the floor, and Hector picked it up also in two or three attempts and restrained himself, just, from shoving it back inside the bird's body cavity. Instead he scraped it off his hands in a sticky heap on the edge of table, and then wiped them abstractedly on his apron.

'Don't worry,' Zillah said, 'it'll be fine. Just bung it in the oven, I would.' Then she kept any further advice to herself, and joined Christian in watching television whilst Hector got on with things. Later on she discovered that the steaming pudding had virtually boiled dry and because, so far, she was winning hands down, she felt quite able to top it up with boiling water without losing face.

At noon, when Hector was getting pinker and more agitated by the moment, the front doorbell rang. Christian ran to answer it, and Zillah heard with surprise and pleasure, his cry of '*Dad!*'

Brilliant timing, she thought. Good old Clive! After she had greeted him and introduced him to Hector, she'd asked about the strange woman who had turned up at the same time, and then for some unaccountable reason had run off again. Hector told her that Wendy was his home decorator, but was painfully shy.

'It's a bit beyond the call of duty, isn't it,' Zillah asked, 'working on Christmas day, I mean?'

'I think she's lonely,' Hector explained.

'Poor woman. That's one thing I've never been, even when I'm alone.'

'Just as well,' Clive said, 'since I'm off again, day after tomorrow. Wouldn't want you to pine away now would we?'

'Not much chance of that.' Zillah said, unsurprised at the prospect of his not too distant departure, but noticing that Hector had visibly brightened.

'Summink smells good,' Clive observed. 'I'm starving.'

Hector felt much easier when Christmas was over, and Clive had once more gone off abroad. He hadn't taken to the man. More than that, he'd been on tenterhooks the whole time in case Clive were to guess the truth about himself and Zillah. Hector was sure he would have been quite capable of duffing him up at a moment's notice if he'd suspected anything. He was a lot younger than Hector and had hands the size of boxing gloves. But it seemed that Clive hadn't suspected anything. He gradually allowed himself to relax.

The only other potential problem was Wendy. When she had appeared unannounced on Christmas day, Hector realised, sinkingly, that she clearly hadn't understood the strictly temporary nature of their association. But, determined not to jeopardise his precious new relationship with Zillah, he'd managed to fob her off, and was vastly relieved when she hadn't even come indoors; turning suddenly and running off. Phew! he thought. That was a close thing!

After Clive's departure, things had settled down as before, with Zillah secretly admitting him to her bed, all unbeknownst to Christian who seemed to assume that he had spent the entirety of each night on the sofa. Everything should have been perfect, but Hector felt uncomfortably unsettled. It wasn't anything specific that he could positively identify. It was just that an indefinable something was missing . . . He considered asking Zillah whether she and Clive had made love in his bed . . . but he really didn't want to know.

It was almost a relief to return to work after the Christmas holiday.

'You doing anything for lunch?' he asked Jess on their first day back.

'Why?'

'Because I thought we might pop over to the pub.'

'Good idea. Why not?'

They walked across the road together and when comfortably seated in an alcove nearest to the fake log fire, Jess asked him, 'How was your Festering Season then, and how is the noble gesture panning out?'

'Noble gesture? Oh I see what you mean. Fine . . . well, OK anyway.'

'Not quite what you'd envisaged?'

'Well Zillah's bruiser of a boyfriend turned up for three days over Christmas and quite frankly we didn't have a lot in common.'

'Must have been a tight fit?'

'What?'

'Squeezing you all into two bedrooms. That is all you've got, isn't it?'

'Oh, that wasn't a problem actually,' Hector said, improvising rapidly. 'Zillah and the boy had my bed and I slept in the single in the spare room. Then when Clive turned up, he moved in with Zillah and the boy slept on the bunk in the cab of the lorry. He loved it. And now of course, we're back to square one again.'

'So, what *is* the problem?' Jess asked.

'Mmmmm?'

'You look fed up.'

'Sorry.'

'Well?'

'Oh, I was just thinking about bloody Clive. He just about ate me out of house and home, and then had the cheek to say to Zillah (when he thought I wasn't listening), that I was . . . Oh never mind.'

'Go on,' Jess urged. 'You can tell me.'

Hector sighed. 'It's nothing really. He just said I was past my sell-by date.'

'*Cheek!* And what did she say?'

'She laughed.'

'Ungrateful bastards, both of them.'

'Oh well, I expect she's afraid to disagree with him. He's a tough sort.' Hector sighed again.

'So it is only skin deep – beauty, that is?'

'Oh I wouldn't say that,' Hector said at once. 'She's a lovely person. I suppose my ideas of suitable behaviour are just rather old fashioned . . .'

'Never mind. Better luck next time, eh?' Jess smiled encouragingly.

Hector refused to smile back. 'That's an odd sort of thing to say. I mean, it isn't as though I had any *special* interest in the woman.'

'No, of course not.'

'I don't know what it is about you, Jess Hazelrigg, but you always seem to twist our conversations around to the personal.'

'I have a morbid fascination with the depths of human depravity and private tragedy,' Jess said. 'That's why I enjoy our little chats so much. Talking of which, what's happened to Wendy lately, d'you know?'

'No idea.'

'It's just that she looked like death this morning, and after only about an hour in Reception, she had to go home. Barry says he's really worried about her.'

'What's it to him?'

'I think he worships from afar.'

'But he's about half her age!'

'Love knows no boundaries, Hector. Surely you understand that?' Jess took off her glasses and began to clean them on the hem of her sweatshirt. Hector turned jokingly to meet her gaze and found himself brought up short by the look in her exposed brown eyes.

'Oh,' he said. 'Right.'

Barry went round to Wendy's house after work and rang the doorbell, stepping backwards to look up at the windows to see whether he was being observed. The curtain in her bedroom twitched, but no one came to the door. He rang the bell again. On the fourth ring the door opened a crack and Wendy's voice said,

'Go away Barry! I'm ill in bed.'

'I just came to see how you are.'

'Thanks, but I can manage.'

'So what's wrong with you then?'

'Oh, I've got a virus the doctor says. I'll be fine once I've taken the antibiotics.'

'But viruses don't respond to . . . Look Wendy, just let me in will you?'

'I can't. I look a mess.'

'I don't give a stuff what you *look* like. It's the real you I care about.'

'Oh . . .' The door opened wider and Wendy peeped out. She was fully dressed. Her eyes were red and puffy and full of tears. ' . . . nobody's ever said that to me before.' She looked utterly pathetic.

Barry stepped forward at once, putting both arms around her, and she began to sob against his chest. 'Come on,' he said, patting her back gently, 'let's go inside and sit down and you can tell me all about it.'

Little by little he got it out of her; all except a name.

'He's had to go abroad on business,' Wendy said, sniffing, 'in . . . indefinitely. And when I offered to give up my job and go with him, he told me he was married to some woman in . . . in Israel, who's a . . . Catholic so he can't get a divorce . . .'

'Poor you,' Barry said comfortingly, holding her hand as they sat side by side on the sofa. He didn't believe a word of it, but was nevertheless affected by her obvious despair. 'What a shame. You must be devastated.'

'I don't know what to do,' Wendy gulped.

'Well, there's not a lot you can do in the circumstances, is there?'

'I thought he loved me, you see.' She took her hand away from his in order to blow her nose on a small pink tissue.

'*The rat*,' Barry muttered.

'What?'

'I'm sure he did (love you, that is), but you know . . . circumstances beyond his control and all that.' He put his arm around her shoulders and squeezed them.

'Yes.'

'It'll all work out in the end, you'll see.'

'Mmmm.' She wiped her eyes again.

'Have you had anything to eat lately?'

'Haven't felt like much,' Wendy admitted.

'How about . . .' Barry felt about in his jacket pocket and produced a packet of crisps, ' . . . one of these. Salt and vinegar?'

Wendy inhaled; half hiccup, half laugh. 'Oh Barry, you're so silly. Fancy thinking a handful of those could mend a broken heart.' But she ate some anyway.

Hector was aware of mixed feelings when Zillah and Christian finally left to go back to their own cottage. As he drove them there, he was forced to admit to himself that it hadn't been, as he had hoped, ten days of unmitigated bliss. There were certainly great advantages to be obtained from a live-in woman like Zillah, there were also notable . . . what was that abominable word that Nigel used all the time? . . . Yes . . . dis-benefits too.

On the plus side, Zillah had been wonderful in bed. She'd slept with him enthusiastically, and (apart from terminal exhaustion) she'd made him feel so desirable, skilful, and *alive*. He thought he had never wanted a woman as much; had never found one who so uninhibitedly enjoyed him. But . . . he couldn't rid himself of the suspicion that she might have slept just as cheerfully with any other man who'd asked her. Could he really marry someone who might well be *promiscuous*?

And then there was Clive. When he had unexpectedly turned up, everything had changed. Hector, who wasn't in the habit of sitting on the reserves bench, found it decidedly humiliating, but valiantly kept up the pretence for Zillah's sake. For some unknown reason, she seemed to be very keen on the brute. Incomprehensible, Hector thought to himself, but if it's a straightforward choice between him and me, then there's surely no contest? She must be bright enough to work that one out. But . . .

Hector gripped the steering wheel with both hands, the better to concentrate his mind. He would have to face up to some uncomfortable thoughts. There was no getting away from the fact that Zillah was not a very suitable prospect as a wife; definitely more mistress material – for bed but not board. But that was not all; it seemed she couldn't cook. She didn't appear to recognise the necessity for housework at all, and she was noticeably deficient in the normal female capacity for self-reproach which, in Hector's view, was the essential cornerstone of a good marriage. How, he wondered, could a man manage such a woman? There were no obvious constraints; no sanctions one could employ. She held all the cards.

And then of course there was the boy to consider. He would be part of the package. Hector would have to be a stepfather to him, would have to get used to having him around all the time, for another nine years at the very least. Would (God forbid!) for Christian's sake, have to be polite to Clive . . .

Then the optimistic side of Hector rose to the fore and he said to himself: Easy! Christian and I like each other. What's the problem? Anyway, Zillah-as-a-guest is probably a totally different reality to Zillah-as-a-wife. As guest, she was probably being super-sensitive; trying not to interfere in my house. But as Mrs Mudgeley . . .

'Here we are,' Zillah said. 'On the left, just here.'

'*Home!*' Christian cried.

Hector braked and drew up outside a run-down cottage. Dead carpets and easy chairs with tide-marks had been dumped in the front garden and were still there. It looked decidedly insanitary. Christian scrambled out of the car without closing the door, and ran round to the back of the house.

'Are you sure it's fit for human habitation?' Hector asked.

'It's fine inside,' Zillah assured him.

'Well, I think I ought just to make sure . . .'

'NO! Stay put Hector. My landlord has had hot-air blowers drying it all out, and he's got us new carpets and chairs and stuff. He rang yesterday to tell me all about it.'

'You never said?'

'Well you were at work at the time. So anyway, thanks for everything. Don't bother seeing us in. We'll be fine.' She opened her door and got out. Then she pulled the two cases and a cardboard box of books from the back seat, and stood them on the road.

'But Zillah,' Hector said, leaning across her seat and looking up at her, 'You haven't given me your phone number?'

'Haven't got one.'

'But I will see you again, soon? We could go out for the odd meal?'

'Somehow I don't think Clive would be too keen on that idea,' Zillah said, starting to close the door. Hector held it open.

'But you're not married to the man!'

'Well that's hardly the point, is it?'

'MUM!' Christian called, running back breathless, 'my bike *is* still in the shed. No one nicked it. Isn't it great!'

'Good,' Zillah smiled round at him. 'Say thank-you to Hector then, and help me carry the bags in.'

'Thanks,' Christian said. 'It was . . . great. Thanks for all the books too.'

'You're welcome.'

''Bye then.'

'Goodbye Zillah,' Hector called, but she was already in the cottage porch with her back to him, and she didn't even turn and wave as he slammed the car door and drove away.

Hector felt miserable and furious all the way back into town. It was Saturday morning and he had the whole weekend ahead, with nothing to take his mind off her casual rejection. He felt badly in need of comfort and reassurance. Then he remembered the expression in a woman's eyes not so very long ago, which had conveyed everything that he now most wanted to feel. So, without further thought, he drove straight to her house and hammered on the door. It wasn't until she opened it, that he began to have qualms.

'Uh, hello Wendy,' he said.

8

JESS drove to Caroline's flat one Saturday evening in early
April. It had been a heavy week and she had been in the
darkroom all that morning, catching up on the backlog of
photo re-prints requested by readers of the *Chronicle*. She was
glad to be up to date, but tired, and ready for a relaxing time
doing nothing special. She and Caroline hadn't seen much of
each other since before Christmas. Both had been so busy at
work.

'Hello,' Caroline said, giving her a hug. 'Come in. How
lovely to see you.' Jess was flattered to notice her Christmas
present hanging on the wall in the kitchen. 'Looks great there,
doesn't it?' Caroline said, following her gaze. 'Pity really, but
I'm sure it will look good anywhere I choose to hang it.'

'Sorry? I'm not with you,' Jess said.

'Glass of wine?' Caroline asked, 'or cider? See, I remembered
this time!'

'Cider would be lovely, thanks.'

'Let's go and sit down comfortably then. I've got lots to tell
you.'

Jess noticed that Caroline herself was not drinking anything,
so she held her glass tentatively, feeling that perhaps she
shouldn't either. As they sat down opposite each other, Caroline said, 'I've been head-hunted,' she looked triumphant, 'by
a firm in London!'

'But you've only been here since December . . .' Jess said.
'So, won't your present company feel a bit . . .?'

'Yes it is tough on them, but that's life, and it's a wonderful
opportunity for me. It's a much bigger operation in London,
masses more scope.'

'I shall really miss you,' Jess said.

'You can come and stay,' Caroline encouraged her.

'Weekends in the big city; visits to the theatre, concerts, to say nothing of shopping.'

'It won't be the same . . . But I am pleased for you. Congratulations.'

'Thank you.' Caroline looked pussy-cat sleek. She didn't seem to have changed in any clearly defined way, but she looked . . . fulfilled? extra assertive? *glossy*. This is where I get left behind, Jess thought sadly.

'But that's not the most important thing,' Caroline said, almost carelessly. 'The best news is that I'm pregnant.'

Jess was astonished. 'So . . . when's it due?' she managed to ask.

'Twenty-first of September or thereabouts. I'm just beginning to feel the bump!' She patted her stomach.

'But what about your new job?'

'I haven't told them yet, but it'll be fine. I'll get myself a nanny for the first few years; no sweat.'

'But . . . are you and Vivian going to get married?'

Caroline gave her an old-fashioned look. 'Good heavens, no,' she said. 'Vivian hates mess. He'd be useless as a father.' Her expression did not invite Jess to enquire further.

'Oh . . . um . . . well what about you? Your life is so ordered, so sophisticated. How do you feel?'

'Ecstatic,' Caroline said simply. 'If you'd told me a year ago that I'd be feeling like this, I'd have laughed in your face, but there you are. That's hormones for you. I've never felt so content. I'm positively cow-like!'

'But won't the new job be very tiring?'

'Probably, but I'll have four months or so before the baby's born, to get settled in. I don't foresee any major problems.'

'Oh.' Jess was unconvinced. 'Good.'

'You're shocked,' Caroline said. 'I'm sorry. I should have led up to it more gradually; not been so abrupt.'

'No . . . no I'm not. I'm just . . . surprised. But I'm so happy for you. It's wonderful news.'

'It does take a bit of getting used to,' Caroline admitted. 'That's why I've been rather antisocial of late. But once it sinks in – it's heaven. Just don't let me get like those other mothers I used to complain about so vehemently, will you? You must stop me if I rabbit on and on about wonderbabe.'

Jess managed a nod and a smile. 'Somehow,' she said, 'I very much doubt you'll have time for all those theatre visits and things. You'll be far too busy.'

'Never!' Caroline retorted cheerfully. 'More cider? No, if there's one thing I'm sure of, it's that this baby is *not* going to take over my life.'

In the absence of Zillah Hector found himself, more and more often these days, thrown back on to Wendy. As he thought this, he acknowledged that it was an unfortunate way of putting it, but accurate nevertheless. The first time he had been back to see her after Christmas – the day he'd taken Zillah home – Wendy had been almost shirty with him! He had hoped that she would have been sensitive to his mood; would have noticed that he was feeling low. Eventually though it did sink in, and she'd cooked him a tasty meal and had soothed his hurt feelings the best way known to man, in bed. Hector, his self-esteem restored, had even remembered the following morning that Wendy was due an explanation for his apparent inhospitality at Christmas.

As he ate the two delicious soft-boiled eggs Wendy had cooked him for breakfast, he dipped the fingers of toast into each perfect runny yolk, and began: 'I believe I owe you an apology for saying the wrong thing on Christmas day.'

'Oh?'

'Yes. You remember, when you arrived at my door at the same time as that slob, Clive? I'm afraid I wasn't at my best. I'd had a simply frantic morning.'

'Really?' Wendy looked wary but interested.

'Yes, really. Zillah – the woman and her son who were made homeless by the flood, you know? Well, she couldn't cook! Can you believe that? And I'm no earthly good in the kitchen. I've never had to be, you see. So I'd kind of taken it for granted that she would help out while she was staying with me. That's not unreasonable, is it?'

'Not at all,' Wendy said. 'It's the least she could have done.'

'Exactly. Well to cut a long story short, she didn't, and I was lumbered with cooking the lot; roast goose, veg, Christmas pudding, everything. So when you arrived, you can understand that I was at my wits' end; not myself at all. I'm sorry I didn't introduce you properly. I must have seemed very rude. I just didn't know whether I was coming or going. Talk about culinary harassment!' Hector waited for Wendy to acknowledge this heroic effort, but she was clearly hoping for more. 'So when you suddenly left,' he went on hurriedly, 'naturally I should have run straight after you. I can see that now. I would have, but I didn't dare leave the kitchen in case the whole place caught fire or exploded or something.' He spread both hands in a charming gesture of male incompetence in the face of superior female expertise.

'Oh,' Wendy said. 'I thought you were just trying to get rid of me.'

'Good heavens, no!'

'You said I was your decorator.'

'No, surely not?'

'Yes you did.'

'How ridiculous of me.' He patted her hand on the table. 'I'm so sorry. What can I have been thinking of?'

'I thought you were ashamed of you and me . . . you know . . .'

'Of our going to bed together?'

'Yes.' Wendy flushed and stared down at her plate.

'You old silly,' Hector said, picking up her hand and squeezing it. 'I was trying to be gallant; to protect your honour . . . I mean I didn't know whether you wanted to acknowledge our relationship so early on, did I? I mean, if I'd said, "This is Wendy, my current lover," you would have been well and truly put on the spot, wouldn't you? I couldn't have risked that.'

'I wouldn't have minded. You could have said I was your girlfriend. You see, I thought that you and . . . that woman . . .'

'Oh no,' Hector said breezily. 'I just felt sorry for her and the boy. That was all.'

'I'm really glad, Hector.' She squeezed his hand in return. 'I was so miserable.' She looked up at him shyly.

'Well,' Hector said, breathing deeply, 'all right now, eh?'

It's not that I really want Wendy in place of Zillah, he told himself; certainly not. It's just that Wendy seems to have the capacity to restore my morale, and as she clearly fancies me rotten, it seems to be a mutually beneficial arrangement. Of course, I'll have to make certain she understands the impermanence of it, but since we're both clearly in need of a bit of nookey . . .

From then on, and without really meaning to commit himself, Hector allowed Wendy to nudge him into a whole series of regular habits. When Hector wasn't on duty, they spent the weekends together in alternate houses. They went out for a meal one night a week, usually Wednesdays. Wendy began to do some of Hector's washing, and ironed his shirts. She even darned a pair of his socks. She's a sweet thing, Hector thought, and she means well, but I have to admit that she isn't exactly challenging.

In view of this crucial deficit, Hector was careful to hang on to his own independence and be alone whenever he felt like it. He also made sure that he didn't have to account for his movements to Wendy. He'd had more than enough of that with Megan. But he did allow her to freshen up the walls of his flat with a lick of paint, and a length or two of wallpaper, being careful, of course, to do all the choosing of colours and styles himself.

Then, when Wendy wasn't around, and when he could wangle a trip out on *Chronicle* business, he would drive to his destination the pretty way, via Zillah's cottage, in the hope of seeing her. The first time he went, he had been lucky. He had caught her by the front gate and had actually spoken to her.

'Look Hector,' she'd said. 'I'm grateful to you for helping us, but that's it. That's as far as it goes. We're fine now. End of story. OK?'

'But Zillah, what about the great times we had in bed. Don't they mean anything to you?'

'They did.'

'Did what?'

'Mean something,' Zillah said. 'In a word: rent.'

After that, Hector didn't try to speak to her any more, but he cruised past regularly, hoping to catch a glimpse, trying to see whether she perhaps looked a little plumper or had taken to wearing smock tops. After all, he reminded himself, they had made love eight times, so it was remotely possible . . . and if it were to turn out to be true, then it would naturally put an entirely new complexion on things. But he didn't see her.

The cottage windows looked blank, and grass now sprouted from the abandoned chairs in the front garden.

Daft sod! Hector admonished himself. Fat chance!

Jess was more often than not out at lunchtime, so she packed a few sandwiches each morning as a matter of course and scoffed them in the Jeep during spare moments. But if she happened to be in, she ate them in the *Chronicle*'s coffee area with whoever else was around. This Thursday the small lobby was full, too full, of the ten or so people who made up the weekly inserter crew, who came in to assemble the paper from its three separately printed sections. The press was thundering away in the basement below them, shaking the whole building. Jess could feel the vibrations on the soles of her feet as she stood by the drinks machine and felt in her pocket for some change. Do I really want to put up with all this cigarette smoke, she wondered, or . . .?

'Jess?' Hector said, at her elbow. 'Got a moment?'

'Sure.' She followed him into the corridor outside.

'Come over to the pub,' he said. 'I need a break from everyone, particularly Nige. He's off for two weeks from Monday and he's getting more like a headless chicken as each day passes. "*You won't forget this?*" and "*Be sure to do that*" and "*Make a point of not . . .*" and so on. Anyone would think I'd never deputised for him before! I don't think he's the ideal News Ed. anyway; far too nervy. I told him – if you can't take the heat, get out of the stable.'

'I'm sure he will have found that most reassuring,' Jess said. 'I'll come, but only for a soft drink or I'll be useless all afternoon.'

'Nonsense,' Hector said. 'You're the least useless person I know.'

Jess walked with a spring in her step down the steep stairs, and out through Reception, smiling at the new girl on the desk (whose name she hadn't caught) and over the road to the George and Pilgrim. There, she and Hector ensconced themselves in a corner by the window, and she unwrapped her sandwiches surreptitiously so that the management wouldn't notice and take offence.

Jess wondered if Hector lunched here most days with his

fellow reporters and Nigel, or whether she was being particularly favoured. She hadn't had a chance to talk to him properly since the last time they'd been here, way back in January, and she was curious to know how the hunt for Morgan's mother might be going. If I had a son, she thought, I certainly wouldn't call him *Morgan*! Then she thought, I must be careful. If I asked impertinent questions he'll probably go all defensive on me, and then I won't discover anything at all.

'D'you come here often?' she asked him.

'Now there's a leading question,' Hector teased her.

'So what's the answer?'

'The answer is no, hardly ever. No time, usually. Today I just felt in need of some undemanding but intelligent company.'

Jess considered a moment and then decided this was a compliment. 'Well, thanks,' she said.

Hector raised half a pint to his lips and sipped it reflectively. Then he put the glass down with a sigh. 'Do you ever think about genetic death?'

'Not a lot, no.'

'Course not. You're young. Why should you? I've been weighing up the pros and cons of fatherhood, you see; trying to analyse it dispassionately, and it still seems to me that wanting children is entirely justifiable. It's selfish, yes, but let's face it there are no *unselfish* reasons for wanting kids, are there? I suppose I've been trying to understand my own motives. It's not that I'm afraid of a lonely old age, or worried about a lack of potency . . . Somehow it's the idea of being the end of the line that depresses me. But in any case, being keen to be a dad can only be a *good* thing, can't it?'

'I suppose we're all victims of the great assumption *when* rather than *if*,' Jess said carefully. 'But it won't be too late for you for years yet? After all, men can go on siring children well into their dotage.'

'True.' Hector looked unconvinced.

'That reminds me,' Jess said. 'Guess who's having a baby – someone you've met.'

'Give up,' Hector said, without trying.

'Caroline Moffat. You remember, my friend from school? You could have knocked me down with a polystyrene rock when she told me! She used to be so anti, and now she's bloody radiant. It's due in September apparently.'

'Really?' Hector said, frowning. 'Have a drink? Go on Jess. I'm having another half. Have a shandy or something innocuous if you must. It's on me.'

'Oh, well all right then. Low alcohol cider, thanks.' Hmmm, Jess thought to herself as she watched Hector going up to the bar. It looks as though poor Hector hasn't got anywhere with the Brakespear woman. He doesn't seem to be having much luck, does he? She wasn't his type anyway. Actually, I can't really think of anyone who would be . . .

When Jess looked up again, Hector was walking back towards her holding the two drinks. He looked preoccupied, as though he were doing mental arithmetic.

Wendy started her afternoon shift early, so that she could overlap with the new girl and keep an eye on her. She didn't altogether trust that Jackie (or whatever her name was). She didn't reckon she'd got a proper grip on the job as yet. Wendy inspected the desks on the far wall, where the public composed their advertisements, to check they had their proper compliment of pens and forms. They hadn't. Jess's file of contact prints was, however, back on the reception desk where it should be, so things were looking up. Last time someone had come in wanting to buy a photo Wendy hadn't been able to find it, and had looked a right charlie.

'Two pens short,' she said, lifting the bar to get behind the counter.

'I dunno,' the new girl said. 'What do they do with them, eat the frigging things? You're in early, aren't you?'

At that moment, Hector and Jess came in together through the swing doors. Hector had his hand resting on Jess's shoulder, where it had naturally fallen as he had ushered her in ahead of him. Jess was laughing, and Hector looked pretty cheerful too until he saw Wendy, when he merely looked surprised.

'You're in early,' he said in passing, and without giving her the secret wink she had come to count on.

'Yes,' Wendy said, 'I . . .' but they were already disappearing upstairs.

'That's the Senior Reporter and the Photographer, right?' asked Jackie. 'Hector and Jane?'

'Hector and Jess,' Wendy said rather shortly.

'Oh, right. It takes a while to work out who's who around here, doesn't it? Are they an item then?'

'*What?*' Wendy turned on her irritably.

'You know – going out together?'

'*No of course they aren't!*'

'Oooh, I'm sorry. Touched a nerve there, have I? I only wond . . .'

'Well stop wondering,' Wendy said. 'You can go now. I can manage.'

'Suit yourself.'

The girl made a big production of collecting up her things and putting on her coat, and then finally she was gone and Wendy was alone. Stupid cow! she thought. What does she know? But the remark had unsettled her. She wished she knew where she was with Hector. Of course she understood his wish that their affair should be kept under wraps at work. It was well known that business and pleasure didn't mix. She didn't mind that so much (although it would be nice to have a ring to flash around), but she still wondered whether Hector was ashamed of his association with her.

It made her feel insecure, and he did nothing to reassure her. He never discussed their future. He never said 'One day we must . . .' or 'Remind me to take you to . . .' or 'That's something I'd love to share with you . . .' He also, puzzlingly, never mentioned children. Wendy couldn't understand that. If, as everyone knew, he was desperate for kids, then why did he never bring them into the conversation? It would be the most natural thing to do after all. Perhaps the gossip about him wasn't true, Wendy wondered, but then again, if not, why did he go and get his sperm tested? And while I'm on that subject, she thought idly, something that's always bothered me – if there's really that many millions of them, then how on earth do they know which ones they've already counted?

Wendy pulled herself together. I'm being silly, she told herself. Of course he wants children. He's probably only waiting for the right moment to bring the subject up. I hope he doesn't wait too long though – I mean, I may be wrong, it's early days, but I've never been late before . . .

She didn't know if she was excited or scared at the possibility. If only Hector had given her some idea of his feelings on the subject. She really didn't know whether he'd be delighted or furious. And how would she break the news to him? Would she say 'the pill' had let her down, or would she confess?

'Can I get some service here?' a sudden man's voice said, making her jump.

'Oh . . .! I didn't see you come in.'

'Well that much is obvious. Now look here . . . What's your name?'

'Miss Bing.'

'Bing? That's not a name, that's a slag-heap! Anyway, never mind all that. What I want to know, Miss Heap, is what you intend doing about this?' he slapped a copy of the previous week's *Chronicle* down on the counter and jabbed a finger at one of the front page stories.

'What's wrong with it?' Wendy asked coldly.

'I'll tell you what's wrong with it. It's all lies, that's what!'

Oh no! Wendy thought wearily, furtively pressing the alarm button under her counter. A fully paid-up member of the awkward squad. That's all I need!

9

THE Somerset Levels are magical towards the end of May, Jess thought, as she walked slowly along one of the moor's rough drove roads. The early morning mist was burning off in the sun and lengthening her view along the rhynes on either side of her, revealing high blue patches of sky above the bare knuckles of pollarded willows. It's worth getting up at six, she thought, just to have the place to myself and to see the flowers of cow-parsley and comfrey and water crowfoot, and the reflections of yellow flags at the water's edge.

A displaying snipe was drumming overhead in a falling arc, making a strange bleating *wuther-wuther* sort of noise. A grey heron, startled at her approach, took off and flapped deliberately away. Skylarks rose straight up from the ground, singing. A sedge warbler only a few feet away erupted briefly from cover in the reeds in a burst of scratchy song, before diving back again.

Jess stopped at a gateway where a perfect spider's web, beaded with dew, glinted in the sunlight. The landscape looked green and fecund. A purposeful group of black and white cows a field away waited beside their corrugated-iron milking bail. She could hear the *putt-putt* of the tractor-driven engine and see a man in white overalls bending down to wash udders or slip on the clusters. A cuckoo called. Swallows swooped and twittered. The air was cool and sweet. Jess inhaled deeply; an addict getting her fix. I ought to come for a walk every day, she thought. Just being here lifts my spirits so wonderfully.

She looked at her watch. It would take half an hour to get to work, so she'd best be starting back now. She had left the Jeep beside one of the many single-track roads that criss-cross the moor and now she drove abstractedly, looking all around out of habit for good subjects to photograph. Soon the ground began to rise gently to one of the many tumps and ridges favoured by the local hamlets and villages, but there were also a few injudiciously-sited cottages along this lower road, only just above the annual inundation level.

Dodgy place to live, she thought, driving past. But they've apparently got away with it for decades – until last winter's freak flood, that is! The first two she passed now looked much the same as usual; dried out, reclaimed, even repainted. But the next one coming up still had jettisoned chairs in its front garden. What a mess!

Jess didn't see the boy who jumped out into the road in front of her, waving his arms, until the very last minute. *What the . . .?* She jammed on her brakes and missed him – just. She wound down the window. 'What the hell d'you think you're d . . .' Then she recognised him. It was the Brakespear woman's son.

'It's my mum,' he gabbled, clutching the handle of the door and wrenching it open. 'You've got to get help. She's fallen down and I can't . . .'

'Hey . . . calm down,' Jess said. 'I'll just pull off the road and then you can show me, OK?' She parked the Jeep in the gateway, grabbed her mobile phone from the passenger seat and followed Christian up the garden path.

'So, when did your mum fall, and where?'

'Down the stairs, just now, over the cat, and she can't get up and I . . .'

'Have you phoned for help?'

'Can't. Haven't got one. That's why I stopped you.'

'It's all right,' Jess said, patting his shoulder. 'Don't worry. I've got a mobile.'

Zillah was still in a heap at the bottom of the stairs when they got inside. Jess saw with relief that she was pale but conscious.

'Aren't you the photographer from the *Chronicle*?' Zillah said. 'Good of you to stop.'

'I didn't have much choice,' Jess said, 'thanks to your kami-kaze son here. So what's the damage?'

Zillah winced. 'I think I've broken my leg, but I'm more worried about the baby.'

'Baby?'

'I'm nearly five months pregnant.'

'I'll ring for an ambulance,' Jess said, pressing buttons on her phone. 'What's your address?'

The ambulance crew took forty minutes to arrive and during that time Jess, guessing that she shouldn't try to move Zillah, made her more comfortable on the floor with cushions, and then ran Christian the short distance to his school.

'Won't you be late for work?' Zillah asked when she got back.

'It's OK. I can phone in.'

'Handy things, those.'

'Well I'm out and about a lot, so I more or less have to have one to keep in touch,' Jess said, wondering why she felt she had to make excuses.

'Clive's got one in his lorry, but of course he's never here when he's needed. You got a man?'

'No,' Jess confessed.

'Very sensible. Ooooh!'

'What?'

Zillah put both hands flat on her stomach, her worried expression transformed into one of delight. 'I felt it move! That's the first time. Can't be much wrong if it's kicking, can there?'

'I'm so glad,' Jess said, but she was thinking, why is it that the whole damn world seems suddenly to be *pregnant*?

Hector enjoyed being Acting News Editor, even if it did mean getting to work at eight thirty each morning. This Monday he sat in Nigel's chair in the long, open-plan Newsroom, running his eyes over the News Diary and relishing the modest amount of power the job afforded him. Behind him on the wall was a board with the date of the paper's next edition marked in at the top, the names of the two duty reporters under it, and below them the six or so stories currently being worked on, each with the initials of the reporter doing them. In front of him was the line of desks which would shortly be staffed by the half dozen reporters and the secretary: On the far side of the room, the Sub-Editors would work at another line of desks, writing the headlines and laying out the copy and advertisements on large screens.

Hector looked around with affection at the rows of standard computers, at the piles of in-trays, phone books and files. The photo board (where Jess's work, plus that of any of the freelance photographers was displayed) was constantly changing, like the distant view of the sea from the west window, but the yellowing maps on the wall had been there for ever, Hector reckoned. It was a comfortable, shabby, familiar place to work and he was entirely happy there. In fact it would never have occurred to him not to work, even though he could certainly have afforded to be a gentleman of leisure. There was a limit to the amount of golf a chap could play.

I'm a journalist because I like contact with people, he told himself, which is why I'd hate to be shut away in a small office all day, doing nothing but admin, like the Editor. I'm unshamedly un-ambitious, but I have to admit I wouldn't mind Nige's job. In general I suppose my life is reasonably rewarding, but there is one thing I simply *must* know . . . the sound of the tannoy distracted him.

'Call for Hector on line ten,' Wendy's voice said.

Hector picked up the phone and pressed a button. 'Hector Mudgeley.'

'There isn't really a call,' Wendy said. 'I just wanted to talk to you.'

Hector looked round to check that he was still alone. 'You're in early?'

'Yes, well I couldn't sleep. Could we have a private chat soon?'

'Why not? But not here of course. Oh yes, that reminds me, I'm afraid we won't be able to go out much while I'm doing Nige's job. He never gets away before seven thirty on Wednesdays.'

'How about Thursdays then?'

'Well I can't promise. I may find errors when I'm checking the pages, so I may have to stay late.'

'Well how about Friday? You should be off by lunchtime then.'

'Let's just play it by ear, eh?'

'And Hector, you will keep an eye on things down here, won't you? Nige always makes sure we're safe. I mean, I don't normally give the general public a thought, but that man last month was so horrible. Fancy calling me a slag-heap!'

'Don't worry old duck,' Hector was feeling benevolent. 'I'll make sure I protect you from all loonies, drunks and weirdos; from everyone except myself in fact.'

Wendy giggled. 'That's nice,' she said. 'I've always wanted someone to look after me, especially now.'

'Why now particularly?'

'Tell you when we meet,' Wendy said. 'It's a secret.'

'Right.' Hector put the phone down. Then his mind reverted briskly to the important question which had been occupying his thoughts for some weeks. Did Jess have Caroline's new address in London? They were friends, so she most probably did. He would just have to ask her, and risk her being nosy about it. He had worked out the dates, and they tallied exactly with her baby being *his*. Could it possibly be so? It would be an extraordinary fluke; a hole in one!

Of course he'd got plenty of time to work out what he was going to do about it. He would also have to make discreet enquiries to discover whether Caroline had been seeing any other men at the same time. That could be tricky . . . but essential. He wasn't going to rear someone else's little bastard, that was for sure! There was also the small problem of recovering from the embarrassment of their last encounter, plus the fact that he wasn't sure he actually *liked* the woman very much. But, if the baby really was his (and conceived in the tower room, under the alphabet frieze, beside the blue elephants to boot), then he owed it to the child to do everything in his power . . .

'Morning Hector.' The secretary had come in, followed by some reporters.

'Oh . . . Morning. Good weekend?' He smiled at her.

'So so. You?'

'Quiet.'

She sat down and started to open the mail, smoothing out press releases into a pile. Hector returned his mind firmly to the job in hand, and began Nigel's routine; listening to news bulletins on the radio, discussing stories with the reporters, putting copy onto advertisements, and (over lunch) reading the rival newspapers. The Newsroom was quiet, but for the clicking of keyboards, the murmur of conversations on telephones, and the occasional laughter and chatter across the desks. Completed copy dropped into the Central News Basket beside him, for his approval. Piles of press releases built up; the used ones on Nigel's future-reference spike, and the discarded ones in his waste bin, as Hector dealt with them. He got himself mugs of coffee from time to time, and sipped them slowly to keep his blood/caffeine level at optimal strength.

Jess came in from the darkroom and dropped a few prints into the photo tray. Hector leafed through them. They were run of the mill stuff; a Rotary Club function, a Lottery winner, a Hospice fundraising walk, and a Model Railway exhibition. Hector checked that all the necessary information was written on their backs, and looked up to find Jess still there.

'Was there something else?' he asked her.

'Only that I saw a friend of yours on my indirect way to work this morning. She's broken her leg, poor thing.'

'Who?' Hector asked, without much interest.

'Zillah Brakespear.'

Hector jerked his head up. 'Oh?'

'Apparently she tripped over their cat and fell downstairs. Christian was just going for help when I happened along. He almost got himself squashed trying to stop me!'

Hector looked concerned. 'Is she all right?'

'Dunno. She went off in an ambulance. I thought I'd pop back this evening to find out.'

'Don't worry,' Hector said at once. 'I'll go. I'd like to.'

'Fine,' Jess said casually. 'Let me know how she is, won't you? Oh, and by the way, there's another bit of news that might interest you. Apparently she's five months pregnant.'

'*What!*' Hector choked and spat out a mouthful of coffee. Then simultaneously the tannoy sounded:

'Call for Hector on line five.'

'Hang on,' Hector croaked, still coughing but detaining Jess with a hand on her arm. He picked up the receiver. '*Kaugh! . . . ker . . . hmmm!* Hector Mudgeley.'

'That throat sounds nasty' Wendy said, 'You should get something for it. It's only me again. Look Hector, can we meet before Friday? I don't think I can wait . . .'

'I'm sorry Madam,' Hector said in as official a voice as he

could manage. 'I'll have to get back to you on that one. Something very important has just come up,' and he put the phone down. 'Wretched woman,' he explained to Jess. 'Some pressure group – keeps on pestering me. What are you looking at me like that for?'

Drat! Hector thought, as he watched the truth dawning in Jess's eyes. She's guessed about Zillah and me. It's written all over her face. Trouble with Jess is, she's far too sharp for her own good.

'Something very important, huh?' Jess said mockingly. 'Well, well, well. Who'd have thought it? I only hope for your sake that Zillah *and Clive* both like the name Morgan.'

Wendy worried all afternoon about what had just 'come up' that was so important to Hector. She wondered if he would take it so seriously, once she had told him her news. She had been agonising about how she was going to break it to him, and kept conducting trial conversations in her head:

Wendy: *'Hector, I've got something very exciting to tell you.'*

Hector: *'What's that then?'*

W: *'I'm late you see, so I've done one of those test things and it's turned out positive.'*

H: *'What's positive? What ARE you on about?'*

No, she thought, that's too vague. I mustn't give him a chance to get stroppy with me before he's got the whole picture. How about coming straight out with it?

W: *'You'll be thrilled to know this. We're going to have a baby.'*

H: *'WHAT?'*

No, too abrupt. I don't want to shock him rigid! Perhaps a more roundabout approach?

W: *'Hector, is it true that you've always wanted to be a dad?'*

H: *'Well, yes it is. How did you know?'*

W: *'Call it intuition.'*

H: *'That's what I love about you Wendy, you're so sensitive.'*

W: *'So if I fell pregnant, you'd be pleased?'*

Hector, kissing her: *'Absolutely over the moon.'*

Yes, Wendy thought. That's the one. She went over it several times to make absolutely sure, and then having decided what to do, she began to work out when she should do it. There was no way she could wait until Friday; the suspense was already killing her. She was going to have to do it today. She knew that the News Editor always went home at five o'clock on Mondays, so there was no reason why Hector should be late. Wendy decided to wait for him after her shift finished, and maybe get him to take her home. Then she would pour him a good-sized whisky and sit him down comfortably, and break the news gently.

Jackie, the receptionist on duty that Monday evening, arrived on time and acted a bit huffy at Wendy's continued presence. Wendy ignored her. Five o'clock came and went and people started saying in passing, 'You still here?' Wendy hung on grimly. Then at last, three quarters of an hour later, Hector appeared, moving so briskly that he was almost out of the main door before she caught up with him. 'Hector?'

'Sorry Wendy, I'm in a bit of a rush.'

'But we've *got* to talk. It won't take long.' It's no use, Wendy thought. It's now or never. She took a deep breath and, lowering her voice carefully she said, 'Look Hector, I really need to know. Is it true you've always wanted to be a father?'

Hector frowned and gestured with his eyebrows towards Jackie's back, in a motion which plainly meant 'not in front of the staff'. 'I'm sorry, Wendy,' he said, 'but I've got to go and see a friend who's had an accident. I'm sure you understand.' And he patted her on the head, and made as if to go.

Wendy felt quite desperate. 'NO!' she cried, clutching at his arm. 'It's YOU who doesn't understand. I'm PREGNANT!'

For a moment Hector looked gobsmacked. Then he pushed her roughly through the swing doors with such energy that she went round a complete turn and a half before she could stop them and emerge into the street. Hector joined her and caught her by the elbow in a painful grip, rushing her away along the pavement and stopping only when they were well clear of the *Chronicle* building.

'For God's sake!' he said incredulously, turning her to face him. 'What are you trying to do to me? It'll be all round everywhere in no time flat now. You know what a mouth that Jackie's got!'

Wendy's news had taken some time to register. Hector had

been so completely preoccupied by fervent hopes about Zillah's baby, that his instinct when Wendy had told him of her condition had been an overwhelming impulse to shut her up. He really did not want the staff at the *Chronicle* to know that he and Wendy were having any sort of a relationship, let alone a sexual one!

Yes, he had to admit it to himself; he was ashamed of her. He liked her well enough, but he definitely didn't want to take things any further than a casual affair. He wasn't the sort of man who fancied the kind of woman who knitted pink covers for lavatory seats. He was a snob, and unashamed of it.

Now, he thought, Caroline has the right sort of social cachet. Zillah, bless her, is really too bohemian, in spite of being bright enough, and so beautiful. But Wendy . . . Hector found he was still clutching her elbow. He loosened his grip and then let go altogether. He looked down at her. Two black streaks of mascara had begun to wend their way down her cheeks on the backs of tears. Oh Lord, Hector thought, she's crying. That's all I need.

'Now let's get this straight,' he said in businesslike tones. 'You think you're pregnant?'

'I know I am,' Wendy said, rubbing her freed elbow with the other hand. 'I did a test and it was positive.'

'But you told me you were on the pill?'

'Yes . . . but it doesn't always work, does it. I'm sorry, Hector. I thought you'd be pleased.'

'You mean . . . you did it on purpose?'

'No! . . . well, I don't know.' Wendy blotted her eyes with a tissue, and refused to meet his.

'Are you even sure it's mine?'

Wendy stared at him with a look of such injured innocence, that even Hector felt ashamed. 'How can you even *ask* me that,' she said, 'of *course* it is.' Then she began sobbing in earnest, and Hector was obliged to lend her his best linen handkerchief to mop up the mess. He walked her back to his car, glancing at his watch as he did so. Then he reluctantly drove her home and saw her to her front door. He couldn't really spare the time, but he owned that he did feel a certain obligation to the woman, even though it was an entirely self-inflicted problem.

'We'll talk soon,' he said, on the doorstep, 'we'll go through all the available options, I promise. But I really do have to go now, quite urgently. And Wendy?'

'Yes, Hector?' She looked up hopefully.

'You know, you've been deliberately deceitful, so you can hardly blame me for feeling less than ecstatic about the mess you're in now, can you?' As he left, Hector felt quite justified in having spoken to her so harshly. He felt disconcertingly that he had been taken unawares, *manipulated*, and it made him feel very angry indeed.

It was only when he was halfway to Zillah's house that he suddenly thought – Good Lord, suppose all three babies are mine? Far from being childless, I might even have a *choice*!

Zillah was unsurprised to see Hector. She had assumed that Jess would have told him of her accident, and that he would be bound to use the excuse to pester her again.

'Zillah!' Hector exclaimed rushing in, his face a picture of concern and anxiety. 'You poor love. How are you?'

'I've been better,' Zillah said. She was sitting on the living room floor on a large beanbag, with the plaster-cast on her ankle stretched out in front of her, watching the news on Channel 4. Christian, who had opened the front door to him, now went back to his bedroom to get on with his homework.

Hector waited until he was out of earshot. 'And the baby?'

'Oh, Jess told you about that?'

'Well of course. Is it all right?'

'Fine.'

Hector let out a breath, blowing both cheeks out like an over-mature cherub. 'Well that is a relief.'

'It is?' Zillah was puzzled.

'Well naturally. I adore children, you know,' Hector said artlessly. 'In fact I've always wanted to be a father.' He cleared a chair near to her, and sat down.

'Really? So why did you have a vasectomy?'

'Oh . . . well . . . yes . . . my first wife, you see . . . She was very much against having children . . . so we . . . 'course it's not infallible. I think statistically it's one in every two thousand that re-connects itself somehow . . . grows back . . . you know. But of course I've never dared to hope . . .'

Heavens! Zillah thought, suddenly seeing a way in which his visit might be turned to her advantage. 'So you reckon that you could be my baby's father?'

'Oh!' Hector said theatrically, 'wouldn't that be splendid!'

'Somehow I don't think Clive would share your enthusiasm,' Zillah said.

'Sod's law, it will turn out to be his,' Hector made a face.

'We could get its blood group tested to find out, I suppose?'

'Better still, we'll get a DNA test!'

'Well yes, but they're pretty expensive aren't they?'

'Oh money's no object,' Hector assured her. 'I've got plenty.' He looked as eager as a spaniel, and almost as appealing.

Zillah knew when she was on to a good thing. 'Fine,' she said, smiling. 'I was coming to that next.'

'Sorry?'

'Well babies are expensive things, you know.'

'Wait!' Hector said, 'first things first. I've got something very important to ask you.' He got out of the chair on to his knees on the dusty floor beside her, and took one of her hands in both of his. 'Zillah,' he said, 'will you do me the honour of becoming my wife?'

Zillah's smile widened. 'Oh I would, Hector, believe me, but I'm afraid I can't.'

'But why? You're not married.'

'Because I'm allergic to marriage in any shape or form.'

'But that's nonsense,' Hector protested.

'Not to me it isn't.'

'But Zillah, cariad, I love you. You must marry me.'

'I'm sorry Hector.'

'But then I can look after you both . . . and Christian too of course.'

'You still can.'

'No, Zillah, I'm old-fashioned enough to want the whole deal. For me it's marriage or nothing.'

'That's a shame.' Zillah's mind worked quickly. 'You see, if I don't get enough support, I might not be able to afford to have this baby at all. It's a dreadful thing to contemplate, but Clive isn't what you'd call a reliable provider, and I'm not yet twenty-four weeks gone, so it would still be legal . . .'

Nothing in this world, she thought, would induce me to get rid of this precious child, but Hector isn't to know that.

'You don't mean abortion?' Hector looked horrified. 'I can't believe someone like you would even *think* of such a thing!'

Zillah sighed. 'Extreme poverty sometimes necessitates drastic measures,' she said quietly.

It worked. Without another word, Hector jumped to his feet and scrabbled about in the inside pocket of his jacket, for his cheque-book.

10

THE news of Wendy's pregnancy (and Hector's part in it) spread swiftly round the *Chronicle* staff like a sharp dose of flu. Surprisingly enough, it wasn't Barry who first told Jess. She would have expected him to be at the forefront of the 'Hey, guess what?' brigade, but he was being uncharacteristically gruff. Poor Barry, Jess thought. I expect he wishes it was his.

As far as Hector was concerned, Jess felt both worried and ambivalent. It seemed as though he had actually achieved his aim, and had begotten at least one baby, possibly two? So now what would he do? Jess was clear as to what ought to happen. Zillah had Clive, so she was all right, but poor Wendy had no one. Hector had a duty to marry her. But, Jess thought, they'd be hopelessly mismatched. Wendy needs someone kind and ordinary and unchallenging. And Hector? Hector needs someone to stand up to him, someone bright who could make him laugh, someone independent who could keep him on his toes . . . someone who could take him with a pinch of salt and yet would understand him.

As she drove towards the country pub where Hector had suggested they should meet for this unprecedented Saturday lunch, Jess wondered why he had invited her there and what he wanted to talk to her about. Perhaps he would ask her advice? It was a flattering thought. He did seem to value her opinion more than she might have expected, given the disparity in their ages. Well, Jess thought comfortably, what's seventeen years when all's said and done? So, what do I do? Should I encourage him to marry Wendy? On the other hand, can I in all conscience tell him all the reasons why he shouldn't? But then again, how would I feel if he did? How the hell did he get mixed up with her anyway? Maybe he doesn't have to *marry* her? He's rich enough to pay her a generous amount of maintenance and leave it at that, surely? I wonder if she's in love with him? He can't possibly love her . . . can he?

Hector was already at the pub when she arrived, sitting outside at a small table in the sun, with a colourful salad and a cool beer in front of him. He looked entirely at ease and greeted her arrival with a wide smile, patting the bench beside him and asking her what she would like to eat and drink. Jess had a salad too, and waited until after it was brought to the table by the publican's wife before starting any serious conversation.

A dark, touzle-headed child of about three arrived at the same time as the food, holding on to his mother's apron and peeking out at them shyly, with small vole-bright eyes.

'Aha!' Hector said, looking down at him. 'And who have we here then? What's your name little boy?' The child hid his face. 'I'll bet it's Marmaduke?' No reply. 'Or Nebuchadnezzar?' Then just as his mother moved off to collect empty glasses from adjacent tables, the child darted forward and landed a puny punch on Hector's thigh.

'NO!' he piped.

Hector bent down and grabbed him by the straps of his dungarees, sweeping him high up over his head, before placing him firmly on his knee. 'I know,' he said, 'it's Rumpelstiltskin.' The boy wriggled, but Hector held on firmly. 'Tell me your name you young scamp,' he said, 'and then I'll let you go.'

'Is that wise . . .?' Jess began, frowning.

'Just getting into practice,' Hector said cheerfully.

Then, as the child opened his mouth to roar in protest, he took a grape from his salad and popped it in. The boy choked, coughed and spat it out, and then began to bellow in earnest.

'Jason?' His mother glanced up from her tray full of dirty glasses.

'Oh, it's Jason, is it?' Hector said, jogging him up and down. 'Hello Jason.' The boy was now trying to bite his hand.

'Let him go, why don't you?' Jess suggested nervously.

'Relax,' Hector reassured her. 'I'm good with children. Where's your Golden Fleece then?' he asked the child, who was by now bright red in the face and struggling furiously. 'You ought to be blond with a name like that.'

'Probably christened before he was born,' Jess observed tartly.

'*Pervert!*' The boy's mother had dumped the tray and now rushed over, snatching him off Hector's knee and bearing him away, wailing.

'Oh well,' Hector said, only slightly abashed. 'Funny how small-minded some people can be, isn't it? You've only got to smile at a child these days, and wallop, you're a paedophile!'

'I think he was frightened,' Jess said.

'Rubbish,' Hector said cheerfully. 'They're like small animals, children, you know. They just need a bit of discipline and then they're fine.'

'Are you quite sure you're really cut out to be a father?' Jess asked, grinning.

Hector's smile vanished. 'Not funny, Jess,' he said. 'OK?'

She felt snubbed. There was a silence, during which they ate their lunch. Jess noticed that the squashed grape was nestling in Hector's crotch, oozing juice, but refrained from mentioning it.

'Lovely weather,' Hector said eventually. 'May is my favourite month.'

'Mine too,' Jess said.

'Jess, have you by any chance . . .' Oh good! Jess thought. At last we're going to get to the point of this meeting. ' . . . got Caroline Moffat's new London address?' Hector finished, looking bland.

'Oh, . . . well . . . yes, but why?'

Hector tapped the side of his nose with an index finger. 'Could you let me have it then?'

'Yes, I suppose so.'

'Oh good.' Hector glanced at his watch. 'Then I really shall have to be making tracks, you know. Busy afternoon ahead.'

Dammit! Jess thought. Is that it? 'You could have asked me for it at work,' she protested, 'instead of dragging me all the way out here. I haven't got it with me anyway. It's in my address book at home.'

'Hoity toity!' Hector pretended to take offence. 'I thought you would appreciate a friendly lunch in the country,' he said. 'How was I to know you'd be so prickly today? If you must know, I've some private business to discuss with Caroline, and

I don't want the busybodies in the Newsroom getting wind of it. OK?'

'You're surely not the father of her baby as well?' Jess exclaimed, bursting into unrestrained laughter.

'RIGHT,' Hector said standing up, suddenly furious. 'That's it. I've had quite enough of your childishness for one day, Ms Hazelrigg. I had thought you mature enough to conduct adult conversations, but I see now that you're just a sniggering schoolgirl. I'm sorry I ever imagined otherwise.' And with that, he angrily dashed the flattened grape off his trousers and strode away. Jess was mortified.

Hector had been infuriated by Jess's levity. He had always thought of her as grown up, so it had come as quite a shock that she could be so juvenile. It was also doubly irritating that she had so speedily jumped to his own conclusion. He could only hope their other colleagues would not be so annoyingly perceptive.

As he drove away from the pub, Hector let out a sigh. Life was getting complicated. He had been precipitate and had almost got himself in way over his head, where Zillah was concerned. Only providence had saved him. Talk about getting carried away! He should never have asked her to marry him *before* ascertaining her baby's paternity. What if she had said 'yes' and the baby had turned out to be Clive's? Hector exhaled in a gesture of relief. So far, the Fates had been on his side, but he mustn't bank on it.

He was sorry though, that he'd fallen out with Jess. She was usually a reliable ally. Perhaps it was just the wrong time of the month? Hector sighed again. So, now he was going to have to go and soothe Wendy. What should he say? It was a blessing his decree absolute hadn't come through yet. It could be useful ammunition if she tried to push him too far. What he had to attempt to achieve, was to hold Wendy off for as long as possible so that he could explore the other more desirable avenues first. In truth, he wasn't keen to commit himself until all the babies were satisfactorily born, given clean bills of health, and paternity-tested. Then, once those formalities had been completed, he would be in a position to make an informed choice – but not until then.

Hector knew Wendy was likely to be unsympathetic to the logic of his position, so he would have to find gentler ways of fobbing her off until a final decision became feasible. A soupçon of reassurance is what's required to sort her out, he thought, as he drew the Jaguar up outside her house.

But, as he arrived at the front door, he remembered something amusing that had happened the day before, which he'd meant to share with Jess over lunch. So when Wendy opened the door, looking apprehensive but pleased to see him, he decided to tell her instead and strode confidently inside smiling broadly.

'Nigel's going to have my guts for garters,' he began, 'I completely missed them when I was checking the pages last Thursday, although of course the Subs should have spotted them. That's their job.'

'What is?' Wendy looked confused. 'What are you on about?'

'Column errors, you know, when a word gets cut in half at the right-hand side of a column and inadvertently makes two new nonsense words. Two beauties slipped through in Friday's *Chronicle. Legend* came out as Leg end, but better still, *Therapists* turned into The rapists!'

The following evening Barry went round to Wendy's house carrying a large bunch of forced roses. His lips moved soundlessly as he rehearsed his lines, and his hands were clammy. He rang the bell and, shifting the bouquet about, wiped his palms surreptitiously on the back pockets of his jeans.

Wendy came to the door. 'Oh . . . Barry.'

'I know,' Barry said, 'you were hoping I was Hector bloody Mudgeley. Think nothing of it. I'm getting used to being a permanent disappointment.'

'Don't be like that,' Wendy said. 'Lovely flowers.'

'They're for you,' Barry said, holding them out. He followed Wendy indoors and waited in the kitchen as she unwrapped the roses and put them into a vase.

'Thanks ever so much,' she said. 'They're lovely.'

'Look Wendy,' Barry said, plunging in. 'I have to ask. Are you going to marry Hector?'

'He was here last night,' Wendy said. 'He says he's going to buy me a ring.' She lifted the corners of her mouth in a determined smile.

'That's as may be, but has he actually *asked* you to marry him?'

'Oh well he can't. Not that it's any business of yours, Barry Poole. His divorce from Megan hasn't come through yet, you see.'

'Oh, very convenient.'

Wendy's bottom lip trembled. 'I think you'd better go,' she said.

'Not until I've said what I came for. Can we sit somewhere?'

'I suppose so.' Wendy led the way into her lounge, and they sat down one on either side of the fireplace.

'Is Hector being kind to you?' Barry demanded. A strangled sob escaped from Wendy. She put her hands up to her mouth and gazed mutely over them at him. 'Come on,' Barry said gently. 'You can tell me. Get it off your chest.'

His sympathy appeared to be Wendy's undoing. She started to cry, and once in full flood appeared unable to stop. Barry moved over to sit next to her, pulling tissues from the box on the table and handing them to her, then piling them in a soggy heap beside the un-lit gas fire once they became smeared with make-up, or saturated, or both. Wendy finally pulled herself together, blew her nose and began, falteringly, to talk. Barry learned that Hector had been acting inconsistently, in a way that Wendy found both bewildering and hurtful. She said she really didn't know whether she was coming or going these days.

'He keeps making jokes,' Wendy gulped. 'I mean, I can take a joke like anyone else, but . . .'

'There's a time and a place for everything?' Barry supplied.

'Yes . . . And then he's really good, you know . . . in bed and that, and we have a terrific time and . . . and then he's really horrible to me afterwards, like it was all a mistake or something, or he wishes he hadn't. So I don't know what to think . . . and now there's the baby . . .'

'When's it due?' Barry asked.

'Middle of December. I'm really worried, Barry. I don't want to end up as a single Mum. I'd never manage . . .' Her eyes and nose were now red and swollen. All traces of make-up had vanished. She looked scared and vulnerable. Barry put a determined arm around her shoulders.

'You won't have to,' he assured her. 'You can marry me instead.'

'But it's Hector's baby.'

'So what? I like babies.'

'But . . .'

'I'm serious Wendy. I want to marry you.' Then Barry's confidence wavered and he added quickly, 'But don't say anything yet; think about it. Yes?' He squeezed her shoulders and she looked up at him with a tremulous smile.

'You haven't any crisps on you, by any chance?' she asked him. 'I'm famished.'

Jess was also feeling confused by Hector's behaviour and by her own reaction to it. One minute he was confiding his innermost thoughts to her, and the next he was biting her head off. She felt hurt and resentful. Then she tried to consider things from Hector's point of view and conceded that, if she was right about his part in Zillah's pregnancy, then the man certainly had a problem. It was no wonder he was a bit tetchy. She could understand his fascination with Zillah; she was a beautiful woman, but Jess would have expected Hector to be more canny than to get involved with someone who already had a partner, especially a man like Clive. And anyway, Zillah seemed to her to be a cold fish; not at all what Hector needed. Jess felt angry with him for being so *dense.*

And now there was Wendy. He ought to have had the sense not to have seduced her of all people! Jess despaired of him but couldn't, quite, dismiss him from her thoughts. Why do I mind so much when Hector's cross with me? she asked herself. And why does his procreative behaviour (which would undoubtedly repel any right-thinking, family-orientated, normal human being) seem to have an undeniable logic about it which I certainly deplore, but which I can also, sort of, understand? Horrible man! she thought crossly. He's not worth all this introspection.

She decided to ignore Hector and his problems in future. Get a life! she told herself sternly. It was easier said than done, in a job as time-consuming as hers. Ah well, she thought, at least my work is enjoyable. I suppose I'm very lucky really.

So the summer went by, and August was all but over before Jess managed to take Caroline up on her offer of a weekend in London. Caroline's house was one of a terrace on three floors plus a basement with railings. It looked much like any other town house outside, but was both elegant and welcoming within. Jess saw her own photograph on the wall almost at once, and was pleased. She discovered her friend to be huge and uncomfortable, but still serene.

'How did your new boss take the news?' Jess asked her that evening.

'She was a bit miffed at first,' Caroline admitted, 'but fine now. I'm off work for this last month thank goodness. Just as well; I feel like a tank!'

'What about getting a nanny?'

'That's all sorted out, luckily. It hasn't been easy. As well as letting her have the basement flat downstairs, I'm even having to buy a car for her.'

'Goodness!'

'You don't know the half of it, Jess. I'm beginning to realise that I'm going to have to plan my life like a military operation. It's going to cost me a small fortune too.'

'Is . . . the father . . . going to be able to help?' Jess asked, choosing her words carefully.

Caroline laughed. 'You really mean, "who is the father?" don't you?'

'Well . . .'

'He's been ringing me up every week since the end of May – making a perfect nuisance of himself. He even arrived on my doorstep a couple of weeks ago.'

'What, to ask you to marry him?'

'No, he didn't go quite that far.' Caroline said drily.

'But . . . do I know him?'

'You gave him my address!'

'OH NO!' Jess coloured deeply. 'Oh my God! I'm . . . so sorry . . . I even joked about it, but I never imagined for one moment . . .!'

'No problem,' Caroline said. 'I'm more than a match for Hector. Don't tell him he definitely *is* the father though, will you? I reckon that by tricking me into the pregnancy in the first place, he's well and truly forfeited any rights he might have had to this baby, and anyway I have absolutely no intention of being beholden to him.'

'You wouldn't marry him then?'

'Heavens, no! Sorry Jess, I know he's a friend of yours.'

'There's something else I think I ought to tell you,' Jess said slowly. 'I didn't tell you the whole story earlier because . . . well, because you said you and Hector hadn't been to bed together . . .'

'Sorry,' Caroline said. 'Stupid pride. Great mistake. It only happened the once, you see. Wonderful isn't it! So what's the big secret then?'

Jess told her, ending with: 'So I suppose Hector must be waiting until all three babies are born, and then I imagine he plans to choose one of you and propose marriage.'

'Cold-blooded bastard!' Caroline was incredulous. 'Real life just doesn't work like that. Has the man no feelings?'

Jess felt obliged to try to explain. 'Well you see, he felt totally betrayed by Megan, his wife; it really devastated him. So maybe he's just been trying to make absolutely sure it couldn't happen again? Underneath, I'm sure he's convinced he's being logical and scientific, and that science is a justification in itself. I know that sounds awful, but he is a decent chap really, honestly . . .'

'Well, you know him far better than I do,' Caroline said. 'The whole idea sounds grotesque to me.'

'He's just desperate for a son to inherit the family title,' Jess said. 'But I'm sure he would never knowingly have fathered three at once. It's just a bizarre fluke.'

Caroline laughed shortly. 'A son, huh? Well according to the tests,' she said, rubbing her bulge complacently, 'mine's a girl, so tough luck!'

'Really?' Jess felt quite light-headed. 'Perhaps they'll all be girls?' she said, giggling. 'Three daughters! Then what on earth will Hector do?'

11

On 25 September, after a long and difficult labour, Caroline produced her daughter and vowed she would never ever again have another baby. Hector turned up at the maternity hospital on the 26th, and assured her that dislocating one's shoulder was far more painful than childbirth.

'How the hell would you know?' Caroline asked.

'I read it somewhere,' Hector told her. He stood by the see-through cot where the baby was sleeping, and peered at it intently. 'He looks a little yellow?' he said in tones of concern.

'Neonatal jaundice,' Caroline said crisply, 'and nothing whatever to worry about. She'll be fine.'

'She?' Hector looked up sharply.

'Yes, "she". There are two kinds of human beings, Hector, or had you forgotten that? So I'm afraid I can't really call her Morgan. Although I suppose I could name her after King Arthur's fairy sister?'

'What?' Hector looked blank.

'You know, Morgan le Fay.'

Hector ignored this. He sat down heavily on the bed and massaged his mouth agitatedly with one hand. He looked shattered. 'This will sound ridiculous,' he said eventually, 'but somehow I never anticipated this. I've been concentrating so much on having a son, you see, I've been . . . so focused . . .'

Caroline almost felt sorry for him. 'Well, never mind,' she said. 'It's not a problem. I'm absolutely thrilled she's a girl. I couldn't be happier.'

'Oh . . . good.'

'She's beautiful, isn't she?'

'Yes . . .' Hector pulled himself together. 'What are you going to call her?'

'Hannah Moffat.'

'You couldn't be persuaded to change your mind and call her Gwladys, my great-grandmother's name, I suppose?'

'I think not,' Caroline said quite gently.

'I could register her for you?' Hector offered.

'No thanks.'

'Well . . . should I contribute to her maintenance . . . a monthly cheque?'

'NO,' Caroline was firm. 'Look, I'm sorry Hector. This baby is nothing whatever to do with you and I won't accept any money. I've a good job and plenty of support. I didn't plan that things should be like this, but that's how they've turned out, and I shall cope in my own way. I'm sorry to be so blunt, but it has to be said.'

'So you'll be all right?'

Caroline saw the beginnings of relief start to creep over Hector's face. 'We'll be fine.'

'Ah,' Hector had rallied himself by now, and stood up to go, smiling bravely. 'No hard feelings then?'

'Absolutely not.'

'By the way,' Hector said, suddenly remembering, 'How did you know about my wanting to call my son Morgan?'

'Doesn't everyone?'

'Can't trust anyone these days,' Hector snorted with disgust. 'Just wait until the next time I see young Hazelrigg!' He moved towards the door.

'Good luck then,' Caroline said.

'And you.' Hector stopped and turned. 'Good luck with what?'

'Well, the next two babies of course.'

Hector turned an unlovely shade of red, opened his mouth to reply, closed it again, raised a hand in a half-hearted valedictory salute, made a dash for the door and was gone.

'Say goodbye to Daddy, Hannah,' Caroline crooned to the sleeping infant. Then she stood Hector's greeting card beside all the rest, called for a nurse to find a vase for his flowers, and settled herself back comfortably on her pillows for a contented nap.

'I've got a bone to pick with you, Jess,' Hector said as soon as he had made sure that the Distribution Manager (who shared her office) was safely in a meeting and unlikely to disturb them. 'There are some very personal things I unwisely told you in confidence, and now I find you've been blabbing them to all and sundry. It isn't good enough. I'm disappointed in you.'

'I haven't been "blabbing" anything to anyone,' Jess countered, stung. 'But if you mean Caroline, then I thought she had a right to know.'

'Well that's where you're wrong,' Hector said. 'Let's get this straight once and for all, shall we? Caroline's baby is not mine. She and I have no "relationship" and it's very unlikely that we shall be seeing each other again. Right? Have you got that?'

'That still leaves Zillah and Wendy,' Jess retorted. 'Particularly poor Wendy!'

'That's none of your bloody business!'

'Perhaps not, but you can't censor my thoughts, and in my opinion it's high time you had some kind of an ethics transplant.'

'And what exactly do you mean by that?'

'You know perfectly well! Examine your conscience, Hector, if you've got one! Now I'm sorry, but I've got to go. I'm late already.' Jess picked up her camera bag and walked out. Hector was left standing in the centre of the room.

Flaming cheek! he thought. Who the hell does she think she is?

But later that evening, he reluctantly allowed the niggling feelings at the back of his mind to emerge and display themselves. It was true, he hadn't been behaving well. Jess was right, blast her! His whole crusade for a son might well have been logical, but it had also been obsessive, and it certainly wasn't ethical. Maybe it had been just as well that Caroline's baby had turned out to be a girl? What a fool he'd been. He might have landed himself with a wife he didn't even *like*! He was lucky to have got off so lightly. And another thing, her baby clearly wasn't his; if it had been, he was sure he would have known at first sight. So now he didn't have to see, or worry about either of them again. Well thank God for that.

But, as Jess had so rudely remarked, that left Zillah and Wendy. I could be in deep trouble here, Hector thought. It's not the sort of thing one can easily buy one's way out of. If only Wendy hadn't *tricked* me.

Then he felt obliged to acknowledge that she had only done what he himself had also been doing, but probably for love, which put him firmly to shame. There was no escaping the facts; he had been well and truly shafted by his own arrow!

Barry was assiduous in his courtship of the gently swelling Wendy. He bought her flowers, carried her heavy shopping, and even took her out for meals when Hector failed to honour his unwritten weekly commitment to her. He tried to persuade her to finish working early, take an extra amount of maternity leave and look after herself properly, but she was surprisingly stubborn and refused to stop until the very last moment. Barry suspected she was afraid, if she disappeared from view, that Hector would simply forget about her. He reckoned she had a point there, so he kept pressing her, but only gently.

Above all, Barry displayed enthusiasm for every aspect of parenthood. 'What'll you call it?' he asked, one evening in October.

'I thought Zara, if it's a girl,' Wendy said. 'Hector wants Gwladys, but I've put my foot down. Imagine the poor little thing going through life as Gwladys with a *w*! 'Course, if it's a boy, it'll be Morgan.'

'Don't you know which it is already?'

'No. I said I didn't want to. I think it should be a surprise. Knowing in advance would spoil it.'

'Is that the only reason?'

'Well,' Wendy admitted, 'not quite the only one. You see if it's a girl, then Hector probably wouldn't marry me, out of disappointment. But if it's a boy, he might marry me just for a son. So either way, I lose out, you see? I just can't risk it. I want him to marry me because he loves me . . .' Her lower lip quivered.

'But why Morgan?' Barry asked hurriedly. 'Sounds more like a sports car?'

'It was Hector's father's father's name; my baby's great-grandfather, and Hector says . . .'

'Morgan Bing, eh?' Barry tried it out. 'He'd get teased rotten at school.'

'No, Morgan Mudgeley,' Wendy said, with a defiant lift of her chin.

'How can you be so confident?' Barry asked. 'There's only a couple of months to go before it's born.'

'Shut *up*, Barry. It's none of your business.'

'But it is, Wendy, it IS. Tell you what, let's make a bargain. If Hector (the bastard) Mudgeley hasn't proposed and got your wedding all arranged by the end of October, right? Then you'll marry me in early December. Yes?'

'But I don't love you, Barry.'

'It'll grow,' Barry assured her. 'Do things my way, and you'll be a proper married woman before the baby's born. I'd even let you call it Morgan if it's a boy. Morgan Poole – can't say fairer than that now, can I?' He felt about in his pocket and held the resulting packet up for inspection. 'Ah, smokey bacon.'

'You'd have to promise not to feed it on crisps?'

'Cross my heart and hope to die.'

Wendy laughed. 'You're daft, you.'

'Make you smile sometimes though, don't I? Which is a damn sight more than handsome-is-as-Hector does.'

'You're a nice boy, Barry.'

'I'd rather be a nice man.'

'All right then, you're a nice man. Let's just wait and see, shall we?'

On 9 October Zillah's second son was born. Hector, who had been telephoning the hospital daily for news on the pretext that he was her brother in New Zealand, finally learned to his joy that the baby had arrived and that he and his mother were both well. HE!

Hector was beside himself with excitement. He rushed out during his lunch hour and bought four blue sleep-suits in assorted sizes, a huge bunch of purple chrysanthemums and a congratulatory card with a stork on the front. He had to force himself to wait until visiting time, dreaming all the while of himself and Zillah in a little, white private room (like the one Caroline had had) surrounded by flowers, holding hands and gazing at their baby boy in mutual joy.

The reality was somewhat different. Zillah was in a large

NHS maternity ward, crowded with visitors and loud with babies. Hector couldn't see her at all at first, and then at the far end he noticed, with a sinking heart, Clive's ginger hair. He was clearly not abroad on business this time, but here, sitting by her bed.

'Hell!' Hector muttered, backing out again in order to consider his options. He decided to postpone the flowers and sleep-suits until a more private occasion, so he put them down carefully on a trolley in the corridor and entered the ward once more. This time he held the card in front of him like a passport, and walked the length of the room pretending to be another delighted dad, like all the others.

Zillah looked wonderful. She was sitting up in bed in a lacy nightdress with her long hair hanging down over her bare shoulders, holding the baby which was well wrapped in a small white cellular blanket. She was looking down at it, and she and Clive didn't appear to be talking. Then Clive looked up and saw him.

'Wotcher,' Clive said, 'if it isn't the Good Samaritan! What brings you here then, as if I couldn't guess?'

'I've brought a card,' Hector said. 'Hello Zillah, how are you?'

'I'm fine,' Zillah said. 'You open it Clive.'

'Oh, another one of these,' Clive said, tearing the envelope and pulling the card out. 'That makes four so far. Must be the most popular design.' He plonked it on the locker by the bed.

'Thanks, Hector,' Zillah said.

'So,' Hector said, craning to see, 'how's the little chap then?'

'He's terrific,' Zillah said, smiling. She pulled the blanket aside a little, so that Hector could get a proper look at the baby. It was quite the ugliest infant that Hector had ever seen, and what hair it had, although wispy, was plainly and undeniably red.

'Brill, eh?' Clive demanded, leaning over and stroking the baby's head with a huge hand. 'Looks the image of my old Mum!' and he grinned cheerfully at Hector and Zillah in turn.

Hector's first reaction was one of wild disappointment, which he struggled manfully to conceal. He smiled gamely at the pink prune in the white blanket, and then turned away.

'Well,' he said, 'best be off then. Just wanted to give you my good wishes. Glad you're OK, Zillah. 'Bye.'

'Goodbye Hector,' Zillah called after him, 'and thanks.'

Hector was so upset that he quite forgot to retrieve his flowers and baby clothes from the trolley in the corridor, and by the time he had got to the front door, remembered them, and gone back again, they had disappeared. He walked slowly back down the stairs, and out into the car park. The weather was bright and sunny and unseasonably warm for October. Hector would have preferred it to be grey, with a chill nip in the air, in tune with his mood. He felt as though his greatest dream had been hopelessly blighted.

It wasn't until he was more than halfway home, that he suddenly remembered something vitally important. According to his father's family lore, Hector's great-aunt (the second Gwladys, sister of Sir Morgan Caradoc), who had died tragically very young, had had beautiful, curly, flaming *red* hair!

After a week or so, this long-disregarded fact began to encourage Hector anew. Zillah's baby wasn't necessarily Clive's. It *could* be his. It was undoubtedly off-putting that the baby was so ugly, but Hector had recently forced himself to watch a TV programme about childbirth (although he had been obliged to go and make a cup of coffee a couple of times, when it had got a bit much . . .) so he now understood that newborn babies were sometimes all red and wrinkled, and that it didn't last.

Accordingly he decided to wait until Zillah was home from hospital, and then visit her again. He drove past the cottage a few times, only to discover, by the oversized presence of the lorry, that Clive seemed to be taking an unnecessarily long paternity leave. Hadn't he got a job to do; money to earn? Hector was impatient to see the baby again and, if it were his, to bond with it as soon as possible, but it wasn't until a couple of weeks had passed, that a chance presented itself.

He walked up the path and rang the bell. He could hear the baby crying, and the sound got louder and louder as Zillah came to the door with it in her arms. Its face was screwed up, mouth wide, gums bared, dribbling and bawling its head off. Zillah looked tired and harassed.

'Oh,' she said. 'Not now Hector. Bad moment.'

'What?' Hector couldn't hear a word she was saying.

'I'm just about to feed him,' Zillah shouted, beginning to shut the door in his face.

'That's fine by me,' Hector said, putting a foot firmly over the threshold.

Zillah sighed and gave up, walking back into her scruffy living room and sitting herself down crossly amongst a litter of dirty mugs, crumpled clothes and cat hairs. Hector brushed off a chair with a fastidious hand and sat down opposite her, watching in fascination as she hitched a breast from under her jersey and popped the enlarged nipple into the child's furious mouth. The ghastly noise ceased abruptly, and contented suckling began.

'Phew!' Hector said. 'That's better. I wonder how many decibels that was?' Zillah didn't answer. 'Where's Christian?'

'At school.'

'Oh yes, of course. How is this little chap then, apart from being hungry?' It didn't look any less ugly this time, Hector was dismayed to see.

'He's fine.'

'Has he been christened yet?'

'No, and he won't be.'

'So there's still time to call him Morgan?'

'You've got to be joking! His name is Florian.'

'Oh come on . . .' Hector chuckled, 'you're not serious?'

'Perfectly,' Zillah said coldly.

'Hasn't he got wonderful little fingernails?' Hector said, changing the subject quickly. 'Perfect miniatures; quite extraordinary.' The dust on the coffee table, he noticed, was thick enough to be aggregating into matted grey caterpillars.

'So what d'you want?' Zillah demanded.

'We still haven't established who's baby he is,' Hector explained. 'My great-aunt had bright red . . .'

'He's Clive's,' Zillah said. 'Any fool can see that!'

'Not necessarily,' Hector insisted. 'Now if you and I and the baby were to get some tests done . . .'

'Out of the question.'

'But you suggested it in the first place!'

'Well I've changed my mind. Clive's been terrific with this baby. He wouldn't hear of tests.'

'Exactly, that's the whole idea. If Clive doesn't hear of them, then he won't worry, will he?'

'No,' Zillah said flatly.

'And you categorically refuse to call him Morgan?'

'I most certainly do.'

'Well that's a great pity,' Hector said, forgetting his recent resolutions all over again in his desire to win against Clive at all costs, 'because I came over here especially to arrange to pay you regular maintenance for my son, but more than that, to ask you again to marry me.'

'Oh well, we can always do with financial help,' Zillah said, softening. 'It's very kind of . . .'

'No marriage; then no money,' Hector said firmly.

Zillah shifted the baby round to the other breast before answering. 'Well that's that then.'

'*Please* Zillah?' Hector pleaded.

'Sorry.'

'Oh well, get lost!' Hector jumped angrily to his feet and flounced out.

Driving back to work, still furious and disillusioned, Hector tried to count his blessings:

1) The baby most probably wasn't his anyway.
2) Zillah, as well as being no cook, was clearly a slattern.
3) He hadn't fancied the prospect of a showdown with Clive.

Ergo, it was all for the best. Oh Lord, he thought, Two down and only one to go. It seems only a moment ago when I had the choice of three! What if Wendy's baby turns out to be another girl? He parked the car beside the *Chronicle* building and walked round to the front, and in through the swing doors.

Wendy was sitting behind the reception desk, and Barry was in front, leaning against it on one elbow. Their faces were close together and they were laughing. They stopped abruptly as he came in. Barry straightened up, smiling triumphantly, and said, 'Ah Hector, I'd like you to be the first person to hear the good news. Wendy and I are getting married.'

12

JESS finally decided that Hector had made his bed and could therefore damn well lie in it. She moved the framed photograph which had stood on her mantlepiece ever since their photo session in Megan's turret house nearly a year before, and looked about for somewhere less conspicuous to keep it. It showed Hector outside the big front door, head and shoulders only, one eyebrow raised ironically with the polished brass knocker gleaming behind his head like a halo. It was one of her best portraits yet. Jess put it into a drawer beside her bed and slid it sadly out of sight. Why is it, she thought, that whenever I get a really good photo of a man, it always seems to be a bad omen?

That reminded her. I'm twenty-four, she thought, and what sort of a love life have I had so far? One shortlived affair when I was twenty-three with a tennis player called Mike, to whom I lost my virginity, of whom I got the ultimate sporting-action shot, but with whom I shared nothing important. The best years of my life are galloping by, and leaving me behind. I should be *doing* something about it. Here I am at home at a loose end on a Saturday afternoon. I should be at a football match with some bloke, or hill-walking, or sharing DIY with him, birdwatching, talking, *anything*. I might be a good photographer, but as a human being I'm a total failure.

The telephone rang, and Jess went into her sitting room to answer it.

'Hello?'

'Jess? This is Vivian Powderham, Caroline's friend, if you remember . . .?'

'Oh Vivian, yes of course I do. How are you?'

'I'm well. I wondered whether you'd care to come out to dinner with me tonight?'

'Me?'

'You.'

'Well . . . yes . . .'

'Are you easy to find? Caroline gave me your phone number but not your address.' Jess told him how to get to her flat. 'Lovely. See you at seven thirty?'

'Fine,' Jess said. 'Great. 'Bye.' She put the phone down and glanced at herself in the mirror above it. She saw a thin, untidy, androgenous sort of person with large glasses and a worried expression. Somehow, she thought, I've got to transform that scarecrow into the ideal dinner-date – feminine without being girly, elegant without being ostentatious, and sexy without being too explicit . . . God! If only it were that easy.

Vivian called for her at exactly half-past seven. He looked, Jess thought, understated but stylish. He was not handsome. His face was too thin, his nose too beaky and his hair too wavy, but he was scrupulously polite and attentive.

'Lovely to see you again,' he said. 'I wasn't sure if you'd remember me, so I had this potted description of myself all ready in case.'

'Tell me anyway,' Jess said.

'Friend of Caroline's who looks like a cross between Bertrand Russell and Jeremy Paxman,' he said. Jess laughed.

As the evening progressed Vivian displayed an attractively wry outlook on life. Jess barely noticed what she was eating; the conversation never flagged long enough. Vivian told her about his art gallery in Bath and the exhibition of portraits which he had mounted recently. He was flattering about those of her photographs he had seen and knowledgeable about the uncertainties of the freelance life, which he nevertheless encouraged her to consider.

'You're wasted on your little provincial newspaper,' he said. 'What do you mostly take pictures of in an average week: Women's Institutes, flower shows, schoolchildren, amateur dramatics?'

'That sort of thing, yes,' Jess agreed, 'and fundraising efforts for charity, local government and parish stuff, accidents, floods, crime, you name it.'

'Doesn't sound very challenging.'

'You'd be surprised,' Jess said. 'Every day is different. Suits me anyway.'

'You must come to the gallery next month,' Vivian said. 'I'm having a specialist photographic exhibition on marine wildlife in all its forms. Quite fascinating; I've learned such a lot of biology.' He leant forward to top up her wine glass and smiled at her. 'But you know, you ought to exhibit some of your stuff. I'm sure it would sell. Caroline thinks so too.'

'Nice idea,' Jess said, smiling back. 'By the way, how is Caroline? I haven't had a chance to go up and see her and baby Hannah yet.'

'I've been once,' Vivian said, 'but to be honest, I find that sort of hands-on parental stuff rather daunting. I'm sure she's a lovely child, as babies go, and Caroline herself is absolutely transformed.' He sipped his wine and looked thoughtful. 'In fact, if I may use a zoological metaphor, it's as though she's metamorphosed into a different life-form altogether. I felt rather out of place as a matter of fact, as though I were still in some kind of irresponsible free-floating larval stage, when she's suddenly become a fully formed adult limpet and stuck herself firmly to a high class rock. Her horizons seem to have shrunk so! We seem to have nothing in common any more.'

'But you'll still be seeing each other?' Jess asked.

'Oh I expect we'll see each other once or twice a year, yes, but somehow I think that will be all.' He seemed entirely philosophical about it.

'So is that why you've asked me out? As a sort of Caroline substitute?'

'Certainly not! Don't underestimate yourself, or me, for that matter.'

'Oh,' Jess said. 'Good.'

But when Vivian dropped her back at her flat later that evening, he made no attempt to 'come in for coffee' or even to kiss her. Jess was disappointed at first but later, lying in bed, decided that she wouldn't have wanted to kiss him anyway. He was good company, but too inoffensive, too refined. It's no good, she thought, he's not for me. I need red-blooded enthusiasm, zest, drive, *passion*!

Hector congratulated himself on not having made a scene in

front of Barry when so gleefully informed of his forthcoming marriage to Wendy. He had managed to say something ambiguous like, 'Really?' and had kept his dignity intact. However, once up the stairs and sitting at his desk, his mind began to work furiously.

I shall have to marry her myself, he thought, and *before* the baby is born too. The little minx! I wouldn't be a bit surprised if she and Barry haven't cooked this whole thing up between them, just to push me into proposing. So maybe I'll hang on until after the birth? But what if Barry really does want to marry her? Jess said he was keen . . . I can't have that fat youth stealing *my* baby. So it may be a girl – so what? Maybe it's ridiculous of me only to have wanted a son all this time? Daughters often get on better with their fathers anyway. A little girl could be very charming . . . but can I bring myself to marry Wendy? Hector forced himself to consider the pros and cons, to be scrupulously honest with himself, and yet pragmatic. He got out his notebook, ruled a column down the centre, and made two lists:

MINUS	PLUS
Wendy isn't clever.	W is an excellent cook.
She isn't well-educated.	She's very tidy and
Not a social asset.	houseproud.
Not the ideal partner for me.	She's fertile.
	She's sweet-looking and
	biddable.

She's having MY BABY – the clincher!

It's all of a piece really, Hector thought. In other words, Wendy isn't my equal intellectually. Maybe that's a good thing. Clever women are notoriously difficult to live with, and I'm not at all keen on this New Man stuff. Wendy is undoubtedly all woman. You wouldn't get her expecting *me* to do the cooking. And the Somerset accent and the social scene? Well, how often do I mix in the sort of circles where that would be a disadvantage? She'd be fine at the golf club with the other wives. What am I fussing about?

But what about love (whatever that is)? Forget it! Hector admonished himself sharply. You're far too old for all that romantic nonsense. After all, you can't expect to have every-thing in this life. Wendy fancies you, and you quite fancy her. That's probably about as good as it gets. But what about loving Zillah? his conscience prompted him. Nah! Hector brushed the thought aside, crossly. That was mere infatuation. Beauty is a gilded trap for the unwary. Just as well some of us have the wit not to fall into it.

The following morning when Hector collected his post at the front door, he discovered that his decree absolute had finally arrived. He was divorced from Megan at last! It must be fate, he thought. I'd better act upon it at once. I shall take Wendy out for a special meal tonight, question her on a few crucial aspects of her family health, and if all is well, get her to forget Barry and marry me instead.

Wendy was trying hard not to examine her own feelings too closely. Barry had worn her down with his entreaties and she had finally said 'Yes'. She wouldn't have to face being a single mum after all, and the relief was wonderful. Barry's delight had been very heartening too. It's what I need, Wendy kept on assuring herself. I need to be loved, and Barry loves me. It's that simple.

She was now determined to stop herself obsessively keeping an eye out for Hector and his comings and goings at work. Instead, she kept her head well down. He clearly wasn't going to propose to her. He didn't want to marry her. It's my own fault, she chided herself guiltily. I trapped him into sleeping with me the first time and now look where it's got me.

'Wendy?' Hector's voice made her jump.

'Oh!'

'Could I have a word?'

Wendy walked across to the end of the Reception desk. 'What about?'

'I want you to come out to dinner with me,' Hector said, keeping his voice low so that Jackie couldn't overhear.

'Oh,' Wendy said, 'well I'm not sure. I am an engaged woman you know.'

'Please,' Hector insisted. 'It's important.'

'Oh well, I suppose we could have just one more meal. I don't suppose Barry . . .'

'Right,' Hector said. 'Pick you up at seven o'clock sharp. OK?' And he opened the door and disappeared upstairs.

Oh dear, Wendy worried. I really ought to tell Barry, but I don't think I'm going to. He'd only be cross, and after all, it's not as though I'm going to make a habit of it. After tonight, that'll be it. She felt sad at the thought, but steeled herself to try to think positively. She would go along with what Hector wanted this last time, and that would round things off tidily. Maybe she did owe him that.

Hector arrived at her house promptly at seven o'clock, dressed in a smart suit and with a bottle of champagne in his hands. He was smiling cheerfully. 'Pop this in the fridge, there's a love,' he said. 'We can drink it when we get back.'

'Oh I'm not drinking these days, Hector. It's bad for the baby.'

Hector frowned. 'Well put it away somewhere, will you? I can't keep carrying it around.'

Wendy did so. Then they got into Hector's Jaguar and set off for the restaurant. 'I feel a bit bad,' Wendy said. 'I haven't told Barry I'm here.'

'Good,' Hector said.

'I haven't changed my mind, Hector. I'm still going to marry Barry. We're buying the ring Saturday.'

'Wendy?' Hector said abruptly, not taking his eyes from the road ahead. 'Is there any madness in your family?'

'What a thing to ask!' Wendy was outraged. 'My family's as good as yours any day.'

'I'm sure it is. So none of your relations have ever suffered from serious mental illness?'

'No way!'

'Or serious illnesses of any other kind?'

'Why?'

'Bear with me, please, Wendy. It's very important.'

'Why is it?'

'Because I say so. Now, have they? Think hard!'

Wendy, remembering her resolve, said obediently, 'Not that I can remember offhand, no.'

'You don't have any diabetes or cystic fibrosis or haemo-philia, or anything like that?'

'No, both my nans and grandads died of old age, and my mum and dad were killed in a gas explosion.'

'Oh . . .' Hector turned towards her for an instant. He looked genuinely sympathetic. 'I'm so sorry. I had no idea.'

'It was years ago,' Wendy said.

'You poor little thing,' Hector said, patting her knee consolingly.

After that, there was no more talk of illness. Hector was very attentive and Wendy began to enjoy herself. They arrived at the best, crowded, restaurant (which Hector usually dismissed as being far too expensive) and were given a table right in the middle. Wendy ordered her favourite meal: prawn cocktail, followed by steak and chips, followed by Black Forest gâteau, and Hector didn't criticise her choice once. Then, as she finally sat back replete, wiping her mouth with the napkin, Hector leant towards her and took her hand.

'I've got something very important to tell you,' he said.

'Oh?' Wendy could feel a burp rising within her, and strove to keep it down.

'I got my decree absolute today,' Hector said, 'so I'm finally divorced.'

'Mmmmm,' Wendy said, letting it out in suppressed form.

'But don't you see?' Hector said excitedly. 'Don't you see where that leaves me? I'm free, Wendy, free to marry you!'

'But . . .' Wendy struggled with the unfairness of life, ' . . . but now I've promised Barry . . .'

'It's not too late,' Hector leant earnestly towards her. 'Ask yourself who is it that you really love? Ask yourself who is the father of your child? Be honest, Wendy!'

'But . . . do you really want to marry me?' Wendy asked, confused.

'I wouldn't be asking you if I didn't, would I?'

'Well, you haven't exactly asked me yet . . .'

Then to Wendy's huge embarrassment, Hector rose to his feet right there in the middle of the posh restaurant, got down rather heavily on one knee and said, 'Please Wendy, would you do me the honour of becoming my wife?'

'*Get up!*' Wendy hissed, blushing. 'Everyone's staring.'

'Not until you've given me your answer,' Hector said, smiling confidently.

Oh God! Wendy agonised inwardly. This is what I've been praying for for so long, and now . . . I am so sorry, Barry. Please forgive me . . .

'Well?' Hector said. 'Hurry up. My knee's killing me.'

'Oh Hector . . .' Tears of happiness started from Wendy's eyes.

'Is that a yes?'

'Yes.'

Hector got to his feet and raised a triumphant thumb to the other diners. There was a desultory scatter of applause. Wendy didn't know where to put herself. 'Wonderful!' Hector said, sitting down again. 'Will you tell Barry, or shall I?'

'Oh,' Wendy said, 'I think I'd better. Poor Barry . . .'

'Poor Barry nothing,' Hector said. 'You're well out of that one. He's a mere child. He'll soon get over it, and I'll lay bets there's somebody not a million miles from him, who will be over the moon at our news.'

'Who?'

'Barry's mother. The poor lad can't even draw breath without her permission. You do realise that you would've had to go and live with her if you'd married him? I don't suppose he got around to mentioning that, though?'

'No,' Wendy agreed. Barry hadn't mentioned it. He had, however, mentioned loving her, several times, which was more than Hector had.

Next morning Barry had a happy time at work casually dropping the news that he and Wendy were getting married soon. He knew that Wendy had suggested delaying the announcement until she had the ring to show off, but Barry couldn't wait. He could scarcely believe his luck, and he revelled in all the exclamations of surprise and delight from his fellows at the *Chronicle*.

'We didn't know you had it in you!' they said.

'You are a dark horse Barry!'

'When's the happy day?'

'What does your mum think, then?'

This last was the only problem. Barry hadn't actually told his mother yet. He decided to do it that evening. He hoped she would be delighted. Hadn't she always said that she lived for his happiness? He hadn't consciously ever been *happy* before. Now he felt as though he could accomplish anything, be anyone he chose, live life to the full. He might even get thinner; give up crisps? He doodled an imaginary headline and the fulsome text below it:

JOURNALIST ACHIEVES DRAMATIC WEIGHT LOSS

14-stone Barry Poole has shed four stone for love. Barry, 21, a graduate trainee on the Westcountry Chronicle, *who recently got a distinction in his shorthand exams and came top in Law, Local Government and Newspaper Practice, plans to pass his Proficiency Test for Senior Reporter in a matter of weeks and move house with his new bride and young baby to pursue a promising career on a national tabloid in the heart of London. 'I'm on my way,' he told our reporter today. 'Nothing can stop me now.'*

Dream on! Barry thought wryly to himself. Sounds good though. He decided to pop down to Reception for a moment just to check that Wendy was all right. Her shift should have started by now, and he didn't want her getting overtired. I'll try to persuade her to stop work straight away, he thought. All this standing about can't be good for her and the baby. He saw her before she noticed him and stood at the doorway at the bottom of the stairs for just a moment, smiling soppily at her profile. Then she looked round and saw him.

'Hello darling,' he said. It sounded a bit stilted, but that was only because he wasn't accustomed to saying the word.

'Oh Barry . . .' Wendy seemed less than glad to see him. In fact she looked tense and unhappy. Barry went over at once and took her arm.

'What's the matter? Are you all right?'

Wendy disengaged her arm gently. 'Yes, I'm fine. There's just . . . just something I've got to say.'

'Don't tell me you've changed your mind?'

'Well not exactly. It's just that . . .'

'You HAVE changed your mind!'

'I'm ever so sorry, Barry. It's not your fault, and I really never meant to hurt you. It's just that Hector's got his divorce through at last and . . . and I do feel that my baby ought to be with . . . its real father . . .'

'Has he asked you to marry him?' Barry demanded, 'Well has he?'

'Yes he has.'

'And you've *agreed*?'

'I'm really sorry, Barry.'

'HOW COULD YOU!' Barry felt his own tears welling up for the first time since he was ten and his father had walked out on his mother and him. So, rather than letting Wendy see him start blubbing, he dashed away from her, punching his way blindly through the swing doors and down the road outside, looking neither left nor right, keeping his head up and his teeth clenched together until he was well away from the *Chronicle* building and the shopping streets, and had reached the steps going down to the beach. Then he marched briskly along the sodden sand away from the quiet out-of-season pier, and the dog walkers, and the men building a bonfire above high water mark for firework night. And not until he was well out of earshot of all but a few tatty gulls did he give vent to his pent-up feelings in a great howl of rage and rejection.

'Jess?' Hector said, putting his head round the corner of the otherwise deserted coffee area. 'You look comfortable. I wish I had the time to read novels at work!'

'I was working until past midnight last night,' Jess retorted. 'I'm entitled to a break with my coffee.'

'Quite right,' Hector said, pressing buttons on the drinks machine and picking up the resulting hot plastic cup rather gingerly. 'Ow!'

'You usually make your coffee in the Newsroom,' Jess observed, putting a finger in her book to mark her place.

'Yes, but today I've a couple of things to tell you.'

'What?'

'Well, firstly it seems that Zillah's baby isn't mine after all. It's Clive's, but far more important than that . . .' He paused for dramatic effect. ' . . . Wendy and I are getting married.'

'You're kidding?'

'No, seriously.'

'But why?'

'Because, as you so trenchantly pointed out, I have a duty to her and the child.'

'But she's marrying Barry.'

'Not now she isn't.'

'But why did you wait until she promised him? It's hardly fair . . .'

'Because I've only just got my decree absolute.'

'But . . . will it work?' Jess protested. 'I mean . . . d'you really think you're compatible?'

'Oh yes. I've done a lot of thinking, Jess, and it's quite obvious that I have to marry Wendy and take full responsibility for our baby.'

'And you've come in here especially to tell me that?'

'Well I felt I owed you a debt of gratitude you see, for showing me the error of my ways. And I hoped you'll be happy to discover that I'm not entirely an ethics-free zone.'

And with that, Hector whipped out his handkerchief, wrapped the top of the plastic cup to make it more bearable to the touch, dipped his head once in a mock bow, and left the room.

Jess watched him leave without a word. Then she shut her mouth firmly and frowned long into her coffee. But when she finally forced herself to begin reading her novel again, she discovered that the words on the page had disconcertingly slipped from their allotted lines, and had wandered at random into a meaningless jumble.

13

JESS, in her reluctant role as wedding photographer, went early to the Register Office to await the arrival of both bride and groom. She was surprised, soon afterwards, to see Barry walking up the path towards her. He looked pale and miserable. 'God, what a dump,' were his first words.

Jess looked round at the ugly prefabricated building which was dwarfed by its concrete car park and bereft of any softening form of plant life, and was obliged to agree with him. Dark clouds were gathering low in the north and there was an unpleasantly sharp edge to the wind. 'Looks like snow,' she said, pulling her scarf more firmly round her neck.

'Nah,' Barry said, 'It never snows in December. It waits until it can kill off all the spring flowers in March.'

'Why did you come?' Jess asked him gently. 'You'll only upset yourself.'

Barry shrugged. 'I still can't believe Wendy will really do it,' he said. 'I told her all about Hector fancying the Moffat woman, and then all about that pretty one who got flooded out. I *told* Wendy what a womaniser he is, but she still says he has a right to be a proper father to his baby. Huh! I'll be willing to bet good money the poor bloody baby won't thank her for it when it grows up. I mean how do you get *through* to someone like that? How d'you tell her she's making the biggest mistake of her life?'

'I don't think you do,' Jess said sadly. 'She wouldn't thank you for it. It would only make her more determined. People seem to have to find things out for themselves, the hard way.'

'So where does that leave me?' Barry demanded.

'I know,' Jess said. 'It's horrible for you. I'm so sorry.'

Barry shivered. 'S'pose I may as well go on in,' he said. 'It's freezing. Very appropriate; piss-awful weather for a piss-awful day. See you.'

Jess rubbed her forearms with her palms to warm herself up. Her coat was usually perfectly adequate, but today seemed particularly raw. She speculated upon what Wendy would wear; some form of off-white perhaps? Then she agonised as to whether she should have told her the whole story about Hector, long since. Jess was sure she didn't know about the other babies. If Wendy hadn't been pregnant herself, she thought, I would have, but then again . . . perhaps not. It's really none of my business.

A car drew up and Ifor Mudgeley, the best man, got out first. Jess pointed her camera and got the two of them, Hector and his brother, walking towards her. They were both solemn, and Hector looked wonderful in his dark suit with a white carnation in his buttonhole.

I much preferred him as a gorilla, Jess thought with a pang.

Then the guests began to arrive all at once, and Jess was fully engaged in trying to get a photograph of everyone attending, so as to get a complete record of the day for the album. When Wendy finally arrived, it was on the arm of her brother who had flown over with his family from Australia especially to give her away. He was the only one who looked properly cheerful, grinning from ear to ear and wishing everyone, 'G'day'.

I'll have to take lots of shots of him, Jess thought, if I'm to get a laugh a page. Wendy caught her eye and smiled. She was clearly apprehensive, but also very determined. She had done her best with her own deeply unflattering shape and the unhelpful ambient temperature, and had managed to find a costume both voluminous and warm, but which still looked bridal. It had been a heroic effort, Jess thought, but the words 'white elephant' still rose irresistibly to mind. Then she thought, *I must not be catty*, and began to concentrate once more on taking photographs.

She took more pictures as everyone gathered in the waiting room. The Registrar was running late, and so they were not admitted to the Wedding Room for a long twenty minutes. Jess amused herself by trying to work out the relationships of the guests to each other and to Hector and Wendy. There seemed to be few blood relations on either side; no mums to cry discreetly into small handkerchiefs, no dads to make inarticulate speeches. If I ever get married, Jess thought, I'll have both. The thought cheered her. She looked across at Barry and wondered how he was doing, and as she did so, he got up and walked purposefully out. Best thing to do, she applauded him silently. Why torture yourself unnecessarily?

'Ladies and Gentlemen,' the Registrar said, appearing at the door of the Wedding Room. 'Would you please come in now.'

The room was square, with a desk at the far end, rows of hard seats facing it, and a rubber plant in each corner. It had been painted magnolia above the dado and a dirty yellow beneath. This place looks more like a transit camp than anything, Jess thought in disgust. A church would be so much more sympathetic, if only it wasn't for the inconvenience of God.

The marriage solemnisation, although deficient in the poetry of the traditional prayerbook, was entirely dignified. Jess, however, missed the ritualistic rhythms of: *For richer for poorer, for better for worse, in sickness and in health, until death us do part*. She was just wondering whether they would all be asked to name *any just cause or impediment why these two should not be joined in Holy Matrimony*, when there was a commotion at the back of the hall. All heads turned, and the Registrar, startled, paused in mid-sentence.

It was Barry. He had burst in and was shouting, 'Wendy! Don't do it! He doesn't love you. *I love you*. WENDY.'

The congregation gaped at him. Wendy went white. Hector flushed brick red. Then Nigel, the News Editor, rose and, stepping smartly sideways from his seat at the end of a row intercepted Barry, catching him firmly by one arm and holding on to him. 'Gerrof!' Barry cried, 'WENDY!'

'Come on, Barry,' Nigel said firmly, 'Let's go,' and he dragged him out.

'Now then,' said the Registrar, 'where were we? Ah yes . . .' And the wedding went on. After that, both Wendy and Hector took deep breaths, made their responses in firm voices and were pronounced man and wife. They bumped noses as they gave each other the customary kiss, laughed shyly, and it was all over.

Later, Jess wished that she'd had the presence of mind to photograph Barry's courageous intervention, but it had happened too quickly. When they all emerged from the Wedding Room Barry was still there, sitting in a corner of the waiting room, crying into a hanky and being talked to encouragingly by Nigel. Jess went over, concerned for him.

'Drunk,' Nigel said briefly, looking up.

'He can't be. He was fine ten minutes ago.'

In answer, Nigel held up a quarter bottle of whisky. It was nearly empty. 'Dutch courage,' he said.

'Oh, poor Barry.' Jess was near to tears herself.

'We'll have to get him home somehow. He certainly can't drive himself. I'd take him, but I haven't got my car. I got a lift here.'

'You could drive him in his car,' Jess suggested, 'and I'll follow in the Jeep, and then I can drive us both on to the reception hotel afterwards. Barry's house isn't too far out of our way.'

'But shouldn't you be busy taking photographs?'

'No. I'm doing the group shots in the hotel. It's not exactly picturesque here.'

'Telling me! Right, let's do it.'

'On second thoughts, perhaps I'd better go first, and warn his Mum.'

When Jess got outside there was a blizzard blowing, and the ground was already covered in a thin layer of snow. Well, well, she thought, so it is a white wedding and no mistake! Then she bit her lip and busied herself in clearing the windows of her Jeep before driving carefully away.

As Jess arrived, she saw that Barry's mother was already engaged in defending her front doorstep from the elements, with a stiff brush. At her approach, she jerked her head up smartly.

'Is something wrong? There's not been an accident? Barry . . .?'

'No, no, everything's fine, Mrs Poole. Nigel's just driving Barry home, and I came on ahead. They'll be here any minute. Barry's just a bit tired and emotional, if you see what I mean.'

'Well he shouldn't be. He had his full eight hours last night. Well, I suppose you'd better come in now you're here. Give your feet a good stamp.' Jess did so. 'I don't know what's got into my Barry these days,' his mother went on. 'He won't talk, he won't go out. He isn't even eating properly. In fact he does nothing but moon around watching rubbishly old videos. It's just not right.' She led the way into their living room and motioned Jess to sit down.

'Oh dear.' Jess wasn't sure how to reply. She looked around, and then idly picked up an empty video case from the floor by her feet and glanced at it to see what kind of thing Barry had been reduced to watching. It was a film she remembered well: *The Graduate*.

'He's had that one on a dozen times if he's watched it once,' Barry's mother complained. 'Don't know what he sees in it. Oh, sounds like him now.'

Barry, supported by Nigel, made a sheepish entrance. 'Hi Mum.'

His mother leant suspiciously towards him and sniffed. 'You're drunk! At half-past eleven in the morning too!' She looked accusingly at Jess. 'You said he was tired!'

'Sorry,' Jess said, standing up again, 'but I'm afraid we have to go.'

'Well!' Nigel remarked, when they were both safely back in the Jeep and on their way to the reception. 'What a carry on, eh?'

'Poor Barry,' Jess said, eyes fixed on the white road ahead. 'He's certainly no Dustin Hoffman!'

'Don't get you?'

'No, it's nothing. Isn't unrequited love sad! I feel so sorry for him.'

'Can't understand it myself,' Nigel admitted. 'If some woman didn't fancy me I'd find it a complete turn-off. I certainly couldn't ever see me doing what young Barry just did; make a total prat of myself.'

'Lucky you,' Jess said.

At the hotel, Jess took picture after picture of Wendy and Hector, Hector and Wendy, Wendy on her own, Hector and his best man, and the bride and groom with assorted family and friends. And Hector smiled and made little jokes and winked at her conspiratorially. It was all quite ghastly. Jess could feel her brittle veneer of control breaking up, and an unprofessional emotion beginning to ooze through the cracks. Lunch was called. She wondered if eating might take her mind off things, so she sat down at an empty place. The table was laid with plates of appetizing smoked salmon, each with its own slice of lemon and little squares of bread and butter. Jess thought, I think I could just about force some of that down. She turned to smile at a relation of Wendy's, who had just made a start on his and picked up her own knife and fork to do the same.

'Uuughhh!' the man expostulated in disgust, spitting out his first mouthful into the white damask napkin provided. 'This ham's off, surely! Tastes just like fish!'

The office Christmas party came and went, without Jess, who couldn't face it and pretended to be ill. Christmas itself was a quiet affair at home with her parents, and when she returned to her flat on 2 January, she discovered a small envelope addressed in Hector's handwriting, amongst her pile of post. Inside was a card, edged with a scalloped border in pale blue:

It's a boy!
Hector and Wendy Mudgeley
are proud to announce
the arrival of their son
MORGAN CARADOC NOEL
on 25 December at 8lbs 2oz.
Mother and baby both well.

Underneath, Hector had scrawled in biro: *Thanks Jess. You were right all along. The eleventh Baronet is <u>beautiful!</u>*

Jess dropped the card face down on to the kitchen table. Then she went slowly into her bedroom, took her photograph of Hector out of the bedside drawer, removed it from its frame, tore it into tiny pieces, and burst into tears.

BOOK TWO

SEVEN YEARS ON . . .

14

NEW year, Jess thought, and time for reflection. It was another good Christmas with Mum and Dad, but I do wish they wouldn't worry so much about my future. These days, heaps of people of my age are single by choice.

Now I'm not going to make any resolutions because I never keep them, but perhaps I ought to do a mini-assessment of the recent past, just so that I can point myself in the right direction for the coming twelve months. So, where am I? I'm thirty one. It's . . . goodness . . . it must be seven years since Hector and Wendy's wedding and I'm still stuck in the same old job. But then, nothing much changes at the *Chronicle*; Nigel's still News Editor, although Barry's now an established Reporter (and heavily-married man). The editorship changed of course, and the new one is OK. I'm not surprised Hector didn't get it, and I don't suppose he was either, really. I wonder if that's what's been depressing him? He's seemed very down lately.

Enough of work; what about me? I like it here, but perhaps it's time to be moving on? I'm never going to have a 'career' as such, if I stay. And what about the rest of my life, my so-called love life? I've had three boyfriends in the last seven years and not one of them turned out to be any good: Dave was terminally boring, Nick chucked me, and Jon was gay – what a pathetic record! Perhaps I'm not destined for passion after all? Maybe I'll consult Hector, she thought. He always talks to me like a Dutch Uncle, and then at the same time I can try to find out what's bugging him.

Jess and Hector had lately taken to meeting for lunch in the pub across the road, whenever they both happened to be in the office at twelve thirty. Sometimes Nigel or some of the Subs joined them, and occasionally Barry. Barry, however, usually had some crisis which demanded his presence. It seemed he either had to rush off home to cope with his dreadful old mother, or go out shopping for his exhausted wife, or babysit one of his children. Four kids! Jess thought, good old Barry! I wonder, if he had managed to marry Wendy (and not Jackie) whether he would have had four with her? I wonder too why Hector and Wendy stopped after only one? It's a little unwise to put all one's creativity into one project, isn't it? Still, Morgan's a beautiful child; looks just like Hector, and life is certainly easier with no sibling rivalry. She sighed. I wonder if I'll ever have any children. I'll have to get a move on if so. But perhaps I haven't got what it takes to be a mother.

'Are you pubbing today?' Hector asked, putting his head round the door.

'Be with you in five minutes,' Jess said. 'You go on.'

When she got to the George and Pilgrim, she found Hector there alone, nursing a double whisky between his palms and idly swirling it around the glass as he stared vacantly into the middle distance.

'Well that's you well and truly scuppered for any actual brain function this afternoon,' she observed, ordering herself a Britvic orange and lemonade. 'You don't usually drink spirits at lunchtime.'

'No,' Hector agreed.

'So why today?'

'Oh I dunno. I suppose I'm feeling rather fed up.'

'Can I ask why?' Jess enquired.

'It's Morgan,' Hector admitted, looking up at her. 'He's having difficulties at school. He still can't read properly, you know, at *seven*! At his age, I was devouring every book I could lay my hands on; it's the best form of escapism there is! And his is the age to be doing it, after all; when he's got all the time in the world and no responsibilities. I don't know. Can't understand him.'

'Perhaps he's a late developer.' Jess suggested. 'What brought this gloom on, anyway?'

'Oh I got him *Scrabble* for Christmas,' Hector said, 'but can I get him to play it? And then when I finally do nail him down, he gets half the letters wrong, even upside-down! He doesn't even try! He doesn't seem to have any ambition – well it's either that, or he's just bone idle.'

'He's still very young,' Jess said.

'That's all very well,' Hector said, 'but it's a tough old world out there. If you're going to be successful, you've got to start young. We had a row about his thank-you letters too. I feel strongly about such things, even though it's obviously much easier to telephone. But would he write any? Would he hell! Even when I typed them all out for him in words of one syllable, he couldn't even *copy* them accurately – full of silly mistakes, made me wild! Anyone would think he was as thick as porridge, but they've just had IQ tests done at his school and he came top, so he's got no excuse! I don't know. I just don't seem able to get through to him.'

'Perhaps you're expecting too much?' Jess suggested.

'Oh that's what Wendy always says, but I'm convinced the more that's expected of you, the better you do. I do have to admit it's been bloody unrewarding so far, though.'

'You're surely not implying that the pleasures of parenthood are overrated?' Jess teased.

Hector refused to rise. 'Not at all. You should try it.'

'I would if I could.' Jess felt downcast.

'Why the doleful look then, Jessy my old boot? I thought I was the only miserable sod around here.'

'Oh I don't know. I never seem to meet anyone; anyone that is, who's not a) already married/getting messily divorced, or b) single-but-certifiable. All the best men seem to have been cornered, and I don't fancy a reject.'

'Quite right,' Hector said. 'You deserve better.'

'Unfortunately, plain worthiness doesn't necessarily attract any prizes.'

'Never mind,' Hector said. 'You've always got me to fall back on, and I've got you. So when we get depressed simultaneously, we can drink together and have a good old moan.' He put out a hand and squeezed her arm encouragingly. 'Cheer up,' he said.

Hector was thinking about Jess as he drove home that evening, and wondered why she hadn't got married long since. She's a lovely person, he thought, sympathetic and easy to talk to, but at the same time absolutely all there; as bright as can be. Perhaps I should have chosen her myself? If she was just a little fatter, she'd be a very attractive shape and with more flattering, more feminine clothes well, who knows . . . we could have had several children too, perhaps?

Hector wondered whether in truth he would have wanted more than one. Maybe at the beginning he had cherished an unrealistic picture of fatherhood? He had envisaged a lot of doing things together; his son learning from him, emulating him, looking up to him. It hadn't been like that at all, at least not so far. Morgan seemed to have spent half his life watching television. The only potentially creative thing he ever did was to draw endlessly repetitive geometric shapes which, as far as Hector could see, required no imagination at all. He hated to think such negative thoughts about his only son, but there was no getting away from it, the boy took after his mother. He was deeply boring.

Hector sighed. His marriage to Wendy was hollow at the centre too. Their sex life had never been the same since Morgan's birth. Wendy seemed to have gone off the boil altogether, and had got very prissy about the whole affair. She'd ended up insisting on a five minute standard performance or nothing, so naturally Hector soon got fed up and had been obliged to seek short-term solace elsewhere. Time I had another no-strings-fling, he thought. I expect it's frustration that's making me so out of sorts, or maybe it's because I'm nearly fifty. Either way, I need something to brighten my existence.

He got out his key and let himself in at his front door. He was late and Wendy was already giving Morgan his tea in the kitchen. Hector patted the top of the child's blond head and pecked Wendy absentmindedly on the cheek.

'How was your day?' Wendy asked him, as usual.

'Oh, so so.'

'Daddy?'

'Yes Morgan?'

'I've got a joke. How d'you keep an idiot in suspense?'

'I don't know. How do you?'

'I'll tell you tomorrow!'

Hector laughed shortly. 'Where did you get that one from, then? School?'

'Yep.'

'Not bad. Better than most of the rubbish you come out with.' Hector turned to smile at Wendy, but she was looking miserable. Oh gawd, he thought. What have I forgotten? Anniversary? Birthday? No . . . He braced himself. 'So, what's up with you?' he enquired dutifully.

'You haven't asked me about *my* day.'

'Well all your days are much of a much-ness, aren't they?'

'Well they wouldn't be if I went back to work.'

'Oh let's not start on that one again, Wendy. There's no need for you to work, and much more important, I don't want my son being a latch-key kid.'

'Daddy? What's a latch . . .'

'Not now Morgan. Mummy and I are talking.'

'Well go on then,' Wendy said.

'Go on what?'

'Ask me.'

Hector sighed and went over to switch the kettle on to make tea. 'Right then, how was your day?' he said with his back to her.

'I went to see Dr Johns,' Wendy said, 'and she says I *have* got to have a hysterectomy after all.'

'Hysterectomy, eh?' Hector said, putting a teabag into his mug and looking for the milk. 'I see . . . Odd word that, isn't it? I've often wondered about its origins. I mean, if an appendectomy is the cutting out of an appendix, then logically a hysterectomy must be the cutting out of hysteria, eh?' he turned to face her, smiling, but caught on his left eyebrow the full force of the empty mug that Wendy had just flung at him. It fell on the floor and smashed into jagged pieces.

'Aaaah!' cried Hector, holding his face 'Why on earth . . .?'

'You don't care!' Wendy shouted. 'I've got to have a *major operation* and you don't give a shit!' and she stormed out.

'POW!' Morgan sang out, looking down at the scattered shards with amazement. 'Bullseye! How'd she DO that? She's useless at throwing straight!'

A new year, Wendy thought as she made supper, big deal!

Will it be any better than the old one? I very much doubt it. Will Hector stop putting Morgan down? Will he be any nicer to me? Will he stop working such long hours and spend more time with his family (and would I even like it if he did)? No, she thought, no to all of them. Perhaps I would have been better off as a single mum after all, or even married to Barry?

Barry was quite clearly a model father. Hector called him 'Poor old Poole the Puppet Pullet', just to show how much he despised a man who would willingly submit to such henpecking. But, Wendy thought, Barry wouldn't have been determined at all costs to buy such a big, draughty, inconvenient old rectory for them to live in, or to use up all her nest-egg from the sale of her own little house. Barry wouldn't have wasted hours on the phone, scouring the country from end to end just to track down that horrible blue elephant wallpaper for Morgan's room. Barry wouldn't have insisted on putting up that irritating alphabet frieze, which was nothing more than a constant reproach to poor Morgan (who could never remember the order in which the letters went).

Oh dear, Wendy thought. I suppose I'll have to explain to Hector about Morgan soon, but I know he'll take it badly . . . I think I'll put it off until after my operation . . .

The thought of her hysterectomy frightened Wendy, but if it helped to get rid of the pain she felt when they infrequently made love, then perhaps it would be worth it. Maybe their married life would improve, and they might even become close again? She clung to this hope as she stirred the white sauce round and round. Maybe deep down Hector was frightened of the operation too, on her behalf? Perhaps that was why he was making jokes? She shouldn't have thrown that mug at him. She could have *blinded* him. Now, every time she saw his poor swollen face and his bruised eye, she would feel guilty and worry whether it was all her own fault for being a bad wife and not allowing him enough sex. Two salt tears dropped into the sauce and Wendy stirred them in.

Hector came downstairs, having just read Morgan a bedtime story. 'Lazy little tyke,' he said. 'We had this agreement; I'd read two pages to him and then he'd read the next one to me, and so on. But when it came to his turn, he just pissed about. Don't understand him. It can't get much simpler than

D-O-G now, can it? A performing horse could manage that, but oh no, not our Morgan. "Bob" was the best he could come up with. Honestly, I despair of him. And to think that Peter Ustinov looked out of a bus at an advertising hoarding at the age of *eighteen months* and read the word OXO. Well!' He shook his head.

'So, what did you say to him?' Wendy asked anxiously.

'Told him straight. If he wants a story, he's got to make an effort too. It's fifty fifty or nothing.'

'Oh Hector . . .' The sauce was just thickening.

'Don't "Oh Hector" me Wendy. You're too soft on the boy.' Wendy took the pan off the heat and turned slowly to face him. Hector registered her tears with surprise. 'So what's the matter with you? If anyone ought to be crying, it should be me.' He fingered his eyebrow, wincing.

'I'm sorry about your eye, Hector, really I am. I never meant . . . I just . . .' Wendy broke down and sobbed briefly into her apron, but when she had got herself under control again, she looked up at Hector. He hadn't moved but she thought she could detect a gleam of compassion beneath the habitual irritation.

'Oh for goodness sake, Wendy. I do care about your operation,' he said gruffly. 'Of course I do. I was just trying to lighten the atmosphere a bit, that's all. So why don't you tell me what the doctor said, eh?'

'He says my womb is retro . . . something,' Wendy said, sniffing. 'It's facing the wrong way and it's crushing my ovaries and that's why it hurts.' She tore off a piece of kitchen towel and blew her nose. 'And it's full of fibroids too, so it's got to come out. He says they do a cut across here . . .' She made a sweeping gesture across the base of her stomach, and Hector winced.

'Yes, well don't let's go into all the gory details,' he said quickly. 'If that's what you need, then of course that's what you must have, and the sooner the better.'

'There's a waiting list of about a year,' Wendy said, 'because I'm not an emergency.'

'Well stuff that!' Hector said at once. 'You'll go privately. They'll have you in and out in a jiffy.'

'Oh Hector, I'd rather not,' Wendy said earnestly. 'It's queue-jumping and it's not right.'

'For Christ's sake woman!' Hector expostulated. 'You need a major operation. You told me so yourself. Well I'll tell you this for nothing, no wife of mine is going to hang about for a whole year, when she could perfectly well get it over and done with in a matter of weeks. Just put that ridiculously outworn socialist dogma behind you, once and for all, will you? I know full well your father was a Trades Unionist way back in the dark ages, but this is now. Things have changed. We've got the money, we're paying for it. End of discussion.'

'But it's against my *principles*, Hector.'

'Nonsense,' Hector said. 'You're probably subconsciously trying to put off the evil hour because you're scared. Quite understandable, but short-sighted. No, the sooner we get you sorted out, the better.'

'I've got a problem,' Hector said to Jess. 'All the company cars are out at the moment, and I need to go and see this dig everyone's so excited about while it's still there and before they build the new road smack through it. I'd go in the Jag, but I'm not risking its sump on those drove roads. They're far too lumpy in the middle.'

'Heavy hint?' Jess said. 'By strange coincidence I'm going out to photograph the trackway this afternoon, and the Chief Archaeologist will be there too, so if you come with me you can interview her while I take my shots.'

'Lovely job,' Hector said. 'Thanks. Let's take our lunch and eat it somewhere scenic on the way, shall we? I'm fed up with being indoors.'

'OK.' Jess glanced at his black eye, intrigued as to how he had come by it. The word going round the Newsroom was that Hector had either been hit by a wayward golf ball, or (snigger) had recently taken up bare-knuckle boxing. Jess waited until they were well out into the countryside and had parked beside a road overlooking the Levels, before she decided to open the subject.

'You really shouldn't play rough games, you know.'

'*What?*' Hector's expression, above a half-bitten ham sandwich, was not encouraging.

'Nothing,' Jess said hastily. 'I'm just worried about you. Your poor eye looks horrible. Does it hurt much?'

'Probably looks worse than it feels,' Hector said, chewing. 'I walked into a door, if you must know.'

'Oh come on, Hector,' Jess teased. 'No one really walks into doors!'

He didn't reply. Instead he stared out at the grey brown January landscape under its feeble sun. Jess followed his gaze. The rhynes were full, but the fields this year had not flooded. As she watched, a farmer with a tractor and trailer was dumping stone to repair one of the droves, and further off, half a dozen swans were clambering out of the water on to a grassy field. When Hector eventually spoke, it was to talk about his family.

'You see that ridge over there?' he said, pointing south-westwards. 'The other side of that hill, on the southern slopes above the Sedgemoor Levels – that's where Zoyland Park used to be; the house my father pulled down so that he could build a factory in Woodspring and get rich.' The bitterness in his voice was heartfelt.

'What was it like?' Jess asked.

'Wonderful,' Hector said simply. 'Elegant. Built by my family in the eighteenth century and lived in by them for six generations.'

'What a sacrilege! Why did your father do it?'

'Oh, lots of reasons. It was an enormous house, and it had gardens and parklands, all very labour-intensive, and he couldn't get live-in staff any more, and it needed far too much costly repair work and upkeep.'

'But why didn't he give it to the National Trust?'

'They don't take on houses that aren't adequately endowed.'

'So, why didn't he open it to the public himself? Places like Chatsworth and Longleat seem to do well enough.'

'Oh that's another kettle of fish altogether; you need special insurance, extra security and God knows what. And anyway he didn't fancy becoming an impoverished museum curator. He wanted to cash-in most of the contents, sell off ninety percent of the land, go into commerce and get rich.'

'And did he?'

'Oh yes. To be fair to him, he wasn't alone in his vandalism. That sort of thing was considered expedient, in those days. In fact I believe about 250 houses of architectural and historic interest were demolished in this country after the second war, or got burnt to the ground for the insurance money! Zoyland Park went in 1953 when Grandpapa died, just as the stock market was rising and other private houses were beginning to flourish. Had Father waited just a few short years . . . but no. Sheer wanton destructiveness!'

Jess got out an apple and bit into it. 'When did your father die? He must have been quite young?'

'In 1983. Yes, he was only 63; maybe it was retribution for the death of the house!'

'You and your brother Ifor would have been all for taking it on, then?'

'*I* would,' Hector corrected her. 'I still hanker after my grandfather's days, when the Mudgeleys were in charge; benevolent guardians of the countryside and its inhabitants. As a system it worked very well. But Ifor's sold out just like our father did. He's all for egalitarianism, anti-snobbery and equal opportunities. Huh!' Hector snorted.

'Is that so bad?'

'Well what's the point of being a bloody baronet if you don't use your title?' Hector demanded. 'That's just perverse *inverted* snobbery! If only I'd been born first . . .'

'Well at least Morgan will be "Sir Morgan" eventually?' Jess said.

'Yes, that's some comfort.'

'So, what happened to the land?'

'Oh a lot got built on, but most is still in agriculture. Part of it is a nature reserve; the low moors bit, and I'm fairly happy about that. I'm on the management committee in fact, and we've made a lot of positive changes to the place. I suppose that's the only good thing about the whole sorry story.' He got out a flask and poured himself a cup of coffee. 'I just wish I could get more campaigning articles into the *Chronicle*. In the good old days when we owned it . . .' He took a gulp of coffee and sighed.

'They mightn't have been good old days for everyone.' Jess suggested.

'I'm not so sure of that,' Hector said. 'At least they all had work then, a regular paypacket, proper housing and their own front doors to close at the end of the day.'

'Or to walk into, if the fancy took them?'

'If you *must* know,' Hector said, tidying up the remains of his lunch, 'Wendy threw a mug at me.' He stared at her challengingly.

'*What?*' Jess began to laugh.

'Damn, I knew I shouldn't have told you,' he said with mock irascibility. He looked at his watch. 'Christ is that the time? We're going to be late. Come on, start her up and let's get going.'

As she drove off, Jess felt in unusually buoyant mood. She tried to analyse why, and concluded that it must be because Hector had begun to confide in her again. In her experience, this was rare, and therefore very beguiling. Most men were famously reluctant to discuss their problems. Her own Dad certainly didn't; for him to do so would have been a sign of weakness and incompetence. Yet here was Hector revealing things about himself and his family, things perhaps he didn't even share with Wendy? Jess felt privileged, *special*. Maybe, she thought, it's more rewarding to be friends with a man than to marry him (unless of course you want his children). Poor Wendy doesn't appear to be getting much fulfilment as a wife. Is it possible that I'm getting the best of Hector? It was a happy thought and Jess drove on, smiling.

But the next day he was avoiding her, she was sure of it. He didn't go over to the pub at lunchtime, and when she went into the Newsroom to deliver photographs or to discuss stories with Nigel, he barely acknowledged her. Jess felt hurt. She tried to think how she might have offended him, but couldn't remember anything bad enough. He surely wasn't sulking because she had laughed at the mug-throwing episode. He wasn't that petty . . . was he?

Just as well I'm not married to Hector, she thought crossly. I never know where I am with the wretched man!

15

IN mid-January, the weekend arrived when Jess was due to go up to London to see Caroline, but she wasn't sure whether she was looking forward to it this time. Over the years she had grown very fond of her, but their friendship was changing inexorably and Jess wanted it to stay the way it had begun. She had always enjoyed Caroline as a mentor: approving, encouraging, laughing at her jokes and drinking wine late into the night putting the world to rights, but these days her friend was permanently distracted and exhausted.

Of course it's necessary to grow up and take on responsibilities, Jess thought, but is this the right way for women to go about it? Isn't this modern feminist ethos for juggling several lives at once every bit as much of a deprivation as being expected to stay brain-dead at home, hoovering behind the furniture? Aren't they simply opposite sides of the same coin?

She didn't envy Caroline and her ilk one bit. They never relaxed. They never had time for trivial pleasures such as putting photographs into albums, writing letters or picking flowers. They were mothers when they were supposed to be bosses, but were obsessed with problems at work whilst playing Happy Families. Whichever role they occupied, they felt guilty. They had holidays certainly, and expensive ones to boot, but even these were high powered. Hannah had to be 'entertained', so Caroline took her to Disneyland, or they went skiing, or they hired a canal boat in France with five other single parents and a few token men, so that the children would learn co-operation, discipline and social skills. It was all such hard work!

Jess worked hard too, but at least she felt that her life was her own some of the time. Did that precious sense of self have to vanish? Did having children inevitably mean a complete derogation of identity? If so, it was to be avoided at all costs.

She remembered the few family holidays she had been on, at Hannah's age. She had made sandcastles, collected shells or investigated rock-pools whilst her parents had read books or gone for walks. The tranquil days had stretched out ahead of her, and hours had elapsed serenely, devoid of any pro-grammed or supervised activity. She supposed her parents must be old-fashioned as well as elderly. It had never occurred to them to entertain her; the very concept would have been anathema.

It seems to me to be totally counterproductive, Jess thought, this raucous trivia which (as current orthodoxy has it) must be drip-fed into children throughout their every waking hour. It's supposed to stimulate their tiny minds, but I think all it does is to make everyone conform to fashionable but intellec-tually vapid stereotypes. It stifles all creativity.

'You sound just like my grandmother!' Caroline teased after supper on the Friday evening, when Hannah had gone unwill-ingly to bed and Jess was trying to propound an edited version of these ideas. 'At least today's children have access to every-thing that's going and have a good social sense and global awareness.'

'True,' Jess agreed, 'and solitary rock-pool gazing certainly doesn't seem to have been much of a foundation for vivid, gregarious encounters, in my experience!'

'No luck with men then?'

'No,' Jess made a face. 'I only attract lame ducks.'

'I never seem to have time to meet new blokes,' Caroline said, 'but I'm bound to admit that it doesn't bother me overmuch.'

'Is work going well then?'

'Not bad, but ageism is beginning to creep up on me. I'm thirty-seven, in my prime, but I'm getting the distinct impression that I'm about to be elbowed out of the way by the "young". It's an uncomfortable feeling; makes me quite manic at times. Insecurity is a high octane fuel for us work-aholics. How about you?'

'I keep wondering whether I should make a move,' Jess said, 'but I like it at the *Chronicle* and there's no particular reason . . .'

'Well,' Caroline offered, 'if you ever want to come to London, you're welcome to rent my basement flat. Since

Hannah grew out of her last live-in nanny, we haven't needed it. I've got a student occupying it at the moment, but he'll be leaving soo . . .' The telephone rang. Caroline got up to answer it and Jess overheard her one-sided conversation.

'Hello? Oh . . . hello. So, what is it this time?'

'No, absolutely not. It's out of the question.'

'She's fine, and she's nothing whatever to do with you, OK?'

'I'm sorry Hector. Listen carefully, because this is my final word on the subject: NO!' Caroline banged the receiver down and turned, frowning, to Jess. 'Guess who.'

'Does he often phone?' Jess felt something uncomfortably like jealousy.

'Not for years and years,' Caroline said, 'but in the last week, twice, well three times now. He says he wants to see Hannah. What's the matter with him, seven year itch?'

'Well,' admitted Jess, 'I suppose you could call it that, but actually in his case it's more like heir-line cracks. H-E-I-R, that is.'

'Uh-oh,' Caroline raised an eyebrow in amusement. 'Having trouble with young Morgan, is he?'

'Yes, he seems very worried about him. Is Hannah reading well?'

'Fluently. It's wonderful when the penny drops, you know. A whole new world opens up to them.'

'Well apparently Morgan is totally clueless about the written word, but bright enough verbally.'

'Probably dyslexic, poor child. It's all the rage,' Caroline said, 'but I can't somehow imagine Hector being very supportive under those circumstances.'

'Oh, I'm sure he would be,' Jess said at once. 'If he knew it was genuine. I don't think he's considered that possibility though . . .'

'If you want my advice,' Caroline said, 'keep well out of it. No parent welcomes any suggestion that its darling child is anything less than perfect.'

'Oh I'm sure Hector wouldn't be so touchy,' Jess said defensively. 'He'd always want what was best for Morgan.'

'Lucky man – he's got a good champion in you.'

'On the contrary,' Jess snapped. 'If you must know, we don't even seem to be on speaking terms, these days.'

On the Sunday evening, travelling home from Paddington, she wondered whether she would want to see quite so much of Caroline in future. She regretted speaking sharply to her. It hadn't been a row, nothing so dramatic, but it was enough to ruffle Jess's composure, as the conversation re-ran itself irritatingly inside her head. She wished she had kept quiet. There was no point in arguing – they had so little in common these days. There was a time, Jess thought, when I assumed that Caroline the High Flyer was about to leave me behind, but now the opposite seems more likely to be true. How strange.

Wendy managed to convince herself that it was because Hector *cared* for her that he was insisting on her having the operation privately, and once this idea had taken hold she felt better able to square it with her conscience and arrive at a less uncomfortable acceptance. She had worried about Morgan and how he would get on whilst she was in hospital. It wasn't so much that Hector couldn't cope with the daily chores. He wouldn't, but that hardly mattered. It was more the fear that in her absence he might demoralise the boy. Morgan was at an impressionable age, and she didn't want him upset. (Any day now, they would have to discuss special schooling . . . but not quite yet . . .) She decided to approach Ifor and his wife June, and was pleased when they cheerfully offered to have him for the eight or nine days that she would be away, or even longer if necessary to allow her to recuperate.

Wendy also undertook a huge cooking session and stocked up the freezer with meals for a fortnight. She cleaned every room in the house, changed the sheets on the beds, put blue-flush in the lavatories, washed the curtains and dusted the tops of the lampshades. At the back of her mind was a tiny voice that said, *What if you don't come round after the operation?* Wendy felt that, in this event, at least she'd have nothing to feel ashamed of.

And now here she was, in her private hospital room, having been brought there at nine thirty by Hector. It was now . . . Wendy looked at her watch . . . five thirty and it had seemed a very long day. A nurse had written *Mrs W. Mudgeley* on a plastic band and had fastened it around her wrist. After some hours a young doctor had showed up, and then the surgeon.

Then no one. Soon she would ring Morgan at Ifor's to check that he was all right. Then at six thirty when Hector would be home from work, she would ring him too. So what now? There was a television, but she didn't feel like watching it. She wished she were in a proper ward with things going on, and other patients to talk to. When she had previously stayed overnight in the Gynae ward for her exploratory laparoscopy, there had been Maureen the hairdresser on one side with her gas curling tongs, and fat Jean on the other with her constant complaints. Wendy hadn't liked either of them much, but at least they were a distraction. She was glad when it was eventually time to telephone.

'Hector, love, it's me.'

'Oh, hello. Hang on a mo. I'll just turn the radio off . . . Hello?'

'How was your day?'

'Pretty good actually. I managed to escape from the Newsroom for almost half of it, and I've done a really good piece on the aerial pollution from that plastics factory I was telling you about. Remember?'

'Oh . . . good . . . Are you all right?'

'Fine. But it's odd being here on my own without you or Morgan.'

'Yes, it would be. Morgan's happy. I rang him just now. He says he and the girls are all dressing up, and he's being a robot.'

'Sounds good.'

'Did you find your supper all right?'

'Yes, I'm putting it in the microwave any minute.'

'I wish I could eat something myself. I'm starving!'

'What? Haven't they brought you any food yet?'

'Of course not! I'm not allowed any supper before the op. I told you.'

'So you did. You all right then?'

'As all right as I'm ever going to be.'

'Well I suppose I'd best be getting on with this cooking business, so . . . well . . . what does one say in these circumstances? Good luck for tomorrow? Hope it all goes well.'

'Thanks.'

'I'll pop in to see you in the evening, OK?'

'Yes.'

'Goodbye for now then, love.'

''Bye.' Wendy put the receiver down slowly. Hector had said 'Good luck for tomorrow' as though she were going to the dentist for a check-up or something equally routine. What if she were to die under the knife? Would he then wish he'd said, 'Darling, just remember one thing, I've always loved you' or maybe, 'Be brave my beloved, I only wish *I* could go through it all for you'. Or even, 'Chin up sweetheart. I'll be thinking of you'.

Tears pricked her eyes, but she sniffed them back. Then she looked at her watch. It was going to be a long night too. She sighed, turned to plump up her pillows and, taking out *Hush Now My Trembling Heart* from her locker, settled back determinedly and began to read.

The day after the operation, Jess felt it was about time she and Hector re-established normal communications, so she went over to talk to him at his desk in the Newsroom.

'How's Wendy?'

'Hard to tell. She was looking yellow and being sick when I saw her last night,' Hector said, barely looking up.

'The poor thing! Was the operation a success though?'

'Oh I assume so. I expect she'll tell me all the gory details soon enough.'

Jess glanced around. Nigel and two of the Reporters nearest to Hector were deep in discussion. Barry and the others were talking on their telephones, and the Subs were too far away to overhear anyway. She decided to risk it.

'Hector,' she said, keeping her voice low, 'I'm sorry if I've upset you, or something?' Hector looked up, frowning. 'I'd never do it on purpose,' Jess said, 'you must know that?'

Hector merely looked puzzled. 'Sorry?' he said. 'I'm not with you.'

'Hector?' called Barry, covering the mouthpiece with his hand. 'I've got a man here who says he saw the fight at the chip shop. On line six. D'you want a word?'

'If I must,' Hector said, picking up his phone. Jess took the hint and slipped out of the Newsroom.

Hector went dutifully to see Wendy again the following

evening. She continued to look pretty dreadful and there was still a gruesome tube coming out from beneath her bedclothes and leading to a bottle of bloody liquid on the floor. Hector sat carefully on the other side where he couldn't see it. Wendy was less drowsy this time, and able to talk.

'They've taken the drip off the back of my hand, thank goodness,' she said, 'and I've even walked!'

'So soon?' Hector asked.

'Well only once round the bed, with a couple of nurses holding me up and carrying my drain. And the Doctor says the op. was all very straightforward and they've left my ovaries in place, so I won't have an early menopause, so that's good, isn't it.'

'I suppose so, yes.'

'And guess how big the lump of fibroids was?'

'No idea.' Hector braced himself for the details.

'Bigger than a grapefruit, they said! So that should make me slimmer, eh?'

'Should do.' Hector sought to dodge the subject. 'Are you in pain?'

'Yes, quite a lot,' Wendy said, wincing. 'But they're giving me painkillers and I'm not moving much, so I reckon it's more uncomfortable than anything. Have you been OK? And Morgan?'

'Both fine,' Hector said. 'Morgan rang me. He's got some rhyme or another that he's dying to recite to you. I'll bring him in in a day or two when you're a bit better.'

'Good.' Wendy yawned and closed her eyes, and after a few minutes when Hector reckoned she was definitely asleep, he tiptoed away. He drove home half-listening to the radio, but after a few moments leaned forward intently and gave it his full attention, driving even worse than usual in consequence.

Once home, he sat for a considerable time staring at the window but unfocused, thinking about the programme he had just heard. Could what they had said be true of him as well? And if so, how could he have got it so wrong for so long? Perhaps he was growing up at last? Or was it just a sign of incipient old age, when beauty ceased to be paramount in a man's assessment of his ideal woman?

Hector had lately been reading a host of popular science

books in an attempt to counteract the bias inculcated in him by his narrow arts education, and the idea of the evolution of human nature by sexual selection currently fascinated him. He saw now that he had been at its mercy all his life, unknowingly swept along by the biological imperative that female beauty signifies youth and health, which together make for optimum breeding of the next generation. It was a cruel fact of nature that kind, clever, *ugly* women were discriminated against most unfairly, in spite of their undeniable worth.

I've done with the breeding bit now, Hector thought, so shouldn't I at last be liberated from the tyranny of my genes? Perhaps that's what maturity is all about. Perhaps that's why I'm dimly beginning to realise what I've been missing all this time. I've been so obtuse, so prejudiced, so *intolerant*. Why didn't it strike me long ago? After all, she has all the qualities I most admire, and I've felt closer to her than to any other woman, for years and years . . . He got up and went to the telephone.

'Jess!'

'Hector? Is that you?'

'Yes, look I'm sorry I couldn't talk to you at work. I'm afraid I've been neglecting you a bit lately. It's not your fault; I just seem to need some space sometimes. But, can I come round and make up for it now?'

'Well I suppose . . . yes, if you like. I've only just got home, and the place is rather a tip, but . . . yes.'

'House-proudness is an overrated virtue,' Hector said carelessly. 'I've always thought so. See you in about half an hour then.'

He ran up the stairs two at a time to the bathroom and gargled energetically with pink mouthwash. He inspected his face in the mirror for flaws and then had a quick shave anyway. He sniffed his armpits, and discovering them to be passably sweet, bounded downstairs again to look for a suitable gift.

His car journey to Jess's flat passed without any conscious effort on his part. The Jaguar drove itself. Hector was suffused with the excitement of the moment. His blood had woken from long torpor and positively roared through his veins. His hands, as they rested nonchalantly on the steering wheel, looked to him to be strong yet sensitive. He felt full of confidence. A long-abandoned tune from his youth rose unbidden into his head and provoked him to spontaneous expression.

'You are the sunshine of my life . . . yeah!' Hector sang, 'Mmm mmm mm mmmmmmm mm mmmmmmmmm . . .' The forgotten words were not crucial. It was the feeling behind them that was so uplifting. He arrived at Jess's door with all his senses heightened as though he'd been breathing pure oxygen.

'Good grief,' she said. 'Champagne! What's all this in aid of?'

'I've been keeping it for years,' Hector explained, 'since before Morgan was born, in fact. And now I've found exactly the right use for it.'

'You have?'

'Well aren't you going to invite me in then?'

Jess took the bottle and moved backwards, but Hector, instead of going past her, stepped jauntily over the threshold and flung both arms round her. Then he held her at arm's length, in order to gauge her reaction. She looked more bemused than ecstatic. His confidence wavered a fraction.

'What's going on?'

'Simple,' Hector said. 'You see I was listening to Radio 4 on my way back from the hospital, and this woman was saying how it's quite possible for some men to be in love for years and years without actually realising it.'

'Sounds pretty far-fetched to me.'

'Not at all!' Hector cried. 'It makes perfect sense. It's a revelation! You see, that's what's been happening to *me*.'

'It has?' Now she merely looked confused.

'Come on, Jess! I didn't exactly expect you to swoon into my waiting arms, but I had hoped for a little more enthusiasm.'

'Well you haven't told me yet who you think you're in love with.'

'Why you of course, who else?' Hector stared into her warm brown eyes and saw with tremendous relief that he wasn't entirely rejected. There was room for hope.

When Hector kissed her, Jess felt mostly confusion and disbelief. He led her through to her sitting room holding her hand and they sat down, smiling rather awkwardly at one another.

'I suddenly feel about sixteen years old,' Hector said.

'You don't look it,' Jess said drily. 'Just as well!'

'Here, pass me the champagne and I'll open it,' he said. Jess did so, and went to find two glasses. Hector tore off the foil and the metal basket and eased the cork out with both thumbs. It made a satisfactory pop.

'Whoops,' he said as the contents fizzed up and overflowed.

'Doesn't matter,' Jess said, catching some in one glass and presenting the other. 'It's a grotty carpet anyway.' She handed the full glass to Hector.

'*Iechyd da cariad*,' he said. 'Cheers, my darling. Here's to us!'

Jess couldn't help but be flattered by this new romantic Hector, but underneath she wondered what on earth was going on. Had he brought the champagne to aid a seduction? Was he hoping she would go to bed with him? As far as she was concerned, there were two significant reasons why she shouldn't: Hector was a married man, and she wasn't on the pill!

She sat on the edge of her seat hugging both arms around her chest, and regarding him seriously. She decided she liked the shape of his nostrils, the curve of his mouth, even the small white scar on his forehead . . . but did she really *fancy* him? Unrequited day-dreams about Hector were one thing, but the actuality was quite another. In her fantasies she had felt a lot of things . . . but apprehension hadn't been one of them.

Hector was taking his time. He seemed to want to talk. Jess put her glass down and, shuffling off her shoes, put her feet up on the futon and leant back.

'I've made so many mistakes,' Hector began. 'You know when famous people are asked about their lives on radio or TV, and they say that, given the chance, they'd do it all over again just the same? I always think that's so bloody conceited! I never believe them. It means they're either too stupid to learn from experience or they're lying through their teeth. No one ever gets it all right, do they? Life's one almighty compromise.'

'With occasional short sharp spells of euphoria, if you're lucky,' Jess agreed.

Hector smiled lovingly at her. 'I want to try to explain things,' he said. 'I want you to understand me. I've changed, you see. Until now I've always seen women as the means to an end; for pleasure, children, whatever, but now . . .'

'Now, what?'

'Well, companionship and friendship are just as important, aren't they? There'd be no need to rush anything. As long as we were together, we could just *be*.'

'You and me, you mean?'

'Yes, you and me.'

'And no one else?'

'Why d'you ask that?' He looked wounded. 'Don't you believe me?'

'Well I was just wondering if it's really positively me you want, rather than simply a change from Wendy, if you understand what I mean?' Hector frowned. 'You see,' Jess said hastily, 'I was at Caroline's when you rang her, so I wondered . . .'

Hector smiled widely. 'Oh, that,' he said. 'No, I haven't the remotest interest in the Moffat woman if that's what you mean. I just wanted to see Hannah. I suppose I still have a sneaking feeling that she might be my daughter, and so I wanted to be sure. What's she like? You've seen her. How would you describe her?'

Jess sat up abruptly and put both feet back on the floor. 'She's very pretty,' she said, 'and very clever at school, but maybe a bit of a show-off, a touch aggressive, even unhappy? It's hard to say. I think she resents her mother leaving her to go to work every morning.'

'Mmmmm,' Hector said. 'Hardly surprising, poor child. Anyway, enough of that. You haven't drunk your champagne. Let me top you up, and then . . . who knows what we might do next, eh?' He smiled at her, a wonderfully open, confiding, *sexy* smile, but Jess felt uncomfortably constrained. What were his real motives? Could it be that having become dissatisfied with Morgan and finding Hannah unavailable to him, he was still out to beget the perfect child . . .?

'No, Hector,' she said slowly. 'I don't think so.'

16

'Saw an old friend of yours in Court this morning,' Barry called to Hector across the desks in the Newsroom.

'I doubt that,' Hector said, without looking up from his computer.

'No, straight up. It'd be hard to forget a name like hers, and I'm sure you haven't. Zillah Brakespear ring a bell, does it?'

Hector looked up sharply. 'What about her?'

'She was in Juvenile Court with her son. Blimey, if ever I've seen a cheeky young thug in the making, it's him.'

'What? Surely not Christian?'

'Nah. He had some really pansy, flowery name. Didn't suit him at all.'

'Florian?'

'That's it. Little devil got let off with a talking-to, because in spite of being big for his age, he is only seven and it was a first offence. He wants to watch it though, next time he'll be slung into care. I just hope my kids . . .'

'But what did he do?' interrupted Hector. He could feel his heart pounding with anxiety.

'Oh, nothing evil, just a spot of TWOC-ing.'

'*What?*'

'Taking Without Owner's Consent. He nicked a car, went for a spin, and was seen dumping it. Not a scratch on it – pretty clever actually – I'm amazed he could reach the pedals. If he hadn't been so conspicuous he'd probably have got away with it, but all that red hair is a dead liability.'

'Was his father in Court?'

'No. They've split up. She said she had no idea where he was. They weren't married anyway, which explains a lot.'

'Hardly worth writing a report on, surely?' Hector said, trying to appear casual.

'What d'you mean? It's my best story this month!' Barry protested. 'Can't identify the brat of course, since he's well under age. Great pity, that. Names make all the difference. Anyway, I just thought you'd be interested.'

'Mmmmm,' Hector said, trying to appear indifferent. He finished typing the story he was on as quickly as he could, and then dropped it into Nigel's basket.

'Any chance of the rest of the afternoon off?' he enquired, 'for personal reasons.'

'Is Wendy all right?' Nigel asked at once.

'Well, yes and no. It's only three days since her operation, and you know how it is . . . I just thought . . .'

'You go,' Nigel said generously. 'We'll manage. Never let it be said . . .'

'Thanks Nige.'

Hector drove the Jaguar as fast as he could to Zillah's cottage, justifying the white lie to himself as he went. He would of course have to go and see Wendy that evening. He also very much wanted to see Jess. He wasn't going to give up on her, not now he'd seen that unmistakable look in her eyes. But this news about Florian had really shaken him, and he simply had to find out what was behind it. He hadn't given the boy much thought in the intervening years. He'd written him off as being Clive's son, but now if he was in trouble and Zillah was having to cope with it alone . . . Well, one visit couldn't hurt. I'll find out what's going on, Hector thought, then collect Morgan and go straight to the hospital for half an hour or so (less if possible), and then drop Morgan back at Ifor's and get away as quickly as I can to see . . . Jess . . . I've been taking things very gently for a whole month, so she's had plenty of time in peace to examine her feelings. Please God, let her say yes, tonight.

He drew up, smiling at the thought, outside Zillah's cottage. The old chairs had gone, but the garden still looked unkempt although, of course, it would hardly look its best in mid-February anyway. It had been unusually gloomy all day, and was now beginning to get dark at least an hour too early. There was a light on inside the cottage and the sound of Radio 3 was audible. Hector banged on the door and flakes of paint fell off.

'Who is it?'

'Hector Mudgeley.'

'Well, well,' Zillah opened the door and stood there impassively. 'Hector Mudgeley, eh? Long time no see.'

'How are you?' Hector asked, noting with shock that she was very pregnant indeed.

'Never better,' Zillah said.

'Can I come in for a chat?'

'No, I'll come out to your car. The boys will be back from school any minute, and I doubt you'd want them joining in.'

'Well, no.' Hector led her down the garden path to the Jaguar and opened the passenger door for her.

'Same old car then?' she said, getting in.

'Naturally. It's a collector's piece.' He got in too, and her scent and nearness reminded him of why he had once lusted after her. 'How are your boys?'

'Oh Christian did really well at school last summer. He's got my dad's brains, I reckon; took nine GCSE's a year early, and now he's sixteen and in the first year of his science A-levels.'

'Very good,' Hector agreed. 'And Florian?'

'Little sod! He's just the opposite. I reckon it's bad blood.' She looked challengingly at him.

'And how is Clive?' (May as well double-check, Hector thought.)

'Oh he buggered off years ago, but it wasn't his blood I meant.'

'But you told me Florian was Clive's?'

'Well I thought he was. Christian definitely is, but since they're so very different in every possible way, it does make you wonder, doesn't it?'

'But no son of mine would steal cars!' Hector protested.

'Aha!' Zillah said. 'So, you *do* know about that. Is that why you're here then, to lecture me for not keeping him under proper control? You should try it sometime. He's slippery as black ice that one.'

'Well maybe I could help?' Hector suggested. 'I've got a boy much the same age as Florian. They might get on well, you never kno . . .'

'Not another vasectomy failure? Don't tell me, his name's Morgan?' Zillah laughed.

'Yes it is, as it happens.'

'So what's wrong with him then, that you need to come sniffing round after Florian?'

'Absolutely nothing,' Hector said, offended. 'It seemed to be my common duty to make sure the child was all right, but if you're just going to sneer . . .'

'Mind you,' Zillah said hurriedly, 'I'm not saying we couldn't do with some help . . .?'

'No,' Hector said. 'This is clearly a mistake. I shouldn't have come.'

'Course, we could always take that paternity test you were so keen on?' she wheedled. 'Then we'd know for sure.'

'Well . . .' Hector wavered.

'He's not such a bad boy,' Zillah encouraged him. 'He's a bit wild, but he's goodhearted really.'

'Can he read?'

'Of course he can! He's not stupid.'

'All right then,' Hector said, making a snap decision. 'It's a deal. I'll find out what we have to do for the test. I think it involves all three of us giving a blood sample. Then I'll let you know, OK?'

'You're on,' Zillah said, opening the car door and getting out just as Christian arrived home on his bicycle. Hector wouldn't have recognised him. He was so tall, and his dark hair was now long and scraped back into an unbecoming ponytail. He didn't appear to remember Hector either, noting him and the car incuriously without a second glance.

'Hi Mum, what's for supper?'

Before she could answer, the school bus drew up and Florian leapt out.

'Hello boys,' Zillah said to them both. 'Good day?' The younger boy, illuminated in the bus's headlights, looked *exactly* like Ifor Mudgeley had at the same age, apart from the hair.

My God, Hector thought with a start. He *could* be mine!

'So, so' Christian answered her over his shoulder, wheeling his bike towards the cottage. Florian said nothing at all. Instead, he twisted his face into a caricature of fear and disgust, then smiled sweetly and followed his brother up the path, slamming the front door behind him.

Zillah, standing by the car and still holding on to the door, raised her eyes to heaven. 'Whilst you're here,' she said to Hector, 'would you like your fortune told? It's what I do these days. I've got a very stylish crystal ball.'

'Not today,' Hector said, so she pushed the door shut and waved him off. It was only after he'd left that Hector remembered he hadn't asked her about the father of her third baby. Had he perhaps been lurking inside the cottage all along. Hector had an uneasy feeling that as usual in his encounters with her, Zillah had come off best.

Jess felt obliged to make a duty call on Wendy, but hoped Hector would be there as well, for moral support. So, knowing that he had left the office early to visit his wife, she bought a bunch of hothouse anemones and a Get-Well card, and drove to the hospital straight after work. However, she found the patient in her room alone, propped up on her pillows and reading a thin book with a lurid cover.

'Oh,' Wendy exclaimed, 'Jess! I didn't expect to see you.'

'Sorry,' Jess said. 'If it's inconvenient, I could come another day?'

'No,' Wendy said. 'I didn't mean that.' Jess watched her as she opened the proffered card. Without her usual make-up she looked quite different. Her hair had been flattened against the pillows and needed a wash, and her face was pale, with large dark patches below the eyes. She had clearly been through an ordeal.

'Lovely card,' Wendy said, looking up, 'and flowers too. Will they go in that vase over there, with the others?'

Jess stuffed them in carefully, one by one. 'So, how are you?' she asked.

'Well I managed a bit of food today,' Wendy said, 'and I've had that horrible drain removed. There was yards and yards of it right inside my stomach, and it didn't half hurt when they dragged it out!'

'Sounds ghastly,' Jess said.

'Yeah, well I wouldn't recommend it,' Wendy smiled weakly.

'I rather thought Hector would be here?' Jess said.

'Oh well, you know Hector,' Wendy said with a martyred look. 'He's probably chasing some story or another. Whatever it is, it will be more important than me.'

Jess was stumped for a reply, her immediate but stifled response being: Well if that's your attitude, I'm surprised he visits you at all!

'Um . . . Is there something I can bring you, books or anything?' she asked, noting the title of *Trembling Heart* without surprise.

'Hector's getting me some magazines today, but I can't seem to take much in,' Wendy said, 'so don't bother, thanks. I feel like my brain's on strike.'

'That'll be because of the anaesthetic, I expect,' Jess said. 'I'm sure it will wear off soon.'

'Certainly hope so,' Wendy said.

After that, there didn't seem to be much to say. Jess wandered over and looked out of the window. There was a good view of the car park and the chimney of the incinerator, but nothing much else. She was about to say that she really ought to be going, when the door burst open and Morgan rushed in, closely followed by his father.

Jess hadn't seen the boy for some time. He was certainly very fetching to look at, and had a lot of Hector in him.

'Mummy!' He rushed over to hug Wendy.

'Hello love! Come and give me a kiss . . . ow! Be careful of my sore tummy . . .'

'Why, hello Jess. This is a nice surprise.' Hector bent to deposit a fleeting kiss on his wife's forehead before straightening up and smiling quizzically at her.

'Listen to this,' Morgan said to them all, screwing up his face in concentration:

> *'We don't care,*
> *We don't care,*
> *People see our underwear,*
> *If it's black or if it's white,*
> *Oh my God, it's dynamite!'*

'Morgan!' Wendy cried, pretending to be shocked. Jess laughed.

'Typical schoolboy stuff,' Hector observed. 'It has all the necessary elements; anarchy, smut, blasphemy and violence!'

'I think it's very good,' Jess said.

'The things they learn at school these days,' Wendy said.

'If you can memorise that nonsense,' Hector said to his son, 'then there's no reason why you shouldn't be able to learn your two-times table, is there?'

'S'different,' Morgan muttered.

'Did you bring the magazines?' Wendy asked.

'Damn!' Hector said. 'Forgot them. Sorry, I'll buy some tomorrow.'

'Oh, Hector!'

'Well,' Jess said hastily, 'I think I'd better be going. 'Bye Wendy.'

'Bye Jess. Thanks for coming.'

'See you,' Hector said, and winked one eye very deliberately.

On the way home, Jess thought hard about herself and Hector, and about Wendy also. She felt sorry for her. Poor stupid Wendy, Jess thought. I know you've had a nasty operation and I do sympathise with you, but you quite obviously haven't got what it takes to keep up with Hector.

And I have? she challenged herself – possibly . . . So what if he did want to have a baby with me, would that really be so offputting? Haven't I always said I wanted children? It's time I made up my mind. Maybe my parents are right, and I won't get many more chances? Would I be stupid to refuse this one? . . . But he's married, so it would be wrong . . . And yet I realise now that I've probably wanted him for *years*. But what about Wendy . . .? Jess went over and over the pros and cons for the rest of the evening and had just concluded that an affair couldn't possibly be justified, when the doorbell rang. It was Hector.

'Can I come in?' he asked.

'Depends.'

'On what?'

'On why you want to?'

'Well, to see you of course.' He gazed steadily at her.

'Sounds reasonable,' Jess said, and opened the door wide.

Hector felt uncharacteristically nervous. He sat on Jess's futon and wondered how he was going to talk her round.

'Whisky?' Jess offered.

'Yes please.'

'Water?'

'About the same again, thanks.' He watched her closely and wondered why he had never really *seen* her before. I've been too hung up on conventional good looks, he thought, too brainwashed by fashion. Here is a woman who appreciates my sense of humour, who is young and slim, and *never tells me what to do*! Why the hell didn't I marry her seven years ago, instead of poor old Wendy?

'Take your specs off a minute,' he said as she sat down opposite him. Jess did so. 'That's better,' Hector said. 'You have the most beautiful eyes, you know. It's a wicked waste to hide them behind such stern glasses. Have you ever considered contact lenses?'

'No,' Jess said firmly.

'Or I believe these days, you can even get short sight permanently cured by laser treatment?'

'NO!'

Hector wanted to say, 'I love you,' but couldn't quite form the words. That sort of tenderness didn't come naturally to him. Maybe later on, in the dark when they were in bed together. 'I think you're wonderful,' he managed.

'But you'd still like to change me?'

'Sorry?' He had hoped she would be looking a little less defensive by this time. Surely his accustomed technique wouldn't let him down – not now when it really mattered?

'Well, you like my eyes but not my glasses. You probably like my figure but not my clothes, or even my intelligence but not my personality?' She jammed her glasses back on to her nose, and glared at him.

'Jess, cariad, why are you suddenly so *cross*?'

'Why d'you think?'

'Well I really have no idea. You're wrong, you know. I love everything about you.' (There – he'd said it!) 'Only say the word, and I'll show you?'

Jess still seemed unimpressed. 'That's just the point.'

'What is?'

'You're a *married man*, Hector. You're not in any position to offer me anything!'

Hector sighed, and spread his hands. 'You're right, of course,' he said. 'But if you were to find that you could love me in return, then such things could be sorted out. Nothing in this life is immutable . . .' He could see her resolution faltering, and continued recklessly, 'and you're wrong you know, I do love your clothes, *everything*. I wish I'd realised this years ago. I can't bear to think how much time I've wasted . . .' She was looking softer, wasn't she? 'You do believe me, don't you?' he begged.

'Well,' Jess began, 'it's so unexpected, you see. It's hard to take in . . .'

'Come and sit next to me.' Hector patted the futon. 'I'm sorry, I've been rushing you. Let's forget everything we've been saying, and just talk. What are you drinking?'

'I've a glass of cider in the kitchen. I'll fetch it.'

When she came back, she sat down beside him and smiled at him shyly. I must take things much more *slowly*, Hector told himself. Jess clearly isn't the sort of woman who leaps into a man's bed on impulse (unlike some I've known!) but when she does, then she really means it. It'll be worth waiting for.

'I know who you remind me of,' he said, reaching out and running his forefinger down the curve of her cheek and jawbone, 'my great-grandmother Gwladys. You've seen my big portrait of her? I've had it in all my various houses (including that dreadful pokey flat where it dwarfed everything and looked ridiculous). It's about the only family heirloom I managed to save, and it looks marvellous now in my study at the old Rectory.' He took a pull at his whisky, and smiled at her. 'Anyway, there's a definite resemblance, by some strange coincidence. She was a famous society beauty in her day, you know?'

'Flattery,' Jess said, grinning sceptically, 'is unlikely to get you anywhere.'

'No, seriously,' Hector said. 'I mean it.' He bent and kissed her cheek. It felt cool. 'And thanks for going to see Wendy. It was good of you.'

'I meant to ask you,' Jess said, 'Why were you so late in getting to the hospital? I thought you'd be there well before me. Nigel said you'd left work soon after two thirty.'

'Ah, well I didn't go straight there,' Hector said. He nuzzled into her neck and made little kissing noises.

Jess was not to be distracted. She leant away. 'So, where did you go?'

'I heard a friend of mine's son was in trouble,' Hector said, 'so I thought I ought to pop over and see how they were.'

'Anyone I know? And what sort of trouble?'

'I'm not sure you'd remember them,' Hector said smoothly, 'but the boy's been in court for "borrowing" a car. I expect it was a one-off thing, a dare or something. There wasn't much point my going over there actually. There was nothing I could do. Oh, Jessie my sweeting, I'm afraid I shall have to go home soon in case Wendy phones, I do wish I didn't have to . . .'

But Jess was tenacious. 'So what's their name?'

'Brakespear,' Hector muttered unwillingly.

'*Zillah* Brakespear?'

'Mmmmm.'

Jess sat forwards abruptly and turned to face him. 'So why didn't you *tell* me straight away?' she demanded.

'Well, it didn't seem that important,' Hector said.

'But you've just told me you love me! Or was I mistaken?'

'No . . . I do . . . I'm sorry Jess . . . but I don't follow . . .'

Jess looked furious. 'It should be obvious,' she cried, looking at him incredulously. 'If we're to have any sort of a relationship, then at the very least, we must be able to *trust* each other!'

Next morning Hector awoke alone in his own house after a troubled night, and decided that come what may, he really did have to *know* whether Florian was his son or not. It might well upset Jess even more, but love wasn't retrospective, so you couldn't be held accountable for absolutely everything you'd done in the past. He wasn't sure how well he'd managed to mollify her the night before. He'd told her over and over again that he wasn't the least bit interested in Zillah, *really*, but Jess had seemed unconvinced. She had assumed that it was Christian who was in trouble and Hector, to his shame, had not disabused her. There would be plenty of time to talk about Florian once the tests had been done. Then he would confess everything, and all would be above board.

Before going to work, Hector telephoned a doctor he was friendly with at the local hospital, and sounded him out on DNA testing. He had to endure a certain amount of ribaldry at his own expense and was warned that it could cost a bit and might take about a month, because it involved matching up the DNA bar-code pattern from the child with those from both its putative parents, and checking that every band in the child was present in one or other of the parents (allowing only a one percent difference for mutations). This sounded fair enough to Hector.

The next stage was to get Zillah to present herself and the boy at the right place and time for their blood samples to be taken. He was pretty sure that this would pose no problem. He was under no illusions as to her motives; she was clearly only in it for the maintenance money. Hector recognised that if the boy turned out to be his, he would be obliged to help pay for his upkeep, but he felt that was as it should be. He wasn't one to shirk his responsibilities. What he hoped was that he would also be granted access to Florian. He was sure he would be able to prevent him from going to the bad, even exert a positive influence; get him reading some good classic books . . . take him to museums and stimulate his interest . . . play *Scrabble*? Hector sighed.

Morgan still doggedly refused to read. He tore through museums without pausing to glance at any of the captions and was bored in five minutes. As for *Scrabble*, it continued to be a non-starter. Hector was becoming more and more worried that there was something genuinely wrong with him – a duff set of genes from his mother or maybe, perish the thought, actual brain damage. He was such a beautiful child too . . .

Five weeks later, Zillah read the letter containing the paternity test result at lunchtime on a Saturday, and let out a whoop of triumph.

'What?' Christian asked.

'Good news,' Zillah said, 'or as you might say, "a nice little earner". Florian? D'you remember the man I was talking to in his car when you got home from school six weeks or so ago?'

'Nah,' Florian said with his mouth full of pizza.

'You mean the old git in the really ancient car?' Christian asked.

'Yes, and less of the "old" if you don't mind. He's the one

who took us in when we were flooded out, don't you remember? He gave you lots of books.'

'What about him?' Florian asked.

'Well,' Zillah said slowly. 'This may come as a bit of a shock to you, but it seems he is your biological father.'

Florian gaped at her. 'Wharrer 'bout Clive?'

'Clive is Christian's dad, Hector is yours, and Johnny-gone-lately is this one's.' She patted her bulge. 'You're lucky. Hector is by far the richest.'

'But I don't want . . .' Florian began

'It's all right, don't worry. You won't have to go and live with him or anything like that. Nothing's going to change. After all, Christian hasn't seen Clive for ages, and this one's never likely even to *meet* its dad, so you'll all three be in the same boat, OK? Just be polite to him when he comes round with the money, and we'll all be fine.'

'Maybe he won't pay up?' Christian observed. 'I mean . . . it wouldn't be much of a return on his investment would it?' He swallowed the last of his lunch and laughed shortly.

'Oh I don't know,' Zillah said, smiling at Florian.

Florian, sensing a tease but not being able to understand it, jumped up from his chair and aimed a volley of punches at Christian, who held him off easily with one arm.

'Hey! Stay cool, OK?' he said. 'There's nothing to get all stressed out about. Three different fathers, eh? Could be a really interesting experiment in genetics. But this Hector bloke hasn't got red hair?'

'No,' Zillah said, 'but he says it's in his family.' She saw a movement outside the window from the corner of her eye and glanced up. 'That's handy, he's here now! You can ask him yourself.' She went to the door to meet Hector, leaving the two boys at the kitchen table.

'Have you had the test results?' Hector asked eagerly. 'I almost came round first thing, but I thought I ought to give you time to break the news.'

'Our post doesn't get here 'til midday,' Zillah said, 'I've only just told Florian this minute.'

'So, how did he take it?'

'Oh pretty much in his stride, I think. He's a fairly laid-back character.'

'Oh good.' He followed her into the kitchen.

'Right, boys,' Zillah said. 'Here he is.'

Florian, still standing next to Christian, turned round to look full at Hector. His wide blue eyes were fringed by long sandy lashes and his face was expressionless as he opened his mouth and spoke firmly and clearly.

'Clive's my dad not you, so you can sodding well fuck off!'

17

IN the days before the paternity test result had arrived, Hector had watched for the appearance of the day's post with anxiety and anticipation. He really did not know what to hope for. Would Florian be another son to invest his interest in, to take the intellectual place of the inadequate Morgan? Or would he turn out to be a disturbed child whom he would never be able to guide towards the ideal? Hector couldn't possibly know, and the uncertainty troubled him. It was, however, vital that Wendy didn't get wind of all this before he had had time to sort it out himself. He must ensure that she didn't open the letter by mistake.

In the event, it was Saturday morning when it arrived and Wendy was still in bed. Hector, thanking the gods for their dispensation, opened it in the kitchen in trepidation. Morgan was also in the room, but Hector knew he wouldn't try to read it over his shoulder. There were some compensations for illiteracy.

He read the letter with impatience. DNA testing was not an exact science but the probability was . . . Hector sat down suddenly at the table and put his head in his hands. He *was* Florian's father! Emotion overwhelmed him. How did he feel? He thought, I knew as soon as I saw him in those lights from the bus! I just knew. Delight struggled awkwardly with the sudden awareness of future complications. Delight won.

'Da . . . ddy?' Morgan began in an irritating whine. 'I'm bored. Why can't you play with me?'

'Tomorrow,' Hector said expansively, carried away by inner joy, 'I'm busy today, but tomorrow I'll take you to see the lions of Longleat. I promise.' Then he folded the letter and stowed it safely in his wallet. And later on today, he thought, as soon as I can get away, I shall rush over and see Zillah!

The next morning Hector regretted his promise to Morgan but felt obliged to abide by it. He drove the boy and his mother to Longleat with his mind very much elsewhere, and it was only when the rhesus monkeys began leaping about all over the roof of his precious Jaguar, that Hector's thoughts properly returned to the present.

'Keep all the car windows *shut*,' he instructed the excited Morgan. 'Hell's teeth! The little bastards had better not scratch my paintwork!' Then the people in the vehicle behind them began feeding the monkeys illicitly with bits of banana, and they all abandoned the Jaguar forthwith.

'I want them to come back so's I can feed them too,' Morgan complained.

'Sorry,' Hector said, 'it's not allowed. Can't you read the notice?'

'But *they* are. It's not fair!'

'There's nothing fair in this world,' Hector said comfortably.

As days out go, it went fairly painlessly. They saw giraffes, zebras, deer, shaggy cattle, camels, lions, tigers and wolves. Even Morgan was impressed. They visited the amusement park near to the Great House and Hector was just beginning to think that it was about time they started making tracks, when Morgan saw the maze, and rushed headlong into it past a large sign which said: EXIT. The first drops of an April shower began to fall.

'Morgan!' Wendy called. 'That's the wrong way . . .' but it was too late. He'd vanished. 'Oh *no*,' she said, turning to Hector. 'Now what do we do?'

'Well there's no point following him,' Hector said. 'We'd only go round in circles. We'll just have to wait until he comes out again.' He glanced at Wendy. She was looking worn out. 'Tell you what,' he said. 'You go back to the car and keep dry. I'll hang on here. I can always get one of the staff to winkle him out if the worst comes to the worst.'

'Well . . . if you're sure?'

'Sure.' There was nowhere to shelter where he could be certain of seeing Morgan emerging, so Hector pulled his coat collar up, stuffed his hands in his pockets and stood it out. In fact he welcomed time to be alone, so that he could think uninterruptedly about Florian.

The child's outburst of swearing the day before had frankly shocked him. Those coarse words issuing from such cherubic lips had been an abomination. Clearly something had to be done, but what? He had given Zillah a cheque to be going on with, but a more formal arrangement would have to be sorted out soon; perhaps a good prep school? Or should he even go the whole hog and offer to adopt Florian to prevent him from going to the bad? No, Wendy would never wear that, and Morgan and Florian might well hate each other on sight. He supposed he could always *leave* Wendy (well provided for, of course) and marry Jess instead. But would Jess be prepared to be a stepmother to Florian? So many imponderables, Hector thought, if this? if that? I need someone to help me sort it all out, there's only one person I want to talk to.

The rain was falling solidly now. Hector could feel it seeping down his neck. Come on Morgan, for God's sake! he thought, and then, why do I of all people have to have a son who can't *read*? There's no justice. Oh there he is at long last . . . Typical – he doesn't even have the grace to look embarrassed!

'*MORGAN!*' he bellowed irritably. 'Over here!'

'Hang on a mo, Jess,' Hector said, putting out an arm to detain her. Nigel and two of the Subs were just going back to work, and the George and Pilgrim was almost empty.

'Well . . .' Jess hesitated. 'I've got a lot on this afternoon.'

'Ten minutes?' Hector suggested. 'That's all I ask.'

'Well all right.' Jess sat down again. Hector wasn't sure how to begin. Jess looked expectant and then, to fill the gap, asked, 'How's Wendy?'

Hector didn't want to be reminded. It was now six weeks since she had come out of hospital and as far as he could see, nothing had changed.

'She went for her final check-up with our GP yesterday,' he said.

'And is she OK?'

'The Doctor asked her if she had "attempted intercourse".'

Jess grinned. '*Have you got to grips with Everest yet, Mrs Mudgeley?*'

'You're not joking,' Hector said with feeling.

'I probably shouldn't ask, but do you and she . . . anymore?'

'Course not!' This wasn't what Hector wanted to discuss at all. 'Look Jess, I've got something I want to tell you.'

'Oh?'

'It happened years ago – seven and a half to be precise, so it has absolutely no bearing on my special feelings for you now. You have to understand that first.'

'What?' Jess looked suspicious.

Hector decided to plunge straight in. 'That boy, Zillah's son who was caught stealing a car, remember? Well it wasn't Christian. It was the younger boy, and well . . . I've discovered he's actually . . . my . . . son. His name's Florian.'

'He's *WHAT*!'

'I'm his father. We, that is Zillah and I, have had DNA tests done.'

'But why now, after all this time?' She frowned. 'And anyway, way back when he was born, you told me the baby was Clive's?'

'Well we both thought he was. You see, I hadn't seen the boy since then, until I heard he'd been in court this February, and then I felt I just had to go and check up on him. When I saw him, I suppose I knew straightaway . . .'

'You never mentioned it?'

'I know. I thought it might be better to wait until I was certain. I mean . . . I might have been mistaken.'

'So where's all this going to end?' Jess cried, holding up her hands to count off the children. 'So far there's been Wendy's, Caroline's, and now Zillah's! How many more of your offspring are likely to come crawling out of the woodwork? I mean it's nothing at all to do with me, but it's still a bit much . . .'

'You're saying Caroline's daughter IS mine?' Hector was triumphant.

Jess blushed scarlet. 'Oh God,' she said. 'I wasn't supposed to . . . it just slipped out. Look, forget I said that, OK? I'm just so confused . . .'

'Is she?' Hector persisted.

'Yes,' Jess said, 'but please don't tell her I said so.'

'Good Lord,' Hector said quietly. So my instincts were right there too, in spite of Caroline's lies. Bloody hell!'

'But where is all this leading?' Jess asked. 'It's only of academic interest, surely?'

'Not at all,' Hector said. 'Children need fathers.'

'But Flossie (or whatever his stupid name is) has Clive, and I'm sure Hannah has any number of substitute fathers.'

'Wrong, I'm afraid. Clive has disappeared, and as for multiple fathers, they can never be substitutes for one proper one.'

'So what are you going to do about it; split yourself three ways?' Jess demanded angrily.

'Jess, darling, don't get cross. I'm sorry to spring it all on you at once. I agree it's a mess, but it all started a long time ago, long before I had the sense to fall in love with you. I was kind of hoping that you'd help me sort it out.'

'What can I do?' Jess shrugged her shoulders.

'Just talk through the options with me; help me to clarify my own thoughts.'

'Go on then . . .'

'Well to start with,' Hector said, sitting back with a sigh, 'I've obviously got to help support Florian. His mother lives on benefit plus a bit here and there from her pottery and some cash-in-hand nowadays from fortune-telling, I believe.'

'You should be consulting her then! But seriously, would the money be a problem?'

'Not really. It's just that I feel I ought to do more – give the boy a better start in life – rescue him, if you see what I mean.'

'But how?'

'Well . . .' Hector shuffled his bottom, ' . . . what if I adopted him?'

'You're joking!' Jess was horrified. 'You can't possibly expect Wendy to take that on! I know if I was in her position, I'd tell you to go to hell!'

'Ah,' Hector said. 'I was afraid you'd think that. Well . . . that rather answers my next question too . . .'

'Anyway,' Jess said, still reeling from the outrageous suggestion, 'from what you've told me of both Morgan and Florian, they'd hardly be likely to get on well together, would they? It'd be a nightmare! Wendy might be a bit thick, but even she wouldn't be that stupid! And what about Zillah's ideas on the subject?'

'I haven't suggested it to her yet. So . . . you think I should pay up and leave things as they are?'

'Well, what other choice do you have?'

'You're probably right,' Hector sighed, 'but I will expect to see something of Florian. I've got to get some reward for maintaining him.'

'Does he know? Have you seen him?'

'Yes, once.'

'And what was his reaction?' Hector told her. Jess laughed. 'The little brat!'

'Look, Jess,' Hector said, glancing at his watch. 'There isn't time now. We've both got work to do, but I thought I might come round to your place at six-ish. There's a lot we need to discuss.'

'I'm not going to bed with you,' Jess said firmly. 'Just as long as that's quite clear.'

'Well . . . if you say so,' Hector agreed. In his experience women nearly always said that, to begin with.

Jess had second thoughts when Hector turned up at her flat with a bottle of claret and a confident smile. She knew she should have put him off, but she did so enjoy his company. She just hoped he was quite clear where she drew the line. They went through into her sitting room and sat down facing each other.

'Where does Wendy think you are?' she asked, to remind him of where his loyalties lay.

'Working.'

'Won't she think it's odd that you're doing extra work all of a sudden?'

'She's been moaning that I work too hard ever since I first married her,' Hector said. 'So if she knew I wasn't working, she ought to be happy.' He looked pleased with himself. 'What a merry little irony.'

'You're horrible to her,' Jess said.

'I know,' Hector looked penitent. 'I'm a shit. It's just that she gets on my nerves so. You can see why, can't you?'

'Mmmmm,' Jess could.

'And anyway I genuinely *have* been working hard on the farm animal rustling story. Apparently it's piglets as well as sheep now. At first I couldn't understand how anyone could steal anything so squealingly vocal as pigs, but it seems they spray them with some sort of gas to shut them up, poor little blighters.'

'Do the police know who's doing it?'

'They're getting very close. Any day now.'

'Can the animals be identified?'

'Seems not. Some farmers are starting to talk about ear-tagging but that sounds a bit like "Never putting anything off, until tomorrow, after the horse has bolted" to me.'

'Do you do it on purpose?' Jess challenged him.

'What?'

'You know very well! Wait while I dream one up . . . yes . . . "You can't make a silk purse without breaking eggs" or "You can't make an omelette out of a sow's ear" – that sort of gibberish!'

'Oh that,' Hector said. 'I just enjoy improving each shining hour.' He smiled seductively. 'I mean, proverbs get so tediously repetitious, don't they. Now then, are we drinking this wine or not?'

After her second glass of claret, Jess appeared to Hector to be more relaxed. He decided to risk it and, leaning over, slipped her glasses off and put them down on the coffee table; pleased when she made no protest. I have never been beaten in this game yet, he thought. This is a tough one, but I'll get there. Then he chided himself for treating Jess as just another potential conquest. She was much more than that. He really did believe he was in love with her! The knowledge both amazed and tickled him.

He set himself the task of charming her. He told her his best jokes, his most ironic anecdotes, and more of his family secrets. He felt he had never before opened up so much, or made himself so potentially vulnerable. Jess's reserve was visibly thawing. The tip of her nose had gone a little pink. Hector bent and kissed it.

'Is it hot, or is it just me?' she asked, blushing. Then she dragged her sweater off over her head and threw it on to a chair. Her hair stood up untidily and she smoothed it down with both hands.

Hector could see the outline of her nipples through her

T-shirt. Didn't she wear a bra? By the looks of things, she would pass the pencil test easily (unlike Wendy) . . .

Hector's trousers felt uncomfortably overstocked. He shifted himself about a bit to relieve the pressure. 'Jessy . . .' he began. She turned limpid eyes towards him and caught her breath. He reached out and stroked her face with the palm of his hand. She began to lean towards him.

'Let's go to bed,' he whispered. Jess frowned.

Damn! he thought, Have I bloody blown it? She's looking embarrassed. I've got carried away and gone too fast. He drew back, all prepared to apologise, but she gave him a reassuring smile.

'Sorry,' she said. 'Bad timing I'm afraid. I've got to go to the loo.'

As she went out, Hector sat forwards with a sigh of relief. She had disrupted the mood he had so carefully been building, but he could soon re-establish it – now that he knew he was going to win . . .

But when Jess returned from the bathroom, he saw at once he was wrong.

'I'm sorry, Hector,' she said. 'This is a mistake.'

By mid-April Wendy was starting to feel more like herself again. She had known her operation was a major one, but hadn't anticipated how long and by how much it would enfeeble her. Now, two months on, she began to be able to contemplate difficult tasks with more equanimity, and the most daunting of these was discussing Morgan's future education with Hector. She would have to do it sooner or later, and probably the sooner the better since Hector kept nagging the poor child about his reading. Perhaps, Wendy thought, perhaps when he understands, he'll lay off him. I certainly hope so.

She chose her moment carefully one Sunday evening after Morgan had gone to bed, and Hector seemed to be in a good mood. She brought him a whisky and sat down on the sofa beside him.

'Hector?'

'Mmmmm.'

'I think we should talk.'

'What about?'

'Morgan.'

'What about him?' Hector asked, looking round at her at last.

'I think I know what his problem might be — with reading, I mean.'

'Morgan's problem, as you so delicately put it, is easily expressed in our wonderful English idiom as plain old-fashioned sloth, apathy and indolence. In other words, he's a dozy idle toad! I love him dearly but . . .'

'But do you?' Wendy put in.

'Do I what?'

'Love Morgan?'

'Well of course I do. He's my son!'

'Yes, but do you actually *like* him?'

'What sort of bloody stupid question is that?' Hector snapped. 'No, don't bother to answer. My programme's just starting.' And he reached for the remote control and zapped the television on.

Oh no! Wendy thought, that's blown it. I must discuss it with him soon, but I can't do it when he's cross. Trouble is, he's cross most of the time these days. Maybe I'll get a chance during the week.

But Hector was not cheerful until the following Friday, when the *Chronicle* came out with his story on the front page:

POLICE SWOOP ON RUSTLER GANG NABS FOUR.

Wendy saw the headline early that evening on a stack of newspapers in the supermarket, which she had put off visiting all day, safe in the knowledge that it remained open late on Fridays. Right! she thought, I'll definitely talk to him tonight. I do hope he isn't home very late. He always used to get off early on the day the paper came out, in the good old days.

She wheeled her trolley up and down the aisles, picking out food more or less at random. She couldn't remember when she had last felt so miserable. She was positive Hector must be having an affair, because when she'd done one of those questionnaire things in her women's magazine, under the headline: *IS YOUR MAN CHEATING ON YOU?* her total score had come to 43 — at the high end of *YES*. But Wendy could not bear to challenge him about it. She really didn't want to know, because all the time she wasn't sure, it might conceivably not be true . . .

She eased her trolley round into the next aisle, holding on to its side with one hand, and on to the bar with the other. It was one of those defective ones which veer sideways whichever way you try to push them. At the far end, she saw a man doing his shopping with four small children, two on foot, and twins side by side in a double trolley. She paused a moment to watch them. The two elder ones were choosing things from the shelves. The two smallest occasionally turned to drop packets in behind themselves. Their father, who had his back to her was laughing – she could hear him – and rearranging things in the trolley, apparently *enjoying* buying groceries. Wendy smiled. They looked like a perfectly adjusted family, as harmonious as a television advertisement. Then she got nearer and saw that the man was Barry. He looked slimmer, more mature, even quite attractive!

'Barry!' she said, going right up to him. 'How are you?'

He looked pleased to see her too. 'How lovely to bump into you,' he said. 'We're fine, as you can see.'

'It must be over a year since I last saw you,' Wendy said.

'Since we stopped having those office parties at Christmas,' Barry agreed. 'Shame about that. I used to enjoy them. Remember that fancy dress one ages ago?'

'Oh yes,' Wendy said, remembering cast-off feathers on the bedroom floor with a pang of nostalgia. 'That was the best of all.'

'So, how's Morgan?'

'Oh he's all right,' Wendy said, and sensing that this sounded rather unenthusiastic, added quickly, 'It's Easter holidays of course. He's away playing at a schoolfriend's house.'

'That's nice,' Barry said. 'My eldest two can't wait to go to proper school, can you?' The two girls nodded their heads gravely. The twin boys in the trolley gurgled happily. 'Well,' Barry said, 'great seeing you again, but I suppose we'd best be getting on. A man's work is never done. I've seriously considered staying late at work, just to get some rest!'

'Lovely to see you,' Wendy said. ''Bye.'

''Bye,' Barry said. 'No, not that coffee, darling. We always have the decaffeinated sort with the red label, don't we?' Then they moved off together.

Wendy found herself standing there, staring after them and feeling emptier than she could have thought possible. She tried to imagine Hector doing the shopping, with or without Morgan, and failed. Then she pulled herself together, picked an unnecessary box of tea bags from the shelf at her elbow, and dropped it into her own trolley. There was no need for her to rush home. Morgan was staying the night with his friend, whose family had bunk beds and were therefore much envied. Wendy was unaccustomed to such freedom, but lacked the spirit to make the most of it. She paid for the food, dumped it in the boot of her little car and then wandered aimlessly round Marks and Spencer until she caught sight of some woman in one of their many mirrors and thought, she looks a mess, and then, *Oh God it's me!*

On the spur of the moment she decided to treat herself to a new hairdo to cheer herself up. But had she enough money? Hector always kept her so short. She checked the contents of her purse – yes, she could just do it. There was a salon in the department store across the road which was also open late, and it wasn't always necessary to book in advance. Wendy went straight there.

When she emerged sometime later with her hair all curly and bouncy and smelling sweet, it was starting to get dark. It was much later than she had intended. Oh well, she thought, it'll serve Hector right if he's home before me for a change, with no supper all ready and waiting.

She saw the police car as soon as she turned in at the bottom of her drive. It was waiting at the top, outside her front door. As she parked beside it and wound down her window, a policewoman got out and approached her.

'Mrs Mudgeley?'

'Yes?'

'I'm looking for Mr Hector Mudgeley, but no one seems to be in.'

'Oh he's probably still at work. Can I help?'

'Excuse me just a minute.' The policewoman turned away and spoke on her radio. Wendy heard her say, 'No, he's not back yet.'

'What's happened?' she asked, beginning to get alarmed.

'It's nothing to worry about,' the policewoman said, 'but there's been a bit of a fire at the *Westcountry Chronicle* building and we need to locate everybody.'

'A fire? But why? How?'

'We think it may have been caused by a small bomb.'

'A bomb! But . . . he must still be there . . . at work . . . Oh my God – *HECTOR!*'

18

JESS was becoming accustomed to Hector waylaying her after work, and wanting to have a drink with her in the pub or go for a private walk by the sea. Sometimes she worked late, and on those occasions on her return home, she would find little notes in her letterbox signed: H.M. XXXXXXX. She became convinced that the man genuinely believed himself to be in love with her.

For her own part, she was still confused, and the only purely positive feelings she had were of relief that she hadn't allowed herself to be seduced that night with claret. Jess thanked the gods for deliverance. She made a firm decision not to have an affair she might be ashamed of. She knew her own limitations well enough – she didn't like subterfuge, and she hated deceit – she would rather remain celibate.

She said as much to Hector, but he still kept coming to see her, even though he wasn't getting anywhere. She could see that she had hurt his pride and was sorry, but she remained adamant.

'I'll divorce Wendy,' he now offered as they walked along a deserted beach, well out of sight of Woodspring. 'Then we can get properly married.'

'On what grounds?' Jess objected. 'What's poor Wendy done to deserve that? And what about Morgan? You surely wouldn't leave him behind too?'

'I *need* you, Jessy,' Hector urged. 'Surely you see that?' Her mobile phone rang suddenly. 'Don't answer that!'

'I must,' Jess said. 'It might be important.' She fished it out of her pocket and pulled up the aerial. 'Jess Hazelrigg?'

It was a regular contact of hers in the fire service. 'Thought you'd like to know,' he said, 'your newspaper's been fire-bombed. If you get down here PDQ, you'll see some fairly dramatic flames.'

'Christ!' Jess gasped. 'Thanks. I'll be right there.' She stuffed the phone back and dragged at Hector's arm. 'We've got to go, Hector. The *Chronicle* building's on fire!'

'Shit!' Hector began to run back towards the road where they had left their vehicles. 'I never thought they'd actually do it.'

'Who?' Jess sprinted beside him.

'Mates of the rustlers. I'd heard they'd made threats, but . . .'

Jess's phone rang again. It was Nigel. 'Yes, isn't it ghastly, I've just heard,' she panted, still running. 'I'm on my way.'

The fire was visible in the evening sky long before they got there. Jess, in her official Jeep and a regular attender at fires and other emergencies, was able to get closer than Hector in his car, being waved through the roadblock and setting-to at once to take photographs. The fire had certainly taken hold. Flames sprouted out of the top windows and roared fiercely. There were loud cracking noises as internal timbers gave way, and the air was thick with the stench of burning paper and plastics. Smuts and ash fell all around. Three fire engines were already fighting the blaze, and another was just arriving, siren blaring. Jess saw familiar faces going about their jobs, as she was herself, but this time it was so different. This time it was her own building that was disintegrating before her eyes . . . She forced herself to concentrate on doing her job and tried to control the shaking of her hands. Then she was briefly interrupted by the police, who ticked her name off on a list of *Chronicle* employees.

'Just checking there's no one missing, who might still be in the building,' he said, running a pencil down his pad. 'That leaves . . . Hector Mudgeley. Everyone else is accounted for.'

'He's OK,' Jess said at once. 'I've just seen him.'

'When was that?'

'Oh, only a few minutes ago. He was . . .' Jess remembered she wasn't supposed to have been with Hector, and had to think quickly. ' . . . in his car driving here. I passed him.'

'Sure it was him?'

'Positive. I'd know that car anywhere.'

There was a crash and a shower of sparks as parts of the

roof fell in. More thick smoke rose into the evening sky. All around was illuminated in the glare of the flames. The crowd went 'Aaaaah!' and were moved further back by a cordon of police. Jess found that she had tears in her eyes at the destruction of it all; the old familiar offices, her precious darkroom, all that valuable equipment . . .

'*JESS!*' someone screamed.

Wendy had burst through the line of policemen and was running towards her, distraught. 'Where's Hector?' she babbled. 'He must have be in there. Have you seen him? He'll be burnt to death! *Oh I can't bear it.* Has the body got a scar on its forehead? They must TELL me, because if it hasn't it isn't Hector. It CAN'T be Hector. *HECTOR . . .!*' and she began to scream again. Two large policemen ran forward and took hold of her by both arms.

'Hector's SAFE,' Jess shouted at her. 'I've just seen him.' But Wendy seemed not to take it in. She fought wildly in her captors' firm grasp, and seemed hell-bent on rushing into the burning building.

'Tell her he's OK,' Jess cried to the policemen. 'What *body* is she on about?'

'There aren't any bodies,' Hector's voice said from behind them. 'The firemen say it's all clear, thank goodness. God, what a mess!'

Wendy wrenched herself free and rushed into his arms. 'HECTOR!' Then she burst into uncontrollable sobs. Hector seemed embarrassed. He patted her on the back a few times.

'All right Wendy. I'm here, OK? Calm down. Everything's under control.' Then he disengaged himself and held her at arm's length and in a cheerful voice, apparently attempting to neutralize her hysteria, said, 'Good Lord! Whatever have you done to your hair?'

It took Wendy some time to get over her anxiety of the night of the fire. She had several nightmares, where she woke crying out for Hector. Hector himself was not helpful or even particularly understanding. He woke the second time, and turned on the light irritably.

'For God's sake, woman! It's only a bad dream. I'm here. There's nothing to get so worked up about. I'm also in the middle of a very difficult time at work. We're all over the place; temporary offices, borrowed computers, printing on somebody else's press in Bristol and Lord knows what else. And then you see fit to murder my sleep as well! It's just not on, you know.' Wendy felt the injustice of this deeply, but tried her best to be understanding. Poor Hector was bound to feel harassed and was also sure to take it out on her.

It also seemed that there was never going to be a good time to discuss Morgan. We must *do* something about him soon, Wendy thought worriedly. The sooner he gets special education, the better. He doesn't complain to me about it, but I can tell he's unhappy at school. I do wish Hector would sometimes stop work for a couple of hours and come to parents' meetings. The teachers all agree with me that there's a problem, and I'm sure he'd take it better coming from them than from me. Maybe I'll get a chance to talk to him tonight.

That evening, however, Hector came home in an odd sort of mood. He wasn't cross and he didn't seem depressed, but he wasn't exactly happy either. If anything he appeared rather on the defensive. Wendy couldn't imagine why.

'Wendy?' he began, 'd'you remember we always said we didn't want Morgan to be too much of an only child and not get properly socialised?'

'Yes,' Wendy said, 'but he's fine. He's got a good friend at school. And while we're on the subject . . .'

'Hang on a minute,' Hector interrupted. 'I've got something I want to discuss with you.'

'What?'

'There's a boy I know, who is going to need a friendly family to stay with for a week or so soon. His mother is having another baby and hasn't any adult to support her, so it would be a great help to her if the seven-year-old could be taken off her hands for a short time.'

'But who are they? How do you know them?'

'I'm coming to that in a minute,' Hector said patiently. 'I just want you to consider how you'd feel about having someone of Morgan's age to stay.'

'Well, it all depends on whether Morgan likes him or not, doesn't it?'

'Oh they'd get on.' Hector seemed assured. 'It would only be for a little while; be good for them both.'

'W . . . ell . . .'

'It would be an act of charity,' Hector encouraged her. 'A good thing to do.'

'But who are they?'

'The boy's name is Florian Brakespear, and he . . .'

'Brakespear? But isn't that the name of that hippy woman who got flooded out that Christmas?'

'Yes it is,' Hector said blandly. 'I wasn't sure you'd remember her.'

'Oh I remember her all right! Can't her lorry driver look after his kid?'

'Oh he's vanished long since,' Hector said. 'Zillah's all on her own now.'

Of course! Wendy thought. *She's the other woman.* It's so obvious!

She nearly came straight out with her thoughts, but native caution tinged with curiosity held her back. 'Barry told me ages ago that you fancied her,' she said, watching to see if his expression changed.

'Poor old Barry,' Hector laughed. 'You can't believe everything he says, now can you?'

'Well, do you?'

'Heavens, no! I just thought you might enjoy having the lad to stay. I know how much you like children. It was always a matter of regret to me that we only had one. I thought this might make it up to you a little.'

Wendy smelt a rat at once, but was intrigued nevertheless. What was Hector up to? She decided she would play along with him a little and perhaps then she might find out. She discovered that she *did* want to know after all; that uncertainty was worse than anything.

'Well, I suppose we could always try it,' she said hesitantly. 'No promises, mind.'

Hector came forward and gave her a hug. 'Good old Wend,' he said. 'I knew I could rely on you.'

'And while we're talking, Hector . . .' Wendy began.

'Sorry love,' Hector said quickly. 'Must just catch the news, OK?' And he sat down with his back to her.

Wendy had a sudden dreadful thought. What if Hector was the father of this new baby of Zillah's?

Jess didn't have nightmares, but she had certainly been unsettled by the fire and its aftermath. It wasn't that she was obliged to share a borrowed darkroom (though that was bad enough), or that she found herself spending more time than usual in travelling between temporary offices to collaborate with her colleagues. These things were irritants but they did not disturb her deep down. It was Wendy's behaviour that had really got to her; the realization that Hector (and the little scar on his forehead) really did belong to *her*, that she knew him far more intimately than she, Jess, did; that she certainly loved him more. She had thought of Wendy as a silly woman who was incapable of intense emotion – the Barbie Doll type whose personality was as superficial as her fluffy sweaters – but she had been shocked by the obvious depth of Wendy's feelings and (if she were really honest with herself), shocked also by Hector's perfunctory words of comfort to her. It wasn't kind. Hector *wasn't* kind!

Jess caught a bad cold which developed into bronchitis, and she had to stay in bed for several days, one of which was her birthday. Her parents rang in the evening to wish her Many Happy Returns, and she pretended she was feeling better than she actually did, in order not to worry her mother.

Her father said, 'Thirty-two eh? Isn't it about time you settled down and gave your mother some grandchildren?'

'Oh come on, Dad,' Jess said. 'You're not supposed to say things like that these days. It's not politically correct.'

'What nonsense. I speak as I find!'

'There's plenty of time,' Jess said.

'Well, don't leave it too long, will you.'

'I won't.'

'Goodbye then, love, and have a happy evening.'

''Bye Dad.'

Jess put the receiver down and lay back, thinking, Forget grandchildren, what about MY life? What am I doing here? There's no future for me with Hector. I definitely don't want him to leave Wendy for me, and I'd hate to be accused of suborning his affections and causing her unhappiness. And there's no one else. Maybe it really is time for me to be moving on.

Perhaps I should go and live in Caroline's basement, she thought, even if our friendship isn't as close as it once was. I must be pragmatic after all, and how else would I be able to afford to live in central London? And I am still very fond of her . . . And it would be an enormous challenge to go freelance . . .

Zillah had her third baby boy at home at the end of April, with expert ease and only minimal help from the midwife and health visitor. Hector, who had called in daily to check on her progress, missed the birth by hours (greatly to his relief) and did not have to get involved. He had expected another one like Florian, and was quite taken aback at the sight of such a handsome baby.

'Isn't he lovely?' Zillah asked proudly. 'I'm calling him Alaric.'

'Oh come now!' protested Hector.

'Why ever not?'

'Well put it this way, it's not a name I'd choose.'

'It's a good thing you're not his father then, isn't it.'

'So who is?' Hector said, glad of the opportunity to ask.

'No one you know. His name's Johnnie.'

'And you don't see him any more?'

'Nope,' Zillah said cheerfully.

'But you're coping all right?'

'Fine.'

'Well I'll borrow Florian this evening then, shall I?'

'If you like.'

'Right. I'll go home and warn Wendy and then I'll be back later.'

Wendy was grumpy on hearing the news. 'It's a bit short notice,' she complained.

'Well babies don't work to timetables,' Hector said.

'And I haven't discussed it with Morgan yet.'

'Then it'll be a nice surprise!'

Both Zillah's boys were home from school by the time Hector got back to her cottage. Christian met him at the door.

'This is a bad idea,' he said.

'Oh I don't think so,' Hector said. 'It'll be a nice break for Florian and give your mother a rest too.'

'But I can look after both of them.'

'I'm sure you can,' Hector said, stepping inside, 'but you don't have to.'

'But . . .' Christian followed Hector into the kitchen. Florian was there eating chocolate.

'Right then, young Florian,' Hector said breezily. 'All set for a few days' holiday? Have you got a bag packed?'

'Piss off!' Florian said sullenly.

'That's no way to react to a good offer,' Hector said mildly. 'Don't reject it out of hand until you know what it entails.'

'It's no good,' Christian said. 'Once he's made his mind up, that's it.' Florian looked gratified at the compliment.

'Well,' Hector said diplomatically. 'I'll just have a word with your mother, shall I?' He knocked on Zillah's bedroom door and went in. 'He doesn't seem keen,' he said to her. 'Can you persuade him?'

'He's an awkward little cuss,' Zillah said. 'I wonder where he gets it from. Tell him to come in here a minute. I'll soon sort him out.'

Hector stayed in the kitchen with Christian whilst Florian was being convinced. Christian was not very talkative, but what he did say was impressive. He was enjoying school, intended to go on to university and then into scientific research of some sort. He wasn't interested in money or cars or status. He wanted to do something worthwhile for mankind.

'I was just the same at your age,' Hector said ingratiatingly, pleased to be getting on so well with him.

'So, what went wrong?'

Hector was saved from having to find an answer by the entrance of Zillah and Florian. She had put on a grubby housecoat and was carrying the new baby in her arms. 'All settled,' she said briskly. 'He knows why I want him to visit you, and he also knows he can come home tomorrow if it doesn't work out.'

'But that's not nearly long enough,' Hector protested. 'Tell you what, Florian. If you stick it out for three days, I'll give you twenty pounds. What d'you say?'

'*Shall we contaminate our fingers with base bribes?*' Christian quoted. '*Julius Caesar*. Did it last year in English.'

'Thank you, Christian,' Zillah said. 'That's quite enough of that.'

'Well?' Hector asked.

'Make it thirty,' Florian said.

'Twenty-five, and that's my final offer.'

'Oh all right then, but only two days.'

Hector laughed. 'You're a tough customer,' he acknowledged. Florian looked pleased.

'Off you go then,' Zillah urged. 'Here's your bag. Have fun, and no swearing, promise?'

'Yeah, yeah,' Florian said.

He picked up his bag, slung it over one shoulder and ambled slowly out of the front door and down the path to Hector's car. Hector followed him, giving a little wave to Zillah and Christian as he went.

'And the best of luck!' Zillah called mockingly.

Hector went round to unlock the passenger door of the Jaguar.

'Hasn't it got central locking?' Florian asked in disgust.

'This is a Classic car' Hector explained. There's nothing new and gimmicky about this old beauty, except the carphone I use for work. He pointed out the walnut fascia and the leather upholstery with pride.

'No electric windows? No tape player?'

'No, thank goodness.'

'There aren't even proper seat belts!'

'Look, Florian,' Hector said sternly, temporarily lapsing from his assumed role of 'understanding parent'. 'If you're coming with me, then come with a good grace, OK? I can't abide whingers.'

Christian watched from the window as Hector and Florian left, and then turned frowning to his mother. 'I don't understand,' he said. 'One minute you're telling Florian he doesn't have to go and live with Hector and the next, you're virtually throwing him out. What's going on?'

Zillah sat down and began to breast-feed the baby. 'It's quite simple,' she said. 'I need money from Hector to maintain his son, and he's more likely to be generous if he thinks he's going to get some access to Florian.'

'But isn't this visit just a one-off?'

'Probably.'

'So what's to prevent Hector stopping the cash flow the moment he stops seeing Florian?'

'Well, once he's started paying a regular amount, he's set a precedent and it'll be that much harder to stop. But if he does, I'll set the Child Support Agency on to him.'

'Do that and you'll get less benefit. I heard the CSA is just an excuse for the government to get their hands on the father's dosh.'

'You're a bit young to be so cynical, aren't you?' Zillah smiled up at him.

'So anyway,' Christian said, ignoring this, 'how did you twist Florian's arm and make him go?'

'I told him Hector's threatened that if he isn't granted any access, he'll start a custody battle and the Judge might make him go and live with Hector full time.'

'But is that true?' Christian was horrified.

'It's a distinct possibility.' Zillah was not about to reveal the implausibility of this to Christian. She desperately needed a break from Florian for a few days, and this was a heaven-sent opportunity.

'But you wouldn't really let him go.'

'Of course not, silly! You and Florian, and now Alaric here, are all my boys. I wouldn't dream of letting anyone else take you over. It just seems time to get Hector to perform some fatherly duties whilst I get a much needed break. He owes it to me.'

'But if Florian only stays with Hector for a couple of days, it won't help much, will it?'

'Maybe not, but at least they'll get to know each other, and once Florian is a real person to Hector, it should be easier to persuade him to shell out.'

'Fleece him, you mean?'

'No. Get him to meet his obligations.'

'But what if Florian plays him up?'

'I've told him why he mustn't. I'm sure he understands.'

'Seems to me the poor little sod's in an impossible position:

(a) Be himself, and then Hector will hate him and won't give us any money, or (b) Be sweet and lovely, and Hector won't give us any money either. He'll love him so much that he'll take us to court and kidnap Florian for ever! How's that for choice? If I was him, I'd definitely go for (a) the aversion therapy, and to hell with the money!'

'I think actually there are more than two possibilities,' Zillah said.

'Name another!' Christian challenged.

'Not for the moment. Just wait and see,' and Zillah smiled again, but enigmatically.

19

WHEN Wendy first saw Florian, he definitely reminded her of someone but she couldn't think who. She didn't know anyone with hair that colour. She wondered if he would have the famous redhead temper. So far at least he was very quiet, barely speaking at all. Perhaps he was shy? Morgan had been excited at the thought of having someone to play with, and had confided to her that he would welcome anyone from a different school, because they wouldn't call him Organ Pudgeley. Poor Morgan, Wendy thought. It's only puppy fat, but children can be so cruel.

Florian's clothes, when he unpacked his duffle bag, looked cheap and worn and there were very few of them. Wendy felt sorry for him. She would have offered him some of Morgan's, the ones he was tired of, but the boy was quite a different shape, taller and much thinner. He needed feeding up, but wasn't in the least puny. At the first supper in Hector and Wendy's house, after he had eaten three helpings of stew and two bowls of ice cream, Morgan had challenged him to an arm wrestling contest at the table and Florian had won easily. Then Hector had wrestled Morgan and let him win a little too obviously, but when he came to compete against Florian, he really had to try to avoid being defeated at first push. Morgan looked on, eyes shining with admiration. Oh good, Wendy thought in relief, they're going to get on. Maybe it won't be so difficult after all.

The following morning Hector ran Florian to his school whilst Wendy took Morgan as usual to his. Morgan was clearly envious of Florian for not having to wear school uniform, which was silly of him, Wendy thought, considering how sweet he looked in his little blazer.

On the second evening Hector was home nice and early,

and they all played snakes and ladders. Florian won, and Wendy privately thought he had cheated, but since Morgan seemed happy she decided to say nothing. She wondered how long he would be staying. Hector had said 'a few days' which meant nothing. Wendy had hoped to get Florian to talk about his family, but he seemed resistant to conversation with adults. He didn't mention Clive at all (which was understandable, since he'd deserted them all), and he was only monosyllabic about his mother, but after he and Morgan had gone to bed in their shared room, Wendy could hear them both chattering away and Morgan giggling. When she went in, to tell them to stop talking and go to sleep, Morgan was pink with excitement and looked somehow furtive. Wendy frowned, but then assuming they were telling each other dirty jokes, smiled to herself and forgot it.

In a funny way she felt rather good about taking Florian in temporarily, as though she were doing a good deed by helping the underprivileged. The boy himself seemed impressed by the number and quality of Morgan's toys. He clearly had nothing like this at home. He apparently hadn't played many board games either, but was very quick on the uptake.

On the third evening Hector got fed up with the two boys larking about in the garage and on the front drive, and produced the *Scrabble* set. Wendy's heart sank. She tried to dissuade him by saying, 'Oh Morgan hates *Scrabble*, don't you love,' but Hector wasn't having any of it.

'He and Florian can both play against me,' he said, 'do a joint effort, pool their letters. I'll still win.'

'Oh no you won't!' Florian countered, rising to the challenge. Then he took over. He was a bit bossy, Wendy thought, but a natural leader. She went to do some cooking and left them to it, and when she came back half an hour later she found Morgan and Florian helpless with laughter and Hector trying unsuccessfully to stifle his.

'What's so funny?' Wendy asked. Morgan pointed. On the well-criss-crossed board in front of them, lay the word BUMHOLE. 'You can't have that!' Wendy cried. 'It isn't in the dictionary so it's not allowed, and anyway it's very *rude!*'

'But it's a triple word score,' Florian protested between giggles.

'That makes no difference. Hector? I'm ashamed of you. You're supposed to be in charge. You're supposed to be preventing . . .' The presence of the boys inhibited Wendy from saying any more, but she felt instinctively that Florian was exerting a malign influence on Morgan, and should be stopped at once.

'Oh I don't know,' Hector said, still smiling. 'I reckon that if intelligence is catching, then we're on to a winner here.' Florian glanced at Wendy unblinkingly. His clear blue eyes looked up at her with an expression that was candid, childlike, *innocent*. Wendy suddenly thought she heard something boiling over in the kitchen, and rushed to see to it.

Later, after both boys had gone to bed, Wendy finally seized the opportunity to speak to Hector. He was sitting back in the sofa, chuckling at Florian's exploits. 'He's a game little chap,' Hector said. 'Of course his upbringing has been hopeless and he's been exposed to foul talk and all sorts of undesirable habits, but he's got *spirit*, if you know what I mean. I have a feeling that his IQ is pretty high. There's a lot of potential there, I'm sure of it.'

'You seem more interested in him than you are in Morgan!' Wendy challenged.

'Rubbish.' Hector brushed the suggestion aside.

'And you still haven't told me where you were on the night of the fire.'

'Sorry?' Hector said. 'Have I missed some vital connection there, or are you just emitting words at random?'

'You were with Zillah Brakespear, weren't you?' Wendy accused him. 'And this baby of hers is yours, isn't it. *That's* the connection!'

Hector laughed. He threw his head back and roared with laughter. 'WRONG!' he chortled, 'on both counts.'

'Stop laughing,' Wendy snapped angrily, 'and swear to me that you aren't having an affair with Zillah.'

'God forbid!' Hector said. 'OK, I swear. I swear her baby isn't mine either. Cross my heart!'

'You really promise?' Wendy pleaded.

'I really promise. What extraordinary ideas you do come up with sometimes. Now come over here you silly sausage and give us a cuddle, eh?'

Wendy allowed herself to be hugged, and they sat back on the sofa together. She studied Hector's face closely. He did seem to her to be completely sincere. She felt as though a great burden of anxiety had been lifted from her, and only now did she realise how crushing the weight had been. Now would be a good time to tell him about Morgan, and really discuss the problem in depth. She turned to him. 'Hector?'

'Wendy?'

'Morgan isn't lazy you know. I'm sure he's got a condition that stops him from being able to read and write and spell easily.'

'What condition? What *are* you on about?'

'Dyslexia.' Wendy crossed her fingers as she said the word.

'There's no such thing,' Hector scoffed at once. 'It's just a trendy middle-class excuse for the thick! You know how it goes: working-class Kevin is just plain stupid, but upwardly-mobile middle-class Tristan is *dyslexic*. Come on Wendy, face facts. Morgan just isn't very clever.'

'You're so wrong!' Wendy said desperately. 'Dyslexia is real. I should know. My brother had it, but no one knew what it was in those days, and then he married into a family that had it too, and now both his sons go to special dyslexic schools in Australia and they've really come on . . .'

'You never told me!' Hector interrupted, suddenly furious, leaping to his feet and pointing an accusing finger at her. 'Before I married you, I asked you if you had any *disabilities* in your family, and you said NO!'

'You said madness, not disability,' Wendy insisted, 'and anyway it's not a disability, it's just a different ability.'

'Splitting hairs!' Hector sneered.

'You don't know,' Wendy shouted. 'You're very ready to criticise, but you don't understand the first thing about it! Morgan's teachers agree with me, and if you ever took the time to come to parents' meetings you'd know that, and you'd understand he needs special tuition!'

'Stop shouting,' Hector said. 'You'll wake the boys.'

'I'll shout all I want in my own house!'

'So what do you expect me to do about it then?' Hector asked wearily.

'I want to have Morgan properly assessed by an educational psychologist.'

'For heaven's sake, Wendy. The child's only *seven*!'

'Yes, but the sooner we know, the sooner he can be helped. He's not happy Hector, and your attitude to him doesn't help.'

'Oh I see. It's all my fault now, is it?'

The door of the sitting room opened and Florian came in, yawning and looking fed up.

'Florian?' Wendy said, disconcerted. 'Can't you sleep?'

'No,' Florian said. 'And I'm off home tomorrow, right? I've bin here three days, an' I want me thirty quid.'

'You want *what*?' Wendy asked.

'All right, Wendy,' Hector said. 'This is between Florian and me. Come on young man. Let's get you back to bed, shall we?' And he took him by the arm and ushered him out of the room.

Wendy slumped back against the sofa and thought bitterly, Great! I knew he wouldn't believe me about Morgan's dyslexia. I must try to convince him.

But when Hector came downstairs again, he said he had work to do, retired to his study and shut the door firmly, so no further discussion was possible.

Next morning Wendy woke suddenly as though a loud crash had roused her. Noises from the road outside were rarely heard in their bedroom at the back of the house, so she wondered if she had imagined it. Hector was solidly asleep beside her and snoring irritatingly. She looked at her watch. It was six thirty. She decided she might as well get up, and in passing quietly opened Morgan's door to check on the boys. Florian was there, in the spare bed, fast asleep, but Morgan's bed was empty and his clothes were missing from his chair. Wendy ran over and shook Florian awake.

'Where's Morgan?'

'Uh? . . . Dunno . . .'

'But did he say where he was going?'

'No.'

'And you can't guess?'

'Nah.'

Wendy tore round the house and the back garden, calling for Morgan. Then she went out of the front door. Hector's precious Jaguar (which no one, not even Wendy herself was allowed to borrow) wasn't in its usual place at the top of their steep drive. Then she saw it, and realized at once what must have happened. The car was slewed sideways at the bottom, with its front end buried in one of the stone gateposts. Wendy rushed down to it and saw with horror that its beautiful, long, shiny bonnet and one wing were badly dented, the front bumper was hanging off and there was a trail of bright green anti-freeze from its fractured radiator. The keys were in the open offside door, but of the driver there was no sign. Wendy ran out into the road and looked wildly up and down. It was empty but for the milkman who was passing in his float. Wendy waved her arms and dashed out in front of him.

'Stop! have you seen a little boy, blond hair, plumpish, wearing a red sweatshirt?'

'Five minutes back? Yes, I reckon I did.'

'Was he hurt?' Wendy gasped. 'Did you see?'

'Shouldn't think so, judging by the speed he was running!'

Zillah met Florian off the school bus that day. 'So, how was it?'

'Fucking awful!' Florian said. 'Hector's bloody old an' Morgan's just a fucking kid!'

'Let's have a little less of the effing and blinding, shall we?'

'Can't help it.' Florian shrugged. 'But I didn't never swear *once* over there.'

'I'm proud of you,' Zillah smiled. 'What's Wendy like?'

'All right. Food were brilliant!'

'And d'you reckon Hector likes you?'

'Oh yeah. He's totally pissed-off wiv Morgan mind,' Florian grinned. 'Gave him a real belting s'morning! Made me late for school an' all.'

'Why?'

''Cos he crashed that stupid old car! Course he weren't really driving it; he don't know how,' Florian made a pitying face. 'Told me he pushed the handbrake down, and nuffing happened – car just creaked a bit – an' then he gets all clever like, trying out the pedals . . .'

'And it was in gear?'

'Musta bin. So he stands on it an' ZOOM! down it goes, YEE . . . EEE . . . POW! *SMASH*! Cor, wish I'd'a bin there!'

'And weren't you?'

'No way,' Florian said virtuously. 'Sleeping in bed, me.'

'But the night before you'd been telling Morgan a few tall stories about driving, perhaps?'

'I might of,' Florian said matter of factly. Zillah raised an eyebrow. 'Not going back there, mind,' he warned. 'Tha's it!'

'You won't have to,' Zillah said. 'But Hector's coming round to talk money tomorrow, so remember to go on being polite, eh?'

'Dunno about that,' Florian said puffing out his cheeks like a middle-aged builder asked to give an estimate. 'I might've fucked off somewhere.'

Both Christian and Florian were absent when Hector arrived the next evening. He was driving a temporary hired car, but Zillah refrained from commenting on it. She had got her argument all worked out and she didn't want any distractions. Hector's first words though, were not what she was expecting.

'I've decided it would be best if I adopted Florian,' he said abruptly. 'He and I seem to get on well, and he's clearly much too much of a handful for you. What do you say?'

'NO,' Zillah said, 'absolutely not.'

'And that's your last word?'

'Certainly is.'

'See you in court then.' He turned to go.

'Wait,' Zillah called. 'Come on, don't be silly. We can talk about this. For a start, what does your wife think?'

'Oh I haven't discussed it with her yet. She's convinced the boy is a bad influence on her precious Morgan, but that's just prejudice. Morgan's a fool with or without Florian in my opinion.'

'But you can't possibly adopt Florian without her consent.'

'Well, no, but I could if I was on my own.'

Zillah laughed. 'You'd be hopeless on your own. You literally can't even boil an egg! No, I've got a better idea. Why don't you pay me a regular monthly whack, and come round once in a while and get your money's worth?'

To her surprise, Hector flinched. 'No,' he said at once. 'Thanks for the offer and all that, but . . . no.'

Zillah studied him calculatingly and reckoned that his demand for adoption was just a try-on, and would never be taken seriously by the authorities anyway. She decided to call his bluff. 'Face it Hector, your idea of adopting Florian was a non-starter from the beginning. Let's be practical and talk about maintenance. How much will you give us a month?'

'I'm not doing a standing order,' Hector warned, 'and if (and only IF) I agree, then I want regular access to Florian. But if you screw up the access, or Florian messes me about, then you'll get nothing from me. Is that understood? I'm staying in charge.'

'All right then,' Zillah agreed (thinking, we'll see about that!). 'I'll jot down the address of my bank so you can send your cheques straight there.'

'I could always bring them round personally?' Hector offered.

'No, I'd rather you didn't,' Zillah said. 'They'd only get lost. They'll be much safer in the bank.' She saw that Hector could appreciate the sense of this. He was looking round her kitchen superciliously as though he had never seen a cobweb before.

They then haggled at length about a suitable figure, with Zillah demanding far more than was reasonable to begin with, in order that Hector should believe he had won by beating her down. It worked perfectly, and she ended up with more than she had hoped for.

'But I must see Florian regularly,' Hector insisted. 'Is that understood?'

'Fine.'

'So, where is he now?'

'Out playing somewhere, I expect.'

'But how am I going to arrange access days? You're still not on the phone, I suppose?'

'Can't afford it. You can just turn up and take pot luck, can't you?'

'That's not very satisfactory,' Hector frowned.

'Well, let's try it for a while and see how it works out.' Zillah smiled her best smile and patted Hector on the arm. 'It'll be fine, you'll see.'

Hector looked only partly convinced. 'I'll be back to see him in a week or so then,' he said.

'Right.'

She watched him walk away down the path to the unfamiliar car, and let out a breath of relief. It *was* going to work out after all. She had banked on Hector's liking for Florian growing large enough to entrap his feelings, but on Florian's difficult nature being awkward enough to dissuade Hector from being determined to have him actually to live with them. For a moment there, she thought she'd miscalculated, and that the first had outweighed the second!

She hadn't been sure either, whether her concern to make sure Florian was properly financed might have been greater than Hector's desire for a new son. In any dispute the person who cares most has the most to lose, and is therefore at a disadvantage. In this case, it seemed that Hector cared more about Florian than she did about the money. Fancy that! Zillah thought.

Jess spent most of May and June assembling a collection of her private photographs for inclusion in an exhibition which Vivian was mounting at his gallery in Bath. She thanked the Fates daily that she'd had the wit to store all her personal negatives at home, rather than at work where they would have been destroyed in the fire. When the exhibition was finally hung in July, she went to help Vivian and his staff put it together, and got home that evening still pink with pleasure at the praise her work had received. It got better. Vivian rang regularly to tell her how it was going, and it was going very well indeed. Jess felt her confidence growing.

This was in marked contrast to her personal life. She had had very little time lately to go for country walks, and to her sorrow had missed the return of her pair of redshanks to the rushy field on the Levels where they habitually bred. Their piping courtship flights lasted only a few days, and were rewarding to witness. Jess felt cheated. She could have used some walks for calm thinking time, to breathe in the good air, and try to decide what to *do* about Hector. He still seemed determined not to give up, as though by sheer perseverance he could force her to change her mind. She had tried avoiding him, but then he waited until late evening and came to her flat instead. Jess was concerned that Wendy would soon discover where he was, and assume the worst.

So, quite often she consented to meet him in the George and Pilgrim, where he drank whisky and was by turns charming and peevish. Jess stuck to orange juice and tried to remain calm. Inevitably their conversations eventually turned either to Hector's problems with Wendy, or to the infuriating lack of spare parts for the Jaguar, or to Florian . . .

'He refuses to see me,' Hector complained. 'I take the trouble to go all the way over to their cottage at Slum-over-Peat, and then I find that he's not there. He's out on his bike, or he's visiting friends, or he's . . . hiding under the bed for all I know, but he won't come with me. I just don't know what to do about him.'

'Back off a bit?' Jess suggested. 'If you put pressure on him, you'll only drive him further away.'

Hector sighed. 'When I think how much I'm paying for the little bastard . . .' he said. 'Somehow I don't like to withold it, although that's what I threatened them with. They do have a moral right to it after all, but . . . it makes me so mad!'

'This isn't just about money though.'

'No, no, not entirely, of course not, but it does come into the equation, Jess. It's bound to.'

'Are you sure it isn't actually about ownership?'

'I'm not with you.'

'Well, put it this way – isn't affection more important?'

'I don't see that it's a choice? Florian's my son.'

'QED' Jess murmured.

'What?'

'Nothing. I'm sorry, Hector, I really ought to be going.'

'Me too I suppose,' Hector said gloomily, 'back to the in-house harridan.'

'Is Wendy being difficult?' Jess asked, getting to her feet.

'Does the sun rise in the east? Of course she is. D'you know, she's still going on about the thirty pounds I slipped Florian months ago. She says I never give her that much! She's a real pain to live with these days.' He sighed. 'Never mind,' he said in her ear as they got to the door. 'At least I've got my Jessy-bootle, even if she won't sleep with me.' He smiled winningly. 'I'd be such a mess without you, you know. You're my oasis in a sea of troubles.'

'Mmm,' Jess said, biting back guilt and irritation, 'that's not much of a compliment actually. Think about it. You make me sound about as useful as a sandcastle in the desert!'

In bed that night she thought, I really don't have any choice now. I've got to move to London to Caroline's basement, and escape all this hassle from Hector. I won't sell my flat, though; I don't want to close down all my options. I'll hang on to it and maybe rent it out to summer visitors, or even use it myself from time to time. I can't go on like this. It really is now or never.

When she finally nerved herself to tell Hector of her decision, he was affectingly distraught. 'But what will I do without you? You can't leave me, Jess,' he implored. 'I *need* you.' Then, when she remained determined, he abruptly changed tactics. 'I've decided to buy that brand-new car I was telling you about,' he said. 'I don't feel the same about the Jag any more, and all those modern gadgets do seem rather useful. Apart from things like electric windows and central locking, they tell me my new one will be alarmed and immobilised. Come to think of it, that's exactly how I feel at this moment! Tell me you're not *serious* about leaving, Jess.'

'I'm so sorry, Hector, but I am. I'll miss you too.'

'But how can I prove to you how much I care? I had a really good offer the other day, you know, and I turned it down for love of you.'

'Who from?'

'Zillah Brakespear.'

Jess almost laughed. 'It's no good, Hector. Emotional blackmail won't work either. I'm sorry but I really do have to go. Surely you can see that? There just isn't any future for me here with you, much as I hate to leave.'

'You'll regret it you know,' Hector said, thwarted and suddenly spiteful. 'No one else is going to fall for you at your age, especially in those clothes!'

Jess gasped. 'Thank you so much for that,' she found the presence of mind to say. 'That really clinches things. Now I couldn't stay, even if I wanted to.'

In the middle of the night Jess awoke with doubts. Perhaps Hector was right. Perhaps she would never find anyone else who would love her. Tears seeped out from under her closed eyelids and ran down her cheeks on to the pillow. Should she go? It wasn't just Hector; there were other excellent reasons for staying. At this moment she had a steady job with a regular salary. Would she be mad, wilfully to throw it all away in order to launch herself into the irregularly paid, seriously dodgy world of the freelance photographer?

Perhaps it would turn out to be the worst mistake of her whole life? Perhaps she would regret it for ever?

Eventually she sat up and put the light on. Then she found a tissue, wiped her eyes, blew her nose and tried to think positively. It might well turn out to be a bad idea, but she was determined to do it anyway. If it all went horribly wrong, she would just have to hope that she could be as blithely insouciant in the face of disaster as the boat owner who once wrote in his ship's Log:

'Bright and beautiful morning. Sank.'

BOOK THREE

AFTER ANOTHER SEVEN
YEARS . . .

20

A T intervals during the next seven years, Jess forgot her relief at having escaped from the burden of Hector's unreasonable expectations, and began to regret never having slept with him. She sometimes saw it as a lost opportunity; perhaps her only chance of love? Gradually however, as her freelance job developed, she became more and more engrossed in it and less and less wistful. Business was good. She'd won a major competition in photojournalism early on, and much subsequent work had flowed from that. I've been lucky, she thought. It was the right decision after all.

She stayed in touch with Hector. He rang her every few months, ostensibly to ask how she was getting on, but actually to unload some of his troubles on to her shoulders. Jess put up with it. She vaguely felt it was the least she could do, but she made a firm decision not to see him in person. It had been upsetting enough to make the break in the first place, and she wasn't about to jeopardise her new found equanimity.

'I've resigned from the *Chronicle*,' Hector said, six months after she had left.

'Why?' she asked, surprised.

'Oh, lots of reasons – I wasn't getting anywhere – the job's changed out of all recognition – the new building is quite ghastly – and anyway I was beginning to feel like a prisoner. I just never got out; spent all day on the bloody phone, and that's no life for anyone.'

'But you were never particularly ambitious, were you? I thought you just enjoyed the ambience of the Newsroom. You clearly weren't in it for the money!'

'A dilettante, eh?' Hector said. 'Probably true, but after you left it wasn't the same. Did you know Barry's the Senior

Reporter now? Seems no time ago that he was the podgy office boy. He's even given up crisps.' He sighed.

'So, what now?'

'Oh, I've joined the family firm as a Director. Mudgeley Goggles is doing rather well at the moment, in fact. We've gone into wraparound sunglasses to protect our customers from all the nasty UV radiation that's currently streaming through the hole in the ozone layer, and it seems to have been a smart move. Funny, really. I always swore I would never get involved . . .'

Poor Hector, Jess thought as she put the receiver down. He sounds so unlike himself, so depressed. This mood seemed to set the tone for the intervening years. Hector was invariably miserable whenever she spoke to him, but worst of all was the day when he telephoned to tell her that Morgan had been 'Statemented' as definitely having Specific Learning Difficulties.

'In other words,' Hector said, 'he's handicapped! I can hardly believe it, Jess, he looks so normal. He was such a beautiful baby too.'

He sounded near to tears. Jess, who had recently done an assignment in a school for dyslexic children, was taken aback at the depth of his defeatism.

'But Hector,' she said. 'It's surely not that bad? Literacy is only a part of life after all, and these days it's less and less necessary. People are already talking to their computers.'

'You don't understand!' Hector said vehemently. 'To me, literacy is *everything*. It's been my living for most of my life. Books are the greatest recreation there is, after all. I have nothing in common with someone who doesn't read, don't you see? It means *I can't relate to my own son!* Put it this way,' he said, 'as far as I'm concerned, if you aren't a fast and fluent reader, then you must be educationally sub-normal. In other words you're mentally deficient!'

'But Hector, that's just nonsense!' Jess protested. 'It's simply wrong. Dyslexics may have difficulty in dealing with symbolic stuff like the written word, but they're really strong on logic and reasoning, and great on things like spatial awareness. They just have weak short-term memories and are slow at reading and writing, but they often have high IQs, and they're certainly not stupid!'

'So, how come you're suddenly such an expert?'

'I've just been working at this school. I wish you could have been there, Hector, their art work was really something.'

'Oh, Morgan's always messing about drawing things, mostly buildings, these days.'

'Well there you are then.'

'It's not enough, Jess. I know it sounds harsh, and I wouldn't say it to anyone else but you, but when a ten-year-old boy can't even recite the months of the year in the correct order, I just feel despair. I feel like washing my hands of the whole fatherhood thing.'

After many such conversations over a long period of time, Jess pondered on the pressures parents bring to bear upon their children, and wondered why some were driven to do it. In her experience, they mostly said they didn't want to pursue their own goals vicariously, but then they tried to do just that. Her own parents hinted heavily, constantly, about the joys of marriage and motherhood.

'You're thirty-nine,' her father had said only the week before. 'You're not getting any younger, you know?'

'You do seem to have an extraordinary facility for stating the painfully bloody obvious,' Jess snapped at last.

'No need for that tone of voice, my girl. We care about you, Jess. It's only natural.'

Jess speculated on whether Hector's reaction towards Morgan could be counted as 'only natural' too. Perhaps if he hadn't built up this cosy fantasy about the father-son relationship, then he mightn't be so disappointed now? But then again, why should parents assume they had the right to be *disappointed* in their children in the first place?

Jess wondered whether there had been any other reasons why Hector had wanted a child. Some men collected status symbols – a smart car, a pretty wife, an elegant house, a pedigree pet or two – and then had to have at least one trophy child to prove their masculinity and complete the set. Perhaps that was it? Of course, she hadn't forgotten the main reason why Hector had been so determined to have a son, but she had always found that one hard to empathise with. No one cares about hereditary titles these days, she thought. They're irrelevant, obsolete, and all the best people play down such things anyway – look at Jonathon Porritt! So, who did Hector imagine he was going to impress? Certainly no one like me, and probably not Wendy either. Caroline? I suppose that might have been a factor when they first met. Jess made a face and smiled to herself.

Caroline could barely believe that she had been made redundant. After all those years of service, all that enthusiasm and inspiration and sheer bloody hard slog that she had put into the company, and now they had been taken over and were downsizing. She was above the 26–35 'employable' age range and therefore not to be kept on. She was shattered. She searched feverishly through the jobs sections of the broadsheet newspapers, avoiding all posts which specified a 'sense of humour' on the grounds that they were the employers most likely to exploit their workers. She knew she had good communication, interpersonal, management and organisational skills. She enjoyed a challenge, had experience, commitment and energy. She was courteous, unflappable, sensitive and flexible – all the buzz-words. She was also highly motivated and had a good track-record, but at forty-four, she was too old. It seemed hopeless.

Jess was a great source of support and help, in spite of being frantically busy and enviably successful. Caroline acknowledged their changing fortunes with a wry smile. She had once suggested in a joke that Jess might buy her house and then rent out the basement to her, to make their role reversal complete. Then she was upset when Jess, for a moment, appeared to consider the idea seriously.

Hannah, at fourteen, predictably saw everything in relation to her own concerns. 'Oh no,' she said. 'You won't be hanging around here all the time now, will you, like a real mother?'

'Thanks, Hannah. Give the knife a good twist while you're about it, why don't you.'

'When I have kids,' Hannah said virtuously, 'I'm going to stay home full-time and look after them properly.'

'Fine,' Caroline said. 'So why don't you get in a little practice now, with the hoover.'

'You're barking!' Hannah said contemptuously. 'I'll get a woman in to do *that*. You do!' Yes, her mother thought. But for how much longer? It's not cheap.

The golden handshake, which had seemed so generous to begin with, now appeared alarmingly finite. They were accustomed to a high standard of living, and Hannah would need a lot of support when she went to university in four years time. Caroline knew that she had to get another job at all costs. She took to going down to the basement of an evening, to discuss her financial worries at length with Jess.

'Well . . . what about Hector?' Jess suggested tentatively. 'He's not short of a few bob.'

'I'd have to be pretty desperate!' Caroline laughed shortly. 'But yes, I suppose as a last resort . . . Funnily enough, Hannah and I were talking about him only last night.'

'Really?'

'Yes. She wanted to know who her father was, so I felt I had to tell her his name, but not much else. I don't *know* much more! Maybe you could talk to her about him one of these days?'

'Well . . . yes. Does she want to meet him?'

'I've said no. Absolutely not. Not until she's eighteen. Then she'll be officially adult and I can't stop her. So . . . how is handsome Hector these days. Does he still phone?'

'Yes, pretty regularly. I think he's lonely.'

'You don't ever wish you'd let him leave Wendy for you?'

'Well . . . very occasionally I do, if I'm honest. I haven't met anyone since him who was such fun to be with . . . and we might have had children together too, I suppose.'

'Well yes, but they can be a constant worry,' Caroline said, sighing. 'Look at me and Hannah. She's my darling only child, and yet now I feel I barely know her. I've missed so much of her childhood, through working all the time, and in five years or so she'll be grown up and gone and that will be it. And now I'm out of a job and wondering whether it was all worth it. D'you remember when I said I wasn't going to let my baby change my life? How could I have been so incredibly naïve! Maybe I should have stayed at home and been a proper mum.'

'Oh I don't know, but then again . . . I probably would

have,' Jess said slowly, 'but then it's easy for me to say that, isn't it, when it's only hypothetical.'

'It might still happen.'

'Face it; it's getting less and less likely.' Jess looked sad.

Caroline changed the subject. 'Does Hector ever see his other son?'

'Florian? Oh that's a saga that runs and runs, and Hector never seems to get anywhere. At first Florian wouldn't see him at all. He just ran away whenever Hector turned up. Then Hector did manage to take him to the cinema a few times, but Florian behaved so badly and used so much foul language that he had to give that up. So then he stopped paying maintenance, and Zillah threatened him with the Child Support Agency, but Hector couldn't allow her to do that so he began paying again, but he still wasn't seeing Florian . . .'

'Hang on,' Caroline interrupted. 'Why didn't Hector just let her go to the CSA if he was prepared to go on paying her anyway?'

'Because Wendy still doesn't know that Florian is Hector's son! Amazing, isn't it?'

'She must be a bit dim, surely? It doesn't sound like much of a marriage. I'm only surprised Hector's stuck it all this time.'

'Well . . . I suppose he feels responsible for her and Morgan, and Wendy is very devoted you know. He likes his creature comforts, does Hector. I suppose he just needs more . . . complexity than Wendy can provide. I think he phones me for a spot of therapy – to get it all off his chest.'

'He phones you because he's still in love with you,' Caroline observed. 'I could do with somebody like that!'

Hector was lonely. He brooded a lot on the unfairness of life. Here he was, three times a father and yet his quest for paternal contentment had got him nowhere. Yes, it was true that Wendy looked after him well. The house was spotless and there was always a meal on the table when he wanted one. She meant well, poor woman, but Hector felt his spirit being eroded away by terminal boredom, which was barely enlivened by sporadic regulation sex.

He wished he had left Wendy seven years before and had gone to London with Jess. He blamed himself for failing to convince Jess of the depth of his feelings when he'd had the chance. It was too late now. She was a high-flyer. She wouldn't have any time for him. She listened patiently and kindly to his troubles each time he telephoned her, but he could tell that she was mostly just humouring him. He was fifty-six and past it.

Over the years he'd learned to live within his own limitations. He knew he didn't want to be alone again; he wouldn't be able to cope. There was nothing for it but to remain shackled to Wendy, but to try and find the odd spark of life and excitement wherever he could. For a short while he'd had an affair with Jackie Poole, slipping round there at lunchtime whilst her kids were at school, but she'd got too demanding so he'd had to give her up. The final straw had been when Barry had come to him all unsuspecting to ask for advice, man to man. Hector experienced an uncomfortable sensation in his guts, which he later identified as guilt. Since Jackie, he'd found no one.

He began to ring Jess more frequently. He liked the sound of her voice.

'Hector? Hello! This is a surprise. You only phoned me last Saturday, didn't you?'

'It was three weeks ago, in fact,' Hector said.

'Really? I don't know where the time goes these days! So, how's things?'

'Oh much as usual.'

'Any news on the Florian front?'

'Only that they've been evicted from that cottage for not paying the rent. God only knows what Zillah does with all my money! The new tenants tell me she's living in a caravan not far away, but I haven't found out where it is yet, so I'm feeling even more hacked-off with them than usual.'

'Oh, poor you,' Jess said.

'Maybe daughters are easier?' Hector suggested.

'Not if Hannah's anything to go by! I gather Caroline finds her very hard work.'

'How are they both?'

'Oh poor Caroline's in a bad way at the moment. She's lost her job and is trying desperately to find another, but it seems almost impossible, in spite of all her qualifications and experience. "Yoof" is everything, it seems.'

Hector sat by the telephone for some time after phoning Jess and then, once he'd made his mind up, he opened his study door and called out, 'Any chance of a coffee, Wend?' and sat back, waiting for it to arrive.

He would give Florian one last chance, he decided. If that didn't work out, then he would wash his hands of him, and Zillah could beat him with the CSA or any other branch of officialdom. He really couldn't give a stuff. And if Wendy found out? Well, he'd just have to put up with the consequences of that.

Whilst he was at his desk, he wrote out the usual cheque for Zillah and then on impulse wrote out a larger one for Caroline. If she was in financial trouble, then this might just be his entrée to a life including Hannah. He wrote each name on an envelope, put both cheques inside, and slipped them into his inside pocket just before Wendy came in with the coffee.

'You haven't forgotten you're taking Morgan over to his friend's this afternoon, have you?' she asked.

'No.' For a change, Hector was looking forward to it. Getting out of the house alone was not as easy as it used to be when he'd had the excuse of a 'story' that needed pursuing. Mudgeley Goggles was very much a nine to five job, and he was conscious that Wendy could always phone Ifor to check up on his whereabouts.

Morgan's friend lived on the southern edge of town, the right side for Hector's purposes. As they drove through the traffic, he tried to get the boy interested in a number-plate game.

'The rules are easy,' he explained. 'You have to look out for any three-letter combination that will make a word by the addition of just one more letter, ignoring the figures of course, and the yearly prefix. OK?' Morgan looked unhappy. 'See? There's one,' Hector pointed. 'It's a good one because it's a word already − RAN − so I get one point to start with. Then I can add an I to it to make RAIN for another two points, or a T to make RANT for a further two, and so on. So I've got five points so far, d'you see? The only other rule is that if you make a rude word or a swear word you get docked ten points. OK? Shall we play it?'

'No,' Morgan said sulkily. 'It's stupid.'

Hector sighed. 'Oh well,' he said, 'please yourself.' He dropped Morgan off with some relief and then drove swiftly out of town towards Zillah's old cottage, hoping that the new people who lived there might by now have found the forwarding address. The place looked better already. Someone had dug the garden and cut the lawn, and there was a new gate with two good hinges at the bottom of the path. Hector swung it open and advanced to the newly-painted front door.

'You could have phoned,' the new female occupant said brightly. 'We've just got connected.'

'Bit late now,' Hector said.

'Yes. Well, I'm ever so sorry. We did have Mrs Brakespear's address. She wrote it down for us on a little scrap of paper, but we haven't used it and now I think the puppy must've eaten it. I looked everywhere after you came last time. Sorry.'

'But can't you remember the name of the place, or anything at all?'

'I think it was over there,' she said, vaguely gesticulating in the general direction of the distant Tor, 'over Glastonbury way'.

'Thanks,' Hector said shortly and went back crossly to his car. He clearly wasn't going to have any luck today. He would have to fall back on his old journalistic skills and track her down through local sources. Luckily he'd kept his contact book in which, over the years, he'd written down the names and phone numbers of everyone he'd ever spoken to, who might be useful to him in future – from the local rat catcher (or rodent operative) to the region's faceless Euro MP. Hector discovered that he was looking forward to doing a bit of detective work again.

By the following weekend he had a pretty good idea of where Zillah might be. He finally managed to escape Wendy's vigilance on the Sunday by saying he was going to take his latest car out for a run to see if he could detect the source of an irritating squeak that had been bothering him. 'Nasty, tatty modern cars,' he complained. 'The Jag never squeaked!'

'It's a lovely car,' Wendy said. 'You know you're chuffed to bits with it. You polish it enough! It's just an excuse to zoom round the place like a boy racer. How about taking Morgan for a ride while you're about it.'

'I don't think so,' Hector said with careful nonchalance. 'He'd only be bored.'

'You mean, you would!'

Hector pretended not to hear her. He got into the car and started it up, pressing buttons to erect the roof aerial and to open the sun-roof and one window. Then, selecting Classic FM, he drove off in a blaze of Kiri Te Kanawa. He was heading for a travellers' camp near Glastonbury.

He found it without too much difficulty, but as he parked he felt distinctly uneasy. Two large mongrels bounded towards him, barking, and a group of youths sitting in the spring sunshine on the steps of an old bus looked definitely threatening. There were half a dozen vans, a few derelict vehicles minus their wheels, and a lot of grey washing hanging limply on lengths of string or draped over bushes. A few daffodils, in a solitary clump surrounded by rubbish, looked like innocents abroad.

'I'm looking for Zillah Brakespear,' Hector called to the youths. One of them said something inaudible and they all sniggered. He got out of his car self-consciously and warily fended the dogs off with the only thing he had to hand, a rolled up copy of the *Westcountry Chronicle*.

The youths turned their backs and ignored him. Out of the corner of his eye Hector noticed something moving. He turned and caught sight of a tall boy with long, red dreadlocks emerging from the furthest caravan.

'Florian?' he called uncertainly. Florian looked startled and then, giving Hector a vigorous V-sign, he started up an ancient motorbike and clattered off. Hector, carefully avoiding the puddles and all too aware of the dogs close behind him, walked across to Florian's caravan and banged on the door. It opened a little way.

'Yeah?' A child of about seven wearing round glasses peered out and said, 'What d'you want?' His index finger was marking his place in a heavy book.

Hector looked up at him. 'Hello Alaric.'

'What do you want?'

'I'm looking for Zillah.'

'She's not here.'

'Do you know when she'll be back?'

'Nope.'

'Well I was hoping to talk to her about Florian.'

'He's not here either.'

'No, I know. So, can I come in for a moment and wait for Zillah?'

'No,' Alaric said, and shut the door firmly. Behind Hector the youths cackled. He turned and saw that the dogs had left him and were now peeing enthusiastically over his car wheels. Then he looked beyond the car and saw someone walking up the path through the freshly greening trees, a slim woman wearing a long flowery skirt and carrying a basket of shopping. Thank God for that! Hector thought, and walked briskly to meet her.

'How did you know I was here?' was the first thing she said.

'You weren't that hard to find,' Hector said. 'I mean, how many other Zillah's do you know? Here, let me carry that for you.'

Zillah handed the basket over to him without thanks and glanced at him dispassionately as they began to walk on towards the camp. 'Well?'

'I've just seen Alaric,' Hector said. 'He must have been deep in a book; rather like a startled mole who's suddenly broken out into the sunlight by mistake!'

'That sounds like my boy,' Zillah said proudly.

'And how's Christian?' Hector enquired, putting off the evil moment when he had to ask about Florian.

'He's great. He's up at Edinburgh, doing a PhD in Genetics.'

'Good God!' Hector said involuntarily.

'Just because we live like this, it doesn't mean we're bone from the neck up,' Zillah said sternly. 'You should endeavour to rise above meaningless stereotypes, you know.'

'So, how's Florian doing then?' Hector asked, challenging this.

'Oh well, pretty much as you'd expect, I shouldn't wonder,' Zillah admitted with a grimace.

'You mean he's in trouble?'

'He's what's officially known these days as a Young Offender – joyriding, mugging, into drugs, well-known to the police, you name it – all in all a well-rounded delinquent.'

'You're joking!'

'Do I look as if I'm laughing?'

'Well, no . . .'

'I always said he had bad blood, didn't I?'

'There's no such thing, surely?'

'So what are you going to do about it then? I take it you had some reason for coming over here?'

'I just wanted to make contact,' Hector said uneasily. 'I think I caught sight of him just now – long hair? On a motorbike?'

'That's him.'

'But he isn't legally old enough to ride one, and he wasn't wearing a crash helmet.'

'Fine,' Zillah said, sighing heavily. 'So you tell him. In fact, I've got a better idea. Why don't you just take him away with you and sort him out? I've had him up to here!' She waved a slim hand near her forehead.

Hector recoiled. 'Well, now I know where you are . . .' he began, weakly.

'Yeah, yeah,' Zillah said.

'I'll come and see Florian again soon, maybe even talk to him.'

'Fat chance.'

'Well . . . anyway . . . best be off . . .'

'If you've got any more spare books,' Zillah said, 'Alaric would be glad of them.'

'Right. I'll see what I can do.' Hector waited by his car until Zillah had got over to her caravan, and then he waved as she turned to shut the door behind her. The huddle of youths regarded him watchfully. He bent a little twitchily under their gaze to unlock the door, and then he saw the damage. Someone had walked the length of his expensive top-of-the-range BMW with a sharp object like a nail in one hand, and had scored a deep groove in its paintwork from end to end. Hector jerked his head up furiously.

The youths stared silently, insolently straight back at him, and Hector, to his eternal shame, dropped his gaze, got into his car and drove sheepishly away.

21

HECTOR arrived outside Caroline's home early one Saturday afternoon and parked his car nearby, going over what he planned to say in his head and hoping against hope that he would at least get inside the house. He walked towards it, looking up at the windows in case Caroline or Hannah might by chance be looking out, but they were blank. He took a steadying breath and rang the doorbell. Nothing happened. He couldn't be sure whether it was ringing somewhere deep within, or whether it was simply broken. He rang it again and hammered on the door with his fist, to make sure. Still no one came. Just my luck! Hector thought bitterly. I drive all the way up to London, and then they aren't bloody well here. I suppose I should have phoned first. But I didn't want to give Caroline the chance to poison the child's mind against me. Maybe I should pop down to the basement instead, and see if Jess is in.

'Can I help you?'

Hector looked all round, but saw nobody.

'Up here,' said the voice. He looked up. A girl was hanging out of the first-floor window, her long mousy hair falling over her face, so he couldn't tell at all what she looked like.

'Oh,' he said, 'I'm . . . er . . . looking for Caroline. You must be Hannah?'

'Yeah. I am. I'm just drying my hair. Mum's out.'

'Well can I come in and wait?'

'Don't think so. I'm not even, like, supposed to *talk* to strange men.'

'I'm not a strange man,' Hector said, craning his neck to see her. 'I'm your father.'

The scene was not at all as he had hoped it might be. He had imagined them sitting side by side on a big squashy sofa, with him leading up to the great revelation very gently, and then Hannah's beautiful eyes filling with tears, and her throwing herself into his arms, and . . .

'You could just be saying that,' Hannah scoffed. 'You might be a multiple rapist or a serial killer.'

'Do I *look* like that sort of a monster?' Hector protested unwisely.

'Yeah, you do actually. Maybe you should get counselling?'

'Look,' Hector said, 'this is silly. Do you know your father's name?'

'Course I do! Hector by name; hector by nature, my mum says. He used to work with Jess, down in Somerset, and when I'm eighteen I'm going to go and find him, and then Mum won't see me for dust!'

'Here,' Hector said, 'catch!' He threw her his wallet. 'Here's proof. Look inside and see who I am.' She caught it, opened it and looked at the name on his credit cards and driving licence.

'Hector Mudgeley!' she said in amazement. 'That's right . . . but . . .'

'But what?'

'You're so *old*,' Hannah said, 'and so un-cool. I'd imagined . . .' She stopped in confusion.

'Are you going to let me in then, or what?'

'Yeah, I suppose I'd better. Hang on.'

Hector pursed his lips as he waited for her to get downstairs. Not another failure, he thought, please God. Then the door opened and Hannah stood there, holding on to it. She was thin and almost as tall as he was. Now that her hair was brushed off her face, he could see that she was quite pretty in a scruffy sort of way. Her clothes seemed to be a mass of unconnected layers and her fingernails were painted black.

'I shouldn't have said that,' she said, giving him back his wallet, 'about you being un-cool, that is.' She made a rueful face.

'That's all right,' Hector said generously. 'I've been called worse things.'

'Come in then.' She led him into their kitchen and he sat down at the table while she made him a cup of coffee.

'I always wanted a dad,' she said shyly.

'And I always wanted a daughter,' Hector lied. 'I was going to call you Gwladys (with a *w*) after your Welsh great-great-grandmother. Would you like to see a picture of the room where you were conceived?'

'Really? Wicked!'

Hector felt about in his inside pocket and produced a sheaf of photographs which he spread out on the table in front of them.

'Oh wow,' Hannah said. 'Blue elephants! Aren't they just the dog's bollocks!'

'I beg your pardon?' Hector expostulated, considerably taken aback.

'You know, solid, sweet as a nut, great?'

'Oh I see. You mean you *like* them?'

'Yeah, course.'

Jess and Caroline got back from shopping soon after four o'clock. 'Come in for a cuppa?' Caroline suggested.

'Love to,' Jess said. She followed her into her kitchen and, unprepared for a sudden stop, cannoned into her back. 'Oh . . . sorry!'

'Hector?' Caroline exclaimed. 'What the fuck are you doing here?'

'Ooooh, Mother, – language!' Hannah said smugly.

'Go up to your room,' Caroline snapped. 'NOW!'

Jess looked around her to see what was going on. Hector was sitting calmly at the kitchen table, nursing a mug of coffee between both hands. Hannah was sitting opposite him, and on the surface between them was a torn-open packet of chocolate biscuits. He looks just the same! Jess thought with a rush of affection; greyer and a bit more jowly, but still good-looking, still the same old Hector. He glanced at Caroline and then turned to wink at her. Jess smiled.

'No I won't,' Hannah said to her mother. 'My dad and me's having a chat for the first time in *fourteen* years, which is all your fault!'

'Hannah, perhaps it might be a good idea if your mother and I sorted out a few things in private?' Hector said to her gently. Hannah looked from one to the other of them and then, noisily scraping back her chair, got grudgingly to her feet.

'Oh all right,' she said. 'I've got things to do anyway,' and she left the room, pushing past Caroline and Jess without another word.

'Right Hector,' Caroline said brusquely. 'I think it's time you were going too. I take a very dim view of people who sneak into other people's houses by conning their children.'

'It was no con,' Hector said. 'Hannah's my daughter.'

'Nice try,' Caroline said, 'but it won't wash, so you can piss off, straight back to yokel county!'

Hector made a face at Jess as if to say – See how I'm being treated? Surely you won't stand for this?

'Why don't you come down to my flat?' she suggested to him, 'and sort things out from there?'

He smiled warmly at her. 'Thanks Jess. It's good to know someone appreciates me.'

Jess turned apologetically to Caroline. 'I'm sorry Caro, I'm not trying to interfere. I just thought . . .'

'Oh take him away!' Caroline snapped. 'Do what you like, just keep him out of my life.' Then she went up to Hector and spoke to him with her face only inches away from his. 'And get this Hector, Hannah isn't interested in you. You've never been a father to her, and it's too late to start now, so there's an end to it. You have absolutely no reason to come here again. Understood?'

'Oh I hear the words,' Hector said calmly. 'It's the sense that eludes me. And you're wrong on the last count. I will have to come here tomorrow, because I've arranged to take Hannah to the pictures.' He got to his feet and walked out of the kitchen.

'Over my dead body!' Caroline shouted furiously after him.

'Fine,' Hector called back. 'Whatever turns you on.'

Jess didn't know whether to follow Hector or try to pacify Caroline. 'I'm so sorry . . .' she began again. 'I . . .'

Caroline turned on her. 'Just get rid of him!' she hissed. 'This has got to be all your fault. How else would he *know*?'

Jess turned and ran after Hector, out of the front door and down the steps between the house and the front railings, which led to her basement.

'You've really landed me in the shit now,' she complained to him. 'She's blaming me for telling you.'

'Don't worry,' Hector said easily. 'I'll put her right tomorrow, when she's had a chance to calm down.' They went inside Jess's flat and he looked around him curiously. 'Oh,' he said, 'where's my favourite futon?'

'I left it behind in the old flat, at the mercy of my summer tenants. It wasn't the most comfortable thing in the world.'

'No,' Hector agreed, 'but it was very *you*, in those days. How often do you go back there? And how come you've never popped in to see me?'

'Don't know really. I always check the flat over at least a couple of times a year. I have a local agent who sees to it the rest of the time. In fact I'm off down there next week, to make sure it's OK for the beginning of the holiday season at Easter.' This is ridiculous, she thought. We're making polite conversation as though we were at a cocktail party!

'It's lovely to see you, Jessy-boot,' Hector said, putting out a hand to pat her arm. 'It's been too long.'

'Yes it has . . .' Jess collected her thoughts. 'But look Hector, what is all this? Why are you suddenly here, and what are your plans?'

'I'm taking Hannah out to see a film,' Hector said. 'It's one she's desperate to see, so she says.'

'But what about Caroline?'

'Oh it wouldn't be her sort of thing at all.'

'STOP IT! I'm being serious. Where are you planning to stay tonight?'

'I've brought a sleeping bag and some rugs. I can kip in the back of the car.'

'Does Wendy know you're here?'

'Not yet. Perhaps I could phone her from here this evening?'

'I think you'd better! So why have you got in touch with Hannah after all this time? It's hardly fair, is it? You can't blame Caroline for being angry.'

'I'm her father.'

'Don't tell me – it's only natural!'

'Well it is, isn't it?'

'So why did you stay away so long then?'

'I can't win, can I? Come on Jess, if you're going to grill

me all night, then at least let's go out somewhere where we can have a good meal and some nice wine at the same time. What d'you say?' He raised an eyebrow at her and smiled disarmingly.

Jess sighed. 'Oh, all right.'

She had almost forgotten how charming Hector could be. She sat opposite him in a small alcove in her favourite restaurant and regarded him over the flame of a flickering candle, with Vivaldi tinkling away discreetly in the background. She felt as though there had been no seven year gap at all; as if nothing had changed.

'You've gone all smart and Londonized.' Hector said approvingly.

'Caroline's influence. She's good at clothes and hair and things.'

'You two are good friends then?'

'Well we were . . . until this afternoon . . .'

'Don't worry,' Hector reassured her. 'She'll get used to the idea. It's not as though I want to steal Hannah from her. I just want to see her once in a while and take her out for the odd treat. Where's the harm in that?'

'Was Hannah polite to you?'

'Eventually, yes, very. Why?'

'Oh, it's just that she's usually rather stroppy.'

'No. I got the impression she was very keen to come out with me.'

'Well, I suppose it will give Caroline a well-deserved rest.'

'There you are then,' Hector said cheerfully. 'Heads, everyone wins; tails, no one loses. Have some more wine?'

He began to tell her about the latest excitements at Mudgeley Goggles, which didn't take long. From there he progressed rapidly on to all aspects of H.M.'s life and times, and he was soon in full journalistic flow, describing his visit to Zillah's caravan and Florian's dreadlocks and motorbike, and the general decrepitude of the camp.

'And did your car still have wheels when you left?' Jess asked, grinning.

'Heaven yes,' Hector said. 'I'm more than a match for your casual yob.'

'Whereabouts is this place?'

'Just outside Glastonbury,' he said, taking a Biro out of his inside pocket and drawing a rough plan on his paper napkin. He pushed it across the table. 'You should visit them. You'd get some winning shots of "alienated youth".'

'Oh I don't have to go to Somerset for that!' Jess said.

When they finally got back to her flat, they were in mellow mood. 'You can't sleep in your car,' she said. 'It's a ridiculous idea.'

'Well, I suppose I could find a hotel . . .' Hector suggested half-heartedly.

'You could stay here with me,' she said. 'In the spare room of course.'

'Thought you'd never ask!' he said, and they both burst out laughing.

In the middle of the night Jess awoke and remembered with a start that Hector was sleeping next door. She had been expecting him to try it on after an hour or so, by coming into her room, looking hopeful. But he hadn't, and now she wasn't sure whether she was relieved or disappointed.

Hannah was pretty sure that Hector wouldn't take her home with him if she simply asked him to. Adults had an irritating habit of sticking together, even when they actively disliked one another. It was obvious that her mother couldn't stand Hector, so that made him a big attraction as far as she was concerned. Once she'd got used to the fact that her father was not only a wrinkly, but near as damn it a crumbly, she could appreciate that Hector might once have been quite tasty. At least she wouldn't be ashamed to be seen going to the odd film with him.

At that first meeting she had decided she liked him, and wanted to know him better, so she'd worked out this neat strategy. Played right, she could score twice with one try! Of the two objectives, of course, escaping from Caroline was her main concern. Hannah smiled to herself. If I pack too much kit, she thought, then Mum'll suss me, so I'll only take the basics in my shoulder bag and then Hector can buy me more stuff when we get there. He's rich enough.

When Hector eventually came up from the basement late on the following morning, Hannah, who had been waiting for him for *hours*, did wonder fleetingly whether he and Jess had spent the night in the same bed together, having sex. But the thought of that was so mind-bogglingly gross that she abruptly banished it from her head, and made herself concentrate on her plan. She and Hector were to go into the West End (in spite of Caroline's protestations) and have lunch wherever she fancied, and then see the film at two o'clock. Hannah hoped she might get Hector to buy her some clothes, but then realized that the shops would most likely be closed on a Sunday. Next time! she promised herself.

The film turned out to be wicked. Hannah was well-pleased she'd chosen it. Hector had looked a bit fazed afterwards, but she reckoned it must be because he hadn't been able to keep up with it. It was probably difficult for someone of his age; you had to make allowances. When they came back to the car to drive back to her house, she put her shoulder bag deliberately on the back seat and covered it up with Hector's rugs and stuff which were already there. Stage one! Then they went inside. Her mother was probably still sulking, Hannah thought, because she hadn't been able to stop her from going out with her dad. She felt a surge of triumph. She'll do more than sulk soon, Hannah thought gleefully. She'll be well gutted.

'I'm going to leave this here for your mother,' Hector said as they went into the front hall. He took a white envelope with Caroline's name on it from his inside pocket and laid it on the hall table.

'What is it?'

'It's a cheque. If I give it to her now she'll probably tear it up, the mood she's in, but I do want her to have it, so will you draw it to her attention?'

'Eh?'

'Will you give it to her after I've left?'

'Oh, right, yeah.'

'Well, I suppose I shall have to be off soon,' Hector said. 'I've so much enjoyed our afternoon together.'

'Me an' all.'

'I'm just going to say goodbye to Jess, OK? And I suppose I'd better have a word with your mother, and then I'll be going, but I'll come and see you again very soon, if you'd like me to?'

'Cool.'

'Right then.' He began to go down the steps to the basement.

'Hector?'

'Hannah?'

'Can I put your stuff in the car?'

'No, it's OK, I'll do it.'

'Well . . . but . . . I'd like to.'

Hector looked up and smiled. 'All right, thanks. I'll chuck it up to you.' After a few moments he emerged from the flat with his overnight bag and called, 'Catch!' and then, 'Keys!' and, 'Oh well done!'

Hannah turned away with the bag, giving a covert clenched fist salute of triumph. Stage two was safe! She walked non-chalantly over the road to where Hector's car was parked, and opened the doors. Then she put the key into the ignition and closed the driver's door. Hector's bag went on to the far end of the back seat above the pile of stuff already there and Hannah, glancing furtively all round to make sure no one was observing her, climbed in beside her shoulder bag, and covered herself completely with the sleeping bag and rugs. It was a large car and there was plenty of room. Hannah made sure she was invisible and then settled down to wait.

It took longer than she had anticipated. She got uncomfortably hot and began to wonder how long she could stick it, and then when she had almost dropped off to sleep through boredom, she heard someone coming. It had occurred to her earlier that she had set things up perfectly for any opportunist passing thief, by leaving the keys so conveniently in the steering column. She had visions of herself being driven off by some startled petty criminal and then held to ransom for millions of pounds . . . well, anything's better than staying at home, she thought. At least I'd see some *action*.

But it was Hector who eventually turned up, and if Hannah had hoped to hear him lamenting the fact that he hadn't been able to say goodbye to her properly, then she was to be disappointed.

'I can't wait any longer,' Hector grumbled. 'She's had her chance. Oh no! The car's open, for God's sake, and she's left the keys in it! Bloody kids are all the same, aren't they; totally irresponsible! Anyone could have nicked it!' He opened the driver's door.

'Is your bag there?' It was Jess's voice.

'Yes, at least she got that right. She could have said goodbye though, don't you think? Ungrateful wretch!'

'Give her time Hector. It must have been a bit of a shock, when you suddenly turned up.'

'Yes, I suppose so. Well, I'd better drag myself away. It's been so good to see you again, *cariad*. Thanks for putting me up. Let's not leave it another seven years, eh?'

''Bye Hector.' There were brief kissing noises.

YUK! Hannah thought.

Then Hector started the engine and they set off. Once air began circulating it got blessedly cooler. Hannah hadn't thought ahead to what the journey might be like, but as it got underway she realised that she was going to learn quite a lot about her unsuspecting parent, from the type of music he enjoyed to the degree of road rage from which he suffered. The music was the worst, Hannah thought, glad that her ears were well-muffled. It was some ghastly soprano screeching away in a foreign language. Why does *anyone* like opera? she wondered. And after all that racket, how can they have the cheek to complain about my heavy metal?

Hannah gathered quite soon that Hector tended towards the continental mode of driving. At first she thought everyone was hooting at him, but then she learned to distinguish the regular blare of Hector's two-tone horn amongst the others, as he carved his way through the London traffic. There was a lot of rapid acceleration and sudden braking, squeals of tyres and hissing of air-brakes. At one point when they were presumably waiting at traffic lights, Hannah heard someone shouting,

'Get yourself some sodding glasses, Grandad!' and then the same voice, 'Oh nice one! Is that your age or your IQ?'

She heard Hector mutter through clenched teeth, 'I'll get you, you stupid bastard . . .' and was abruptly pressed into the back of the seat as he stepped hard on the gas, and then very nearly thrown forwards into the foot-well as he unexpectedly jammed on the brakes. 'CUNT!' Hector shouted.

Hannah took as firm a grip as she could on the edge of the

seat and lay there, ears pricked, wondering if she was going to learn any new words. She rather doubted it actually. Hector's generation's vocabulary was pretty lame in her estimation. She did, however, begin to wonder whether she would reach her destination in one piece. Veg out! she advised herself. Relax! He's managed to survive this long as a driver, what's another few hours?

Once on to the motorway, things got easier and Hannah almost dozed off again. I'll wait until he's safely in a service station, she thought, before I show myself. He's not exactly laid-back, and I don't want to be the cause of a multiple pile-up. She hoped, however, that Hector's bladder would prove to be weaker than her own. She'd forgotten to go before stowing away, and she was already feeling the need . . .

After they had been driving for about an hour and a half, she felt the car slowing down and heard the sound of progress-ively lower gears being engaged. They turned a few corners at a gentler speed and finally, in the nick of time as far as Hannah was concerned, they came to a halt.

She threw off the sleeping bag and rugs and sat up, stretching. 'Thank God we've stopped at last,' she said. 'I'm bursting for a pee!'

Hector's expression in the mirror was one of comical horror. He whipped his head round to stare at her. 'What the hell . . .?'

'I wanted to come with you,' Hannah explained, 'and I didn't think you'd let me.'

'Too bloody right!'

'Gotta have a leak,' Hannah said quickly, opening the door. 'Back in a mo.'

She worried as she hurried into the Welcome Break, that Hector might simply drive off and abandon her. He didn't. When she got back, he was still sitting in his car looking displeased, but resigned.

'I ought to take you straight back to London,' he said, sighing, 'but there isn't time. Damn it, Hannah! What on earth am I supposed to do with you?'

'Take me home to your place.'

'It's not that easy.'

'Why? Are you ashamed of me?'

'No, of course not, you noodle.'

'So, what's the problem?'

'The problem, as you so simplistically put it, is this: what on earth am I going to say to my wife?'

22

WENDY examined her reflected head and shoulders carefully to detect the latest of the accumulating
imperfections of age, and realized for the first time, sadly, that
the term 'turtle neck' no longer applied solely to woolly
jumpers. She turned away from the bathroom mirror feeling
old and unloved. I shall be fifty next year, she thought. What
shall I do if he leaves me?

When Hector had gone off with no explanation, Wendy
hadn't known what to think. Perhaps he already had left her?
Where had he gone? How could she find out? She couldn't
look at any of their annotated phone bills to discover the
numbers he habitually rang, because he always paid them
without reference to her and then locked them up in one of
his filing cabinets. She decided she would press the redial
button on the telephone in his study, just in case his last call
had been to his bit-on-the-side. She had done this several
times previously without success. Once, surprisingly, it had
been Barry's number and afterwards she'd wished she had
thought in advance of something plausible to say. But since
she hadn't, she'd had to disguise her voice and pretend it was
a wrong number. Wendy had felt very sad about that. She
would have liked a chat, but somehow she could never quite
bring herself to phone him deliberately, in case she got Jackie
instead.

This time, re-dialling got her a woman's voice on an answerphone. 'I'm sorry I can't talk to you at the moment,' it said.
'If you want to leave a message for Jess Hazelrigg, please do
so after the beep. Thank you.'

Wendy put the phone down without speaking and thought,
JESS? Surely not!

She didn't know what to do. Suppose she were to ring Jess's

number, and Hector wasn't there? She couldn't think of a convincing lie and she shrank from explaining the real situation to Jess, so she spent the rest of the day in a state of suppressed anxiety, functioning like an automaton. She took Morgan to his Saturday swimming lesson. She did one load of washing and two of ironing. She hoovered the house. She waited and waited for the telephone to ring and eventually, that evening, it did.

'It's me.'

'Hector! Where *are* you?'

'In London.'

'But why? Who are you with? When are you coming home? And why didn't you *tell* me first? I've been worried sick!'

'Calm down, Wendy, everything's fine. I just need some space, OK? I'll be back tomorrow evening.'

'But why did you go to London in the first place?'

'I don't know. It was an impulse. I'm sorry, I should have discussed it with you.'

'Are you seeing Jess?'

'No,' Hector said very casually. 'Haven't been in touch with her for years. Why d'you ask?'

'No reason.'

It *must* be her, Wendy thought as she put the phone down. Why else would he lie? She slumped on to the floor beside the phone, put her face in both hands and wept. She was now so unloveable that her husband even preferred *Jess* to her. Tears trickled through her fingers and down her arms, making the sleeves of her cardigan all wet inside. Wendy couldn't understand how Hector could fancy someone like Jess! Perhaps she'd changed? Of course she had the advantage of comparative youth. I was attractive ten years ago, Wendy thought, wiping her eyes. It's so unfair! Perhaps it's a judgement on me for deceiving Hector into marrying me? Maybe I should have married Barry instead, when I had the chance?

Barry – she hadn't given him a thought in years. He was still young. He must only be thirty-five or so, but even he wouldn't fancy her now. She remembered how keen he had been on her fourteen years ago, and how she hadn't taken him seriously at all. She knew now how he must have felt, and was sorry that she had treated him so casually. She should have been kinder. She thought about him on and off all Sunday morning, and wished she could think of a way to make it up to him. Then, on impulse, when Morgan had gone out with a friend and the house was empty, she looked up his phone number in the book and dialled it. If it's Jackie or one of the kids, Wendy thought, I'll just put the phone down. But it was Barry himself who answered.

'Barry? Hello, it's Wendy Mudgeley.'

'Hello!' He sounded genuinely pleased to hear her.

'This is probably a silly question, but do you know Jess Hazelrigg's address in London?' I don't need it, Wendy thought. It's only a pretext, but Barry isn't to know that.

'Sorry, no,' Barry said. 'I gather she's been doing pretty well for herself though. Why?'

'Oh it's not important,' Wendy said. 'How's things with you?'

'Bit tough at the moment actually,' Barry said. 'Jackie's . . . away and now Mum's died, so I'm having to cope with all the children single-handed. It's a bit like having both feet nailed to the floor.'

'I'm *so* sorry,' Wendy sympathised, 'I had no idea! Poor you! Can I help at all? Would you like to bring them over here for tea tomorrow, for instance?'

'Well that's really kind Wendy, but my two eldest are due to go to a birthday party in Bristol, and of course Muggins here has to take them, but thanks very much for asking.'

'It would be nice to meet up sometime,' Wendy suggested tentatively.

'Yes it would. We must arrange it.'

'Yes, well . . . goodbye then.'

''Bye Wendy. Good to talk to you.'

He doesn't really want to see me, she thought. He's just being polite.

The afternoon dragged by. It was sunny outside but there was a cold north wind. Wendy went out to dig up some dandelions from the border in the front garden, so that the flowers wouldn't go to seed and spread themselves everywhere. Gradually, in spite of the chill, she became absorbed in her task. As she worked, a bright yellow brimstone butterfly, the first of the season, fluttered by. A robin sang in the cherry tree above her head, and Wendy began to feel her heart slow down to a more tranquil beat. She breathed in the cool air, and brushed the hair out of her eyes with the backs of her soil-caked hands.

Once upon a time, she thought, I used to varnish my nails every other day, and grow them all long and sophisticated. Now they're less than half that length and all filled up black with dirt! She didn't quite know why she'd taken to gardening. She had never been in the least interested in it until she'd turned forty. Then she had sown seeds from a free packet on the front of one of her women's magazines, and had watched them grow and transform themselves into bright summer flowers. She had made something beautiful from almost nothing. It felt like magic. Wendy knew Hector didn't appreciate beauty – one spring she had planted out a whole bed of snapdragons, taking care to get the spaces between them exactly right, and he'd stood behind her and jeered. 'You should get a job in municipal gardening,' he'd said. 'They'd love those serried ranks.'

If she had known then that serried meant 'close set', she might have been able to think up a cutting reply, but of course she hadn't, so she couldn't. She sighed, and decided to try to forget about Hector at least for the rest of that day.

It finally began to get dark and, unusually for her, Wendy couldn't be bothered to change out of her gardening clothes. She brushed the loose soil from her knees, changed into more comfortable slippers, washed her hands, and then lounged in front of the television with Morgan and a glass of hock from her wine box. She remembered she hadn't yet taken anything out to un-freeze for supper, but didn't do anything about it. Morgan had requested spaghetti and convenience sauce out of a jar, so Hector could damn well eat the same. Why should she put herself out? Oh dear, she thought, looking down at her dirty trousers. Is this what they mean by 'letting yourself go'? Is this the beginning of the end?

At eight o'clock, after she and Morgan had eaten their supper and were again slouched in front of the box, they heard the front door opening and Hector coming in. About bloody time! Wendy thought, looking at her watch. I'll wait until

Morgan's gone to bed, and then he's going to have one hell of a lot of explaining to do.

But there were voices in the hall. Hector had some woman with him. Oh no! Wendy thought horrified. I look a complete and utter mess for the first time in my entire life and Hector has to choose this moment to bring visitors home without even warning me. I'll kill him!

'Do I look really mucky?' she asked Morgan anxiously.

'Well, you've got this big smudge of something on your forehead,' he said. 'I was going to tell you.'

Then the sitting-room door opened and Hector came in, and behind him was a skinny, defiant looking girl of about Morgan's age, wearing crumpled clothes and large black boots. Hector himself looked belligerent, and Wendy's heart sank. She recognised this attitude as a favourite strategy of his for countering criticism; attack always being his preferred form of defence.

'Ah, Wendy and Morgan,' Hector said firmly, putting an arm around the girl. 'I don't believe you've met my daughter Hannah?'

'I'm going to call the police,' Caroline announced at ten o'clock. 'There's still no reply from Hector's number, just a sodding answerphone. It's quite obvious to me that the bloody man's kidnapped her!'

'But Hector wouldn't do a thing like that,' Jess protested.

'So where is Hannah? We've looked everywhere. We've phoned all her friends. What other explanation is there?'

'But I saw him leave,' Jess said, 'and she wasn't with him, and anyway it would be virtually impossible to make Hannah go anywhere she didn't want to, without an almighty struggle and a lot of noise. Someone would have noticed!'

'No,' Caroline said despairingly. 'You don't understand. I didn't mean kidnapped as in "against her will". She probably hid in the boot for the first five minutes. That's why I'm feeling so desperate. I have this dreadful certainty that Hannah would do *anything* to get away from me.' She began to cry messily and with great gasping breaths. 'I've failed,' she sobbed, 'failed at the most important thing in life – being a mother!'

'No . . .' Jess soothed her, putting both arms around her,

and holding her tightly. 'You haven't, of course you haven't. It's all my fault. I'm so, so sorry. If only I hadn't let on that Hannah was Hector's daughter, then none of this would have happened.' She sounded tearful too.

After a moment or two, Caroline sniffed loudly and pulled back a little, so that she could meet her friend's eyes. 'It would probably all have come to the same thing in the end,' she admitted. 'I'm sorry I blamed you earlier. If I'm honest, I've known for some time that Hannah was just waiting for an excuse to get away from me. It's just . . . just that I can't believe that any responsible adult would connive at it with her. How could Hector do it? It's *sick*!'

'But I don't suppose . . .' Jess was interrupted by the sound of the telephone ringing. Caroline let out a muffled scream and almost pushed Jess over in her haste to disengage herself and rush to answer it.

'Sorry, sorry. Hello? . . . Oh Hannah darling! I've been so *worried*. Are you all right? Where are you?'

'In Somerset, at Hector's house,' Hannah sounded sulky. 'He made me phone you. Calm down, will you? It's no big deal.'

'What on earth do you mean? A man kidnaps you and . . .'

'Get real, Mum! It was no kidnap. I stowed away on the back seat of his car. He was, like, ballistic when he found out.'

'Ohhh . . .' Caroline felt about for the nearest chair and sank into it. There was a brief silence.

'You OK?' Hannah asked. 'Like you haven't fainted or nothing?'

'A fat lot you care,' Caroline managed to say.

'What d'you mean? I'm calling you, aren't I?'

'But I've been trying Hector's number for *hours*, and all I got was his damned machine!'

'Yeah, well, he switched it over when we got here. He said he needed quiet space, 'cos we had, like, stuff to discuss.'

'But you are all right?'

'Well I'm totally wrecked and the journey here was a bunch of arse, but yeah, I'm OK.'

After the first tremendous relief of discovering that Hannah was safe and well, Caroline began to be curious about the kind of reception that had awaited her. 'What's Hector's family like?'

'Oh Morgan's not exactly cool, but he's wicked at drawing. He's mad for it! You should see the stuff he does. He is SO talented.'

'And Wendy?'

'Well she was well gutted at first. Seems she didn't know nothing about me, nor Florian, Hector's other son. Hector'd decided to, like, give it to her straight, see, but Wendy just ran upstairs, and we could hear her bawling right through the ceiling. And then Hector wen' up and they had one heck of a row, like shouting and chucking stuff, and then she comes down all swollen up round the eyes, and she goes, "I'm sorry Hannah, this isn't any fault of yours," and I'm like, "That's OK," and then she makes us this huge bowl of spaghetti and stuff, like nothing's happened. It was well weird, I can tell you!'

'And what about Hector?'

'Oh he's toughing it out. He's the dog's, is Hector.'

'*PLEASE* Hannah! Do endeavour to talk proper English. All this mock Cockney street-speak is getting more than a little tedious. It's so *limited*!'

'Yeah, yeah.'

'So,' Caroline said briskly, 'when are you coming home? Get Hector to put you on a train, and I'll meet you at Paddington. Yes?'

'No way.'

'Whatever do you mean?'

'Just that. I like it here. The food's pukkah. I've never had a dad nor brothers before. End of story.'

'Now come on, Hannah. Don't be ridic . . .'

'Leave it, Mum, OK? It's been a long day and I'm wrecked. Oh, one more thing . . .'

'What?'

'Hector's showed me this huge portrait of my great-great-grandmother, yeah? On his study wall? So my name's not Hannah Moffat no more. Everyone's got to call me Gwladys Mudgeley. Right?' And she put the phone down.

Jess didn't know quite how to help Caroline. She felt guilty for having precipitated the crisis, and yet she knew logically that it wasn't her fault. It was Hector they should be blaming.

Jess supposed that she ought to feel antagonistic towards him as a result, and thought she did, but then again . . . This is no time for introspection, she thought wearily. I shall have to try to help sort things out, but first I'm going to make us both a milky drink to go to bed with. There's nothing more we can do tonight.

On her way out of the kitchen she noticed an envelope on the hall table, and went to investigate. It was in fact two envelopes. One had got caught under the unclosed flap of the other, and had become stuck there. Jess separated them out and saw that the outer one was for Caroline, but the inner one was addressed, also in Hector's writing, to Zillah Brakespear! Jess carried them both in to Caroline with the two mugs of hot chocolate.

'If he thinks he can buy me off . . .!' Caroline began, taking out the cheque. 'I've a good mind to tear it up!' Then she looked at it and hesitated.

'Is it for a lot?' Jess asked.

'It's pretty generous, yes.' Caroline admitted.

'Don't do anything rash,' Jess suggested. 'Wait until tomorrow, eh?' Then she produced the other envelope. 'I expect this is a cheque too. It got stuck to yours. I suppose Hector can't have noticed.'

'Zillah Brakespear,' Caroline read. 'Why don't we open it and see how much he's paying her!'

'Oh well . . .' Jess demurred, but Caroline had already torn the envelope, and was taking out Zillah's cheque.

'That's interesting,' she said. 'It's for an awful lot less.'

'He probably pays monthly,' Jess said. 'I wonder if she's missed it yet.'

'Oh he can always write her another one.'

'I've got a better idea,' Jess said. 'I could take it over to her when I'm down there next weekend, dealing with my flat. Hector's told me where she lives and I'd like to see her again, and maybe even meet the ghastly Florian!'

'If I wasn't so desperate to get myself a job, I'd come too,' Caroline said, 'but I daren't stop looking. Everything's such a mess! What am I going to do, Jess? How am I ever going to get Hannah back? I tell you something – first thing tomorrow, I really am going to phone the police!

The next morning Caroline did just that. She looks terrible, Jess thought, watching her, and feeling for her friend. I doubt if she's slept at all. She doesn't seem to be having much luck with the police either.

Finally, after an increasingly acrimonious conversation in which Caroline was reduced to shouting down the phone, she crashed the receiver down and rested her forehead on the tips of her fingers.

'No joy,' Jess said. It wasn't a question.

'They say it's a domestic problem,' Caroline said, 'and is therefore outside their remit. Can you believe that? The moment I told them Hannah was with her father, they completely lost interest. So what the hell do we do now?'

'I suppose you could try talking to her on the phone again?'

'You don't know Hannah like I do. Once she's decided to do something, she can be *so* stubborn. Even when she's made the most ghastly mistake, she'd die rather than admit as much to me. She can't bear to be in the wrong.'

'Well, maybe we should leave it as it is for a while?' Jess suggested. 'It's school holidays, so it's not crucial, and I'm sure Hector won't let her come to any harm.'

'I don't seem to have much choice in the matter,' Caroline said bitterly. 'God! Children – who'd have them!'

'It's funny,' Jess said, 'but now we know Hannah's safe, I'm starting to feel most sorry for Wendy in all this. Imagine what it must be like for her.'

'Yes, in spite of everything, she made Hannah some supper last night,' Caroline said, agreeing. 'You're right. That was pretty heroic. You can't blame someone for having been born, but I'm willing to bet that in those circumstances, most of us would have!'

'So you needn't worry any more, OK?' Jess said comfortingly. 'Hannah's perfectly all right for the time being.'

Even so, it was a long week. Jess had a lot of work on. Caroline was at last called to a couple of interviews. They compared notes each evening.

'Today's inquisition went well,' Caroline said. 'I almost dare to hope . . .'

'When will you hear?'

'They're seeing more candidates early next week in

Edinburgh, so I'm having to contain my impatience. Oh by the way, I got through to Hannah on the phone this afternoon.'

'And?'

'She says she's fine. It sounds as though Wendy isn't holding up too well though. Hannah says she's been spending a lot of time in bed, and when she does appear, she's quite obviously been crying. Apparently she's had to go to her doctor for sleeping pills.'

'Poor thing!'

'I know.'

'But Hannah's OK, that's good. Any hints about her eventually coming home?'

'None. It's like some ridiculous comedy routine. She won't answer unless I call her Gwladys, *Gwladys . . .!* And she won't discuss the future at all . . .'

'But she's happy? Couldn't you pretend to yourself that she's on holiday?'

Caroline sighed. 'It's not that easy. I need to *see* her; talk face to face.'

'So, come down to Somerset with me tomorrow.'

'I *can't* Jess. What if somebody phones about a job? I daren't leave London, just in case.'

'Well they're hardly likely to do so over the weekend, are they? Come with me, Caro. Have a break yourself. You can help me with the flat and then we can walk by the sea again, and go and see Zillah in her camp, as well as going to Hector's to sort Hannah out. Go on, spoil yourself – say you'll come?'

'Oh, what the hell,' Caroline said, giving in. 'Let's do it!'

23

Jess and Caroline left London very early on Saturday, driving westwards along the M4 and then south down the M5. It was a bright clear morning and still early in the year, being the week before Easter, but the lambs they saw in the fields alongside the motorway were already chunky and well past the charming stage.

'There are one or two things I've definitely got to do,' Jess said. 'I wouldn't mind popping into the *Chronicle* to see whoever's there, but the most important thing is to make sure the flat is clean and fully equipped for the season. I do like to see to it myself to make sure it really is done properly.'

'You should learn to delegate,' Caroline said.

'Should I?' Jess said. 'Why? Why is it that mastering the art of delegation is always considered to be such a virtue?'

'Well . . . I don't know really. I can't say I've ever analysed it, but it's clearly much more efficient. After all, no one should be indispensable.'

'Why?'

'Well it's obvious . . .'

'Because we've all been brainwashed into thinking we're just tiny cogs in the huge wheel of industry, and one cog is very much like another?'

'We can't all be rugged individualists like you, Jess!'

'Why not?'

'You sound just like Hannah used to, when she was at the "why" stage! Not that I was ever there long enough to give her proper answers,' Caroline sighed. 'That was certainly one hugely important thing that I delegated – the bringing up of my daughter – and look where it's got me.' She bit her lip.

'This is only a hiccup,' Jess said. 'You'll see. It'll all work out.'

'When we get there,' Caroline said, 'I'll phone Hannah straight away to tell her we're coming to see her.'

'Do it now if you like,' Jess said, indicating her mobile phone.

'No . . . she won't be up yet. I'll wait until we get there.'

When they arrived, and Caroline had taken a few deep breaths to calm herself, she did telephone Hannah, wandering round the small kitchen whilst Jess made coffee and some toast for breakfast. It sounded like an unsatisfactory conversation, but Jess could hear only half of it.

'Could I speak to Hannah please?'

'But this is Hector Mudgeley's number?'

'Oh for heavens sake, *Gwladys* then!'

'Darling? How are you? Well I just thought I'd phone . . .'

'No I'm here, in Somerset, at Jess's flat. We thought we'd come round . . .'

'But Hannah . . .'

'But *Gwladys*, I'm not interfering. I just . . .' Caroline put the phone down slowly. 'She hung up on me,' she said. 'She doesn't want to see us. She says if we go round there today, she'll run off! So what the hell do we do now?'

'Drink this,' Jess said, putting down a mug of coffee. 'It's a tricky one, isn't it. How about getting on with the boring stuff today, and waiting until tomorrow to go to Hector's?'

'I wanted to see Hannah *at once*,' Caroline said, 'but I suppose you're right.' She took a gulp of coffee. 'Oh dear, patience never was my forte.'

But soon afterwards she pulled herself together and elected to begin on the housework. Jess, who had always admired her, now saw that her regard was well-deserved for although Caroline was clearly worried and upset, she was still able to discipline herself to get on with the job in hand.

'Why don't you go round to the *Chronicle* now?' Caroline suggested, 'while I make a start on this.'

'Well, if you're sure?' Jess said. 'Great. I'll be as quick as I can.'

It was years since Caroline had dusted anything. As she went round the flat she felt rather like a child playing at being grown up, and the thought entertained her. Jess, as promised, was soon back.

'Hoovering is quite fun for a change, isn't it,' Caroline remarked to her, as she pounded up and down the carpet in the living room.

'*Fun?* It's the thing I most loathe doing!'

'How was the *Chronicle*?'

'Oh fine. Nigel was there on weekend duty. It was lovely to see him, but strange to be back in that atmosphere again. The new building even smells like the old one now. Some sad news though; Nige says last month's best unused headline was: *Nightmare Mother-in-law Drives Wife into Arms of Vicar*. It sounds right up Barry's street; the sort of story he most loves to write, but for one thing.'

'What?'

'It's his wife, Jackie, who's run off! So Barry's been left to bring up the four children on his own, and the horrible irony is that his awful old mother, who was the cause of all the bother, died the week after Jackie left! Poor Barry. Life always seems to shit on him from a great height. He's having to work part-time and is even thinking of giving up his job altogether and living on social security.'

'That's dreadful.'

'I know. Certainly makes you think. Now, what's next?'

They went out and bought some more plates and mugs, and collected current leaflets from the Tourist Office. They took blankets to the launderette, and replaced three light bulbs. They bought a plunger to unblock the lavatory, and had two extra keys cut. And then they went for a long walk by the sea to unwind, and to work up an appetite for supper.

The tide was in, and the sun glinted on the incoming waves as they spread their line of foam on the sand in a brief fizz of white with each gentle approach. The two friends walked there, where the sand was damp and firm underfoot, and they stared out over the Bristol Channel at the pair of islands, one steep and one flat, which today were blue-sharp in outline. The smell of the sea lingered in their nostrils, and the cool breeze lifted their hair and waved it around their faces. Herring gulls hung overhead, trumpeting. Behind them, nearer to the pier, the first families of the season sat, wrapped in anoraks and eating ice creams, but the beach ahead was empty and inviting.

'Race you to that washed-up oil drum!' Jess challenged, beginning to run.

'Cheat!' Caroline cried, starting after her.

'What d'you fancy – Chinese, Indian or Italian?' Jess asked breathlessly as they got there together, and stopped to admire the view.

'Indian,' Caroline said at once. 'I could murder a biryani. D'you know, Jess, if I wasn't so worried about Hannah, this could be the best weekend I've had in years!'

Caroline woke next morning puzzled as to where she was, and for a split second before she remembered about Hannah, she felt gloriously free. Then, guiltily, she decided that whatever Hannah/Gwladys said, she couldn't put it off any longer. She must attempt to see her at once.

At breakfast she began to get cold feet again and Jess, alert to this possibility, suggested they might first go over towards Glastonbury, find Zillah's camp and give her the cheque.

'And then,' she promised, 'we'll go and sort out Hector and Co.'

It took about an hour to reach Zillah, but Caroline was happy to sit back and be driven, able to look at the view and to notice with pleasure a single heron on guard beside one of the many drainage ditches.

'I wonder why they're called that?' she said to Jess, as she commented on it in passing. 'The ditches, I mean – spelt r-h-y-n-e-s but pronounced 'reens'. She was looking forward to meeting Zillah, and intrigued to discover what Hector's other teenage bastard would be like. But in this last, she was to be disappointed. Florian was not there.

'He's never here,' Zillah explained. 'Even if he had a ball and chain attached to both ankles, he'd find some way of disappearing.'

She had seemed pleased to see Jess after the initial blankness of pre-recognition, and Caroline was relieved about this, because her first impressions of the camp were unequivocally negative. As they arrived it had come on to rain, a sudden April shower which transformed the ground in the centre of the camp, in moments, into a mudbath. Zillah hadn't seemed to notice the state of their shoes as she welcomed them inside, and Caroline, having looked about her at first for somewhere to wipe her feet, realised pretty soon that it was her own unsuitable ensemble that needed protecting from Zillah's caravan, rather than the other way around.

'Would you like to try some of this,' Zillah offered, producing a half-full bottle and three tumblers. 'Dandelion wine.'

'I wouldn't,' counselled an earnest child in glasses, from a bunk high on the wall. 'Tastes like cough mixture!'

'This is Alaric,' Zillah said. 'Off you go now, and read in the other room, OK?' The boy climbed down with a good grace, holding a large book in one hand. Caroline noticed with amazement that it was *War and Peace, volume two.*

'Is that the sort of thing he always reads?' she asked when he had gone and shut the door behind him.

'Yes,' Zillah said matter-of-factly. 'He's a genius. My eldest is pretty bright too. My only mistake was in letting Hector father the middle one.'

'Mine too,' Caroline said, charmed out of her usual reserve by the other woman's unexpected candour. 'My only one, that is.'

'Really?' Zillah looked interested. 'Boy or girl?'

'She's a girl. Her name's Hannah.'

'Easy or difficult?'

'Well just at the moment, very difficult indeed!'

'There you are,' Zillah said triumphantly. 'Bad blood! I always said so.'

Caroline smiled at her. She was certainly a good-looking woman – late thirties, early forties? She was living in a total hugger-mugger, even a slum, and yet she seemed completely assured and unapologetic about it. She didn't rush round frantically trying to tidy things away, saying 'Oh dear, you've caught me at a bad moment. I was just about to spring clean' as a lesser person might have done. She didn't even clear spaces for them to sit down, but seemed happy that they should push piles of clothes and books aside themselves for that purpose. Caroline, to her surprise, found this refreshingly admirable. Here was someone entirely comfortable in herself, who didn't give a damn what anyone else thought. She smiled again and drank deeply of the home-made wine. It was rather sweet for her taste, but still welcome. A tortoiseshell kitten roused itself from its sleep further along her bench seat and seemed inclined to arrange itself more comfortably on her lap. Caroline edged away and fended it off, but the kitten persisted.

'Push her down,' Zillah advised. 'Or you'll get hairs all over yourself.' She seemed to be waiting for them to declare their purpose.

'We came to give you this,' Jess said, handing over the cheque. 'It got mixed up with Caroline's one, by mistake.'

'Well, thank God for that!' Zillah exclaimed, taking it. 'About time too! I've been on my beam ends this month. I've even tried going up to the phone box and ringing Hector's house, but his wife always answers the damn thing so I've just had to put it down. I've been getting desperate, I can tell you!'

'Oh dear,' Jess said. 'I'm sorry to hear . . .'

'Florian's in trouble again you see. There's this huge fine to pay for his truancy from school, and no way I can cover it. And why should I? I reckon Hector should cough up. More wine?' Caroline accepted a top up. 'Does he pay you monthly?' Zillah asked her.

'He hasn't paid me anything until recently. I didn't want to be beholden.'

'I'd take whatever's going,' Zillah advised at once. 'He's rich enough!'

'But he's never tried to dodge his responsibilities,' Jess put in.

'Mmmm' Zillah said. 'That's a moot point. I've a good mind to go round there and have it out with him face to face. If I had transport I would! I've only held back this far out of consideration for Wendy, because she was nice to Florian years ago.' She sipped her wine. 'What's she like?'

'We think she's having a bad time,' Jess said. 'She's only just found out about Hannah and Florian, and it seems she's really upset.'

'Oh he's finally told her, has he?' Zillah said. 'I was always amazed she didn't guess, way back, but there you are. Funny how easily people can be conned, isn't it? And it's not only the Wendys of this world who fall for it! What is it about Hector, do you suppose? I'll admit he's sexy . . .'

'And he has a certain obvious charm,' Caroline said.

'He's entertaining,' Jess said defensively. 'And I've certainly not been conned by him.' She'd gone pink.

'Mmmm' Zillah said again. 'Perhaps you could speak to him for me then?'

Caroline drained her glass and put it down. She was beginning to feel almost comfortable in this grotty caravan. So, I'll be covered in dust and hairs when I leave, she thought. So what? She looked at Jess, who was smiling at the kitten as it tried to scale the curtains. She caught her eye and raised an eyebrow.

'Well, I suppose we'd better be off,' Jess said, taking the hint and getting up.

'Look Zillah,' Caroline said on impulse, 'why don't you come too? We're going over to Hector's now, to try to persuade my daughter to come home. You could help us to teach him a lesson.'

'But,' Jess said quickly, 'what about Alaric?'

'Oh he's very sensible,' Zillah said. 'I could ask Rose in the next van to keep an eye, but he can make his own lunch, no bother.'

'So will you?' Caroline was keen to co-opt all available moral support.

'Well, how would I get home?'

'Oh we'd give you a lift back, of course, wouldn't we Jess.'

'Well . . . yes I . . .'

'Right,' Zillah said crisply. 'Let's go.'

Ever since Hector had sprung his daughter on her without warning and then selfishly, to 'make a clean breast of everything', had told her at the same time that Florian was his son, Wendy had felt bewildered and wretched. It was as though the whole world, which she had always known and trusted, had suddenly been revealed to be a mirage, and everybody but her had known it all along. She felt betrayed and despised and, yes, stupid too. She didn't know what to say, how to react, what to *do*.

Her first action had been to scream at Hector, but eventually she'd thought about the girl downstairs, and how she must be feeling, and how it wasn't *her* fault. So Wendy had made a supreme effort to act with dignity, and had cooked them some supper. She couldn't understand half of what the girl said, but she and Morgan seemed to hit it off at once, mostly on account of his drawings. Hannah/Gwladys seemed to think they were remarkable. She said Morgan ought to train as an architect; that he could be famous! They were getting on so well together that Hector was beginning to look miffed. Wendy almost smiled.

But then, as the days went by, all the negative aspects of the situation caught up with her, and she was overcome with despair. She began staying in bed, sleepless and unable to stop weeping. She couldn't bear to go out, and so Hector was obliged to do the shopping. She wasn't hungry, and the very thought of cooking made her ill so she stopped doing any. She saw the confusion on the faces of those around her and, for once, she couldn't care. Everything seemed futile, hopeless. She found even the smallest decision too hard to make. Depression had closed in around her and had crushed all her initiative. What was the point? Her husband didn't love her. Her son didn't need her. She didn't want to have to face another day.

After Hannah had been with them for a week, things came to a head for Wendy. She felt she couldn't go on. Her home, her privacy, her *life* had been invaded and she was expected to behave as though nothing had happened. How long would Hannah stay? Would Hector expect Florian to join them too? How would she cope? Why *should* she cope? But where would she go if she couldn't? She had a car, but no money and no convenient relatives or friends to escape to (except for Ifor and June who might side with Hector). She felt trapped, and it was unendurable.

It was mid-morning, and the Sunday papers lay in roughly folded heaps where Hector had left them. Hannah and Morgan had gone out for a walk by the sea. Hector, clearly quite unable to deal with this new boneless Wendy, had brought her up a cup of tea.

'D'you need anything?' he asked, assuming a *you-know-I'm-useless-at-this-sort-of-thing-but-you're-putting-me-in-an-impossible-position-and-I'm-doing-my-absolute-best* sort of expression. Wendy knew that he expected her to rally at this and become normal again, but she hadn't the will or the energy even to try.

'No.'

'Well, is there anything I can do?'

'No.'

'Oh . . . well you see it's just that Ifor's invited me to play golf at his club today. We arranged it weeks ago, but I don't like to leave you like this.' Wendy said nothing. She didn't care whether he stayed or went. It was all the same to her. 'So . . . will you be OK, if I go?'

'Yes.'

'You're sure?'

'Yes.'

'Well . . .' Hector was looking infinitely relieved. 'I'll go then, but I won't be long, I promise.'

Wendy watched without emotion as he escaped thankfully from her. She waited for ten minutes to make sure he really had gone, and then she went into the bathroom and got her bottle of sleeping pills. With an odd flash of the old Wendy, she decided she didn't want to die in her nightie in bed, but fully clothed and decent downstairs. So she dressed and went down into the front room. Then she sat on the sofa with a half-bottle of Hector's whisky, and began deliberately to swallow all the pills.

Jess drove Caroline and Zillah back northwards, trying to concentrate on her driving, but feeling muddled and anxious. She could appreciate that Hector was behaving badly; there was no gainsaying that. But she still couldn't believe that he was being deliberately cruel . . . well yes, sometimes he wasn't exactly kind . . . but there was nothing actively mal-evolent about him. He hadn't got himself into these situations on purpose – they had somehow come about by unfortunate tricks of fate. They weren't entirely his fault. Jess wasn't at all keen on this coming confrontation, but in Zillah's caravan she had felt outvoted. If Wendy was really as upset as Hannah had said, then perhaps it was more than a little unwise . . .? And knowing Hector, he'd slip imperturbably away, and they'd be left (as ever) to cope with the mess he'd left behind.

But, Jess thought, why is it that I still feel so partisan? I can't seem to help it. I suppose I must be fond of the man. I certainly don't want to see him humiliated. Oh dear . . . She glanced round. Caroline and Zillah seemed to be getting on very well indeed. That dandelion wine must be an excellent social lubricant, Jess thought. I'm sure they have nothing in common, except Hector.

When they arrived at Hector's house and drove up his steep drive, the only car parked at the top was a small hatchback which had to be Wendy's. Jess began to hope rather fervently that Hector wouldn't be at home. She could feel her chest all tight with apprehension, and her hands were suddenly clammy. We shouldn't have come, she thought. It's a mistake. She hung back as the others got out, went to the front door and rang the bell. Jess expected that the sound of three slammed car doors and the noise of the bell would elicit some response from those inside, but no one came. She began to relax a fraction.

'Trust Hannah not to be here,' Caroline said rather shakily.

Zillah rang the bell again and hammered on the door. Still no one.

Jess felt ridiculously relieved. 'Oh well,' she said, 'better luck next time, eh?' But Zillah had walked over and was holding up her hands to her face so she could peer in through one of the front windows.

'There's someone here,' she called, 'a woman lying on a sofa.'

'Must be Wendy,' Jess said. 'Is she asleep? Don't let's wake her . . .'

'No,' Zillah said, knocking on the glass. 'She's not moving. She doesn't look right to me. I'm going inside to make sure. I'll break in if necessary.'

'Oh,' Jess protested, 'do you really think we sh . . .?'

But Zillah had run to the front door and was turning the handle. It opened, and she went inside. Jess and Caroline looked at each other, eyebrows raised. Then they heard Zillah shout and were galvanised into motion themselves. They ran indoors. Wendy, pale and unconscious, was sprawled on the sofa. Her half-shut eyes revealed two white half-moons with no visible irises.

'Overdose,' Zilla said, indicating the empty pill bottle and the half-drunk whisky.

'Oh my God!' Jess cried. 'We must get an ambulance!'

'Better idea,' Caroline said, 'and quicker. We'll drive her straight to Casualty. Here, help me carry her out to the car. Bring the pill bottle!'

Even with three of them working together, Wendy was remarkably heavy and floppy. They managed to ease her into the back seat of Jess's car, and Zillah got in as well to support her head. Jess was about to get into the driving seat, when Caroline stopped her.

'No, I'll drive, and Zillah can look after Wendy. You stay here, Jess. Someone has to break the news to Hector, and you're the best person for that job.'

'But . . .' Jess began, 'what about Hannah?'

'Hannah can wait. This is more important.'

'But . . .' Jess said again. Caroline was inside her car and had started the engine. 'You'll let me know what . . .?' Jess's voice tailed off.

'We'll see you at the hospital,' Caroline called, winding down the window and moving off, 'just as soon as you and Hector can make it. OK?'

Then they were gone. Jess sat down suddenly on the front doorstep, feeling weak and shivery and utterly useless.

24

HECTOR got back from golf in a good mood. It had been a hard fought match but he had played better than usual, and his final putt had been a positive triumph! He hummed to himself as he drove up his drive with a flourish. Then he remembered Wendy as he parked in front of the garage, and thought, Oh Lord, I hope to goodness she's got herself together by now. I just don't know what to say to the woman when she's in this mood. He got out of the car and was just closing the door, when Morgan dashed out of the house, followed by Hannah.

'Dad!' Morgan shouted, 'we've got to go to the hospital *NOW*! Mum's O.D.'d'

'What?' Hector didn't understand. 'Jess? What are you doing here?' She had also emerged. She looked pale and agitated.

'Drive us to the hospital, Hector,' she said. 'I'll explain as we go.'

After she had told him what Wendy had done, Hector was astonished. He couldn't believe that his wife would try to *kill* herself. He said so over and over again, shaking his head in disbelief as he irritably negotiated the crawling Sunday afternoon traffic.

'You sound, like, cross.' Hannah observed from the back seat.

'I'm UPSET,' Hector retorted, glaring at her through the rear-view mirror. 'Of course I'm bloody upset!'

He became even more belligerent when the lorry in front of them had a minor collision with a bus going in the opposite direction and blocked the road, holding them up for all of five minutes. When the four of them, stressed and anxious, finally got to Casualty, they found Caroline and Zillah sitting side by side, waiting.

'She's going to be all right,' Caroline said at once, rising to greet them. 'We got her here in time. They've just told us.'

'You mean she isn't going to die?' Morgan asked.

'No, she'll be all right.'

Morgan sat down suddenly on one of the waiting room chairs and knuckled his eyelids, and Hannah, ignoring her mother, sat down too and put an arm around his shoulders.

'Phew . . .!' Hector said, letting out a long breath. 'Well, that is a relief!' He glanced round. The women seemed to be looking at him strangely. 'I can't imagine how you all came to be there at the crucial moment,' he said. 'But thank goodness you were!'

'Oh . . . I'm just so, so thankful she'll be OK,' Jess said in a wobbly voice. 'If Zillah hadn't thought to look through that window . . . I dread to think . . .' Then she went over and hugged Caroline. 'And you were wonderful!'

Hector saw to his surprise that they were both in tears.

'Look,' Zillah said, standing up also, 'I need to talk to you about money, Hector Mudgeley, but now is clearly not the time. I must get home to Alaric.'

'I'll drive you,' Jess said at once. 'What about you, Caroline?'

'I've got to be back in London tonight, I'm afraid,' Caroline said. 'I daren't stay away any longer. Will you come with me, Hannah?'

'*Gwladys*,' Hannah said without looking up. 'Of course not. Can't you see I'm needed here?'

Caroline sighed and prepared to leave, patting her eyes with a tissue from her handbag without smearing her make-up. Jess put an arm through hers and then, reaching for Zillah, linked up with her too, and the three women thus united said their goodbyes.

'Well thanks again,' Hector said. 'I don't know quite what we should have done without you . . .' He was relieved when they'd gone. It had felt almost as if they were ganging up on him! He went over to the desk and asked to see his wife. 'In a little while,' he was told, so he went back to sit beside Morgan and Hannah.

Morgan had now recovered himself enough to ask, 'Why did she do it, Dad?'

'Who knows,' Hector said sadly. 'Mysterious are the minds of womenkind.'

'She did it,' Hannah said, turning on him furiously, 'because of me and Florian. *Like, it's OBVIOUS!'*

As Jess drove Zillah and Caroline away from the hospital, she decided she would remain in Somerset for at least one more day. Work would have to be juggled to fit in somehow. She needed to satisfy herself that Wendy was really all right, and Hector too.

'Let's take Zillah home first,' Caroline suggested, 'and then go back to your flat to collect my things, and then perhaps you could put me on a train, unless you're planning on driving straight back to London yourself, that is?'

'No,' Jess said. 'I'm staying on for a while.'

The journey back to Zillah's camp was a much more subdued affair than the outward one. They stopped *en route* for a quick bite of lunch, and Caroline wanted to hear what had happened to Jess after she and Zillah had taken Wendy to hospital.

'I waited for what seemed like an eternity,' Jess told her, 'and then Morgan and Hannah got back literally minutes before Hector arrived. The kids were all for leaving a note for him and taking Wendy's car to go straight to Casualty, but luckily he turned up in the nick of time. It would have been so horrible for him to have found out that way.'

'Oh I don't know,' Caroline said rather acidly, sipping coffee and swallowing. 'He didn't seem exactly distraught, did he.'

Jess ignored this. 'I must ask you,' she said to Zillah, 'what made you look through that front window? Thank goodness you did, but why?'

'I had a premonition,' Zillah said, simply.

After that, no one felt much like small talk, so they finished their sandwiches and got back on the road. When they finally arrived and drew up by Zillah's caravan, they found Florian sitting nonchalantly on an upturned bucket, drawing lazily on a spliff, with Alaric sitting astride the motorbike, giggling.

'Where have you *been*?' Zillah said to him, getting out of the car.

'Oh, here and there,' Florian said easily. 'But I'm back now, aren't I?'

'Only just!' Alaric slipped in. 'This bike's red ho . . .' Florian quelled him with a look.

'And I told you not to smoke dope here!' Zillah said sharply.

'So I'll go somewhere else,' Florian replied equably. 'No sweat.' He got to his feet and wandered off a little way, a tall, thin figure in dirty jeans and a holey, black T-shirt.

His hair looks matted like a shrunken jersey! Jess thought. How does he wash it? Maybe he doesn't! I'm so glad I don't have to struggle with a son like that.

'Well,' Zillah said to them, at the open car window, 'that's that, then.'

'I'm sorry it all turned out to be so pointless for you,' Jess said.

'Can't be helped. Come and see me next time you're passing?'

'Right. Thanks.'

As Jess and Caroline prepared to go, two huge mongrels bounded round the vans and made straight for their car. 'Watch out!' Jess called. Caroline let out a squeak of alarm, and they both rapidly wound up their windows. As they drove away, Jess looked in her mirror and saw that Florian had taken charge, and both dogs were now lying on their backs in front of him as he squatted down on the dusty ground, tickling their tummies.

'Well, I'm not going back there in a hurry!' Caroline said with feeling.

'Me neither. How d'you think Florian can afford drugs?'

By the time they got back to Jess's flat, and Caroline had packed her things, and they'd phoned for the time of the next train to London, Jess was beginning to feel quite exhausted. She drove her friend to the railway station, and waited for the train to leave. Caroline slid down the window and leant out.

'Thanks for coming,' Jess said. 'I'm only sorry it's been such a wash-out from your point of view – about Hannah, I mean.'

Caroline made a rueful face. 'Oh well,' she said. 'I suppose I should be grateful she's not Florian!' Jess managed a smile. 'Take care,' Caroline said, 'and I'll see you when you get back.'

The guard raised an arm and blew his whistle. Jess reached

up to give her a kiss, and then the carriage began to move. She waved, feeling the tears rising in her eyes, and by the time the train had gathered momentum, she found she was crying in earnest. She walked slowly away, keeping her head down so no one would notice.

The flat seemed very empty when she got back to it. She poured herself a long drink, using up all that was left in Caroline's bottle of gin, and adding vermouth and tonic to finish them off too. Then she sat in solitary confusion in an armchair and tried to recover her habitual optimism. At least, she said to herself firmly, at least Wendy didn't *die*.

The next morning she felt only marginally better. She waited until a reasonably social hour and then rang Hector's number.

'Hello? Is that Morgan? Is your father in?'

When Hector came to the phone he grumbled, 'Jess? It's only half-past eight! I thought for a moment there was another crisis!'

'Sorry,' Jess apologised. 'I just wanted to know how you are?'

'Angry,' Hector said. 'We've been burgled! Must have happened when we were at the hospital. Someone left the front door open.'

'Oh no!' Jess felt immediately guilt-stricken. 'Was much taken?'

'Only stuff that could be carried easily: Wendy's jewellery, some money, credit cards, that sort of thing. I suppose I should be grateful he didn't carry off the telly or the video or my computer as well!'

'Do the police know who did it?'

'Unfortunately, yes. They seem to have a pretty good idea. A youth with long red hair (would you believe?) was seen riding down my drive on a motorbike. No prizes for guessing who that might be!'

'Oh dear, Hector, I'm so sorry. Have they caught him yet?'

'Don't know, and can't say I care very much either. It's Zillah I feel sorry for (apart from myself, that is!).'

'Yes . . . Does Wendy know?'

'Not yet. I don't want her any more upset.'

'No, of course not. When are you going in to see her?'

'Ten-ish. Want to come?'

'No . . . you'd better go on your own. Maybe I'll go this afternoon.'

'Come round here, why don't you? I'd pop over to yours, but for the kids, and the fact that I told the police I'd be here.'

'No Hector . . . I don't think so, not for the moment anyway. So, how was Wendy when you saw her last night?'

'Bit groggy, but entirely *compos mentis*, thank God.'

'Was she very unhappy still?'

'Well she certainly wasn't a barrel of laughs, but they're giving her anti-depressants, and they're organizing some counselling, psychotherapy, that sort of thing. They reckon that should sort her out.'

'Oh,' Jess said, 'good.'

'If you change your mind, Jessy-boot,' Hector said. 'Do come. I could do with your company.'

'Right,' Jess said. ''Bye.' She put the phone down. I will go and lend Hector some solidarity, she thought to herself, but first I should like to see Wendy.

When Wendy had initially regained consciousness in the late afternoon of her 'cry for help', her inability even to end things satisfactorily weighed as heavily upon her as all her other deficiencies. I'm so useless, she thought despairingly. I can't even make a go of killing myself!

However, at least in hospital you didn't have to make any effort. You could just lie there and everything would be done for you. Hector had got her a private room, of course, and for once she was reconciled to the privilege. Some of the nurses were really kind. Pills and sympathy, Wendy thought, beats tea any day.

But there was one nurse who clearly considered attempted suicide to be a sin, and was very disapproving of her. Wendy gained the distinct impression that she believed hospital beds should be reserved for people who were ill through no fault of their own. Her attitude made Wendy feel angry. I've just as much right! she thought. Who does she think she is?

She was still cross the following morning, and she found she was strengthened by it. She discovered to her surprise that feeling angry could be a positive experience. She had got some of her spirit back! She began to think, I don't have to put up with things. I *can* say what *I* want. I don't have to stay with Hector . . .

But this thought frightened her with its implications for future decisions and change. It wasn't the time to be thinking like this. She wasn't yet strong enough to cope. She tried to stop thinking at all. The pills they had given her were making her drowsy. She clutched at sleep gratefully.

When she next awoke, it was to find Hector sitting on her bed.

'I've just seen the first swallow of the year,' he said cheerfully. Wendy closed her eyes again. 'Don't tell me,' he said. 'I know one swallow doesn't make a silver lining, but it's a start isn't it?'

'Stop it, Hector,' Wendy said, eyes still closed.

'Sorry?'

'If you're going to talk at all, then say something that really matters.'

'I was just trying to cheer you up,' Hector said.

'Well don't!' Wendy opened her eyes. Hector was looking hurt. Don't let him get to you like that! Wendy counselled herself. Don't automatically feel you have to look after him. *You're* the one who needs love and attention. If he won't give you any, then to hell with him! She closed her eyes again.

'So, how are you, Wend?'

'I've just tried to kill myself,' Wendy said. 'How d'you think I am?'

'Well,' Hector said, 'I really don't know. That's why I asked.' There was a silence. 'Well, what shall we talk about then?'

'Tell me what's been happening. Is Morgan all right?'

'Well he was worried naturally, but he's OK now. He's written you this letter. I'll bring him to see you tomorrow. D'you know Wend, I really do think this architecture career of his might work out. Wouldn't that be wonderful?'

'I love Morgan for what he is, not for what he does,' Wendy said.

'Yes, well . . . so do I of course . . . but . . .' Hector subsided into silence again.

Wendy began to feel that for once in their relationship she had the upper hand, and it gave her a *frisson* of pleasure. She opened her eyes to watch Hector squirm some more, and then relented fractionally. 'What about you?' she asked.

'Oh, I'm all right, well except for the bur . . .'

'The what?'

'Nothing,' Hector said hastily.

'Come on Hector, spit it out!'

'Well I don't want to upset you . . .'

'Why break the habit of a lifetime?'

'Don't be like that, Wendy. I'm doing my best.'

'So what were you going to say?'

'Oh it's nothing much. We had a few small things nicked from the house. I've cancelled all the credit cards, so it's no big deal.'

'They won't catch whoever did it,' Wendy said wearily. 'They never do these days.'

'I thought you'd be all upset.'

'Why? I'll tell you something, Hector, nearly dying really brings home to you what's important and what isn't. But I don't suppose you'd understand a thing like that.'

'Of course I would!' Hector said, stung. 'And anyway, you're wrong in this instance. They *do* know who did it.'

'Who?'

'Florian.'

Wendy began to laugh weakly, and then it increased until she was shaking all over and nearly choking with uncontrollable mirth.

'You're hysterical!' Hector exclaimed in alarm, jumping to his feet and ringing for a nurse.

'Can't be . . .' Wendy gasped hoarsely, trying to get some air between coughing fits. 'I had it all . . . cut out . . . remember?' Then the nurse came and gave her a sedative, and she vaguely saw Hector being escorted out of the room, before succumbing once more to blessed oblivion.

The next time she awoke, it was to find the nurse bending over her.

'Your sister's here to see you, Mrs Mudgeley.'

'Haven't got a sister,' Wendy said crossly, and heard the nurse saying, 'She's still a little confused. I'll leave you two together.' Wendy opened her eyes properly. 'Jess?'

'Sorry, I didn't mean to wake you. Sorry about the "sister"

stuff too, but I wanted to see you, and they wouldn't let non-family members in.'

This was a new Jess, Wendy saw, with a designer haircut, and wearing smart clothes, even some subtle make-up. It was a great improvement. No wonder Hector . . .

'You must be feeling dreadful,' Jess said. 'Poor you. But thank goodness you look a lot better than you did!'

'I'm not with you?'

'When we found you, I mean,' Jess said.

'*You* found me?'

'Yes. Didn't Hector tell you?' Wendy made a dismissive movement with her head. 'Actually,' Jess ventured, 'I was afraid you might be very annoyed to have been discovered before . . . you know.'

Wendy frowned. 'No,' she said. 'I'm not quite sure what I feel yet, but it isn't annoyed.'

'Oh, that's a relief!'

'So tell me,' Wendy asked. 'What happened?' She motioned her to sit on the bed, and encouraged her to relate the whole story. 'Great!' Wendy said, when she'd finished. 'Isn't that bloody typical? I owe my life to Hector's three fancy women!' Jess looked taken aback. 'I guessed,' Wendy said, looking challengingly at her. 'I'm not completely stupid!'

'Oh no,' Jess said at once. 'It's not like that at all. Hector and I have never been lovers. Really and truly!' She looked so open and honest, that Wendy's certainty wavered.

'You're trying to tell me that you're *just good friends*?' I mean to say, Wendy thought, why have you come here if you aren't feeling guilty?

'Yes.' Jess frowned and looked at her shoes. Then she straightened up. 'To be honest, it might well have been more, but we felt we . . . so we didn't.' She stopped in confusion.

'Oh I SEE,' Wendy said. 'Hector tried it on, and you weren't having any. Is that it?'

'Well . . . not exactly . . .' Jess looked extremely uncomfortable.

She's either lying, Wendy thought, or she's trying to protect Hector. Either way, she isn't on my side. Then she thought, I'm ill. I don't have to put up with anything I don't want to.

'Before you go,' she said, 'answer me one thing. Was it you

who kept ringing Hector, and putting the phone down when I answered?'

'No,' Jess said.

'Well, who then?'

'It was probably Zillah, wanting to speak to Hector about money.'

Wendy snorted. 'And when I think how short the bloody man's kept me, over the years . . .'

'Must have been tough.'

'You don't know the half of it,' Wendy retorted, closing her eyes and lying back on her pillows.

'Well,' Jess said uncertainly. 'I'm so glad you're all right. Well of course I don't mean all right, exactly . . . but, you know. Um . . . perhaps I'd better be going . . . I don't want to tire you out.'

'You want Hector?' Wendy said suddenly, surprising even herself. She opened her eyes wide and started straight at Jess. 'You take him! I'm finished with the bastard!'

'Oh, but . . .' Jess now looked rattled.

'And pass me that letter, over there. It's from Morgan and I haven't read it yet.' Jess obediently handed it over. Wendy tore it open, and read:

Dere mum – I hop yore alrit. Hanna worris that it her faught butt I sed yoo woodent blaym her aw floryine. Get well and cume hom soon. lots of luve morgan XXX.

'Well, I'd better be going . . .' Jess began again nervously.

'Stay and read this!' Wendy ordered. She felt extraordinarily powerful. Jess took the letter from her and read it obediently. 'Oh, poor Hannah,' she said. 'You don't . . .?'

'Blame her? Of course not. Will you talk to her, Jess? Explain it's nothing whatever to do with her.'

'I'll certainly try,' Jess assured her. 'Wasn't it good of Morgan to write to you on her account.'

'You don't know how good,' Wendy said. 'He *never* writes letters.'

'Talking of which,' Jess said. 'Here's my address in London.' She wrote it quickly on a page from her notebook, tore it off and offered it to Wendy.

'What for?'

'Well, I sort of feel I'd like to help. For instance, you might need a temporary bolt-hole . . .'

'Doubt it,' Wendy said, making no attempt to take it. Jess hesitated and then put it down on the end of the bed.

'Did you really mean it?' Jess ventured. 'The bit about being finished with Hector?' She looked more confused than hopeful, Wendy noticed.

'I've really no idea,' Wendy said. 'But if I am, then one thing's for sure: it'll be him that leaves our house, not me and Morgan. After all the work I've put into it, I'm not giving it up for anyone! Anyway, it's always the wife and children that get the house.'

'Not always,' Jess said. 'Not in Barry's case.'

'What d'you mean?' So Jess told her about Barry's marriage breaking up.

'I never did like that Jackie,' Wendy said, and as she spoke, her whole body began to tingle and feel as if it was part of a real person again. She felt suddenly – what was the word? . . . Yes . . . – *worthy* again. Would it last? Was this a renewal of hope? What if she and Barry . . . ? She closed her eyes, the better to savour this outside chance.

'I'm sorry,' Jess said. 'I've exhausted you. I must go.'

Wendy kept her eyes shut and heard her leaving and the door closing behind her. Then she sat up and read Jess's address, before folding it carefully and putting it in her handbag. You never know when I might need this, she thought. It *is* worth going on. I wasn't meant to die.

25

AFTER Jess had left Wendy, she felt relieved but also upset.
Of course she was glad that Wendy had survived, but she
had been affected by her anger, and was also apprehensive at
the thought of a freshly semi-detached Hector. She would
have to go and see him, of course, but only briefly to say
goodbye, and then she would drive straight back home to
London. I've got loads of work to get on with, she thought.
That should distract me.

Hector was delighted to see her. He enveloped her in a
bear-hug at the door. 'Thank goodness you're here!'

'I can't stay, Hector. I've only come to say goodbye.' Jess
saw a movement on the landing above, but couldn't tell who
it was. 'I just wanted to make sure you're all right.'

'Well it isn't every week one's wife attempts suicide,' Hector
said, making a brave gesture, 'but under the circumstances . . .'

'Of course,' Jess said. 'And the kids?'

'Well they're my only source of hope really. Hannah's a bit
of a handful as you'd expect, but *at last* I've begun to get closer
to Morgan.'

'Oh good!'

'It is. I have to say this, Jess, even though he is my son (so
it seems like boasting), but he really does appear to have an
extraordinary talent!'

'That's great, Hector. I'm so glad.'

'But you don't have to go yet, surely?'

''Fraid so. I've loads of work on, and I only came down for
the weekend.'

'Well maybe I could come up to London and visit you
sometime soon? Ifor and family have offered to take Wendy
and the youngsters for a short while to give me a break.' He

lowered his voice, 'I'm looking forward to it actually. It's been damned hard work ever since Wendy's been . . . ill.'

'Yes, I'm sure.'

'But won't you come in for a coffee? You can surely spare ten minutes?'

'Well . . .' Jess weakened. 'Oh all right. Thanks.'

She sat at the kitchen table and tried to assess her feelings. What if Wendy really did throw Hector out? What if they eventually separated for good?

I don't want to get involved in their break up, she decided. I can't face having anything to do with it, so I must make sure I keep my distance until it's all resolved, one way or the other. And then, who knows?

'You're looking very fierce all of a sudden, *cariad*?' Hector said, handing her a mug of coffee. 'Biscuit?'

'No thanks. I don't feel fierce, just confused I suppose.'

'Tell me, Jess,' Hector said, leaning forward intently. 'Do you know why Wendy did it? It's a complete mystery to me.'

'Well . . .' Jess began slowly, 'I suppose she felt betrayed . . .'

'But Caroline and Zillah are ancient history, as far as I'm concerned,' Hector said. 'Surely she understands that?'

'I don't think that's the point, Hector. It's all to do with a lack of trust, and deceit and . . . things like that.'

Hector sighed deeply. 'So, what now?'

'I don't know. That has to be between you and Wendy.'

'But you won't desert me, will you, Jess? After all, we go back a long way.' He put his hand over hers on the table, and smiled into her eyes.

Jess withdrew smartly. 'I'm sorry, I really ought to be off.' She got to her feet and hung her bag over one shoulder.

'But you haven't finished your coffee.'

'Sorry.'

'But Jess – we should talk.'

'So give me a ring, if you want to.' Jess almost ran out of the room into the hall, and collided with someone carrying a bag. It was Hannah. 'Ow!'

'Sorry,' Hannah said. 'Are you going back to London?'

'Yes.'

'Wicked!' Hannah said. 'Can I cadge a lift?'

'Yes of course!'

'You're not leaving me as well?' Hector asked, looking desolate. 'I thought you were happy here.'

'Yeah, well you know . . .' Hannah said.

''Bye Hector,' Jess said, giving him a peck on the cheek.

Then she and Hannah got into her car and drove off down the steep drive. Jess's last sight of Hector in her mirror was of a forlorn figure standing alone outside his large house, with one hand raised in valediction.

'Have a tissue?' Hannah said, proffering one.

'Thanks. Hold these for me a mo, will you?' Jess took her glasses off one-handed, and blotted each eye in turn. 'Are you Gwladys or Hannah these days?'

'Hannah. Gwladys is totally *lame*,' Hannah said in disgust.

'Oh,' Jess said. 'Good.' She glanced sideways at Hannah's profile. Her thin face was set in determination, but Jess could detect more than a little disillusionment in her expression as well. 'So, why did you decide to leave?'

''Cos it was a bunch of arse there.'

'What d'you mean?'

'He treated me like a bloody *skivvy*,' Hannah said. 'Soon as Wendy stopped doing all the housework and cooking and stuff, Hector expected me to do it. ME! And he goes,' (she put on an affected Hector-ish accent) '*Normal communication with you appears to be quite impossible. Now if you were to attempt Standard English, we might get somewhere*, and I'm, like, *WHAT*?' She shook her head in disbelief. Jess pursed her lips firmly to stop herself from smiling.

'Morgan will miss you?' she suggested.

'Morgan's cool,' Hannah assured her. 'He won't be that bothered. I'll bet he's still in his room right now, drawing away! Like, he knows where he's at. He'll be fine.'

'Your mum will be overjoyed to see you.'

'I doubt that.'

'Oh Hannah, she *will*. She loves you to bits.'

'Yeah?'

'Yes, really.' Jess worried about how she would broach the subject of guilt, responsibility and Wendy, as she had promised, without upsetting Hannah, but it came up naturally sometime later, when they'd stopped for some food.

273

'People can't help being born?' Hannah said, hesitating over a plate of egg and chips.

'Of course not. Look, Hannah, Wendy asked me to give you a message.'

'Yeah?' Hannah looked wary.

'She says what she did is absolutely NOT your fault, or Florian's. It's entirely between her and Hector.'

'Is that right?'

'Yes, honestly.'

'Cool!' She took a huge mouthful of chips, looked up at Jess and even smiled.

They made it back to London in good time, and Jess watched as Hannah ran up the steps to her front door, and straight inside without bothering to close it behind her. Then she heard, with satisfaction, Caroline's delighted cry of '*Hannah!*' before going down into her basement flat. Home at last.

For the next few days Jess was frantically busy catching up with her work, but each night before she went to sleep, she lay in bed and wondered where her life was going. Would she ever achieve a good relationship with a man, and have children with him? Or, were men an optional extra? She rather liked the idea of living alone, and taking lovers when she felt like it. Caroline certainly seemed to manage that sort of arrangement very efficiently, but then she never got emotionally involved with any of her men. Could I be so detached? Jess wondered. Would I even want to be?

Do I know what I really want? Do I actually hanker after children? I don't believe I do, now. If I had some, I couldn't possibly go on working the way I do. I think I'm beginning to come round to the idea that women ought to make a *choice* between having a career and having babies (women like Caroline and me that is, who have the luxury of choice). It doesn't seem to work when people try to do both.

But what about this biological clock that's supposed to be ticking away inside all of us women? Then she thought, it's all nonsense – we're just brainwashed into thinking that we're not *fulfilled* unless we've given birth. That may well be a reality for the majority, but for a growing minority of us, it simply isn't true! She lay, staring into nothing for a while, and then she thought, I may not want children, but I do need something more than just work. I'd like a satisfactory emotional life, so I *do* need a man. But should it be someone like Hector? And on this question, and still irresolute, she fell asleep.

Caroline came round the following evening. 'Thanks again for bringing Hannah home,' she said. 'I think I was too incoherent the other night to thank you properly. I'm just SO grateful.'

'It was entirely her idea,' Jess said. 'I didn't earn any brownie points.'

'You OK?'

'Just about,' Jess said. 'I've been doing a lot of thinking.'

'What about?'

'Oh, my life and what to do with it. The usual problems.'

'And?'

'No . . .' Jess said slowly, 'I can't say I've come to any conclusions at all.'

'You will,' Caroline assured her. 'I've always found the hardest decisions in life tend to be made *for* one, by circumstances. You just have to trust in the Fates. Anyway, I can't stay. Just wanted to share two bits of good news.'

'Yes?' Jess encouraged her.

'The first is that Vivian's moving to London, so it looks as though I'll be seeing more of him. The second is that I got that job!'

Jess rushed to hug her. 'Congratulations!'

'Thank you.'

'You must be so chuffed!'

'I am,' Caroline said happily. 'Now, must dash. I just had to tell you straight away.'

'I am SO pleased,' Jess called after her. The telephone rang and startled her. 'Hello?'

'Jess? It's me.'

'Oh Hector, how's things?'

'Dire. Look Jess, I really need to talk to you. Could I come up next weekend? Ideally I'd like to have made it this Saturday – the day after tomorrow – but it's no good. There's still too much Wendy and I have to sort out . . .'

'But what's wrong? Is Wendy ill again?'

'No, just the opposite; she appears to have made a remarkable recovery. The doctors are delighted with her.'

'So what's the problem?'

'She only wants a *divorce*! That's what's wrong. Honestly Jess, I just don't know what to think. There've been so many times over the years when I would have jumped at the chance, but now . . . just when Morgan and I are getting on so well . . . I just don't know what to do for the best. I really need to talk to you, Jessy-boot. There isn't anybody else who understands me half as well. How about if I ring you tomorrow? I'll have more time then.'

'But . . . would it be such a good idea?'

'Who cares! I'm drowning Jess, and you're my only life-belt. Don't let me down.'

'Well, if you put it like that . . .'

'Good on you, *cariad*. Who knows, this whole mess might be a blessing in disguise for both of us.' Then he hung up.

Jess sat and frowned at the floor. Had Hector really meant what she thought he had? Was she wrong, or had she just been nominated as First Reserve, in the expectation of Wife No. 1 retiring from the scene? She found the sudden possibility of actually getting what she (secretly) thought she'd always wanted daunting in the extreme. Then gradually, it began to grow on her.

Next evening, and every one after that, Hector telephoned, and they had long talks. Jess found herself inexorably drawn into the arguments which were raging between him and Wendy, and she was often confused, unsure which of them she felt the most sympathy for. Hector, of course, took it for granted that she would unhesitatingly side with him.

At first Jess got the distinct impression that it was only his self-esteem that was hurt, because Wendy wanted to divorce *him*, and that, had it been the other way around, he would have been much less upset. She gathered that Wendy had changed, and become assertive and distinctly unfeminine. Hector complained that, after all he had done for her, she was now rejecting him, and he didn't understand it. Then later he seemed to be trying to convince himself that divorce might be the right thing to do after all, but only on condition that he would keep custody of his son.

'Well of course I see your point,' Jess said. 'But Morgan's fourteen now, isn't he? In five or six years he'll be grown up and leaving home anyway. And five years is nothing!'

'So you do think divorce is the answer?'

'No, Hector, I didn't say that.'

'I'm sorry, Jess. I know I shouldn't ask. It isn't fair. And I'm not trying to put pressure on you. I just love listening to the sound of your voice.'

She put the phone down after this conversation, sighing. There was no doubt about it, she was *fond* of the man. Perhaps eventually she and Hector . . .? After all, she would hate the thought of him being alone and miserable. And they had known each other for a long time, and they rubbed along together so easily and laughed at the same things . . . When you thought about it like that, it would be a lost opportunity if they ended up apart, wouldn't it? Jess warmed to the idea.

But then a few days later, he said something unsettling. 'Maybe I should jack-in Mudgeley Goggles and come to London to seek my fortune. I could lodge with you for a while, couldn't I, Jess?' And she had this alarming vision of Hector, permanently unemployed, bored rigid, needing constant attention, expecting regular meals, and hurt if she had to spend any time at all away working. And she felt the panic rising within her; found herself saying something sharp and unkind to him, like:

'You're a bit old to be Dick Whittington, aren't you?'

So she alternated uncomfortably between these two extremes, looking forward almost fearfully to the impending weekend when Hector would arrive; wondering if she should cancel his visit, knowing that when she saw him, all her doubts and niggling feelings of caution and unease would probably be swept aside by the force of his personality, and the comfortable *safe* feeling of his companionship. But maybe that's what I *need*, she mused. Or is it?

Then unexpectedly on Thursday, and again on Friday evening, Hector didn't phone. Jess wondered what was going on. She debated whether she should ring him instead, but decided against it. It was a welcome breathing space.

On Saturday morning she woke with feelings of foreboding

and thought, Oh Lord! It's today! However, it wasn't Hector who arrived on her doorstep at noon.

'Oh!' Jess said, opening the door. Her welcoming smile dropped abruptly. ' . . . Wendy?'

'It's OK,' Wendy said. 'Hector's fine, and he knows I'm here.'

'Oh . . . good.'

'So, can I come in for a moment?'

'Yes . . . sorry. I was just a bit surprised.' Jess led the way inside. 'Would you like a coffee or anything?'

'Cup of tea'd be nice,' Wendy said.

'Come into the kitchen then.'

Wendy sat herself down at Jess's scrubbed pine table. She had a new smooth, grown-up hairstyle. In fact she looked remarkably self-possessed. 'I gather your job's going well,' she said. 'Making lots of money.'

'Not bad, yes,' Jess admitted.

'I fancy getting a job,' Wendy said. 'Part-time of course, because of Morgan.'

'Good idea,' Jess agreed. 'I'm sure it's a mistake for mothers to work full-time.' She put Wendy's tea down in front of her but remained standing, leaning against the wall.

'You are?' Wendy seemed surprised.

'On reflection, yes.'

'Poor Barry's found he can't even work part-time, you know? He nearly killed himself trying!' Wendy made a gesture of self-mockery at the unintentional irony. 'So he's had to give up journalism altogether. Such a shame; he loved his job, did Barry.'

Jess wondered where all this was leading, but she bided her time. 'Have you spoken to him?' she asked.

'Oh yes,' Wendy said. 'I've seen quite a lot of him just lately – wanted to see if there was anything I could do to help him, you know.'

'And was there?'

'Well, to be honest, not a lot. He's so busy coping with all those kiddies, he hasn't a moment to call his own. But he was pleased I tried.'

'I'm sure he was.'

Jess drank her coffee and regarded Wendy over the rim of

her mug. Wendy put hers down, and looked straight up at her. 'Hector's been talking about marrying you, after our divorce goes through,' she said.

'Oh . . .!' Jess said, startled by her directness.

'Does that mean he hasn't got round to asking you yet?'

'Well . . . no. It's news to me!'

'But would you?'

'No! . . . well, perhaps . . . Oh *I* don't know!' Jess felt exasperated.

'Mmmm,' Wendy said. 'I thought as much. He was only trying to make me jealous. He's been dead against divorce all along in actual fact, but then he's a man – he has his pride.' Jess nodded in a way she hoped was encouraging. 'Course,' Wendy went on, 'I blame myself for a lot of our problems. When you've been together as long as me and Hector have, you get so's you take each other for granted. But I've had plenty of time to think lately, and I reckon I haven't been attending to his . . . needs . . . enough, if you understand my meaning?' Jess nodded again, mutely. 'So,' Wendy said, warming to her subject, 'we've made this mutual decision and I wanted you to hear it straight, face to face, so you'd understand. OK?'

'Well, yes.'

'It's like this then – We've been married for over fourteen years, right? And we've got a lovely home, and marriage is never easy at the best of times. But I do love him (always have), so I've decided to work at it, and Hector's promised to try harder too. And I'm definitely going to go for a job, so's I'll have some money of my own. And this way, Morgan won't suffer, which is the most important thing. So the upshot is; I'm NOT going to divorce Hector after all!' Jess stared in admiration at this new, determined Wendy.

As far as problem-solving was concerned, Jess had always known that the best way to discover what you *really* wanted, was to let someone else cast the die for you. Then, judging by whether you felt instantly liberated or immediately regretful, your true inclinations became clear. In that moment, she knew at once that she valued her career and her independence above everything; that she would never have been able to cope with all the complications that go with *passion*. She sat down opposite Hector's wife, put her elbows on the table, and cupped her chin in her hands.

'Thank you, Wendy,' she said. 'I think you've just saved my life.'

'And now you can save mine,' Wendy said.

'How?'

'By letting me talk to you?'

'Well . . . yes of course . . . but I don't know quite . . .?'

'You're closer to Hector than anybody else but me,' Wendy said firmly. 'So I know you'll understand. I just want to get it all off my chest. Right?'

'By all means,' Jess said. She was feeling so irresponsibly generous, she would have agreed to anything. It was an emotion she was beginning to identify as relief . . .

So Wendy talked, and Jess made her cups of tea (and later lunch), and occasionally said encouraging things like, 'Yes,' and 'Mmmmm,' and 'Oh I do understand,' and also, 'Really?' and, 'Good Lord!' and, 'He *didn't*?' And when, from time to time, Wendy's eyes began to leak, Jess handed her tissues without comment, and the tears dried up very soon, but the talking went on.

Jess rang for pizzas for their supper, and pressed Wendy to stay the night. 'You can always phone Hector to tell him.'

'D'you know?' Wendy said, 'I think I will!'

After supper, they sat on opposite sofas with their shoes off and their feet up, drinking gin and tonic. 'I'm so glad you came,' Jess said.

'So'm I,' Wendy agreed. 'I feel ever so much better.'

'But there's still one thing that bothers me.'

'What?'

'Well, I think I do understand why you love Hector,' Jess said, frowning, 'in spite of the way he's treated you. And if you're sure he's really sincere in his promise to do better in future . . .?'

'Oh he IS,' Wendy assured her.

' . . . But I suppose I'm just a bit concerned that, as usual, he's getting it all his own way – d'you see what I mean? You've been through all this together, and he's been totally selfish and done exactly what *he* wants, over the years, and then in spite of everything, he ends up with all the prizes – you and Morgan. In other words, he's won!'

'Oh no he hasn't!' Wendy giggled. Jess looked across at her in surprise. 'I shouldn't laugh,' Wendy said. 'I know it's not nice, but I can't help it!'

'What?'

'Well, this was what turned everything around, you see. Hector was so upset, and I comforted him, and well . . . one thing led to another, and it was brilliant!' She took a hefty swig of gin and sat back, laughing.

'Go on,' Jess urged, 'the suspense is killing me!'

'Well,' Wendy said, 'I suppose I can kind of appreciate how devastated he's feeling, since it's SO IMPORTANT to him. But I don't properly understand *why*? I reckon it's a load of nonsense myself.'

'*What* is? You're doing this on purpose!' Jess said, laughing too. 'More gin?' She poured them both another glass.

'OK, I'll start at the beginning,' Wendy said. 'It was Thursday – day before yesterday. Right? And we all three went over to Ifor's house for tea, and guess what? My sister-in-law June (who's forty *five*) turns out to be eighteen weeks *pregnant*! She said she would have told us earlier, but she was that embarrassed! So now she's had this amniocentesis test done, and it seems the baby's fit and healthy, and . . .'

'Don't tell me,' Jess interrupted, shaking her head. 'It's a boy, yes? A son and heir? The eleventh Baronet, no less!'

'Got it in one!' Wendy whooped, and they both collapsed in laughter.

Jess wiped the tears from her eyes and held her glass high. 'A toast!' she cried. 'To him. To US. To the future!'

The End.

A SELECTED LIST FROM ARROW

ALL ARROW BOOKS ARE AVAILABLE THROUGH MAIL ORDER OR FROM YOUR LOCAL BOOKSHOP AND NEWSAGENT.

PLEASE SEND CHEQUE/EUROCHEQUE/POSTAL ORDER (STERLING ONLY) ACCESS, VISA, MASTERCARD, DINERS CARD, SWITCH OR AMEX.

EXPIRY DATE .... SIGNATURE ....

PLEASE ALLOW 75 PENCE PER BOOK FOR POST AND PACKING U.K.

OVERSEAS CUSTOMERS PLEASE ALLOW £1.00 PER COPY FOR POST AND PACKING.

ALL ORDERS TO:
ARROW BOOKS, BOOKS BY POST, TBS LIMITED, THE BOOK SERVICE, COLCHESTER ROAD, FRATING GREEN, COLCHESTER, ESSEX CO7 7DW.

NAME ....

ADDRESS ....

....

Please allow 28 days for delivery. Please tick box if you do not wish to receive any additional information ☐

Prices and availability subject to change without notice.